NO LIMITS

ELLIE MARNEY

Bearded Lady Press
elliemarney@gmail.com
Australia

ISBN-13: 978-0-6480885-1-6
Cover Design by www.ebooklaunch.com

For Grant Saltmarsh
Ave atque vale

1

harris

Blue-and-red lights swirling over a windscreen white-out, and the siren sounds exactly like the guitar feedback loop on an Arctic Monkeys track.

Through it all, the haze of people talking, people moving, people's breath in my face, my own hair in my mouth, the rancid taste of vomit and a blur of fast noise –

'...*gethimouttathe...*'

'...*just easy now...*'

'...*transfer, but Mildura won't...*'

– and a constant slow thump in my head, like the heavy beat of night-club bass. I'd like it to shut up now, but it doesn't. It can't, although I've got no fucking idea how I know this.

'...*lift him up and onto a trolley...*'

'...*two, three – that's it, nice and...*'

'...*stabilised, if you'll take...*'

Firm hands hold me steady so I don't tip. Sense of movement, the ka-chunk of wheels over bumps in the floor. Reverb travels up my bum and back, through the rest of me, so I vibrate into the bed I'm lying on. Then – the glare, the whiteness. Those lights, thrown right in your face.

'...*get them off and have a look, don't...*'

'...*wait for Doctor McGaven? He's only just arrived, so...*'

'...*keep pressure on, gimme the scissors...*'

Sudden draught on my skin. It travels up from ankle to shin to thigh – my thigh, fuck – so fast I don't realise I'm cold until the gooseflesh rises. Now everything hurts, hurts *bad*, the pain in my leg like a crosscut saw on bone. Fighting against it forces my mouth open. I hear a long lowing moan somewhere far away, like bulls roaring for food, lost love, the end of fences, the open road –

'...*his arms in, Nick, for god's sake!*'

'...*holding him, I'm holding him, just cut off the...*'

'...*theatre's clear, if you want to do a CT we should...*'

'*Wait!*' someone says. 'I know him! I know him. Just let me get in there.'

Sight returns without warning and there's a face above me. Dark eyes, white teeth, brown skin, pulled-back hair a little frizzed from sweat and effort. The girl smiles at me, smooths my forehead.

'Harris! Hey, Harris, it's okay. You're all right, yeah? You're gonna be fine.' Something red smeared on the girl's face, near her cheekbone. She swipes at it with the back of one gloved hand. 'It's okay, mate. We've got you.'

My lips, swollen and gummed-up, move to no effect. Words are so dry they won't come.

'Shh, don't try to talk yet,' the girl says. 'We're gonna go to sleep now, okay? Just watch my face, that's it. We're gonna have a rest. Watch me count – ten, nine, eight, seven...'

Her nose is strong and her bottom lip is full. I got no idea who she is. Her lip is round and powerful and pillowy. I stare at it, sink into it, sink back like I'm falling, clouds soaking me up, all the noise, all the blood, calm and quiet and soft and –

*

Me and Rachel are on a bright white beach, someplace the air is really soft. Sand trickles between my toes. The moon is still out, in that way it sometimes is in real life, hanging up in the blue sky like half a Jatz cracker. I'm playing with Rachel's hair, and she's letting me...

I wake up to the smell of Tang.

Tang is this fluoro-orange powder you stir with water into something that's supposed to taste like juice. What it actually tastes like is Fanta that's gone flat in the bottle, if you let the bottle sit in a hot car all day. The powder has a bitter chemical graininess. Mix it up with vodka and it's almost bearable.

We used to go into Five Mile for immediate needs – bread, milk, tobacco, baked beans, eggs – and there'd be half a dozen dusty packets of Tang sitting next to the antacids. For years I thought it was some special thing they used to stock for the exclusive use of my father. Later, I realised I was right. Nobody will drink that shit except my dad.

Which means I know straightaway who's breathing on me, even if the voice isn't already too familiar.

'Harris. Harris, come on, mate.'

I try to ignore the jet-fuel burn of vodka and Tang. Go back to the beach dream.

'Harris, wake up. Get up.'

Throat's so parched I can't even make the obvious response, *Get fucked.*

He flicks my face with the backs of his fingers.

If there's one thing my dad excels at, it's being a pain in the arse. He can be a pain in the arse all fucking day, not even break a sweat.

He keeps flicking.

'Harris, we're gonna get you outta here, mate. Hospital's no place for you.' He leans closer, whispering. 'I know we've had our disagreements, son, but we can discuss that later.'

I don't know what he's talking about for a second. Then it comes back to me, like an ice-water drench. I groan, shift my head.

'That's it, boy. Wakey wakey. Coppers already gimme your bag, with your stuff from the Watts place. Just crack open those eyes and we're outta here –'

There's a mechanical hiss, a shuffle, and I feel how the air in the room has shifted. Someone else in here now. A large someone, I reckon.

'Hands off, if you don't mind, Mr Derwent.' A large voice, for a large someone. Female. Full-throated and brassy. A Bette Midler voice.

'He's me son.' Dad's got that narky tone. Automatic Defensive Aggro mode. 'Do what I like with me own son.'

'Not really, no. He's on the ward, so he's my responsibility at the moment.'

Bette, I bloody love you. Did you ever know that you're my hero?

'I was waking him up,' Dad says. 'He's been sleeping for ages –'

'He's recovering from the anaesthetic,' she says matter-of-factly. 'He's only just out of surgery, he's in no shape to be getting up. Leave him be, Mr Derwent.'

Bette moves nearby. I hear the *scritch scritch* of chafing polyester. The wheeze in her breathing. She must be right beside me, her quilted padding against my dad's barbed wire.

'Come on, Dennis,' she says. 'Your boy's not going anywhere. Look at him, eh? Come on out of the ward, I'll find you a coffee. You can have a smoke out in the ambulance bay. No more trying to wake him, or I'll have to ask less nicely, okay?'

More scritching, the shuffle of shoes on lino, taking the smell of Tang away. Herding my father towards the door, please god.

4

'I just wanted him to see me. Know I'm here and stuff...' and bullshit bullshit bullshit, Dad lays it on like this all the way out. I stop listening after the first bit.

The door hisses shut and I'm in the clear. I can prise my eyes open for a peek around.

Hard to tell what time it is, but I'm gonna say night. The lights are dim. Everything in the gloomy room is powder blue – a dilapidated shade of blue, like Mr Metcalfe's old ute. Now Dad's gone, the smell of antiseptic slices its way up into my nostrils.

My eyes remember how to focus. A privacy curtain is pulled aside to my right. Two other shadowed beds lie empty. The vent blows air-con cold, the sheet over me is starched, and I'm not wearing a shirt. I don't think I'm wearing jocks, either.

I must be on some cool drugs, because I feel okay. I mean, not fighting fit or nothing, but I don't feel too bad. About as good as you can feel lying in a hospital bed without your jocks.

My gaze runs down to the humped shape over my left leg.

I make my hand – the one without the IV tubing stuck in it – work enough to flick the sheet up. Catch sight of my Betadine-yellow leg, the cage over it. The sickly gleam of plastic that's *coming out of my skin*, Jesus Christ.

I finally figure it out.

I am not okay. This is not a dream. I got shot. I'm in hospital, just out of surgery. Rachel's gone. I'm back in the country, back in Ouyen, flat on my back, at my father's mercy.

I'm fucked.

Well and truly.

2

amie

'Right – I've covered wards, I've covered theatre, I've covered Urgent Care, I've covered discharges. Are we all on the same page? Yes? Excellent. What haven't I covered? Um...'

'Needs,' Nick pipes up. 'And CNAs.'

'Oh, right. Needs. Hang on, let me check...'

'Mrs Dougherty in Three has paperwork for Needs.'

Barb folds through a few sheets on her clipboard. 'Mrs Dougherty in Three...yes, has paperwork saying no penicillin. Everybody got that? No penicillin for Three. And Mr Krane in Twelve has no deep reclining, no prone. Breathing problems. So don't lie him flat for linen changes, or he'll go all gaspy.'

'I spotted him yesterday arvo having a ciggie out in the car park.' Mel hooks her thumbs into her utility belt. 'He seemed fine, then.'

'You saw him having a ciggie? Christ, Mel, would you let me know if my respiratory patients are out smoking?'

'Sure.' Mel shrugs. 'Sorry, I didn't know.' She makes a face, catches Nick's eye.

Nick shakes his head at her, grinning. 'Yeah, Mel. Who can we trust to keep an eye on things if security won't?' Mel gives him the finger, rolls her eyes.

Barb flaps her pages at them. 'Behave. What else was it?'

'CNAs,' I say, waving my hand.

Barb beams at me. 'Course, sorry. You've got obs in Three, Seven, Nine, Twelve and...um, that's it. Three, Seven, Nine and Twelve. Come back after that, we'll get you on breakfast, and then linen.'

I give her the thumbs-up.

'Oh, and a word about Seven. Actually, this isn't just for Amie, it's for everyone. Everybody looking here? Right. Most of you know what's going on with Seven. It's a police case, so don't get bothered if you see the constabulary at some point. Derrin Blunt has said he'll pop by for some questions after breakfast –'

I wave again. 'Actually, Dad said it's looking more like after lunch.'

'Oh? Right. So Sergeant Blunt will be in after lunch, might have Jared Capshaw or other officers with him. No emergency, just as you were. There was a bit of, y'know, flailing around when Harris first came in, but no aggro. Also not ambulatory, and he's on Endone, so he's gonna be groggy for a fair while.'

'Is that the business out of Five Mile?' Mel asks.

Barb nods. 'Yes, it is, and no wild speculation, if you don't mind. I'm sure we'll all hear about it in the papers. One last thing – please don't engage with Harris's father, Mr Derwent. You'll be in your grave before you win that one. Just call me, and I'll come deal with him, okay? I can't ban immediate next-of-kin from the ward as long as he's behaving himself, even if he is visiting with a lidful. But if you see or experience him being troublesome, report it.'

'I caught him pinching the patient on the arm,' Nick says.

'Did you? Great. I mean, not great, but you know, write it up. And that's it, folks.' Barb catches every eye around the staff room. 'Go make the hospital work.'

She flaps her clipboard at us like she's shooing chooks out of a pen – in a tiny rural facility like Ouyen hospital, professional manners tend to get a bit casual. We rise as a jumbled group off our chairs, while she drops down into hers. The white plastic creaks, the moulded arm-rests spreading to accommodate her bulk. Her face is flushed beneath her skullcap of sweaty brown hair. She's not wheezing today, though. That's a good sign.

'Get you anything?' I make the offer casual. 'Need some chasing done before I go on obs?'

'Oh, bless.' Barb passes me her clipboard, with assorted paperwork. 'Could you take that to the admin desk and say I'll do handover in five? I just need a little coffee first.'

'I'll say ten, and I'll bring you the coffee.' I tuck the clipboard under my arm. 'And I'll text Dad, see if I can get a better idea of when he's coming in.'

'Amie, you're a doll.'

I go make her a cup of instant coffee at the bench. When I bring the cup over, Barb's face is looking better, less pink. This is the moment she gets to rest before she bundles into her car for the drive back to Patchewollock.

Nick's already pulling on the straps of his backpack, throwing his scarf around his neck. I grab him before he heads out the door.

'Any more excitement I missed?'

'Not really.' He helps me straighten my staff lanyard, which is tangled over my collar. 'You saw it all yesterday morning. Harris did his puking in Recovery, apparently, while he was still on half-hourly obs. When I came on night duty the only thing I had to worry about was his dad. Real piece of work, that one.'

'How come you had night duty? Did you put your name down for extra shifts?'

'Yeah.' Nick shrugs. 'My car's just about ready to crap itself. It's

8

time I bought something decent instead of relying on Grant's hand-me-downs.'

'Hey, don't knock hand-me-downs. Hand-me-downs are cheap.'

'Yeah, but the difference is, if yours dies in the middle of the road you can get it fixed for nothing.'

'Dad could have a look?' But it's only half an offer. I don't know how busy Dad will be over this Five Mile business. He might not have time to fiddle about with other people's engines for the next few days.

'Nice of you,' Nick says, but the look on his face tells me he's already made up his mind. 'Anything you need before I go?'

'World peace? A cure for cancer?'

'Hilarious.'

'Dunno, is there anything?'

'Go say hullo to Mrs D, she gets lonely. And you'll wanna drop in on your mate during obs.'

'Harris isn't my mate,' I point out.

'You knew him when he came in.'

'He was in pain when he came in. I was just helping him out. I mean, yes, aeons ago I played netball when he was in under-17s, but –'

'Glorious sporting years, I'm sure. But they're clearing the drain in his leg this morning.'

'Ouch.'

'Maybe go distract him with footy nostalgia.' Nick makes a face, which just looks tired. 'Dickhead Derwent. Don't know how he managed to get himself shot in the leg. Self-inflicted, probably.'

'Hey. Give him a break.' I push at Nick's arm.

'Right. If you're gonna abuse me, I'm off.' But there's no rancour in his voice. He's obviously too knackered, and he's just not that kind of guy. 'Have fun, see you Wednesday.'

'Text me about the pub after work.'

'Will do. Cheers, babe.'

I drop the clipboard off to the admin desk, text Dad with the question, and collect Spot, the blood pressure machine. Obs is a pretty simple gig: pulling Spot along the hall, going into rooms to say hello, open curtains. Take temperature, pulse, blood pressure, check respiration rate, tidy up a little. It's a lull; the night duty staff are giving their final instructions and saying their goodbyes, and the earlies staff are still yawning as they come on the ward. Patients not already roused by the breakfast bustle are starting to wake.

Mrs Dougherty in Three wants the loo, and then a blanket. She has wispy-white hair and cold fingers. 'How's your dad, Amita?'

She's also one of the only people I know who calls me by my given name. 'He's good, Mrs Dougherty.'

'When's he gonna give up the police work and come take me away from all this, eh?'

'I'll tell him you're still available, Mrs D.' I grin, tuck the blanket around her, let her know I'll come with her brekky in a bit.

I don't know what to expect in room Seven. I haven't seen Harris Derwent since he arrived with such dramatic flourish: paddy wagon lights blueing up the whole bay in a frantic, hands-on, this-is-a-fucking-emergency scene. He was barely conscious then. It's not like he'll recognise me now.

The room is still dim. It smells like sweat and antiseptic in here. There's a bulky figure on the bed, obscured by the sheet-covered cage over the lower half of him. My shoes are rubber-soled so they don't make any noise at all as I move closer to the other bed's nightstand and reach for the lamp.

As soon as I flick the switch, I hear a sigh.

'Could you please turn off that fucking light?'

His bed is half-reclined. He's all lank blonde hair and whitened tan. I'm seeing a lot of him: he's shirtless, with the sheet rucked down to his hips. Working in a hospital, you find yourself dealing with people in various states of distress and undress. It's kind of weird, seeing people you know personally when they're so vulnerable. Six months into this job it's something I'm still getting used to.

'Sure.' I turn the light off. 'What happened to your gown?'

Harris doesn't reply. Then I nearly step on the wadded blue paper gown on the floor. He's pulled it off himself. Maybe it was uncomfortable, all scrunched to accommodate the cage over his leg.

'Are you cold? You look cold.'

His eyes are winced closed. A plate of quartered hospital sandwiches and a cuppa sit untouched on the trolley at the bedside. I wonder if he's still too groggy or nauseated to eat. But his recovery period was last night; he should try to eat. It's the best way to regain strength after surgery.

I carefully fold up the sheet and blanket so they're covering his chest. Nice chest, although it's not really my job to notice. From what I hear, Harris Derwent gets his chest admired on a pretty regular basis anyway. I keep my eyes firmly elsewhere while I'm fixing the blanket.

He turns his head towards me. 'Do I know you?'

I lose what to say for a second. His eyes are very green and glazed, and he looks horribly tired. Which is fair – I went home exhausted after yesterday's shift, although nothing much happened after that one emergency. But even one emergency can do that to you.

'I-I was here when you first arrived,' I finally get out. 'Yesterday morning. You came in with Jared Capshaw –'

'You counted me down.' His voice is rough from the intubation. 'Yeah.'

He remembers me. What else does he remember?

'Do you know where you are? You're in Ouyen hospital. You've had surgery on the bullet wound in your thigh.' I try to think of more detail so he can orient himself. 'You've been pretty out of it since you came in. Your leg –'

'What about the others?' His eyes hunt around, as if he thinks they might be in here with us. 'Rachel...'

'You were the only one admitted.' I frown. 'D'you want me to chase it up for you? Is there someone you need to contact? Your dad's been in –'

'No.' The word comes out short and flat. 'Don't contact my dad.'

'Okay... But he's already been in once and he'll probably come in again later. He seems pretty keen to see you.'

Harris closes his eyes and his whole body sinks, boneless. 'Fine. Whatever.'

I squint at him. His hollow cheeks are covered in dark gold stubble. He was nearly an hour in surgery, and he would've been recovering from sedation all afternoon, into the evening. More drugs would've seen him through the night. Maybe this is really the first time he's communicated since he arrived.

I think about what he's communicating.

'D'you want me to stall him?' I say quietly. 'I could maybe hold him over until the afternoon...'

Harris blinks up at me. 'You can do that?'

I nod.

He holds my gaze for a moment before sinking into the bed again. This time, he looks more relaxed. 'Thank you.'

'Is he bothering you? Barb can ban him from the ward if –'

'No. That'll just piss him off.' He stretches his neck, grimacing.

12

'Dad... Dad can be hard work. That's just the way he is.'

Which is what people say about you – the thought comes before I can stop myself. At least I don't say it out loud.

*

For the next couple of days, Harris has a barrage of visitors.

A stocky Melbourne cop with a ginger crewcut drops by, along with some skinny English guy in a suit. Not to mention the local police, and by that I mean my dad and Jared Capshaw. Dad came back from that first interview with Harris wearing a very grim expression. Melbourne police involvement always makes him edgy.

I ask Dad if there's any word about what happened because, after a one-paragraph mention in the local paper, there's been no more information, and the rest of the staff have all been trying to pick my brains. Everything is gossip fodder in a small town.

'It was some Melbourne police op.' Dad spreads his hands. 'One of the Watts kids   do you remember Rachel Watts? Yeah, she and her boyfriend got into trouble with some goons at the Five Mile quarry. Harris swooped in, trying to help out, and ended up getting shot for his efforts.'

'Didn't Harris go to Melbourne with Rachel's brother for a while?'

'Yeah, Mike Watts and Harris are mates. I guess that's how Harris got involved.'

Harris doesn't exactly have a reputation as a hero. I try to imagine him swooping in. Can't picture it. 'Are you sure he wasn't with the goons?'

Dad shrugs. 'Look, I don't actually have many details about it. Harris Derwent was one of the good guys, that's all I know.'

'Harris was helping the cops?' That gives my eyebrows a

13

workout. 'No way.'

'Yes way – but please don't use that phrasing when you explain it to the hospital staff,' Dad says with a grimace.

He gives me a quick sound-bite to repeat: Harris and a couple of other kids got caught in the crossfire of a police operation at the Five Mile quarry, but everyone's okay, Melbourne police have the person responsible in custody, and Harris isn't a suspect. That's enough to shut everyone up, and it's all I have the energy for after dealing with Mr Derwent since Sunday. Harris's dad always seems to be lurking around, ready to take advantage of every moment his son is left alone. He's rude, unpredictably short-tempered, and even though it's none of my business, I don't like him.

When his dad *isn't* around, an outside call is patched through to Harris's bedside phone. He talks to whoever it is for a long time. His voice works to sound upbeat, saying things like, 'Nah, I'm good. Yep, it's all sorted. Just a couple more days. I'll tell your dad if there's anything I need. No, no bullshit, I swear'. Then his tone softens as he says, 'Hey, it's okay. Don't feel bad. I'm just glad you're all right…' I hear this while I'm taking away his meal tray, on which a lot of food has been moved around but nothing much has been eaten.

On Tuesday, Michael Watts's dad comes during visiting hours. I haven't seen the family since I heard they moved to Melbourne. I'm cleaning up in the bathroom and catch the end of a stilted conversation where Mr Watts asks Harris if he's doing all right, and does he need anything, and has he got a place to stay. Harris answers *yes, no, sure*, to everything.

I exit the bathroom with the rubbish, and see Terry Watts pressing a roll of fifties into Harris's hand. Harris looks as if he'd rather take a pair of pliers to his own fingernails than accept the money, but he nods and holds onto it anyway. When Terry finally leaves, Harris turns on his side, like he'd curl up in a ball if only his leg wasn't in the way.

I think he might be in some sort of delayed shock. Also the drugs we're pumping into him can cause nausea. He kind of zones out for a while there, becomes unresponsive if I come in to serve meals or tidy up. I don't push him, but I mention it to Barb.

I've resigned myself to being ignored while I'm changing the pillowcases. Which means it's an absolute surprise when I go in later that afternoon and Harris speaks to me.

'Thank you.' His voice comes out raspy. I don't know if that's the drugs, or lack of voluntary use.

'That's okay.' I think I'd better take it slow. 'You all right?'

He doesn't seem to know if he's really got it in him to reply. He just shrugs. I nod – I don't understand, but I get it.

'Look, I'm sorry I haven't been able to help more with keeping visitors away.' He knows who I mean by *visitors*. 'Usually the charge nurse bosses people around. She's much better trained.' I give him a little grin, testing the waters.

He shakes his head. 'Not your fault. Sorry you have to deal with it.'

'Don't worry about it.' That's the second time he's covered for his dad's behaviour, I notice. 'I'm Amie, by the way. If you need anything.'

I replace the pillow and notice him trying to keep his eyes trained away from my boobs as I lean over him. Which means at least some of him is back online. When the patients start checking you out, you know they're returning to normalcy.

'I know you from someplace else, don't I?' he says suddenly.

'Um, maybe from school?' My final year of high school is still hanging off me like a loose thread. I've only been legally allowed to buy drinks at the pub for six months. 'I went to Ouyen Secondary, too.'

Harris still looks mystified.

I explain further. 'You went through the year above, with Simmo. And uh, Della and Jo and Chrissy.' I keep my eyes averted when I say that. Harris's rep with the girls is legendary, but he doesn't need to know I've heard about it. 'Or maybe you remember me from from West Mallee FNL?' I slip the second pillow out from under the freshly-changed one, trying not to roll his head. 'I played netball when you were playing footy. It was a few years ago...'

'The sarge's kid?'

I sigh, quietly enough that he won't notice. 'Yeah, that's me.'

He squints up. 'Was that the under-17s?'

'Yeah. I only played for two seasons. You gave it away the year after I started. You used to play half forward with Michael Watts.'

He closes his eyes, and I wonder if his leg is hurting him. 'Yeah, I played with Mike.'

I get a strong memory then of Harris taking a one-armed specky in the middle of some game...was it when they played Mildura South? I don't remember the opposition. But I remember how Harris looked in that moment: muscled shoulders lifted and arms reaching high, sun-bleached hair whipping back, stretched to his full height. You couldn't help but admire the scenery. I know a few of the netball chicks actually cried when he quit footy.

'You were a gun.' I clear my throat. Hopefully I'm not blushing. 'Top notch. That's why I remembered you. Wasn't there talk of you being scouted?'

'That was only a rumour,' he rasps.

I'm pretty sure it was more than a rumour, but I let it lie. 'So why'd you give it away?'

His eyes take on a strange sightlessness, and I know he's not looking at the inside of this hospital room. The pause goes on for a moment too long.

'Harris?'

'Just did.' He turns his head.

He clearly doesn't want to talk about this. I have no idea why. Most of the guys I know talk about their old footy victories a hundred times a day. Now Harris looks low, as if the whole conversation has depressed him. Damnit.

Then he blinks suddenly and talks again. 'So you finished school last year?'

'Um, yeah.' I bundle up the dirty pillowcases in both hands. 'Did a CNA course over the summer, and now here I am.'

'So you're a nurse? Or a, what...'

'A Certified Nursing Assistant. Just a fancy name for a trainee.' I scan the sheets above his leg. The linen will be tricky, but not impossible. 'I've got to change your bed sheets, too.'

Harris startles a little. 'How the hell you gonna do that?'

'Watch me.' I grin.

It takes about five minutes. I peel the fitted sheet down from the top at the same time as I unroll the new sheet, slipping it beneath his neck and shoulders, careful of his IV. When I get to his hips, I have to slide an arm under him and lift him in sections until the new sheet is cooling the skin of his back.

He's heavy, and I won't say he smells nice – he hasn't let us bathe him since he came in – but he has a distinct scent I associate with maleness. I've always thought if guys knew how appealing their own scent was to girls, they wouldn't use so much pongy aftershave. His skin is fine-pored and smooth, but he also feels clammy to touch; I'll have to report that.

He jerks when I slip my arm under his waist. I'd put it down to nerves, but this is *Harris Derwent* we're talking about, the slayer of Five Mile... I file it under 'normal embarrassment' – I know he's not wearing any jocks.

The sheet goes down pretty easily on his right side, everything kept modest because of the top-sheeted cage. Then I move over to his left. 'Can you lift your butt?'

'I got nothing on,' he warns.

I try not to grin: definitely normal embarrassment. I tug a side of the top sheet over to spill onto his lap. 'Will that spare your blushes?'

He's blushing anyway, but he nods.

'Good. Now lift up, just a little.'

He braces his right foot, tenses, and lifts enough to give his hips a few centimetres of clearance off the bed. I whip the dirty sheet down and shimmy in the clean one.

'Excellent. Down.' I replace the top sheet by laying it over the cage above the existing one, then drawing the old sheet away. 'There you go. Just like magic.'

'Great.' He's panting. That tiny bit of effort has made him break out in a sweat.

'You all right?'

'Yeah. Fine.'

I keep an eye on his face as I unfold a fresh blanket over the top of him. 'How's your leg?'

'Dunno. You tell me.' He shivers, rubs his hip under the blanket. 'The doctor hasn't said anything except I was lucky, and that I'll be on crutches for a while.'

I nod. 'You were, you know. Incredibly lucky. The bullet went clean through without hitting bone, or any major blood vessels. You could've lost your leg, or bled out.'

'Crutches sound like a good option, then.'

'Really good. Like, unbelievably good. The only things you have to worry about now are physio and risk of infection. That's why they've got the drain in.' I pause. 'But I'll ask the RNs, see if I can get you more information.'

'Thanks.'

I examine his face. 'Anything else you need? Are you in pain?'

He shrugs awkwardly. 'I'm due another dose tonight.'

I narrow my eyes. He's frowning, and his forehead has a light sheen. Since I started working here I've learned that patients aren't always the best judge of how much pain they can handle. Male patients, particularly, whinge about minor injuries like they're dying, but almost never admit to serious pain. I'm gonna have to make this easy for him.

'Gimme a number,' I say. 'If one is 'Shit, I've stubbed my toe', and ten is 'Please god, make it stop', where are you?'

He takes a breath and looks away, across the room.

'Hey.' I tap him on the arm. 'Don't whitewash it. Just tell me.'

His throat moves as he swallows, and he doesn't say anything.

I study him, see the lines on his forehead, the furrows of tension around his eyes and mouth. I abandon the laundry trolley and walk out of the room.

It takes me a few minutes to find Barb and fill her in on the problem.

'Well, how long has he been like this?' She sighs and grabs a pair of gloves from the wall dispenser as we walk. 'Hasn't anybody else noticed the poor bugger's been suffering?'

'He's been out of surgery, what, two days?' I hand her a wrapped syringe. 'Look, he's not the most forthcoming patient, maybe he's just been real quiet about it.'

'Mmph,' she says, and loads the syringe.

We enter Harris's room together and I can tell he recognises Barb.

'Hello there, Mr Derwent.' Barb uncaps the syringe as she moves to the other side of his bed. 'Amie tells me you're struggling a bit.'

'Could be,' he says. He's still panting a little. I feel like a fool not to have noticed before now.

'Well, you know, that's why the Good Lord gave us analgesics,' Barb says. 'Also, we have that nifty little buzzer beside your bed. All the mod cons here. So next time you're doing it tough, give us a bell, all right?' She grabs the tube of his drip with one meaty hand.

He nods just as she depresses the plunger. His face instantly releases – hard lines softening and lips opening as the pain recedes. The sight of his reaction gives me a little shiver. I get over myself, grab a towel and smooth his hair back off his forehead.

'Dummy,' I say softly.

'Thank you,' he says, and I think he really means it this time. His voice has gone thick, liquid.

'Well spotted,' Barb says to me. 'I'll have someone come in to check his blood pressure and do some obs, and then maybe we'll have a talk about the drug sheet. He shouldn't be getting so much breakthrough pain at this point.'

As Barb heads out, I move to stuff the dirty linen in my cart; I've still got beds to change in Twelve. Harris snags my wrist as I'm turning.

'Hey.' He's slurring his consonants. 'M'sorry for being an arsehole patient.'

'You've been in pain.' I shrug. 'Pain can make people a little crazy.'

He's still holding my wrist. His fingers are warm, shaky, and a little sweaty. His eyes glow like green neon, the pupils mere pinpricks. 'I knew you were the sarge's kid. He's an okay bloke. I know I see him a bit more than he'd like, but he's awright.'

I've heard Dad talk about Harris, on occasion. I don't know if all the things Dad had to say about him were as complimentary.

'Well, I'm glad you think so.' I gently extricate my wrist, patting his hand as I go. 'Now start getting better, and you'll be kicking the footy again in no time.'

'Yeah, okay,' Harris sighs. His eyes close.

I think of something then. 'Harris, when you're checked out of here, do you have a place to go?'

'Dad,' he says softly. 'Dad'll want me back.'

It's not until I'm out in the hall with the trolley that I realise he didn't really answer the question.

3

harris

Years ago, this mate of mine had a dog for round-ups that got poisoned when she ate fox bait. When we dragged her out from under their old house, her body was stiff and stretched, her mouth a death-grin, her exposed belly white and vulnerable.

That's how I've felt since I arrived in hospital, like someone stretched my skin taut. These last two days have been shit. Police interviews, and talking with Rachel on the phone, dealing with her dad...

The business at the quarry. That's what the sarge called it. Thing is, I wouldna been anywhere near the quarry, my former place of employment, if I'd known it was gonna turn into a total fuck-up. But Mike's sister, Rachel, needed a hand. By unfortunate coincidence, I've had a thing for Rachel for years. It was during the quarry business that I realised Rachel's in no way interested. So I've been chewing over that concept while the pain chewed through me.

Meanwhile, my own dad's been hovering around like a blow-fly over roadkill. Today my leg was throbbing with a false heartbeat and I'd had enough. I gave myself permission to be a bastard for a while, let myself drift.

Then Amie Blunt arrived to change the sheets. She asked me about the pain – no idea how she knew – and came back with Bette, she of the scritchy polyester pants and the brassy voice. The name tag on her bosom read *Barbara Dunne*. She pumped a shot into my IV line and the pain was magically, amazingly gone. The relief made me want to weep and cheer at the same time.

Now it's night. Don't know when we got through afternoon, but it's pretty dark in here. I'm lying flat, feeling floaty, just listening. The hospital has a muffled quiet by evening. You can hear faint beeps from other rooms, the hum of the air-conditioning. It's like being underwater.

So I hear it when someone raises their voice down the hall. A ruckus in Admissions, maybe. I can't make out words. I lie here, trying to work out what's going on from the wailing. The noise masks the beat of fast-moving footsteps, which is why I'm caught by surprise when Amie Blunt ducks into my room.

She closes the door, turns, and leans her spine against it. Could be she's just something I'm dreaming up because of the drugs I'm on. But I can see details that tell me she's real. Her hair, dark and shiny, is slipping out of her plait; she rakes it back. Her hands are shaking, and she's breathing hard.

'Amie?' My voice comes out rough.

She jumps, the whites of her eyes flashing. 'Oh, sorry. Sorry, I thought you were asleep. I wouldn't have come in if I'd known you were –'

'You okay?' Her voice is tight and her movements are small, jerky. Doesn't take a genius to figure things out, which is good cos I'm no genius at the moment. 'You're upset.'

'No, I'm...' She stops. Takes a breath, releases it. 'Yes.'

'Okay,' I say.

She swipes her palms down her work pants, closes her eyes. 'I just need a minute.'

'Not a problem.' I'm hardly gonna say no after what she did for me this arvo. I wriggle myself up. 'What's happening?'

'You shouldn't be moving.' She says it on automatic as she looks over. 'Just a... A bad case.'

'Oh.'

'Craig Davies was admitted,' she blurts out.

'What?' I blink.

'You know him?' She looks away to the other side of the room. 'He was...messy. Off his face on ice. Barb had him transferred to Mildura for treatment.'

Ice. Fuck.

A mate – well, he's my dealer, but he's still a mate – slipped me some in a bong during a bonfire night about a year ago, and it nearly took the top of my skull off. Holidaying in your head is one thing, but ice turns you into a fucking lunatic. Blind paranoia and rage, and a hefty dose of crazed energy that leaves you champing at the insides of your mouth...

It's the closest I've ever been to feeling like I'd slipped into my father's skin. It scared the shit out of me. I've never wanted to be near the stuff since.

'I know Craig.' I sound dazed. Or maybe it's just surprise: Craig's the last person I would've pinned as an ice user.

Amie's eyes are shadowed. 'He attacked his sister.'

'What?' Now I'm sitting up, as up as I can manage.

'I can't...' Amie shakes her head. Her cheeks are still blanched. 'I can't talk about it. I shouldn't have said anything.'

'His sister, Clare?'

Amie nods, very small.

My voice comes out strangled. 'She's *eleven*.'

'I know. I saw them...' She looks down, pressing her lips together, as if she's trying to stop herself from crying.

'Are you okay?'

'Yeah. I just need to catch my breath.' She makes a brief humourless laugh. 'I'm not really used to this nursing thing yet. I have to get a bit tougher.'

'Siddown.' I nod my chin at the chair near my bed.

She shakes her head. 'Thanks, but it's okay. I'll be okay.' She looks around suddenly, like she's just realised where she is. 'Damn, I should go.'

'Relax, mate. Give yourself a minute. I'm sure there's plenty of people out there who can hold the fort.'

Amie sighs, sinks her head back against the door. 'God, I'm kind of crap at this, aren't I?'

I frown and smile at the same time, ease back on the pillows. 'What are you talking about? You're a good nurse.'

Amie snorts.

'You are,' I say. 'You handle my dad like a champ. And you were great with me this arvo.'

'You don't have to keep apologising for your dad, Harris. And the nursing...' She straightens, rubs at her forehead. 'I don't know sometimes.'

'You always wanted to do this kinda work?' I don't know why, but I feel the urge to keep her talking. Being high sometimes makes me chatty. Amie looks like she needs a chat, and I don't mind the company.

She shrugs. Some of the colour is returning to her face. 'I guess. My mum did it. I know the life.'

'Not your dream job, though?'

She laughs softly, but it's a proper laugh this time. 'I'm a few decades too late for that. My dream job would be to work with Ansel Adams.'

I dunno who that is. I like seeing Amie laugh, though. Good-looking chick. Gotta admit, whenever she's in the room it's a struggle to keep my eyes off her rack. I look at her plait now instead, which is flopped over her shoulder. Her hair must be long when it's loose – the plait is a thick rope. Her eyebrows are dark and her skin is an even light brown, like a really nice tan, and everyone knows the sarge's wife was Indian, or Pakistani, or something like that.

She takes a step closer, tucking in her work shirt at the back. I catch her scent, which I remember from when she changed my sheets earlier – some sort of flower shampoo. 'What was *your* dream job? When you were a kid?'

The question takes me by surprise. I have to think about it. 'Um, I dunno. I think I wanted to be Matthew Richardson.'

'The Richmond footy hero? Makes sense.' She smiles, tilts her head. 'You never said anything.'

'What's that?'

'About having a senior sergeant for a father. You never said anything. Everyone makes stupid jokes about staying on the right side of the law...'

I shrug. 'I'm not everyone.'

Well, of course I never made a joke. She didn't think I noticed, but I saw her expression this afternoon when I made the connection between her and her dad. I know what that's like: having everyone raise their eyebrows when they hear your name, cos of what your parent did.

'Well...thanks. For not making a joke out of it.' She bites her lip. 'I'd really better go. You should sleep. I'll see you tomorrow.'

She eases the door of the room open, pokes her head out, slips through. The door sighs as it closes behind her. I sigh, too.

Maybe Amie and me can cut a deal. I won't make jokes about the cop thing, if she'll stop asking about the footy thing. I haven't played footy in three years. Thinking about it just makes me feel like crap. And I'm worried a genuine answer might pop out of my mouth if she keeps pushing.

Better not to talk about it. Better not to remember what it feels like to run hard on the freezing winter ground with a slippery ball in your hands, judging the kick. Having a whole team of mates calling for you to belt it their way. Leaping for a mark, with the sky so close that you...

Shit.

I'm not gonna explain it to her. How Dad was being smart about it. How Saturday was match day, so bruises that appeared on Sunday could be explained away by the clashes at footy the day before.

That was where I collided with Simmo's head.

I got that in the game.

Mike was the only one who never bought the bullshit. He'd give me a look if he saw my busted fingers, or the bruises over my ribs. But it didn't matter. By the time I was sixteen, logic won out over passion.

Why'd I give it away? Because I figured it out. Footy was beautiful. Footy was pointless.

I could never win.

*

'D'you remember when we used to go yabbying?'

Dad's voice wakes me. For a second I wonder where I am, then everything slams back into focus. It's Wednesday. My leg aches from this morning's physio session. There's a bitter taste in the back of my throat.

Dad's standing over by the window, looking out.

'I used to shoot a rabbit the night before,' he says, 'and you'd wake up keen as mustard. Grab the bucket and get the net from under the house. You were always so bloody excited to go. Even if I made you carry the rabbit.'

He sounds like he's talking to himself, but I think he knows I'm awake, the same way I know whenever he's in the room. Psychic tension.

'We'd walk to the rez,' he says. 'Take our time. Find a nice shady spot on the bank to sit and bait the net. Stretch our legs while we waited for the net to fill up.'

The feel of it comes back to me. Hot sun baking my skin, flies on my lips, the weedy decomposing smell of the reservoir.

'I remember,' I say softly. 'You'd have a coldie and a smoke while we waited.'

Dad nods at the window. 'You used to draw in the mud with sticks. Build those little mounds of stones.'

'You never let me skim them.' I remember that, too. He used to cuff me over the head, say I'd stop the yabbies from coming.

Dad grins. 'When the flies got too much for us we'd haul in the net.'

I think of the mud-streaked bodies of the yabbies. The green and purple and blue of their shells, the way their giant pincers snapped helplessly. Out of their element, their glistening armour was just extra weight to carry around. I always felt sorry for them, especially the big ones. They'd survived so long in the murky underwater pecking-order of the dam, grown to such a size, and there they were, floundering in the net: defeated warriors. It almost felt mean to take them home and eat them.

'They were nice-sized yabbies,' I say.

'Bloody great eating,' Dad agrees. 'Into the pot, then onto the newspaper on the table. Bit of vinegar, salt...' He shakes his head and makes that sound that always reminds me of horses nickering.

I wonder where this is all going. The yabby memory is from ten years ago, but I've got fresher ones. Less pleasant ones. There's still a bruise on my cheekbone from when we fought over the rifle

I borrowed to help Rachel. Dad was pissed about it; the rifle was unlicensed, so the sarge confiscated it.

'We had some good times, didn't we, Harris?' Dad turns around. 'We haven't always seen eye-to-eye, but there were good times.'

'Sure, there were good times,' I say slowly.

And there were. Like when I'd ride on the tray of the ute, jouncing down to Five Mile. Or when Dad and I would sit together of an evening, on the couch at home, watching quiz shows and competing to see who could answer the questions on the telly first. Or my best memory: Dad working on an engine in the shed, showing me where to use the tools, the radio oozing out some daggy seventies song in the background as the cool afternoon bled the heat out of the shed walls.

Those memories have a clear crystalline bite. They could've happened yesterday. But I remember them so well because they were standouts. Like a leaping redfin on your line, they jump up easily from the grey background.

At the moment, Dad's only focused on the fact I've replied in the affirmative. To Dad, being agreed with is the only acceptable response.

'Yeah, there were good times,' Dad says, nodding. 'Which is why I'm gonna ask you to do this. I know, I know... We have our barneys, and you were keen to move to Melbourne. But this is important, Harris.'

I get a cold clench in my gut. 'What're you talking about?'

Dad presses his point. 'It's bigger than you and me. Bigger than a few spats.'

'Dad –'

'I'm sick, Harris,' Dad says. He looks right at me. 'Cancer.'

I feel sick, too. It wells up suddenly, like a vat of acid, red and bubbling.

'You've got cancer.' I stare at Dad, only half-believing. This could be a trick. I wouldn't put it past him.

His voice goes quiet. 'It's for real, Harris. I've gotta come in for treatment.'

'*Bull*shit.' The word explodes out of me before I can stop it.

'I said it's for real. I'm not lying.' Dad sighs. 'I'm seeing Doc Clifford. She wants me to start a course of chemo after Christmas. Until then I'm on some kinda medicine to get the ball rolling. I mean, look at me, yeah? I'm dropping weight, I've cut back on the cigs... I dunno what else I can say to convince you, Harris, but it's true.'

My head is sloshing around with the combination of this morning's drugs and now this news. I can't seem to process. My dad has cancer. He might be dying. I don't know what to feel.

'And that's what I wanna ask you,' Dad goes on. 'That's all I need. It's what kids do for their old folks – stick around when the going's tough.'

That's when it all comes clear. When I finally understand what Dad wants, and what it'll mean.

'You want me to come home.' My voice is flat. 'To stay with you.'

'While I go through treatment, yeah. If you do that, things'll be different. I'll mend me ways. Stop ragging you. But I need you home now, son. You'll have to get back on your feet, and I'll be on my medicine. We can look after each other.'

Look after each other. Those words have a whole different meaning under Dad's roof. I remember plenty of times he's 'looked after' me – usually it happened when I wasn't doing as I was told, or doing it fast enough, or sometimes when I was getting up to strife, or resisting him. I've got enough memories of those times that only the really painful ones stick out now.

It's not like it's been all one way, either. I always thought it was impossible to stand up for myself, then when I got tall, I found my fight. I did it out of anger, or out of desperation, or just to save my sanity. Does that make me a bad person? I dunno.

What I do know is that since I hit puberty, me and Dad in combination can't be anything but wrong. Oil and water, chalk and cheese, fuel and flame; some things just shouldn't be mixed.

'I think you're fucking crazy.' I stare at him. 'I'm crook, you're crook. How're we s'posed to help each other? What, you want me to –'

'*I want you to do something good for me!*' Dad's face is livid. He realises he's bellowed, lowers his voice, which I can see takes some effort. 'I want you to do what a son should. Take care of me before I go into the ground. I'm tryin' to talk reasonable with you, but you can't even do that!'

The bed I'm in seems to have turned into malleable plastic. I can feel the pillows under me, the padding I've shrunk into. My whole body is tense – I try to relax my thigh, which is throbbing again. Dad's flare-ups do this to me, every time.

But I'm stuck here on this bed. I can't get up and walk away. I've just gotta take the hit, and hope there's still enough spring left in me to bounce back.

I start slow. 'If you're seeing a doc about it –'

'It eats you up from the inside.' Dad glowers at the floor. 'Nothing smells good, nothing tastes good... And it hurts. It's hard to get up in the morning sometimes.'

I close my eyes. 'Dad, I dunno. This is...'

This is what? Insane? Stupid? All of the above? I got away from Dad once. Going back would end me. It's not gonna happen. No fucking way.

'Look, I'll sweeten the pot,' Dad says suddenly. 'I'll come clean with you.'

My eyes open. 'What?'

'Come back home. That's all I'm asking. If you do that…I'll tell you where to find your mother.'

The silence in the room now is a glaring contrast to Dad's bellow of a moment ago. I truly feel as if my lungs have stopped working.

It takes me a whole minute to push words out my throat. 'You know where she is?'

'Yes.'

I absorb this for a second. Make my throat work again. 'And Kelly?'

'They're together.'

Together – my mum and my sister are together.

'I know you've been hunting around for them,' Dad says. 'I know you've been trying to track them down.'

I won't ask him how he knows this.

'I'll give you contacts for them.' Dad looks at the sheets on my bed. 'Once I go into hospital, you can get in touch with them –'

'I want to get in touch with them now.'

'Harris.' Dad meets my eyes. This isn't something we've ever discussed before. I might be okay with sticking up for myself, but I've never been brave enough to broach this topic.

Dad shifts his stance, and I flinch.

'Come home, son,' Dad says softly.

I hold his gaze for a long time before I nod.

4

amie

'A Brazilian.'

'Not in a million years.'

Roberta snorts on the other end of the phone. 'You're telling me you wouldn't even try it? Even if it's on special?'

'The hair is there for a reason, Robbie. Not to mention *ouch*.' I have a thought. 'God, tell me your mum isn't doing it.'

'Ew! *Please*. Mum makes Pam do all the waxing treatments. Anyway, I'm not gonna tell her I'm getting one, and neither are you.'

I laugh. 'You're safe, because I'd never have that conversation with your mum, like, ever. And for the record, I think you're totally bonkers.'

'Gotta try everything once,' Roberta says, and I can hear her grinning. 'Maybe next time you come up here to Mildy, I'll bring you to the salon. You might change your mind...'

'Not a chance,' I say, still laughing.

'So how's things at the hospital with Nick?' She says it casually, so I know she's softened me up with the Brazilian joke.

'Fine.' I pick at a bald patch on the knee of my jeans. 'We're not twelve, Robbie.'

'I know. But I'm pretty sure he's still into you.'

My cheeks warm. 'We broke up ages ago, Rob, and we decided that together. Anyway, I like what we have now. Me and Nick get along great. Everything's friendly.'

'Good. I mean, I know Nick's not a jerk. I figured he'd be all right.' Robbie sounds satisfied. But her next question is more tentative. 'And is your dad doing okay?'

This is the question she should have prefaced with the Brazilian joke. I swallow before replying. 'He's fine. No more dizzy spells. He knows this is his last year on the force, he's already talked to the Mildura CO about it.'

'That must be a relief.'

'Yeah.' I sound upbeat, but I'm not sure. What will Dad do if he's not a copper? 'Anyway, he's on medication for his heart. The doctor says...' I pause, struggling to keep my tone light.

'Ames? What does the doctor say?'

I shake it off. 'Nothing. Dad'll be okay. I'm keeping an eye on him.'

Once I finish on the phone with Robbie, I take off for Pink Lakes with the camera. It's not the best time of the day for shooting, but it'll do.

Last month, I went through a phase of shooting close-ups of old metal – gate bolts, padlocks, faucets, rusty flakes peeling and broken. Now I'm a bit hung up on native mistletoe. Tight frames of dripping sap, of sticky green tendrils burrowing their way into bark, smothering the new growth... I don't know exactly what's drawn my eye, but I find the subject fascinating.

Time seems to move differently in certain places, and Pink Lakes is one of them. The salt pans throw the light up in the air: everything seems to glow like a Martian landscape. Sometimes I get so focused I'll take shot after shot, and only realise when I look through the viewfinder that the sun's gone down and I've lost the light.

Time moves differently in hospitals as well. Depending on the roster, I work four or five shifts per week. Anything can happen in between. Some days I go in and the patient I've been seeing in a certain room is gone. Recovered and checked out, or moved to another ward. Sometimes you know they'll be back. Sometimes it's like they've disappeared, snapped out of existence.

Mrs Dougherty's angina clears and she returns to Aged Care. Kevin Monaghan comes into A&E having nearly completely ring-barked his left thumb after a fence-wire accident. He stays overnight. Monday to Friday is generally pretty sedate. In that time we get the usual complement of geriatric cases, a whiplash patient from a minor fender bender near Sea Lake, and an infant with febrile convulsions. Friday night through to Sunday afternoon is the busiest period. We see kids who've banged themselves around playing junior sport, as well as people who've waited all week to come in after injuring themselves, and a number of DFOs (drunk, fell over).

Harris Derwent won't get to see that. He's due for discharge today. He's moved from the bed to a wheelchair and now onto crutches, in his five days on the ward. He's been examined by the physio and sits in a chair for meals. It was weird when I came on shift and saw him standing again for the first time – I'd forgotten how tall he is. Pushing six foot, and broad in the shoulders.

I go in to collect his tray and he's wearing a faded black T-shirt and navy trackie pants, standing – crutch-supported – by the window that looks out onto the back car park. Far as I know, the only thing to see out there is a series of external vents for the hospital air-conditioning and the plastic milk crates where Barb and a couple of the other die-hard smokers sit during their break. Barb isn't out there now. She's here, in the room, and so is Harris's dad.

Dennis Derwent looks the same as all the blokes I know locally who do the heavy lifting and hard slog of day-to-day farm work.

He wears the same kind of jeans and boots and flannie shirts. He isn't any more physically imposing. But he's intimidating. He gives off a strange energy, like an acrid smell. His muscles are always tense, his eyes narrowed. He reminds me of a guard dog: hackles raised, ready to snap.

Maybe all the time spent looking through a viewfinder has honed my eye, but to me it's very clear, the family resemblance between father and son. They don't have matching eye colour, and Harris is stubbled while his dad is smooth-faced, but they both have strong full-forward builds, although Dennis seems leaner, as if he's lost weight. Dennis is dark-haired, close-cropped; Harris's messy blonde surfer hair stands out as an almost deliberate point of difference. But together like this, their similarities are more striking. Harris has the same slow-twitch muscle, the same tanned skin. Harris also seems tense. He doesn't have his dad's intimidating presence, but he has the same sense of contained energy.

Dennis sits back in the hospital chair in his son's room, legs loose and knees akimbo, rolling a cigarette. His tobacco pouch rests on his thigh. Barb seems to be trying to keep his attention on her.

'...so yes, he's ready to go, except for the paperwork. But he's going to need time to rest, and a bit of looking after when he gets home.'

'Yep. No worries.' Dennis is focused on his smoke, dressing the paper with the brown threads.

'He has to stay off that leg for a while, and keep doing the wound-dressing we talked about –'

'He'll be right once he gets home.' Dennis licks the edge of his rolling paper. 'You'll be right, won't you, Harris?'

It doesn't quite sound like a question. Harris is still looking out the window.

'Yeah,' he says, over his shoulder. 'Yeah, I'll be right.'

'See?' Dennis slips the cigarette into the corner of his mouth as he looks at Barb. 'He said he'll be right. He'll be fine.'

I'm not really supposed to be party to this conversation. I'm just the clean-up lady, the silent unnoticed servant. I slip over to the trolley by the window on Harris's near side and tidy the rubbish on the tray.

Barb talks on behind me. 'Is that true, Harris? If I sign you out and give you some wound-dressing stuff, will you be okay at home?' She gives the words a strange emphasis.

Harris turns his head to reply and sees me there, my fingers busy on the tray. When our eyes meet, it's like they get stuck together. And while his expression is frozen in neutral, there's a whole world of stuff in his green gaze that worries me. I don't recognise everything in there, but I know it's a far cry from the relief most patients feel when they check out and return home.

We share that moment of recognition. Then Harris swallows, blinks, and turns back to the window.

'Sure,' he says. 'All good.'

Barb makes a little sigh. 'All rightie.'

I lift the tray and escape.

Harris goes home an hour later. I carry his duffel bag for him as he hobbles behind his father towards the sliding glass doors. Harris has to hunch his shoulders over the crutches. It makes him look smaller.

His dad opens the passenger door of a beat-up white Toyota ute and Harris clambers his way in. The afternoon light is fading, taking on a cool blue-grey tone from the shadow of the pergola above the ambulance bay. Harris takes his bag, props it on his right leg as I help wrangle his crutches into the cab.

'Cheers.' He only looks at me once, and it's a quick glance.

He pulls the door shut, still not looking at me, as his dad starts the engine. I get that feeling, like the person I'm trying to engage with is uncomfortable because of something I said or did. It rankles me. I'm damned if know what I've done to make Harris Derwent feel uncomfortable.

Then I think about what I saw back in his room. What I saw in Harris's face. And I realise something: that is a secret part of him. Something he never shows anybody.

A powerful urge wells up inside me to reach out and grab the door handle of the Toyota and yank it open again. But I don't do that. Mainly because I have no idea what I would say after that point. 'Get out of the car'? Or 'Don't go home with your dad'? And what would happen then?

I don't know. I don't know what else I can do, so I just stand silent on the pavement as Mr Derwent revs the engine. Harris sits in the passenger seat, his face turned forward. His profile doesn't give anything away as the old ute eases out, drives off.

Barb moves to stand beside me. She scratches the back of her neck as she watches the ute turn onto Britt Street. 'Hm. Not exactly what you'd call an ideal outcome.'

'Why did he do that?' I'm thinking of Harris's expression. 'Why did he even agree to go home?'

'Who can say?' Barb shifts her weight from one foot to the other. 'Sweetie, I've worked at this hospital for seventeen years. Worked with your mum in theatre, worked A&E... Seventeen years is a long time. Some things just curl your hair. You don't get used to them, and maybe that's how it's supposed to be.'

'So you knew.' I didn't mean it to come out so accusing.

Barb doesn't seem to take it personally. 'Every time that boy came in to A&E, I wanted to punch his father in the face. I tried reporting it, and I wasn't the only one. But Dennis always had Harris cleaned up and polite when Social Services came knocking. That kid...'

'He's not a kid now,' I point out. 'He's nineteen.'

'That's right. And he's old enough to make his own choice. He chose that.'

A mental image of Dennis Derwent, casually rolling a cigarette, clashes in my mind with an image of Harris, white-faced and sweaty when I prodded him to give me a number. I don't know Harris, not really. I can't hope to understand why he did this. But I have a sick feeling I know what it will mean for him.

'Maybe he doesn't think he's got choices,' I say.

Barb shakes her head as she turns away. 'Lord only knows, Amie. Lord only knows.'

*

I have to pick up groceries from the Ouyen IGA before heading home. It's the same list every time: tins of fruit punch, bacon rashers wrapped in paper, cartons of milk... Harris Derwent's blank hard profile lingers in my mind the whole time I'm shopping. Ten minutes past the sign for Walpcup in the warm car I catch sight of my house though the windscreen. That's when I finally start to feel better.

Sometimes, in books, you read about a girl – it's always a girl – described as 'plain'. It's kind of an old-fashioned term. It's supposed to mean someone who has a nice personality but isn't much chop in the looks department. Our house is plain. Painted weatherboard with an attached carport, an old picket fence with a creaky wire gate, grass growing high. An old Holden carcass sits on bricks between the carport and the fence – Dad periodically raids it for parts when he's working on fix-it jobs.

But my whole body relaxes when I see the ramshackle yard, the dun-white walls. It's home. It's mine – mine and Dad's. I never feel anxious or afraid returning to it, the way Harris Derwent felt returning to his.

I'm lucky, I realise as I pull the handbrake. Home is a haven for me. Not everybody has it so good.

The squad car is parked in the driveway, which means Dad's home for lunch. The heavy bags of groceries make me lumber awkwardly down the hallway and into our tiny kitchen. Dad's keys, wallet, and phone are on the table. His jacket is hanging over the back of a chair. I dump the green bags on the lino floor, grab Dad's phone and wander out through the back door to the roofed concrete area near the outside laundry.

Dad's got his blue uniform sleeves rolled to his elbows and an apron on. The apron is a faded pink floral number, an ancient one of Mum's. Dad always wears an apron over his uniform when he's tinkering – he has a terrible habit of wiping his hands on his front when he's working on cars. I've tried to break him of it, but I think it's an unconscious thing.

'Dad, your phone.' I stand on the top step and hold the offending item out.

'Hey, love. What?' He looks over and blinks. He's got a fanbelt, like a big black licorice strap, in one gnarled hand. 'Oh bugger. Was it on the kitchen table?'

'Jared's gonna have a heart attack if you miss another call. And I've had enough medical emergencies for today. Did you take your pills?'

'Yeah, sorry.' He winces in apology. 'How was work?'

'Oh, y'know, fine. Have you eaten?' He's supposed to eat with his pills.

'Not yet. Just wanted to find a match for this bit of rubbish.' He waggles the fan belt.

'I'll make you an omelette.'

'That'd be great, love, thanks.'

Dad and I have this incredibly boring gendered division of

household labour, where Dad fixes the cars and plumbing and electrics and stuff, and I do all the grocery shopping. But we both take turns making meals and doing laundry and tidying. It's a flexible system – we both work nights at various times, so it has to be – but it seems to keep the house functioning okay. And me and Dad, of course. We function okay, too.

Once I've changed out of my nurse-wear and into a T-shirt and jeans, I go back and wash my hands at the kitchen sink before cracking eggs into a bowl. Dad clomps up the steps as soon as the aroma of bacon omelette starts wafting around.

'You good?' I watch him as he washes his hands at the sink. He's looking a bit grizzled today, and his greying hair needs a cut. He uses the potato brush to get the grease out from under his nails, which makes me wince, but he's obviously thinking about other things. He often comes home to tinker when he's got a particularly knotty problem he's trying to work out.

He kisses the top of my head as he dries his hands. 'Yep, I'm good.'

I slip the omelette onto a plate, set it on the table. 'So what's going on?'

'Ah, nothing.' I can see that's not true just by his expression, so I wait it out. 'Well, something. You know, there's always something.'

I nod. This much I've learned.

Dad fesses up as he shuffles into a chair at the table. 'The Donovan boy. He's gone missing again.'

'But they brought him back!'

'Well, he got hold of some more gear. I'd say Snowie Geraldson tuned him up.' Dad sighs, picks up his fork. 'Gavin tore up the house looking for cash and now he's pissed off in his mum's car. They know where he's gone –'

'To Mildura, to get more drugs.'

'Yeah. But there's about a dozen places he could be, and his father wants me to do some asking around up there. So I might be heading up this arvo.'

Shit – that means Dad won't be home until late. And he looks peaky already.

'You won't get him back before evening,' I point out.

'I know.'

'So why don't you get the Mildura blokes to search this afternoon, then go up tomorrow morning?'

Dad shrugs. 'It's not their job, to go hunting for Patchewollock kids who've gone out on a tear. They've got plenty to do already. And his mum's worried.'

'She's right to be worried.' I pour myself a glass of juice, sit at the table. 'She should have a talk with Mrs Davies. Jesus, I don't know if I could deal with that. Having a son who's slowly losing his mind.'

'It's not...' Dad frowns, considering how to phrase it. 'Gavin's not a bad person. Craig's not a bad person, either.'

'I know he's not a bad person. He's a nice person, Craig. And Gavin and his little brother came to the Walpe Christmas do, just last year, remember? He was chatting up the girls, helping with the barbeque... He's a nice kid. I don't get it.'

'Drugs make people do bad things.' Dad concentrates on his plate. 'This drug in particular.'

I nod and sip my juice, but the conversation has made me sad. Or maybe I'm still feeling sad from dealing with the Harris thing. I'm not sure.

'So work's going okay?' Dad scrapes up eggs with the edge of his fork, but he's no fool. I'm only quiet when I'm pensive like this.

I shrug. 'It was okay. A bit horrible at the end, when I had to watch Harris Derwent go home with his father.'

'Dennis took him back?' Dad straightens, pushes his empty plate forward. 'Yeah, not exactly the happy homecoming, I imagine.'

'That's what Barb said.' It annoys me that I helped manage the guy's care for five days, but apparently I'm the only person who's not up to speed on the situation. 'How long has that been going on?'

'Longer than I would've liked.' Dad shakes his head. 'Probably feels like forever to Harris.'

'Why didn't you do anything about it?'

It's not like the way I spoke to Barb; I really do sound accusing this time. Barb's hog-tied, to some extent. She can make recommendations, but there's a limit to what she can do.

Dad's a copper, though. He's in a position of authority. He has more power in a situation like this.

'It's not so simple, love.' He angles his head to hold my eyes. 'You know what it's like – I get a call-out for a domestic and by the time me and Jared rock up, everyone's gone quiet. Or the wife has started defending the bloke who's bashing her, and the kids are told to keep their mouths shut. It's a bloody complicated business.'

I take a sip of my drink, feeling dry-mouthed and frustrated. 'But Harris isn't a minor anymore. Why'd he go home? What would make him go back to that?'

'We might never know. Maybe Dennis has got something over him, or something there keeps pulling him back.' Dad turns in his chair, leaning one elbow on the table. 'It's a shame, yeah? Dennis is a complete bastard, but Harris... Funny kid. Personable, y'know? But obviously not quite a hundred percent. I remember about six years ago he started pinching stuff around Five Mile, getting into strife in other ways. Lots of attention-seeking stunts, I guess, which stands to reason. Stole that ute out of Shane

Morang's front yard – remember that? You might have been too young...'

'No, I remember. That was a big deal, wasn't it?'

'Too right it was a big deal. New generator sitting under a tarp in the back of the tray and along comes this snot-nosed thirteen year old, decides to take the whole thing for a joy-ride.'

'Was he charged?'

'No, but he came bloody close. I had Shane in the back office at the station for about an hour, talking him out of it.'

'What did Dennis say?'

Dad doesn't reply for a moment, and it's as if the light in the kitchen has shifted. The lines of wear on his face suddenly look like shadowed gouges.

'Don't know if you want to hear it,' he says finally.

He's right: I don't know if I want to hear it. Just looking at Dad's face is enough. But it's all tied up in what I saw, what I felt this afternoon. Somehow, I have to know.

My voice comes out quiet. 'What happened?'

'Well, it was years ago, but...' Dad traces the edge of the table with the flat of his thumb. 'Dennis collected Harris from the station the day before, so I went up there to see what the outcome was. Dennis kept me talking in the front yard – it's a broken-down old place, I figured he didn't want me sitting in his kitchen, y'know?'

I nod. Lots of rural folk keep up outward appearances, but the insides of their houses reveal the quiet poverty of farming life. And not everyone is comfortable with the local constabulary in their kitchen.

'Anyway,' Dad continues, 'I just had a bad feeling. I couldn't see Harris around. I didn't want to get Dennis any more riled, but I asked to see his boy, made some excuse. So Dennis goes in, gets Harris to come out.'

I've already steeled myself to hear the worst, but the look on Dad's face still makes me shiver.

Dad sighs out through his nose. 'Well, he was knocked around, I could see that. Big shiner on one eye, and he was moving funny. He wasn't like he is now – this was before he got a bit of height and meat on. He was just this skinny little bugger, with about two inches of ankle showing where he was growing out of his jeans. I said to him, *Harris, are you okay?* Like, of course he wasn't okay, why was I even asking? But he said he was fine. That he fell off his mate's dirtbike.'

Dad shakes his head. I can see it's hurting him to remember, and the hurt is because the situation made him feel powerless. And I totally get that.

'Well, I didn't want to get him in more trouble. Bad enough I'd even shown up in Dennis's yard. But I asked him anyway, straight out – *Harris, did your dad lay into you?* And he just looked at me. He didn't say anything, but his face...'

Suddenly I can imagine this picture with frightening clarity. Because Harris would've worn the same expression then as he did on Tuesday, when I asked him whether he was in pain.

Don't whitewash it. Just tell me.

Now I understand why it was so impossible for him to answer. The idea makes me sick. It's weird, too, knowing this personal stuff about Harris. I can picture the scene so vividly, it makes me feel like a voyeur.

I have to swallow before I can speak again. 'What did you do?'

'Wasn't anything I *could* do,' Dad says softly. 'Had to get back in the squad car and drive away. Praying the whole time that Dennis wouldn't make Harris pay for me showing up. That was the worst part – knowing I might've caused more harm just by visiting.'

'That's... Dad, that's awful.'

'Yeah. They're the times you really hate the job.' He sighs again, and I know his thoughts have strayed. Now he's thinking of another lost boy, and the efforts he'll have to make to find him. 'Look, are you gonna be right tonight if I go to Mildura?'

'I'll be fine, don't worry about me. But if you finish later than nine-thirty, you should stay the night with the Murphy's.'

'Amie, it's only an hour back from Mildura –'

'Seriously, Dad, just think about the time before you get in the car to drive home. I don't want to worry about you writing yourself off because you had a dizzy spell, or fell asleep behind the wheel.' I drain my glass, stand up to take the dirty crockery to the sink. 'I might go out with the camera for a bit this arvo. Call Nani and say hi.'

'Sounds good. Okay, I'd better move.' He stands up, collects his stuff off the table, then stops when he looks down to put his keys in his pocket. 'Shit, I've still got this bloody apron on.'

I can't help but grin. 'You look nice in floral.'

'Matches my eyes.' He unties the apron, looking sheepish, before pecking me on the cheek. 'See you later on, love.'

Once Dad's driven off and I've finished rinsing the dishes, I go back to my room and flop on the bed. But I can't nap now, it's too late in the day, and my mind is too busy. Harris Derwent's face keeps materialising inside my skull. I drag on my boots, grab my camera and my keys, close the front door behind me.

Don't whitewash it. I feel stupid for having said that, now I've got Harris's full story. *Just tell me.* As if it were easy. As if he would. He's probably so used to hiding his hurt, it's weird to talk about it.

And maybe – now that he's living with his father again – talking is too dangerous.

5

harris

Grant Denyer has challenged us to name Ten Things You'd Find On A Beach Holiday.

'Sand,' Dad says.

'Sea.'

'Fish.' Dad spits out the answers. 'Crabs.'

I look at him. 'That's two.'

'Shut up. I got 'em right. Have another go.'

I sigh. 'I dunno... Flies?'

Flies is wrong.

'Dickhead.' Dad nudges me, eyes focused on the screen. 'Never been to the beach – how would *you* know?'

The television shouts back at him. I lift my stubby by its glass neck, stare out the living room window. Night has come. The living room is lit by the hanging bulb in the ceiling, and Dad strains forward on the edge of the couch, elbows on his knees, his hands hanging down.

The studio audience laughs at something.

'Move those plates,' Dad says in the lull.

I inhale. Here we go again. 'Easier if you do it.'

'I'm watching me show.' Dad snatches his tobacco pouch off the coffee table.

I ignore him, take another pull from my bottle.

'Harris, move your arse and move those plates.'

I look at him. I'd say *You can't be serious*, but he can be and he is. He's deadly serious. I found out the hard way yesterday.

I clench my jaw. Get one crutch under me so I can haul myself up off the spongy couch. Put the crutch in my left armpit, steady myself, lean for the dirty plates.

'Get outta the way,' Dad says. 'I can't see the telly.'

'This is the only way I can do it,' I say through my teeth.

The lurch to the kitchen takes forever. I clatter the plates into the sink, rest my arse on the edge of the kitchen table. My leg aches.

'Get me pills!' Dad calls.

I close my eyes. I think I might be stuck in a re-run. Not *Family Feud*. Some sort of gothic horror-comedy. I can't believe I'm back here. I can't believe I said yes.

This is crazy. I'm no help to Dad like this anyway. These last four days, I've crutched around the house doing a poor impersonation of helping to keep the place running. Dad expects the house to be warm at night, he expects water to be in the taps, the toilet to flush, dinner to appear on the table. How he expects all these things to magically happen, I have no fucking idea.

It's the same technique he used with my mother. His expectation is a fixed unchanging weight and an explosive fury follows when his expectations aren't met. I'm so over it I can't think straight. This is why I left, this is why I swore I'd never come back. Dad doesn't want a son, he just wants a compliant servant –

'Don't forget me pills!' Dad bawls from the living room. He's finished with beer, started on vodka about an hour ago.

I grab the packet of medicine off the kitchen bench and stagger back through to the living room, chuck the packet on the coffee table.

'Here's your bloody pills. I'm going to bed.' It's six-thirty in the evening.

'Good on ya,' Dad says.

I lean for my other crutch, get it under me, limp off down the hall.

Inside my room, I close the door and rest on it to catch my breath. Easier to breathe on the bed, though. I hobble over, put my crutches aside and lie back. The bed is too narrow, too short. It's the same one I've had since I was twelve.

What's my mum doing now? I'm trying to keep my mind on the prize. I imagine Mum making dinner for herself and my sister. Something nutritious and colourful, not the shrivelled sausages and mashed potato and blanched carrots she always served up under Dad's orders. Maybe she's making salad, or pancakes. Maybe she's coming home from work, and she's tired, and my sister helps her, and they make dinner together...

I try to imagine Kelly, but I can't picture her any way except the way she looked when she and Mum left: all pudgy fists and soft two-year-old hair. Which is dumb, because she'll be thirteen now. I wonder if her hair went dark or if it stayed blonde, like mine. Like Mum's. I wonder if she even remembers who I am.

It's the same question I ask myself about my mother, sometimes. Does she remember me? Does she think about me, like I think about her? Did she know what it would mean when she left me behind?

Of course she knew. But she didn't have a choice. On bad days, I have to remind myself of that.

I push my heels against the baseboard, tuck my arms up under my head. My muscles feel tight. When Dad went in to Five Mile today, I searched the house again for clues. Dad hasn't told me anything useful yet. He could be lying about knowing where Mum is. She's been impossible to track online. She might've remarried, or just flown under the radar to avoid him. Shit, I wouldn't be surprised if she's taken out a no-contact order against my dad, or even changed her name.

But I have a feeling Dad knows exactly where my mother is. He's probably planning to drip-feed me the info until he goes in for chemo, and then – when he's practically in the hospital foyer – he'll finally tell me the truth. I think Dad's gonna lean hard on that leverage. He knows there's no fucking way I'd be staying here without it.

Because here feels dangerous. I have to be on my guard all the time.

Before now, there's always been an out. I've been able to rely on being a taller, heavier opponent. If things got serious, I could always walk away. Go to a mate's place or squat somewhere until things blew over. I used to crash at Mike's sometimes. I even slept at the quarry once. I think Mark West, my old boss there, understood more than he let on.

But now that's not the case. I can't walk distances on my crutches. I can't drive away in the ute because it's a manual and I can't handle the clutch with my bung leg. Most importantly, I can't hold my own with Dad physically, and he knows it.

I push myself up, stumble to the door, shove the back of the only chair in the room – an old wooden one – under the door handle. Then I take out the tiny foil of pot from the cavity under my old footy trophy and roll up. Lie back on the bed again, stare at the ceiling, and smoke the joint as the August dark settles around and inside the house. The pressed tin patterns high above me are smeared with dust.

When I was a kid, I realised something: nobody wants to hear your bullshit sob story. Everyone's got their own lives, their own troubles. Folks like to know the gossip, but they don't like to be asked to do anything about it.

So usually I keep my own counsel. But this whole situation would be easier if I could hash it out with somebody. I could call Rachel – I think about that for three long seconds, discount it. I'm past that, past the 'What Would Rachel Do?' stage. I could call Mike, but it's kind of the same thing – and he's not here, he's *there*, where I can't be. Melbourne is a long way from Five Mile. Right now, I think you could measure the distance in light years.

My thigh is tender, throbbing and annoyingly itchy by turns. I think again about Amie Blunt at the hospital, the way I ignored her on the day I left. It was a bastard act, but she made me feel exposed. I can handle people's scorn but not their pity. My hackles were up that day, though. Maybe I read it all wrong.

I study the tin on the ceiling. You'd need a lot of pressure to stamp those designs into the metal. Maybe I'm being tempered here. Maybe this is character-building. Maybe, when I meet my mum and my sister again, I'll be a stronger, more decent person...

I slow my breathing, and try not to wonder whether the price I'm paying for the info about my mum and my sister is too high.

*

'The pub,' I say.

'What?'

'I wanna go to the pub.' I rub a hand across my mouth, slouch in my chair at the kitchen table.

I'm itchy with old sweat, and my stubble has grown into a full-blown beard, but shaving is awkward and I can't take a shower. The shower is outside, under the same tin roof as the toilet and laundry tubs. Navigating the stairs is a pain in the arse. Plus I'm not supposed to get the bandage wet. I tried wrapping my leg in plastic, but it didn't work. I even tried standing under the spray with my foot up on a chair. Couldn't keep my balance. I ended up crawling over the concrete for my crutches, buck naked and sopping. Got so fucking angry, I slammed my crutch through the wood-veneer door.

It just reminded me of all the times I'd spent there, shivering in the dark while Dad raged through the house, knowing I couldn't hide forever –

I feel like a kid again. Helpless. Hopeless. Is it the injury, or is it being in this house, being near Dad? Fuck, I don't know. All I know for sure is, I stink, and if I have to sit on that moth-eaten couch watching TV for one more meaningless night, I'm gonna fucking explode.

'C'mon, Dad.' I make my voice encouraging. 'Let's go to the pub. Stuff baked beans on toast – we could get a counter meal. Have a beer. Three beers.'

'Got beer.' Dad sits across from me at the kitchen table while we're waiting for the baked beans to heat. 'In the fridge.'

And vodka. And Tang. Just the memory of the smell makes me wanna heave.

'I want a UDL,' I say, traitorous. 'Bourbon and coke. Play a game of pool or something. Haven't you had enough of the telly?'

'Play pool on crutches, can ya?' He's giving me the look I recognise. The fucking-with-you look.

I glare back, try not to sound desperate. This won't work if I sound desperate. 'People'll think you've disappeared. They'll think we've gone stir-crazy and offed each other.' If I don't get outta here soon, that could still happen.

'On tap might be nice,' Dad says contemplatively.

'Yeah,' I say. 'Foam on top. Roast beef and gravy. Mushy peas. Might run into a few mates, have a gasbag.'

Dad's eyes narrow. Running into mates wouldn't be part of the plan. He likes us independent. As in: isolated, exiled.

Undefended.

'Actually, it's Monday, isn't it?' I backtrack quickly. 'So it'll probably be dead quiet. Col will be pleased to see us. Bit of business on a Monday night.' I sugar-coat it further. 'He might let us order on tick. I can pay him next weekend, he knows I'm good for it.'

I'm not good for it. I'm not good for anything. I'm a fucking good-for-nothing, but I don't care at this point. I'll lie my arse off to Colin Geraldson – local publican and owner-manager of the Five Flags – if it means I get one measly night outta this hole. Col might even believe me when I say I'll pay up later; he knows he won't get more than a sniff off Dad. I might look like the better of two shit options.

'You're good for it, are you?' Dad glowers at me over the rim of his glass. 'Good for two pub meals and a booze-up. You weren't much good for groceries last Wednesday.'

'*Next* weekend – didn't I just say next weekend?' I take a neat swallow out of my own glass. Electrolyte powder mixed with water: it's pretty disgusting, but I told Barb at the hospital I'd stay hydrated. 'Mark West still owes me some cash from my last pay. Haven't managed to catch up with him about it yet.'

Lie, lie, lie. Terry Watts gave me enough to cover the hospital excess, and the wound-care supplies and antibiotics for the week just gone. I got a few fifties left, then no idea where my next dollar's coming from. Sure as hell not from Mark West. He's a good bloke and he's spotted me enough already.

But Dad doesn't need to know that.

I stand up awkwardly, grab my crutches. 'C'mon, then. We going or what?'

Dad makes me stand there while he knocks back the dregs in his glass. Tongues his front teeth. Makes a big sigh, like this is some kind of major life decision.

Then he stands up and snatches his keys. 'All right.'

My suppressed whoop of triumph gurgles in my throat. This is not a victory. My father is driving me to the pub. Negotiating it with him, bringing him around to it, has made me break out in a sweat. Life isn't supposed to be this much hard work, is it?

But the clean air outside the house is almost enough consolation. The breeze lifting the hair off the back of my neck smells of mallee bark with a touch of iron from the old corrugated sheets rusting by the front stairs. I don't stand and enjoy it – my leg and arms will tire too fast, and I don't want Dad's momentum to slow – but I lift my chin to give the cool air access, wipe my face on my shoulder before climbing into the ute.

I chew my thumbnail on the way down Sandbag Road to the Five Mile turn-off. Dad sits quiet as we jolt along, then he leans forward and switches on the radio. Orchestra and the mournful guitars of Chicago swell in the cab.

Dad makes a teeth-sucking noise. 'Fuckin' hate this song.'

I'm tempted to ask why he doesn't change the station, but I know he won't do that. This car only has one station: Dad's.

'Yeah,' I say. 'Not my favourite.'

'Reminds me of your mother.'

I freeze. This is the first time he's brought her up. I wet my bottom lip, decide to take the chance while I've got it. 'S'pose she's still living in Adelaide, then. Her and Kelly.'

'S'pose so.' Dad drives on, looking steadily ahead. 'All the support requests came from there.'

Support requests? I'm not sure which I find more incredible, the fact we're discussing this, or the fact that anybody could ever imagine my father complying with child support requirements.

'That was a while ago, though,' Dad goes on quietly. 'Haven't heard anything for a couple of years, at least.'

'She's still alive, though?' I'm shocked by how thick my words come out.

'Guess so.' Dad shrugs. 'The mail was from a PO box. She could be dead in a ditch, but I guess I wouldna got letters then.'

'You're gonna write down the forwarding address and stuff, are you?' Doubt in my tone.

'I'll give you everything I got,' Dad says. 'When the time comes. It's been a couple of years, like I said, but I can get in touch with people who'll know.'

'Right.'

He glances at me. 'I said I'd do it and I will.'

I roll down the window to get some air, blow away the sting in my eyes. My crutches are propped on my right, near the gear shift, so they're not bumping my injury. There's the added advantage: they provide a useful barrier between me and Dad. Feeling protected, I decide to go for it.

'Did Mum ever ask about me? In letters or anything?' I have to look out the window as I say it.

The silence in the cab now can't be masked by radio music over the speakers. It's deeper than any old Cold Chisel song, deeper than the hollow gong in your guts after a quarry explosion. I get a terrible sense of having crossed a line and my eyes drag sideways against my will.

Dad's not looking at me, though. He's looking through the windscreen. I'd hate to think what he's really seeing.

'I've told you plenty of times already,' he says softly. 'Anthea knew the rules.'

The softness doesn't fool me. His voice is full of menace and he's gripping the steering wheel. If this was happening at home, I'd be laid out on the floor by now.

'We split it fair and square,' Dad goes on. 'She took her stuff, I got the house. She got the girl, I got the boy. I told her never to come back. And if she tried to find you, to take what was mine by right...'

His eyes lock on mine.

'...I said I'd fucking kill you myself before I let that happen.'

Dad pulls the handbrake and I realise we've rolled to a stop. All my skin is cold. My throat is too dry to spit.

'Right. Let's go have a beer.' Dad pushes out of the cab, doesn't wait for me to follow.

I sit there for a full minute before I can move. The hair on my arms is still standing up when I hobble my way into the pub.

The inside of the Five Flags seems surreal after the conversation I've just had. There's the long solid bar, with Col Geraldson pulling beers for a few local boys. There's the pool room, the dark drinking tables with the wooden chairs, the jukebox in the corner. A few other blokes in workboots and jeans are slugging back their drinks.

My brain and my body aren't playing nice, neither of them cooperating as I crutch over to where my father is quietly arguing with Col at the bar. I feel like I'm moving through molasses.

'...don't wanna be rude, Dennis, but I can't serve you until you've fixed up the tab,' Col says.

Colin Geraldson is burly – when he played centre half back in his younger days his nickname actually was Burly Geraldson – and he's not just the local publican, but our landlord. He doesn't look unkind but he's not a guy you wanna cross. His current expression is like a brick wall.

'I've got it,' I say quickly. I reach for my wallet and fish out one of the last of Terry Watts's fifties.

'See? Harris has got it.' Dad has a note of victory in his voice. I don't look at his face; he'll be smirking. Even being close to him is making my gooseflesh rise.

Col appraises me before sliding the fifty off the bar, grabbing two pint glasses. 'Fine then. But I'm cutting you off after the cash is gone.'

'Harris wants a UDL,' Dad says.

Col sighs and puts back one of the glasses.

Once Dad's got his beer and moved off to a table, Col finds me a can of bourbon and coke, speaks quietly. 'You know I can't keep serving you unless Dennis pays his tab.'

We're both watching my father. I nod, resigned. 'How much does he owe? Maybe I could fix it up, so he's not –'

'A grand,' Col says. 'He owes me a grand, Harris. The tab here, plus two months' rent on the house.'

I stare.

Col nods grimly. 'And another grand in utilities, I hear. He might owe some money at Metcalfe's as well. You didn't know about that, did you? Your dad's been racking up a few bills lately.'

For fuck's sake. That isn't 'racking up a few bills'. That's a solid debt. And the worst thing is, it's kind of my fault. Dad's been crapping out on everybody all over town in my absence and part of me knew he'd do it. When I left for Melbourne with Mike and Rachel, I figured I'd cut loose. Dad would have to sink or swim without me.

But now I'm back here, back in the mess he's made. He's *my* father. He's my responsibility.

'Something else you should know,' Col goes on, disguising our chat with a wipedown of the bar. 'Your dad's in hock to some bookie in Mildura. Don't know all the details. But from what I've heard, he could be neck-deep.'

'Neck-deep?' My voice is hoarse. 'How much are we talking?'

Col shrugs. 'Dunno. Could be as high as five grand.'

Seven grand, total. *Seven thousand* dollars.

Dad will never cover that. He might scrape together enough for the local bills, but if he's in trouble with a bookie, things could get dirty real fast. And he's gonna drag me down with him if I don't do something about it.

But it's bigger than I'd anticipated. Seven grand is more than I can possibly repay. The size of it makes me feel like a tiny boat rolling on a giant sea.

I rub my forehead. 'Jesus. Thanks for telling me, Col. I can't pay you tonight. I don't...' I don't know how I'm gonna pay at all. I try to screw my head on straight. 'Look, I'll get you what you're owed somehow. Let me sort it out, yeah? Just give me a few weeks to find it.'

Col looks at me, nods, moves along the bar to serve another customer. I turn around, lean against the wood, pop the ring tab on my can. The first long slug is to anchor me. The second is to help get my mind around this fucking ridiculous concept: I'm broke, I'm injured, I'm unemployed, and I've just taken on a seven thousand dollar debt.

This is insane. My father has lost the plot. What the hell is he doing, getting in deep with a bookie? How did he manage to rack up such a huge tab? How in hell am I gonna pay it back?

I'm jerked out of my contemplation of the pub's wooden floorboards by a slap on the shoulder. The slap knocks me off balance; I right myself before I slip off the bar.

'Hazza!' Snowie Geraldson grins at me, opens out his hands.

'Snow.' The colour has dribbled out of my voice but I give pleasantries a try. 'Hey, man, good to see you.'

'Shit, mate, they told me you'd been wounded in action but I didn't believe it.' Snowie gestures at my leg, and the crutches, just as one of them slips off the bar and clatters to the floor. 'You should be at a table, yeah? You want your crutch back?'

'Yeah, cheers.'

Snowie retrieves my crutch, and between the two of us we get me to a table. One of the pub regulars puts some grey-bearded Jimmy Barnes song on the jukebox. Jesus, don't people here get enough of Jimmy Barnes?

'Mate, you look like death warmed over,' Snowie says. 'Get some booze into you, that's it. What's been going on?'

Skinny, with a loud-coloured silky shirt that practically screams *I Am Not A Farmer*, Snowie Geraldson is Colin's second kid, and the only one who's stayed local. Snowie's a year older than me and, in a shocking break with the tradition of country nicknames – where redheads are called Bluey, and tall men are called Shorty – Snowie's hair is actually snow-coloured: white-blond and upstanding. He's always had fair hair, but I think he bleaches it now.

He listens while I give him the heavily edited version of how I got shot in the leg, whistling at the emergency bits. Snowie always does a good impression of listening to what you've got to say. When I'm done he buys me a beer. I wouldn't trust him as far as I could throw him, but Snowie's an okay guy.

He's also my dealer.

'So, no goodie bags to tide you over?' he asks, waggling his eyebrows.

'Nah, mate. Not exactly cashed up at the moment.'

'And I'm guessing Col told you the bad news.' His eyes flick towards the bar. Snowie and his father call each other by their first names, something I've never quite understood, but each to their own. 'Your dad got up to a bit of mischief while you were in Melbourne, eh? Got in a bit of a pickle.'

'Yeah, from being too pickled,' I quip. Thinking about the debt still makes me feel sick.

Snowie shakes his head. 'Hard call, mate. Feelin' your pain there – I'm trying to help Col keep the pub propped up. Been working in Mildura to make some extra dough. This place...' He waves a hand to encompass the bar, the pool room, the whole palaver. 'Well, it's not quite holding its own at the mo.'

'I thought the pub was doing okay?'

'Yeah, not so much. Lotsa people have left town. Lotsa businesses are hurting – ask Bev Metcalfe at the grocery how much she owes the bank. These old joints have got heaps of problems too – broken plumbing, shitty wiring. Be all right if it was just the business, but the upkeep's a killer.'

I finally catch on. 'That's why Col's calling in my dad's debt.'

'Yep.' Snowie makes a snort. 'Can't give beer away for free, eh? Col loves this place. It's all he knows. But if he can't make it pay...'

So I'm not the only kid in town trying to help a parent stay solvent. That makes me feel slightly better, somehow.

I lean back in my chair. 'And you're working in Mildura? What's the job?'

Snowie grins. 'Let's just say I got irons in a few different fires. I'm still around on a Friday night if you need anything.' He winks at me.

'I'll let you know.' I sigh. 'Be a bit easier if some rich relative died and left us a few handy million, yeah?'

'Too right. If I win the lotto or something, I'll give you a call.' Snowie laughs, nods at my drink. 'Anyway, get that into ya. Can't be depressed on your birthday.'

'What?'

'Well, you were rockin' it up big this time last year...'

'It's the ninth of August?' My face must look pained.

'Yeah, mate.' Snowie stands up. 'You have that one, and I'll get your next UDL on the house, while Dad's still feeling generous. That's a good pressie.'

He slaps my back, moves away to talk to another mate at the bar. I look at my can. It's my birthday. I'm twenty years old today.

Twenty years old, and I feel like I'm a hundred.

6

amie

I finally catch up with Nick and Robbie on a morning I have free in my part-time roster. Robbie's come down from Mildura for the day to see her dad and Nick's just come off night shift. We end up at the bakery. Somehow, if it's morning coffee, everyone ends up at the bakery, even though it's mainly for tourists who want to gobble a vanilla slice on their way through Ouyen as they head for more exciting towns like Swan Hill or Mildura or Shepparton.

Robbie's hug is as warm and genuine as she is. She smells of nail polish and perming solution. Nick's black hair is flat, and his windbreaker bunches to his elbows. He looks a bit shattered after coming off work.

He stretches back in his aluminium café chair and rubs his arms as he finishes telling us about it. 'So yeah, the extras are busting my arse. I've only taken two this week and I'm bloody knackered.'

'Come work at the salon,' Robbie offers, scooping up froth from the top of her cappuccino with her spoon. 'We're open six days now, from eight until seven. I swear to god, Mum's working herself to death. Remind me never to open my own small business. But hey, you can have my shifts if you want them.' She grins at the idea.

Nick makes a face. 'Brazilians and chest waxes? Thanks, Rob, that's real generous.'

I snort at the mention of Brazilians.

'Couldn't be worse than bedpans and vomit,' Robbie counters.

'I guess.' Nick shrugs. 'Nah, I love nursing. I'm in it for the long haul. Not like you, missy, just dipping your toe.' He raises his chin at me.

'Mm, I haven't made my mind up yet.' I slurp my coffee. 'But hey, at least one of us has found a calling.'

'I'm just trying to figure out how people like Barb do it full time for so many years.'

'You'll get there. You have to build up your stamina.' I squint at him. 'But the extras are for what? You're really trying to get some cash together for this new car?'

'Yes. And I'm really trying to sell the Subaru. No joy yet.' He tilts forward to sugar his coffee. His long blunt fingers destroy three paper tubes before he's happy.

Robbie raises her eyebrows at him. 'Procrastinating much?'

'Shut up.' He glares at her.

'Wimp. Are you going to tell her or not?'

I glance between the two of them. 'What? What's going on?'

Nick gives Robbie a look, stretches his long legs under the table. 'I'm moving to Melbourne, Ames. That's why I need a new car. I know I've talked about moving before, but I'm actually making plans now. Grant's gonna help me set up a place to live.'

'Really?' The bottom drops out of my world a little, but I force my expression into neutral. The day is bright, sunny. 'Well...that's great. Geez, why were you putting off telling me?'

'He thought you'd be pissed,' Robbie confides.

'I'm not pissed, that's crazy.' I'm a bit pissed. Not enough to spoil Nick's mood, though. 'I'm happy for you. But what will I do at the hospital without you?'

He grins. 'Be awesome, like usual? Spread your little brand of joy on the ward? The patients love you, Ames, and you're good at it. You're even good at putting up with the nongs, like Harris Derwent.'

'Harris Derwent was on the ward?' Robbie presses one hand to her chest. 'Holy shit. Is he still hot as the sun?'

'He was a patient. You don't ogle patients.' I frown at Nick. 'And he's not a nong. He's an okay guy.' I see Nick's eyebrows. 'Fine, then, don't believe me. But whatever his rep, he was an all-right person at the hospital. What have you got against Harris anyway?'

'Apart from the fact he's a smart-arse brain-dead man-whore? Nothing.'

Robbie waves her teaspoon. 'Hey, the queue for the smart-arse brain-dead man-whores starts behind me, okay?'

I laugh, but I feel bad for Harris. And the idea of Nick moving away settles on me, like a dark scratchy quilt. 'So you really want to leave Ouyen? For good?'

Nick puts down his mug, his eyes intent. 'Mum and Dad are here. It'll always be the place I grew up and the place I come back to – it's in my bones. But I want to see different places, try different things. I can't stay, Ames. Not for my family, not for anybody. I have to go, even if it's just to see if I can do it.'

I remind myself this was inevitable. Nick's been talking about it for ages. And around here, the question is always whether to go or stay. This year I've seen two other friends, Shelley and Peta, make the switch to city living, and Robbie moved to Mildura when her mum got divorced and started the salon business. It's one of the conditions of rural friendship: that you hold on tight, and when the time comes, you hug hard...and let go.

It doesn't make the sting less painful.

But Nick has already gone on. '...so Melbourne would be a good start. And you should be looking further afield, too.'

I baulk. 'Come again?'

'You should be thinking about where you want to go from here.' Nick leans forward. 'Amie, you know what I'm talking about. Since your mum died it's like you're glued in place.'

'Hon, he's right.' Robbie nods, sipping her coffee. 'You do seem a little rusted on.'

'What?' I stare between my two best friends. 'Where's all this coming from?'

'Now who's procrastinating?' Nick levels a glare at Robbie.

She presses her lips before looking at me properly. 'Amie, don't be mad, okay? But me and Nick have kind of been scheming on your behalf.'

I frown at them warily. 'You've been scheming to get me to Melbourne? I can't do that. You know I can't do that.'

'This isn't about Melbourne,' Robbie admits. She reaches into her bag and pulls out a purple document folder, places it on the table. 'It's about this.'

I blink between them, blink at the folder. 'Okay, I'm...confused.'

'Remember all those AusArt scholarships and stuff the school guidance counsellor sent you links for at the end of last year? And you were all, *Oh, this looks so cool but it'll never happen*? Well...'

'Me and Robbie submitted your photos to a residency program.' Nick gets it all out in a rush. 'It's an overseas study grant, and you would be awesome at it, and we really just want you to give it a chance.'

I gape. 'You submitted my *photos*?'

Robbie jumps in, pulling out sheets from the folder. 'Yeah, check it out. It looks fantastic! You get to choose the place you want to go, and all you have to do is agree to an interview.'

'An interview.' I'm still gaping. 'Are you *kidding*?'

'Amie, come on.' Nick looks at me sternly. 'Your photos are amazing.'

Robbie nods. 'Sweetie, we're not trying to be the boss of you or anything, but you *have* to know you're talented. And it would be sad if you wasted that because you weren't given the right opportunity.'

'I can't...' I really can't. My brain just isn't keeping up.

'Robbie found the links from last year.' Nick's face turns pinker as he explains. 'And she sent them to me, and...the whole thing kind of snowballed.'

'First we joked about it, then Nick wrote an application for you, but we still weren't really thinking about it like a real *thing*...' Robbie says, taking up the story, '...until we got the email –'

'Which said you'd been shortlisted,' Nick finishes.

Robbie nods. 'Which said you'd been shortlisted, yeah. So you just have to fill in the forms, and sign up for an interview, and you'll be good to go!'

There's a long pause as my head spins its wheels. Nick and Robbie are both looking at me expectantly. I don't know what to say, or even if I can form words. My friends are nuts. *Nuts.* They're so nuts, it's making my eyes well up. And a residency. A *shortlisting*. Ohmigod –

'Ames.' Robbie grabs my shoulder. 'Amie, say something, you look like you're going into shock. Oh my god, Nick, is she okay?'

'Amie, I'm sorry.' Nick holds my hand across the table. 'We really didn't mean to freak you out. But would you at least think about it?'

I try to clear my throat by taking a long slug of my coffee. 'Guys, I appreciate you did this. Really. It's...a surprise.'

'A good surprise?' Robbie looks so hopeful.

I hate to bring her down. 'It's lovely you did it. But –'

'Here come the buts.' Robbie looks at Nick.

'*But* I can't just pick up and go overseas! With Dad's condition, and my extended family here, and –'

'It's okay, it's really okay.' Nick shushes Rob with a raised hand. 'I know you're dealing with stuff, and you don't have to make a decision right this second. We're just asking you to have a go. That's all.'

'Right.' Robbie looks like she wants to say more but is restraining herself. She passes me the purple folder. 'I'll forward you all the emails and stuff. Just...have a look at it.'

'Please?' Nick makes the puppy dog eyes. He has beautiful eyes, so it's pretty effective.

I hold the folder gingerly. 'Okay, I'll look.' Robbie cheers, and I stare her down. 'But I really don't –'

'Don't overthink it,' Nick says. 'Just go with your gut. And don't worry if it sounds crazy. You should do something crazy at least once a day.'

I roll my eyes. 'That's your suggestion, is it?'

'I'm a nurse. That's my medical recommendation.' He grins.

My friends are certifiable but they love me, and they mean well. I've missed Robbie since she moved to Mildura and now I'm going to miss Nick when he leaves. Goddamnit. Even though his departure is still only in the planning stages, I already feel lonely.

And the idea of a residency is...well, it's amazing, but it's impossible. I planned to go overseas once – my plans changed. And now I can't go anywhere. That's not me being rusted on, that's just reality.

That's the way it has to be.

*

I'm turning the key in the lock, mulling over Nick and Robbie's 'surprise' and Nick's decision to leave, when the landline rings.

66

'Hello?' I answer with a query, even though I know who's calling. There's only one person who rings our landline.

'Amita, it is Nani.'

'Hi, Nani-ji.' Her voice always makes me smile. 'Is it sunny over there today?'

'It is a lovely fresh day, dearest. The weather is getting warmer. I went to the market with Hansa yesterday. I had to take off my cardigan.'

'Did you have a nice time at the market?'

'Yes, indeed, thank you. A woman there is selling fresh paneer. Many women now don't make their own paneer. They say it's time-consuming. Well, of course it's time-consuming, that's what cooking is about. Amita, are you oiling your hair like we discussed?'

I sigh and smile at the same time, let my bag slip off my shoulder onto the floor. 'Nani-ji, it's only August.'

'August, yes, we are coming into Spring. And you know Jasminder's wedding is nearly here. You should have nice hair at the wedding.'

The wedding. Jas is my twenty-two-year-old cousin and she's getting married to a twenty-five-year-old irrigation scientist. The wedding preparations have been driving me a bit crazy. Nani wants me to go to Mildura for all of them. They'll go for days and I'll have to take time off work, not to mention leaving Dad here on his own, but I can't just say no. It's family.

'I'll do my best to have nice hair at the wedding, Nani-ji,' I say dutifully.

'Amita, is there something troubling you?'

I laugh as I sink onto the armchair near the phone. 'How do you always *know*?'

'I am your grandmother, it is my job to know. Now tell me.'

'My friend, Nick? You remember him? Well…he's moving away.'

'This is the boy you walked with.'

'Yes, we dated.' I smile and nod, even though she can't see me. 'Nick's talked about moving to Melbourne before, but this time he sounds serious.'

'He has a place to go in the city?'

'His older brother, Grant, lives there. In Collingwood.'

'Two sons – such a blessing!' I hear her bangles tinkle; the phone is in the living room of my aunt's house, and I'm pretty sure she's just lifted an acknowledging hand towards the large portrait of Guru Nanak above the mantlepiece there. 'And this boy who is your friend, he is alone in Ouyen?'

My cheeks warm. 'Nick's not alone. He's got the rest of his family, and he's got me.'

'But you are not walking together anymore,' Nani points out.

I grin ruefully. 'No, we're still broken up, last time I checked. We get on better as friends.'

'So he looks for a new life and someone of his own. Amita, you cannot stop the tide. It is a normal thing, this leaving.'

'I know, Nani-ji. But I just...'

'You will miss him.'

I think about it. 'I've got other mates, but Nick's my best friend at the hospital. It'll be hard without him.'

'Most certainly it will be hard. But if his family is here, he will be back. And if you are a true friend, you will want him to be happy. Do you believe he will be happy in the city?'

I don't have to think too hard about that. 'Yes,' I admit. 'Yes, I think he'll be great in the city.'

'Then go to him and give him a gift of parting and wish him well. Maybe it is his destiny to be in Melbourne. You cannot stand in the way of destiny.'

'I guess.' I try to smile. Then I think of the residency and my face falls. 'So what's *my* destiny?'

She answers quickly, with utter certainty. 'To meet a handsome Sikh man at your cousin's wedding, and fall deeply in love, and give your Nani many great-grandchildren for cuddling.'

I can't help but laugh. 'I think you should talk to Jas about the great-grandchildren before you talk to me.' I try not to sigh into the phone when I continue. 'Everyone really wants me up there for the wedding?'

'Of course they want you here! What a thing to say. I want you. Hansa and the girls want you. Apu wants you here also.'

'That's...nice.' Apu is my grandmother's pet name for my grandfather, Anupam. Who died before I was born. Before Nani ever moved to Australia, in fact. She talks about my grandfather a lot, which isn't unusual. What's unusual is that, in our most recent phone calls, she's started talking about him as if he's still alive and well and chatting to her on a daily basis.

'The wedding is in a month,' Nani goes on. 'That is barely time enough to prepare. And I want you to come to gurdwara with me and help with langar.'

'Tell me the dates again and I'll see what I can arrange with work.'

She tells me, after finding her glasses. I see her in my mind's eye as though she's right in front of me: a slightly shrunken-looking woman in a pale peach-coloured salwar kameez, with grey hair pulled back in a tidy braid. Her glasses will be balanced on her nose and she'll have her feet up on a cushioned footstool in front of the wing-backed chair in the lounge room. I gave her the footstool three years ago for her sixty-eighth birthday. A cup of tea will be settled on the little table at her left.

'And Mehndi Night!' she exclaims. 'You must come to Mehndi Night or your cousins will miss you.'

I think my cousins will do fine without me, but I agree to come to Mehndi Night anyway because it'll be one of the more enjoyable activities related to the wedding.

We chat for a bit longer before saying our goodbyes. Resting the phone back in its cradle, I think about how Nani talked about my grandfather. She wasn't acting like this last month when I visited. But that was a month ago.

I need to try to visit her every fortnight like I used to. Stay on top of things. Last year, with exams followed by the CNA course straight after, I was often too exhausted on the weekends to drive to Mildura. But that's no excuse. Nani and the family depend on me.

Suddenly I'm filled with a desire to see Nani. Her arms are bony, but strong when they hug you. Her eyes are always a little starry. I hope she's not tiring herself out with all the flurry over this wedding business.

Dad lets himself through the front door and a flare of sunlight invades the hall, illuminates the spot where I'm sitting.

'Hey, you're here,' he says, taking off his sidearm. That's always the first thing he does when he comes home. 'Thought you'd be out with the camera.'

'Not yet.' I pull my bag onto my lap as I sit up. 'Just finished on the phone with Nani.'

'Uh-huh.'

'I'm a bit worried about her.'

'What, is she not all right?'

Dad frustrates me sometimes. It's like he can't bear to say the word 'sick'. In both our minds, sickness leads inevitably to something worse. For Dad, the aversion to talking about it, even thinking about it, is more severe. It's made it hard to get straight answers out of him about his heart condition, and it's wearing at times, considering I work in a hospital.

Dad cares about Nani, though. He isn't as close with my aunt's family since Mum's death, but Nani is different. She's the closest direct link he has to my mother, apart from me. Nani is important.

'Her health is fine,' I say patiently. 'But she talks about Nanaa like he's still around.'

Dad hangs up his utility belt on the hat-stand in the hall. 'Maybe, in her mind, he is.'

'Doesn't that bother you?'

He pauses before replying. 'I don't think it's awful.'

A little knife slices through my heart. Sometimes it's these tiny moments that get you. Or maybe it's just been a shit week. First the business with Harris Derwent, and Craig Davies, then Nick and Robbie's announcements, and now Nani…

I know why Dad doesn't think it's awful to believe the person who you loved most in the world is still around. Even after four years I wish I could get up one morning and see my mother preparing breakfast in the kitchen. The wishing makes a small, but very deep, glassy-black wound inside me every time I let it. But I don't let it as much as I used to.

'Nick's leaving Ouyen,' I blurt out.

Dad walks over and pats my shoulder gently. 'Nothing you weren't expecting, eh?'

'No, I know. But…'

'Imagine you'll be telling me the same thing one day. Y'know, studying in Melbourne, or Adelaide maybe. What kids do.'

I consider the residency concept for one second – tantalising, terrifying, impossible – before shaking my head at him. 'Dad, *I'm* not leaving.'

Dad takes his hand away. 'Okay. Right. Well, come on then. Help me out the back for a second? I wanna move that engine block winch.'

Out in the workshop Dad tosses me gloves, gives instructions. The winch is easy, and physical, and I don't need to think about anything else for a while. Which is good – I'm done thinking for the day.

I try to let go of my conversations with Robbie and Nick and Nani, concentrate on the rough weight of the metal and the smell of grease. Then I wash up and collect everything I need for a shoot, and go lose myself in the minute texture of mistletoe, the squirming smother of its growth.

7

harris

Dad cuffs me in the kitchen, for the third time, and that's when I decide to go.

I can't stay here anymore, I can't do it. I've been through this so many times already: the energy in the air, the building tension. We've performed all the drama in these scenarios before.

The small retaliations have started: Dad moving my crutches, banging into me in the kitchen, picking at me for no reason until I snap back. The cuffing – like this morning, when I got in his way at the sink – is the current stage in a predictable cycle. The next stage is when the damage gets done.

And I'm in no shape to be dealing with it, so I'm basically defenceless. I can hardly balance on my crutches and the throbbing in my thigh over the last few days has been keeping me awake at night. I thought the bloody thing would've healed by now. I'm out of pain meds, so I'm screwed.

By the time Friday comes around, all I can think about is getting outta this house, even for a few hours. The smell of it, the hum in the rooms, the way Dad stalks around... If I don't get some space soon, I'm gonna go fucking nuts.

So I have a few beers with Dad in the late afternoon to move things along. Wait out the hours before he crashes on the couch in front of the telly. When he's good and snoring, I grab my crutches and close the screen door behind me as quietly as I can.

The cool breeze on the front porch is a relief, but it's not enough. I wobble my way down the stairs. I guess I've had more than a few beers.

The ute's parked right up near the house but I can't drive it, of course. I've always thought Dad's insistence that his vehicles be manual was a vaguely cool retro thing. Now it's just another barrier to leaving.

Well, fuck it. Fuck the ute. I've walked to the Five Flags from here before. And it's a clear full-moon night, I'll be able to see where I'm going.

I'm on the road before I think about it too long.

I've got my jacket on and my wallet in my pocket, I don't need anything else. My leg is hurting, but at least I'm not lying in bed feeling like I'm suffocating, trying to ignore the pain. I swing through my crutches to keep up momentum. I've done crazier shit than this.

For the first thirty minutes, I'm savouring it. The moonlit road I'm on, the smell of the wheat in the paddocks, the sneaky jubilation. After that, I start to forget where I'm going. The *crrunch-crrunch* of my rubber crutch-stops slipping on the sandy gravel becomes a monotonous soundtrack. I'm sweating under my clothes; in combination with the cold night air, it burns and chills me in turn.

By the halfway point, my armpits are aching and my leg pulses in time with my swaying gait. I run my tongue over my parched lips. Right now, the only plan is to make it to somewhere I can get a drink. It doesn't even have to be alcoholic.

I'm not in my room at home, though. I'm not trapped. I feel apprehensively, excitingly free.

I get into Five Mile…maybe an hour later, maybe more, I've totally lost track. My head is throbbing and my leg is dragging, but I don't care: I've made it. When I push through the door of the Flags and up to the bar, I feel like celebrating.

Because it's a Friday night, I'm not the only person in a celebratory mood. It's after nine, but the bar is loud, well-populated.

Col Geraldson is taking beer orders faster than he can serve them. 'Back again, Harris?'

'Yes, yes, I am.' I smile wide as I lean my crutches on the wooden ledge, pull my wallet out of my jacket pocket and throw it on the bar. 'I'd like to get completely shit-faced, thanks very much.'

Col just raises his eyebrows. 'Okay, then. Sounds good.'

My T-shirt is sticking to me, and that first long cold pull from my glass is like sex. Christ, I needed that. I slam the rest, bang the empty glass down, break out in goosebumps. There's another beer already waiting for me. It tastes almost as good as the first.

Thirst slaked at last, I turn around to see what's happening in the pub. Joe Krane is arm-wrestling with Taylor Schmidt to a lot of raucous laughter and shouting. A bunch of old-timers nearby is threatening to tip a beer on them. A couple of guys from Murrayville are standing in the pool-room doorway, holding their cues and having a smoke, yelling encouragement. Some dickhead has put Jackie Onassis on the jukebox; the brassy chorus is belting out so hard, Col's forced to lean over the bar to hear the orders.

I spot Snowie Geraldson's white mop and Hawaiian shirt. He's holding court at one of the tables, flags me over. Col sends a UDL down the bar and I stick it in the waistband of my jeans so I can manage my crutches, finally make it to the table. 'Fuck, is it loud enough in here?'

Snowie laughs. 'You wanna hear a joke? What's a redneck's last words?'

I know this one. '"Hold my beer and watch this"?'

'Ah, shit, mate, you stole my punchline!'

'It's old as the hills, ya dumb bastard.' I crack my can, hold it up for admiration. 'Mate – this is living. Right here.' I sink about half of it in the first swallow. My throat seems to go dry the moment I stop drinking.

'Nice one.' Snowie grins, slides a glass across the table in my direction. 'Here you go, get that into ya.'

It's a shot of vodka, from the bottle he's got on his right. I'm not usually a vodka-drinking man, but tonight any contributions to the 'Get Harris Wasted' fund are gratefully received.

I down the shot, pass the glass back with my eyes watering. 'Cheers.'

'Bottoms up.' Snowie pours, belts back a shot of his own.

I gesture around the pub. 'To be honest, I'm buggered if I know what you and your dad are worried about. Place seems to be roaring along.'

Snowie scans the pub, makes a rueful smile. 'You know what they say. Everything looks together until it all falls to shit. Jesus, don't get me started.' He scratches the back of his neck. 'Anyway, I wanted to talk to you. Glad you came by.'

As if I rock up every Friday night on crutches, half-tanked, covered in dust, hair stringy with sweat. Which, okay, sometimes I do, minus the crutches. Whatever.

'Talk away,' I say, helping myself to a handful of peanuts from the open packet he's got on the table. Can't recall having dinner, and peanuts look good right now.

'You know how I said I was working in Mildura? Said I had a few things going on, right?' He offers me another shot, which I accept, and pours his own follow-up. 'Well, if you're interested, there's something we can do to help each other out.'

I knock back my shot, raise my eyebrows at him, nice and high.

I might be a few drinks in, but I'm pretty sure there was a meaningful gap somewhere between 'I've got a job in Mildura' and 'we can help each other out'.

'What's the connection?' I ask. 'Whatcha saying?'

Snowie leans forward on the table. His hair glows above his gleaming eyes. 'I'm hooked up in Mildura, mate. I got access to good stuff. Good suppliers. And I got contacts up there, now. It wasn't hard.'

'Well, yay.' I wave my can in front of my face. Snowie's tried before to get me to deal pot around town. I've always preferred to be my own man. I'll score for myself, maybe help out a mate, but I don't broker. 'Plenty of local folks here'll put their hands up.'

'But that's what I'm talking about, ya dope. I don't need mates down here. I need mates in Mildura.' Snowie's gaze is intent as he tears a cardboard coaster to pieces with his fingers. 'There's jobs available, hey. I've been setting something up. And I need blokes around who can help out. You could make a little moolah to sort out your old man's problem.'

For a second I think he knows about Dad's cancer and I'm struck dumb. Then it sinks in that he's talking about the outstanding bills. Possibly the more pressing concern. If I don't sort out the bookie, there'll be unwelcome knocks on the door. And if the tab here isn't tidied up, Dad will be a bear to live with for the next five months without his regular doses of beer and vodka.

If I go back. That's still up in the air at the moment.

'Well...' My hands are getting nice and loose. 'Job offers. Sounds good. But I'm not exactly at the top of my form right now, yeah? Not in the peak of fitness or anything.'

Snowie shakes his head. 'Not a problem, mate, not a problem. You'll be right soon, and I need guys who're trustworthy. You've always been pretty solid.' He lifts his head, sees someone at the bar. 'Ando! Hey, Ando, get over here.'

A hulking figure detaches itself from the bar, makes its way over to our table. Marcus Anderson looks like someone took a member of the Hitler Youth and a WWE wrestler and mashed them together – he's tall, with a blond buzzcut, and bulging with muscle under his black Jim Beam T-shirt. In about ten years, he's gonna look like a flabby gorilla.

Snowie and Ando have been tight since Ando moved here about three years ago. I'm not in love with the guy: he's got a steely quiet and constantly looks as if he's sizing you up for a fight. He and Snowie get up to mischief when they're together. But he's loyal – generally, where Snowie goes, Ando goes too.

'Your dad's calling for you,' Ando says to Snow, as he puts his beer on our table.

'Ah, shit.' Snowie scribbles something on what's left of the coaster and shoves it at me as he rises. 'There's me new number, anyway. One sec.'

He disappears to help behind the bar. Ando gives me the once-over as he leans back in his chair. 'Snowie gave you his number, did he? You thinking of coming on board?'

'Dunno.' I shrug. 'Dunno what I'm getting on board with, for a start.'

'Not hard to understand, is it?' Ando takes a pull from his glass. 'Good job, easy money. No busting your arse hauling rocks, or whatever you were doing at the quarry.'

'Shot firing,' I correct. 'Blowing shit up.' There was some rock hauling involved but I'm not gonna elaborate.

Ando gives me a little smile. 'This is better. Just courier packages. Here, there – driving around.'

I try to focus on him for a second. 'Shifting product, is that what you're saying?'

He lifts one massive shoulder. 'If you're worried about the risk from the cops, do something else. Run messages. Go-between stuff.'

Drug runner. That's what all this vague language is referring to. That's what Ando and Snowie are talking about. Hardly the job of my dreams. The offer is tantalising all the same, because it's an offer. And because of the money – how else am I gonna sort out Dad's money issues?

But I can't pay off Dad's debts if I'm stuck in the local lock-up, either.

'Nice working environment, is it?' I smile. 'Lots of obliging ladies and helpful police officers, plus all the mull you can smoke?'

Ando grins like an eel. 'Nah, mate. Not mull. We've moved on a little way from that. Scaled up.'

His grin makes my nerves ping alive, because I know what he's talking about. There's pot, and there's pills, but there's only one party in Mildura that everyone wants a piece of: crystal meth. And I don't want a bar of it.

I let my smile freeze in place. 'Scaled up, yeah?' If Snowie's into dealing ice with the big boys in Mildura, he's getting into some serious shit. 'Sounds, um, lucrative.'

'Like you wouldn't believe.' Ando gives me a wink as he finishes his beer.

Snowie rocks back up to the table and I almost startle.

'Col managing okay now, Snow?' I ask.

'I was just filling Harris in a bit,' Ando says to Snowie.

'Right.' Snowie eyes him, then me. 'Yeah, I reckon you're a good fit for the job, Harris, what do you think?'

'Um, dunno.' I take a pull from my can to shield my face. 'Nice to have options, though.'

'He'd have to be able to hold his own,' Ando says. 'Gotta have a bit of clout sometimes, eh?'

'Shit, Harris can hold his own,' Snowie says, slapping my shoulder. 'You've got a bit of that martial-arts stuff from Westie, haven't ya? And look at him – he fucking walked all the way here on crutches! He's a legend.'

'I am a legend,' I agree, half to myself. How many drinks have I had now?

79

'Show me what you got, then.' Ando rises out of his chair.

'Piss off, Ando!' Snowie's laughing. 'You're gonna take a swing inside my dad's pub?'

'Nah, mate. Outside,' Ando puts his hands on his hips and lifts his chin at me. His grin looks less friendly now. 'Whaddya say we take it outside, so old Col doesn't have a heart attack, yeah?'

I can't believe this is real. 'You seriously wanna have a go? Outside the pub?'

'I wanna see if you can handle yourself,' Ando says. 'Call it a job interview.'

'Not exactly interview-ready,' I say, tapping my crutches.

But then I see someone come into the pub, someone I'd really prefer not to be dealing with now. It's Mark West. It hadn't occurred to me that Westie might be at the pub. But it's a Friday night, so it bloody should have.

Tall and solid, Westie's a big-arsed bastard with a beer gut and an unruly black mullet. He rolls through the door with Matt Tringle from my old work. I keep my head down. I don't want to exchange glances with the bloke whose trust I exploited when I helped Rachel out with that business at the quarry. Who I still haven't had a chance to apologise to.

If Westie's coming into the pub, I really want to be going out.

'Uh, yeah, outside sounds good,' I say to Ando, and I swing around to list out of my chair, grab my crutches. As Westie reaches the bar, I make as swift an exit as I can.

Snowie whoops. 'Ah, shit, I wanna see this! You bloody crazy-man!'

He half-tumbles with me out the door onto the front pavement. Long fluoro lights make the pub façade glow – the empty street beyond seems extra dark. The brisk night air blasts my senses, leaves me shivering. Ando's voice sounds behind me and I turn.

'Been looking forward to this.' Ando's radiating satisfaction. I guess I pissed him off some time in the past.

I gesture at my crutches. There's still a chance I can talk him out of it. 'You serious? How's this gonna work? You're gonna punch the crippled guy and I'm gonna fall over, is that it?'

'Nah, mate,' Snowie says, adjudicating. 'It's knock-knock, yeah? You can go first. You're okay balancing on that leg of yours, aren't ya? Put the crutches down.'

I'm struggling with the logic. 'I'm gonna stand here on one leg?'

'Hold one crutch,' Ando offers. 'And I promise not to hit that hard.' That eel-grin again.

Oddly enough, I don't trust him. 'One shot, huh?'

'Two shots each.' Snowie's grinning, too. I'm starting to wonder if he's really on my side. 'Aw, c'mon Harris, it'll be all over in five seconds!'

I look at Ando. 'One crutch. And two shots.'

'Yup.' Ando is smiling ear to ear.

'And not the leg.'

'Right.' Ando lifts a finger. 'Not the leg.'

'I'll hold him to that,' Snowie says, all solemn.

Like this is a thing, a real thing. And it bloody *is*, because I'm handing my right crutch to Snowie. Balancing on my good right leg while I try to put some weight on my left foot, which is – Jesus, so painful. I think my leg is swollen. I can feel it every time I put my foot down. This is a dumb, dumb idea. But I'm in the middle of it now.

I raise my fist, try to imagine landing it. 'This is fucking ridiculous.'

'Stop ya moaning!' Snowie says. 'Just sink one!'

I wind up and punch, my knuckles connecting with Ando's rock-like gut. But my arms are limp, and I've got no manoeuvrability. I can't even stretch and lean for more power. It's a pretty pathetic effort.

And now it's my turn to take a hit.

'You gotta stand still,' Ando says, stepping closer.

'Well, fuck, I can weave a little, can't I?' I'm getting cranky, now. And there's a strong possibility I was weaving before I ditched my crutch. 'Unless you just want an easy target.'

That, according to Ando's face, seems to be the preferred option. But he shrugs. I'm the one with the handicap. He doesn't want the victory to appear too hollow.

'Plant your feet,' Snowie advises.

'Thanks.' I roll my eyes. The day I take tips from Snowie about how to take a punch will be the day I fucking die.

But the first hit from Ando, to my solar plexus, makes me *feel* like I'm dying. He catches me off guard while I'm still eye rolling, and lands a solid jab to my diaphragm. The shock forces the breath out of me, pushes me into Snowie. A flush ripples up my face. My skin feels like liniment, hot and cold together.

'Fuck. Way to go a bloke, when he's not ready.' I cough it out.

'Then get ready for the next one,' Ando says.

He raises his fist, but Snowie steps in. 'Harris's turn, mate.'

'Right. Still taking turns, are we?' I cough again. It's no effort to keep my voice dry.

Ando shrugs. 'I guess you can –'

I don't wait to hear what Ando guesses I can do. I just do it, while he's still talking. My jab clips him smack on the shnozz. It's a better punch than last time – I wasn't thinking too much about it, I just threw it. Ando's head snaps back, and when he lowers his chin there's a thin line of blood leaking out one nostril.

My leg aches but I laugh. Can't help myself. Ando looks like one of those red-faced bulls in a cartoon. He's not best pleased.

'That was you, was it?' he says. 'You're all done?'

'Yep.' I should really stop grinning. It's only making things worse.

'Right.' Ando squares up. 'My turn. Knock-knock, bitch.'

'Hold on, I'm gettin' outta the way.' Snowie leaps aside.

And now I'm listing here, watching Ando wind up. This is not aimed at my gut. He's coming right for my head.

Nothing can prepare you for a full punch to the face. Getting hit in training is not the same – you're not trying to knock each other out of the ring with any malicious intent, you've got your gloves on. Knuckles bashing into your cheekbone and mouth at a million miles an hour is something entirely different.

The punch smashes a shower of drizzling fireworks into my head. I go down, of course, and I'm just glad I fall on my right side. If I fell on my injured leg now I'd black out. The pain seems to bounce around behind my eyes and my whole body resonates. But anger boils up from inside, too. Pain seems to do this to me sometimes, and Ando's pissed me off now.

I find my crutch somewhere, lever up. Struggle to my feet. 'Gimme another one.'

'You've had your two shots, mate,' Snowie says. 'You're done.'

I spit on the concrete, look right at Ando. 'Gimme another one, you weak fuck.'

'You sure about that?' Ando says quietly.

'Nah, mate, game's over.' Snowie holds out a hand. 'You're a legend. Point proved.'

'Absolutely,' I say, which could be a reply to either of them. I don't know who I'm talking to right now. My eyes are popping stars and my head's ready to explode.

Ando shrugs. 'You asked for it.'

He lifts his arm while Snowie's saying, 'Nah, mate, ah, shit – Col! Col, we've got a little situation out here!' and then Ando's fist slams into the other side of my face and I'm thrown backwards by the force of the punch.

Rockets go off behind my eyelids. I bounce off Snowie, then the outside wall of the pub, manage to catch the lintel of the door so I don't slither all the way to the ground. I get a nauseating feeling, like my bones are rearranging under my skin – my cheekbone and nose disappear for a second, then boom back to life. Someone grabs me under the armpits before I faceplant.

'Ando, I think he's had enough.' A big arm hoists me up as my head hangs down.

'I'm good,' I slur. Blood spatters on the concrete step when I talk. I see a pair of acid-resistant boots that look vaguely familiar. 'Ah, geez...Westie, is that you?'

'Yeah, you silly bugger,' Mark West says. He props me back against the wall. 'Well, aren't you a sight for sore eyes, eh? Shit. What a mess.'

I'm breathing through one nostril, and blood is rusty in my mouth. 'I was... Me and Snowie...'

'Yeah, no worries,' Snowie says. 'Thanks for that, Westie, we can sort it out.'

'Looks like Harris needs a stretcher,' Westie says. 'Ando, why don't you rack off for a bit, hey? Snowie, get us a towel.'

'We were just foolin' around,' Ando says.

'Well, you're all pissed as farts, so I'm not surprised it ended in tears,' Westie says. 'Harris? Hey, Harris, mate...'

Snowie comes back with a bar towel. 'Put that on his mouth. And Harris, I got your UDL.'

I take a slug of that first. Fumbling for the towel, I keel forward onto my left leg. A bolt of sheer agony streaks up from my toes to my neck. It makes me cry out. The world tilts at a crazy angle.

'Whoah, there.' Westie grabs me again. 'Jesus. Are you running a fever, Harris? Mate, you're a bit hot.'

I fight the urge to vomit, make a sick grin with my eyes closed. 'Mark, if I'd known you felt that way about me...'

'You dickhead.' Westie snorts, pulls me away from the wall, steers me to hobble into the street where his black Hilux is parked a few bays down. 'Snowie, I'm taking him to Ouyen. I reckon he needs the doc.'

'I'm fine,' I gasp. Westie's bulk keeps the weight off my bad leg.

'He said he's fine!' Snowie throws up his hands.

Westie shrugs. 'Better safe than sorry, eh? Tell your dad I'll drop back later.'

As Westie pushes me into the cab of the Hilux, I make myself give Snowie the thumbs up. 'It's all good, Snow. Don't you worry. The legend will return.'

'No hard feelings,' Ando calls. 'You're all right, Harris.'

I nod my appreciation – he's come around to my way of thinking – but that only makes me feel like spewing again. Westie opens the driver's side door and climbs into the cab.

'I'm missing something. I'm missing...' I pat my front with one hand. 'Where's me crutches?'

'In the tray.' Westie jerks a thumb back behind us. 'Come on, ya dopey bastard. Let's get you to the hospital.'

I lie my head back. The car rumbles beneath me as we reverse out of the bay. 'I'm sorry for the mess, Westie. And I didn't mean to fuck up at the quarry –'

'Harris, forget it. Everything's insured, remember? It all worked out okay.' Westie laughs. 'Shit, mate, you sure know how to raise a ruckus, hey?'

'Yes,' I agree. 'Yes, I do.'

The car ride goes by in a blur – we're moving through time and space at warp speed. I ask him to stop on the way and I hang my head out the window and fight the heaves. Then we arrive, and I think Westie is carrying me. Actually I'm not sure, because I don't know whether the concrete is up or down. I keep my eyes closed.

But I can smell Westie cos he stinks of Lynx, and someone's setting me down in a chair but...whoah, okay, the chair's got wheels. We're moving, we're coasting. A bright friendly voice someplace nearby starts talking when we've stopped. It takes me a second to place the voice, the face.

'Hey, I know you,' I say, which is actually an achievement in itself. Knowing that I know her. Also the speaking. Because putting words together is hard work.

'Yep, you know me,' Amie says, and she's wearing this tight

amiable smile. She has her badge on and her hair pulled back and she's looking me over. 'How're you going, Harris?'

'Amie? Sarge's kid?' Wow, I'm really together with the words and the speaking tonight.

'Yep, that's me.' Her smile grows tighter but her fingers on my wrist feel more gentle. 'Hey, have you had enough of this UDL?'

Which is funny, because until she mentioned it I hadn't even remembered I was holding it. 'I'm self-medicating,' I say, and my laugh turns into a hiccup.

'I can see that.' Amie slips the can out of my grip. 'How's about I hold onto this for you?'

'I haven't finished me drink,' I point out.

'Actually, I think you have. But I'll put it right here for you, okay?' She sits the can on the metal nightstand near the bed.

Yep, there's a bed right there with clean white sheets. The only downside is, the bed looks high. I got no idea how I'm supposed to be getting onto that. Which I think for a second might be what Amie and Westie are discussing, until I zone back in.

'Is this how you found him?' Amie says, and Westie says, 'I found him outside the Five Flags, getting his arse handed to him by Snowie Geraldson's mate. Got no fucking idea how he managed to get to that point –'

'Oi, oi.' I snap my fingers with my arm extended. 'Mind your French in front of the girls, Westie. You'll make Amie blush.' I wouldn't mind seeing Amie blush again. I look at my hand and wonder whether I could reach the can on the nightstand if I stretch far enough.

'Oh, I've heard a few naughty words in my time, Harris. Don't you worry.' Amie pushes my arm down and says, 'Look, I don't need the doctor to tell me his temp is high. So that's not from a fistfight and it's got nothing to do with him being pissed. Is that why you brought him in?' but I don't think she's talking to me.

'I think he's crook,' Westie says. 'He can't keep his weight on that leg, and I don't think that's from being ploughed, either.'

'You did the right thing,' Amie says. 'Can you stay for a tic, until we figure out what's the matter? I've got an idea what it might be but we need the charge nurse to check him out and I might have to get some details for the forms.'

'I can stay as long as you need,' Westie says.

'Thanks.' Amie turns around to me and says, 'Harris? Hey, Harris, we need to have a look at your leg, mate. You think that'd be okay?'

'Sounds good.' My voice is sloppy but the words are still working.

'Can we get you up on the bed to have a look? Mark, can you help me get him –'

'Yep, no probs,' Westie says, then he's grabbing me out of the wheelchair. My legs fall out from underneath me – this standing-up business is trickier than it looks.

Something occurs to me suddenly. 'Westie, y'know...I think I might be a bit pissed.'

'Bloody Einstein, you are,' Westie says, then he shoves hard and my arse is up on a higher seat than the one I had before.

'That's it, that's great,' Amie says. 'Now let me get in there...'

Amie swings my legs over, pushes down on my shoulders. This bed is not as soft as it looked from lower down. But that's not the priority as Amie starts unzipping my fly.

'Whoah, wait a sec –' I get out, but now she's tugging my jeans down. The top of my Bonds trunks peel back enough to flash hair, and I make a grab for her hand. '*Hey –*'

'I can take them off or I can cut them off. What would you prefer?' she says, and she gives me a look. But the room has started spinning so I let go of her hand. The air on my legs is cold, and I shiver. Someone works at my boots, then my jeans are all the way off.

'Okay, right.' Amie's voice sounds strangled. 'Harris, the dressing on your leg is looking kind of crusty, so I'm gonna remove it.'

I nod with my eyes closed.

'Yeah, that doesn't look good,' Westie says, from somewhere a bit further away. I hear the snip of scissors, then everything sounds further away as the dressing is pulled off my skin. My hands clutch the sides of the bed.

Amie's speaking with this fast authoritative voice, now. 'Mark, could you please go down to the admin desk and say we need the charge nurse to come here straightaway? Like, immediately? Thanks.' She lays something over my hips, covering me, before squeezing my hand. 'Harris, you look pretty sick, mate.'

'I...' Nausea barrels into me. 'There was a fight...'

'Sure,' Amie says. 'But the site of your surgery is really inflamed. The charge nurse is going to examine you, all right?'

I can't stop shivering. 'It was hurting at the pub.'

'I'll bet it was hurting for a while before that, too, am I right? It's gonna be okay. It's good you came in.'

Amie scoots around as another lady arrives to stand on the other side of me, and they start talking. Amie's doing a lot of nodding, which makes me seasick. I roll sideways suddenly – there's a quick movement as someone slips a bucket near my head close enough for me to hurl. My stomach cramps and the smell of regurgitated booze makes me gag and retch again. My hair is pulled back gently off my face.

'Well, he's clearly got cellulitis all up that thigh, but let me have a look first,' the other lady says, and Amie wipes my face with a damp cloth as I groan back onto the bed.

'Hey,' she says. 'Hey.' Somehow the sound of her voice helps me settle. 'Harris, it's okay. You've had a bit to drink, so it's probably better out than in.'

'At the Five Flags.' I breathe slowly through the shudders.

'How'd you end up at the pub, Harris?'

'Ah, I jus'…' I wave a hand, but she's asked the right question. She's pinpointed exactly where this whole night started. 'I jus' couldn't deal with Dad, y'know?'

She's looking right into my eyes, nodding. Her face looks very sad and soft. 'So you decided to go, was that it?'

'Yeah. I crutched it to the Flags –'

'You walked all the way there?' She glances across at the nurse, back to me. 'Wow. That's, what, about eight kay?'

'Yeah.' I snort, raise my eyebrows with my eyes closed, remembering. 'Yeah, s'a fair way…'

'Did you have sore arms after that?'

'Sure… My armpits got pretty sore…'

'You must've really needed that drink,' she says drily.

'Hah, yeah. Ow.' Something's going on with my leg, the charge nurse is doing something painful. 'Hey, whatcha –'

'Harris.' Amie's fingers on my chin draw my face back around. 'Look up at me here, that's it. So what happened at the pub? You got into a blue with someone?'

'Yeah…' The pain in my leg makes it hard to focus. 'Um, yeah, well, I was jus' talkin' to Snowie. His mate…'

'His mate belted you, did he?'

'Snowie, he's –' Lancing heat shoots up my thigh. My hand jerks towards my leg, what's going on there.

Amie reels it back. 'Tell me about Snowie,' she says.

I have to concentrate to talk. 'He's…he's visiting home and he's…he's talkin' about some work maybe. Asks me if I can handle myself and I say yeah, and Ando says…Ando says he'll be the man to find out.'

'Right,' Amie says, her eyes narrowing. 'So did he?'

'Did he what?' I gasp, catch my breath, keep my gaze on Amie.

'Did Ando find out if you could handle yourself?' she asks patiently, clasping my wrist, nodding for me to go on like she really wants to hear the end of the story.

I look at her, my vision juddering. 'Shit, yeah, I guess – fucking hell –'

'I'm admitting him,' the charge nurse says. 'I think it's abscessed, but page Dr McGaven. It's his case. If he needs to go back into theatre he'll want to know early. Can you wait while I call Barb?'

Amie nods, then the charge nurse says something else but I don't hear it. I close my eyes again and give in to the black.

*

Burning.

My whole body throbs with my pulse, my eyelids feel hot, my throat is rough from spewing, and my stomach is sore from contracting. My leg feels like it's on fire. This is shit. I thought hospital was supposed to make you better.

If I wanted to pay more attention I could hear what the doctor and the nurses are saying about me. Lots of half-whispered, urgent-looking conversations are going on. But I don't know if I have the energy to give a toss.

Nothing feels quite real. The anonymous scenery in here – the blue walls, the window, the curtains, the door – it all seems like part of a dream. Makes sense, I guess: I keep slipping into a doze, jerking awake. Different nurses arrive at intervals to put shots in my IV line, or try to coax me to drink a little water. The water always comes straight back up.

Dad – Dad hasn't showed. He might still be laid out, too pissed to drive. Or maybe he's sulking. Or maybe he's dragging it out.

Letting me stew in my juices for a while. When he thinks I've dwelled long enough on how screwed I am and how he'll react – how he'll retaliate – he'll rock up to the hospital and barge his way back in. Unless...

Unless I don't let him.

I could slip into sleep, relax into it, sink...and just keep sinking. I already feel so heavy, and my head aches all the time. The idea of just letting the dark well carry me deep is appealing. And it's got me curious. What if it's only a matter of not resisting?

I could do it. I could slide from my father's grasp, like a fish in a creek. And the amazing thing is, I don't think it would even take much effort. It would be a letting go of effort, in fact.

The concept has been waving to me all day, at the side of my vision, like a curtain blowing back in a gentle breeze. It sits there, waiting.

Patient.

'Harris.' Someone's supporting my head. 'Harris, come on, now. Sip.'

I don't want to.

'Sip. Come on.' The angle of the thing against my lip changes. 'Harris, you're ticking me off now.'

The water'll just come back up, I want to say.

'Harris, look at me. Open your eyes.'

I do. Because it's Amie and because I'd like to see her. But she doesn't look happy to see me. She looks really pissed off, actually.

She waves sheets of paper in the air. 'When I left here last night you were responding to treatment. Now you're febrile, you're still hypotensive, you're vomiting, not taking fluids. Your acuity is for shit.'

I don't know what any of that means.

'You're bloody...' Her cheeks flush as she makes a frustrated screwed-up face. 'Start *fighting*! For god's sake, Harris!'

I think about explaining it to her. I've had twenty years of fighting, and I'm so fucking tired. What would it matter if I stopped fighting? What business is it of hers anyway?

She must see something in my expression because she stops waving the papers. She puts them back on the clipboard then she finds a chair. I watch her drag it closer until she's sitting by the side of the bed.

'You look *bad*, Harris,' she says softly. 'What are you doing?'

I don't know what I'm doing. Far as I can see, I'm not doing anything. Maybe she thinks that's a problem.

She bites her lip. 'Will you talk to me? Can you talk?'

I swallow. Test out my throat. It hurts.

'Sip,' Amie commands.

That helps.

'Now talk.'

'Nothin' to say.' My voice sounds like powdered sand.

'Oh, I think there's plenty.' She pushes my hair back. 'You just don't want to dredge it up, do you?'

I close my eyes.

'Oh, no no no,' Amie says. She squeezes my hand. 'No you don't. Speak to me, Harris. Tell me something real. You talk a good game, but you never say anything I don't already know. Gimme something honest.'

I just look at her.

'You don't want to, do you? How can I...?' She scans the room. Her face gets this desperate searching expression before her eyes come back to mine. 'Okay. This is how we're gonna do it. I'll tell you something, then you'll tell me something. All right?'

She sits for a moment with her hands in her lap. Her eyes lose focus, like she's seeing inside herself. She's not in uniform, I suddenly notice: she's wearing jeans, and a pale pink shirt. Her eyes are brown, liquid. Her hair is so dark, the colour of charcoal, and the room is quiet in the dusk.

'I went to the beach when I was thirteen,' Amie says suddenly. 'With Mum and Dad. It was gorgeous. We stayed for a week. I loved the...the vastness of it. The ocean, the swell. It made me feel invincible and insignificant all at the same time. D'you know what I mean?'

I don't know. I've never been to the sea.

'There was this shop near the beach,' Amie goes on, 'I guess it must've been a souvenir shop. They sold milk and bread and stuff, but they also sold second-hand novels, and postcards...oh my god, these terrible postcards. Old-style sexist ones, with naked women and some jaunty message. *Wish you were here, it's hot and wet* – that sort of thing. You can imagine the pictures.'

She smiles faintly. She's sitting forward now, her hands on the sheet. Her fingers pick together, sparring like small restless animals as she looks at something else, something within.

'There was a shelf with all these little shell sculptures, y'know? Shells glued together. I thought they were adorable. They were really tacky, of course – little shell people waving, drinking beers, smoking pipes. But the most glamorous things in the shop were these bottles of coloured sand. The sand was in layers, like a piece of marble cake. I wanted one of those sand bottles *so* badly. It was like an itch. I had to have one...'

She swallows. 'The day before we left, Mum took me to the shop and bought me one. Just a small one, a little bottle with a cork stopper. I was so happy to have it, I crooned over it all the way home. And, y'know, I think it was just a wonderful distraction. Because all the way home, my Mum and Dad were talking about Mum's treatment, and how long it would take, and when she'd be in hospital, and how the recovery process would go...which didn't happen, of course, cos she never made it out of surgery. So all the time they're talking, I'm sitting in the back seat of the car looking at my little bottle of marbled sand –'

She stops. Examines her hands.

'That was the last holiday I had with both my parents. Before my mum passed. And I still have the little bottle. It's on my dresser, at home, with the cork stopper...' She peters out, shrugs. Makes this brave almost-smile. 'Anyway, that's me. Now it's your turn.'

I don't know what to say after that, or where to look except straight at her. The pause stretches, pulls taut, then she lowers her head to meet my eyes. Her breath is warm on my face.

'Your dad can't come to the ward, Harris,' she says softly. 'He tried to come after visiting hours last night, and he was bombed. He abused the staff, so Barb banned him from the hospital. If he tries to get in again, security will turn him back.'

Suddenly it's like something clicks inside me – tumblers turn, and the lock breaks. And I tell her.

'I can't live there anymore,' I whisper.

'At your dad's?' Amie asks.

'He's sick. Cancer. He wants me to stay. But I think he...' I shudder, close my eyes. 'I think we might kill each other if I stay.'

Amie doesn't say anything. She squeezes my hand gently, strokes my knuckles with her thumb until I open my eyes. It's the first time anyone has touched me with gentleness since...since the last time I was here at the hospital, I guess. I get a sudden flash of the way Amie slipped her arm under me when she changed my sheets that time.

'It's okay,' she whispers. She touches my bruised cheek. 'We'll work it out, Harris. We'll figure it out.'

It's such a relief to say it to someone, to hear any kind of reassurance, I can't even be embarrassed. My body is filled with this trembling energy that takes whole heartbeats to settle.

Amie stays with me until the nausea subsides, until I've

managed to take in some fluids, until I fall asleep. I don't know what happens after that.

8

amie

I honestly thought Harris was going to die.

He looked worse than the first time he was admitted, ticked all the boxes for septic shock. The prognosis for that is bad, like really bad: mortality can be as high as eighty percent. Barb kept putting a hand on my shoulder and reminding me that Harris wasn't my patient, that I was just a trainee, that none of this was my fault.

It just reminded me of the opportunity I'd had to speak up when he left last time with his dad. What has Harris endured over the last fortnight? What the hell happened to him?

I should have said something earlier. I should have acted.

He teetered for fourteen hours. Part of me understood that if Barb was really worried, she would have transferred him straight to Mildura ICU. But I've seen it before: patients who come in looking okay can take a sudden perilous turn. Like three months ago, with Mr Janssen – he'd seemed fine, then he had a secondary stroke, deteriorated within the space of hours, and we lost him.

And it wasn't only a physical battle with Harris. His eyes looked dead. Sometimes it's the mental and emotional war that takes more effort. He didn't look like he had any effort left to give.

When I came off night shift, he was responding to treatment from people way more qualified than me, so I went home. But what he said when he was admitted gave me a bad feeling. I ended up coming in for my shift early on Saturday evening so I could see how he was getting on.

Which is how I came to be verbally abusing a patient, then telling him one of the most personal painful memories of my whole life. If Barb had caught me she'd have had my head, not to mention my lanyard. *Don't get caught up in it, it's not your job to save the world* – that's her mantra.

In this case, though, I couldn't be detached.

Harris started taking fluids again, and keeping them down. I stayed with him until it was time for me to go on duty, then I slipped into the staff toilets to change into my work clothes. My whole body was shaking from holding that conversation with Harris inside myself. I was tired and distracted on shift, and Harris's words seemed to echo in the hospital halls: *I think we might kill each other if I stay.*

But by Sunday morning, he appeared to have turned a corner. Seeing him get his strength back was an enormous relief. Every time I passed his room, a tiny nuclear charge went off beneath my ribs.

Now it's Monday – he's sitting up and eating a bit, and when I go in to check his case notes, there's a chance to talk. Not talk-talk: neither of us has acknowledged the things we said to each other on Saturday evening. Some things have their own moment. Take them out of that moment and they tarnish, like precious metals exposed to the harsh air.

But I can broach the subject of him getting regular attention when he's discharged this time. Not that he's enthusiastic about it.

'Check-ups? Seriously?'

I look at him once, before turning back to check his antibiotic IV. 'You tried to walk halfway across the Mallee on a badly infected post-op injury, then you got into a fist fight at the pub... You're not taking proper care of it, Harris, or you wouldn't be in here again. Which means we've gotta make sure it's taken care of.'

His face turns to granite. 'I'm not a charity case.'

His expression is so cold and glowering, I'm reminded why half the blokes in the district prefer to stay on his good side. It also makes something inside me ache: he really doesn't get it.

I feel my own expression soften. 'Harris, it's got nothing to do with that. This is a hospital. We have a duty of care. Barb'd rather cut off her own arm before she'd let you walk outta here, knowing you could be back next week.'

'That's not –'

'Listen. If your leg gets infected again, that could be it. You could lose your leg.' I try to convey the heart of it. 'We're trying to look after you, mate. Do the right thing by you. Same as how we wouldn't leave you dying outside on the street.'

He takes this idea in. The wary suspicion in his eyes starts to fade. 'Okay, then.'

I force myself to grin. 'Jeez, don't mind me. Just trying to help you out here.'

'I don't need helping out.' He says it with less conviction.

'You'd look a bit different with one leg.'

'Shut up.' He sighs. 'Fine, okay. Whatever. Check-ups.'

'I'll talk to Barb about it. See if we can make it a bit easier for you, yeah?' I don't wait for him to reply. 'Now – lunch. Will you try to eat more?'

Harris makes a face. 'I guess.'

I consider the congealing items on his tray. 'Tell you what – I'll warm this up for you. You eat half of it, then for dinner I'll bring you chicken and chips from that joint on Main Street, okay?'

'How you gonna get that?'

He's squinting at me, but if there's one thing I know about guys from all the time I've spent with my dad, it's that their mood and their appetite go together hand in glove. I can practically see Harris salivating.

'I'm going up there for a slice of pizza later.' I keep my voice nice and casual, but I'm pretty sure the word *pizza* is now pinballing around inside his head, to devastating effect. 'Didn't bring dinner in tonight, thought I'd pick something up on my break. Do we have a deal?'

Harris looks at the lunch tray, looks at me. The tip of his tongue skitters over his lower lip. 'Pizza.'

'Or chicken.' I shrug. 'Up to you. Hospital will cover it. I just thought you might like something a little more...'

'A little more. Yeah.' He glances at the tray again, like he's wishing the plate held a nice juicy porterhouse.

'Here, let me take that.' I don't give him time to think too long. 'Won't take a second to warm it up.'

'Thanks.'

I shrug again. 'It's my job.'

It's not really my job – convincing patients they should let us look after them, buying dinner for them so they won't have to put up with the nutritious-but-lousy stuff the hospital provides – but I'd do it for anyone who needed it. Harris needs it. I've dispensed lollipops and bandaids: this is the same thing, just on a slightly larger scale.

By Tuesday, Harris is almost back to normal. He's reached that point which is a drag for patients and a reassuring sign for nurses everywhere – he's bored. I catch him lying in bed, flicking through television channels on the monitor in random frustration. *Flick flick flick.*

He clicks the 'Off' button and tosses the remote down, then stares at the ceiling until he realises I've entered the room. His face – still bruised from the fistfight – gets this neutral alert expression, which I've figured out is just window dressing.

'Hey, um, yeah,' he says. 'What's happening?'

I shrug. 'Nothing. Just came by to see how you're going. Had enough of the TV?'

'Yeah.' He prods the remote. 'Sports report's over. Now it's just daytime soaps, local news...all the usual crap.'

'You're getting a lot of interruptions for physio and dressing-changes and stuff,' I note.

'Yeah.' His shoulders do a little shuffle.

'Something else you want to do? Crosswords? Or maybe you've got a book to read or something?'

'A book?' His eyes are amused. 'Nah, didn't really think to bring my library bag with me.'

'Well, there's books in the lounge area, I could bring you a couple.' I frown. 'They're mainly old Mills&Boon paperbacks, though. Might not be your thing.'

'Don't you think I'm a true romantic?' he says.

I've managed to get a grin out of him at least. 'They're not exactly *Romeo and Juliet*. More heaving bosoms and guys with airbrushed chest hair.'

'Heaving bosoms, eh? Now you're tempting me.' He shifts on the bed, makes a grimace.

'Are you in pain?' I ask quickly.

He shakes his head. 'Nah, mate, it's fine. Just can't help but be uncomfortable sometimes, that's all. If I'm feeling crap again I'll let you know.'

'Good.' My shoulders release. He trusts me this much, that's something. 'Hey, if you don't want to read romance novels, I could bring in a few books from home. Or magazines. My dad has a lot of old car magazines.'

'Your dad?'

'Yeah. Y'know – my father. The police sergeant.' I grin.

Harris's eyebrows look like they're on stilts. 'And he'd lend me his magazines?'

'Sure. He wouldn't miss them. He's got loads. They just sit around the house gathering dust, until I put them in the woodstove.'

Next time I'm on shift I carry a generous stack of magazines into Harris's room. Let the pile thump onto the tray trolley beside his bed so he can hear the weight of potential enjoyment in the pages.

He pushes himself up on the pillows. 'These are all from your dad?'

'I put a few others in,' I say. 'I get a lot of *National Geographic* mags from the op shop, thought you might like to have a look. The pictures are pretty cool, and the articles are interesting. And I found some other old ones – fishing, gardening – from the lounge room.'

'Gardening?' His lips quirk up. 'You looked at me lately? You think I do a lot of gardening? Jesus, I think we should go back to the heaving bosoms.'

'No *Playboy*, if you were wondering.'

He shakes his head sadly. 'I'll just have to hope they've done a few features on naked tribeswomen in *National Geographic*, I guess.'

He's *definitely* coming back online.

There are other clues as well. Barb said he's arcing up in physio – depressed patients generally don't whinge, just suffer in silence – and he's chatting with the other nurses sometimes. I'd like to see him eat more, but let's face it, it's hospital food. At least he's talking, even smiling on occasion. He has a really good smile. It starts as a kind of wicked grin, then widens into this crinkly-eyed authentic happiness that somehow makes me happy as well.

I start to feel confident the despair I saw in him when he was admitted was just a blip on the radar. When I go in to help Nick with a dressing change on Wednesday, Harris is sitting on the edge of the bed, leafing through a *National Geographic* and kicking his legs.

'See? Boobies.' He holds up a double-page photo spread – a really gorgeous one, actually of elderly Choco Embera women laughing over a cookfire.

I grin. 'I knew you'd find them somewhere.'

'Hold still, please,' Nick says. He extends a hand for the extra gauze I pass him.

'That's looking good,' I say, checking the wound over his shoulder.

'Good enough to invite to the dance on Saturday night,' Harris quips.

'No dancing,' Nick says. 'And no kicking, thanks.'

'Can't help it,' Harris says. 'I got the wriggles.'

Nick makes an exasperated sound out his nose.

Harris is wearing a threadbare white T-shirt and a pair of footy shorts Barb got for him at the op shop on Maine Street. They fit him nicely, I notice. But I don't think he's going to be playing footy for a while. The wound in his thigh is now a gouged depression – I know Dr McGaven had to excise some abscessed tissue. It might be months before Harris regains full use of his leg.

He leans back on his hands and looks at the ceiling for the messy bits of the redressing process. 'La la la, yeah, ow.'

'Do you want a local?' Nick asks, losing patience.

'No, I don't want a fucking local, I just want it done.'

'Harris,' I warn.

'What? I can't complain if it hurts?'

'Complaints cost twenty bucks extra,' Nick says. 'There – straighten your knee. Yep, that's it. I'm done.'

'I'll clean up,' I offer.

'Great, thanks, I've gotta see Mrs Martinelli in Two.' Nick walks out.

'He hates me,' Harris says, after an interval.

'No, he doesn't,' I scoff, but I'm already thinking up excuses for Nick's rudeness. 'He's just...got stuff happening. He's distracted.'

'It's no big deal,' Harris says. 'I'm not crying about it.'

I snort. 'I think you're reading too much into it. Proper nurses are supposed to be detached.'

'I'm not saying he's not professional. He just hates me.'

'He doesn't hate you. He just –'

'Doesn't like me. At all. Which, if you think about it, is pretty much the definition of hating somebody.'

I shake my head as I collect the scissors and sterile packaging. 'You're being paranoid. Nick's a good guy.'

'I'm not saying he's not.' Harris tosses the *National Geographic* back onto the pile at the foot of the bed, then does a double take at me. 'Hang on – he's Nick Partridge.'

'Yes.'

'Who you went out with for a while,' Harris says, tilting his head to catch my eye.

I squint at him. 'How'd you know that?'

'I heard about it.'

'Okay. So?'

'So he knows you. He's probably looking out for you. Am I right?'

I fumble all the gauze and paper tape scraps into the kidney dish on the tray. 'Nick's a mate. He was already working at the hospital when I started –'

'Sure, he helps you out at work. But what I mean is, he's

probably wondering what the fuck I'm doing, talking to you.' Harris leans back on his hands. 'He doesn't want his ex-sweetie getting too friendly with a guy like me.'

It's my turn to double take. 'It's none of his business. And what would he have against you?'

'Nothing.' Harris lifts one shoulder, almost like an apology. 'He just figures I'm a local dickhead who bongs it up on the weekends and gets into punch-ups at the pub, and he thinks I'm not the kind of guy you wanna be giving the time of day to.'

I can't look at him, because that assessment is pretty much exactly what I heard from Nick. 'But...that's unfair. He doesn't know anything about you.'

'He thinks he knows enough.' Harris's look is weighted. 'He probably knows how I ended up back here, right?'

I match his look to reassure him. 'He doesn't know about your dad. He knows about the fight.'

'Right. Which means he's heard I'm friendly with Snowie Geraldson. That'd be enough to get his back up.'

'That's...' *Bizarre*, I want to say. But it would explain a lot. My forehead screws up. 'Look, I think you're barking up the wrong tree, but whatever.'

Harris makes a face that suggests he believes it's not only the right tree, but it's a pretty well-marked tree. I think about what he's just said, remember my dad a few weeks back talking about Gavin Donovan. *I'd say Snowie Geraldson tuned him up.* I knew about Snowie's rep, but until I heard about the fight I didn't know Harris was involved with him.

Now I'm curious. 'Why are you friends with Snowie anyway?'

'I'll be friends with anybody who buys me a beer.' Harris looks over, makes a flat snort at my expression. 'I'm joking. You know his dad owns the Five Flags... Well, I've spent a fair bit of time at the pub.'

'Pub mates?'

'I guess. Snowie's okay.' He sees my expression change. 'No, really, he's okay. I mean, he's an idiot – and that's coming from me, King of the Idiots, so I can speak with authority, yeah? But I've known him since primary school. I just can't bring myself to see him like other people see him.'

'Right.'

Harris leans to catch my eye. 'He's not called Snowie, y'know. His real name is Gerald.'

That makes me pause. 'Gerald Geraldson?'

'Yep.' He grins. 'And he's always been friendly, so...'

'You're friendly back. I get it.' I steady the tray as I lift it. I'm taking a gamble with my next comment but I think it might be accurate. 'You never thought he was just being friendly because you're a customer?'

Harris wriggles himself back onto the pillow-end of the bed. 'Sure, maybe that's true. But Snowie's got his own shit to deal with. I'm not gonna hang more on him.'

That's something else I need to talk to him about. My voice goes quiet. 'Harris, have you figured out how you're going to deal with *your* shit, once you get out of here?'

He grabs a copy of *Home and Garden* and flicks through it, studiously avoiding my eyes. 'I'm working on it.'

Once I've left Harris's room and binned all the rubbish, I head for Barb's office. She's bustling inside one of the glass-fronted cubicles near the staff room. I scan around to make sure nobody needs me before walking through the open door.

'Harris Derwent,' I say, by way of hello. 'He's due for discharge on Friday, and he needs follow-ups. I don't know who with, but... I mean, what he really needs is domiciliary care –'

'Good afternoon to you, too.' Barb is elbow-deep in paperwork at the desk. 'And I'm aware of Mr Derwent's circumstances.'

'I know.' I stop, straighten up. 'Sorry. I just... His living situation is shitful, Barb. I know he lives too far away for us to visit, but –'

'I understand,' Barb interrupts, still sorting paper. Her head bobs. 'What he needs is a structured appointment schedule for post-release care.'

'But will he keep to it? And if he's seen by rotating staff members, won't he just find it easy to skip appointments unnoticed?' I sigh, push back my hair that's come loose from my ponytail. 'I don't know. Maybe it's just because I know him, I know what's going on behind the scenes. I'm really worried he's gonna leave here, go and get himself all banged around again, then before you know it we'll be sending him up to Mildura for an amputation assessment.'

Barb has obviously been listening with more than one ear. She's still standing behind the desk, files in hand, but she's stopped making a paper-tornado.

'Do you think he can be persuaded to change his living arrangements?' Her voice is quiet, thoughtful. 'If he was living nearby, we could schedule him to come in once a week for the next month, on a set time and day.'

'Would Harris quit his dad's place, you mean?' My forehead screws up at the concept. It's a very attractive concept. I don't want to get too married to it.

Barb shrugs. 'I could try to put the thumbscrews on Dennis to bring him in for appointments, but I don't know how far I'd get –'

'I'll talk to Harris.' I grasp the lintel to steady myself at the idea. Harris may not be very approachable on the topic of his dad, but if I'm going to say something, now's the time. 'I'll see what I can do. It's really up to him, though, isn't it?'

Barb looks at me gravely. 'Yes, love, it is.'

'If he had a place to stay...' My hand goes up to my bottom lip before I'm even aware of it. I'm racking my brain now. 'Let me ask around. I can have a go, right?'

'No harm in it, love. But you'll still have to talk to Harris,' Barb reminds me. 'That'll be the biggest hurdle.'

'Yeah.' I grimace.

'If we can get him closer... *If* we can get him closer, then we'll talk about it. And talk some more about scheduling you for the appointments.'

'*Me?*' My eyes dart back to Barb's. 'But I'm not an RN. I can't assess him properly, I just change the dressings –'

'– which is exactly what you'll be doing every time he comes in.' Barb holds my gaze. 'Look, this isn't my standard approach. Normally, if you've got a needy patient known to you personally, I'd tell you to back off. But in this case, if Harris sees someone he knows it might be an advantage. If he needs assessment you can refer him, and he'll be here on the ward if there's a problem. One of us can check things over before you let him go, if you're not confident.'

'But I'm not –'

'You're what he's used to,' Barb points out. 'He seems to trust you. He's much more likely to come in regularly if he can see someone he's comfortable with. At least you care whether he makes the appointments.' She gives me a speculative look. 'You do *care*, don't you?'

I press my lips together before replying. It's a lot of responsibility. I might have to change my shifts, and it's more nursing – real nursing – than I've been expected to do before. But it's Harris...

'Yeah,' I say. 'Yeah, I do.'

Barb gives me a meaningful look. 'If we manage to set this up, though, there's something I want you to remember. Harris is a person, not a project. You can't save people, Amie – I've told you that, time and again. You can only give them the encouragement they need to save themselves. Don't let yourself get too involved.' Her cheeks go round as she smiles. 'But I'm sure you'll be sensible about it. You're the most sensible girl I know.'

When I get back out into the admissions area, I look up the hallway. Everything in the hospital is blue: blue-grey carpet, pale blue walls, blue admissions desk. Barb says the patients find it soothing. I glance down at myself, at my navy work pants and teal-coloured uniform shirt. Standing completely still like this, I could almost be part of the furniture.

Barb is right – I *am* sensible. And dependable, trustworthy, responsible... I am all those things. I mean, between my job and my family I kind of have to be. It's why I haven't even looked at the purple folder Robbie gave me. Because I'm sensible, and the photography residency is just a flight of fancy.

Being sensible is part of what makes me a model trainee. It's the only way I can juggle all the needs of the people who rely on me. Being sensible is *necessary*.

I should find it reassuring that Barb thinks of me this way.

*

'Yeah, I guess so,' Mark West says, contemplating the coffee in his mug. 'Only for a month, you said?'

'Yeah. Just a month.' I'm trying to keep a lid on my fizzing excitement. 'Barb Dunne at the hospital said he'll need regular appointments for four weeks, but after that he should be back on his feet.'

'Harris is an okay bloke.' Mark nods at me, nods at Dad across the other side of the workshop. 'I mean, he's a bit of a wild man, but he's young. I did plenty of stupid shit when I was young – pardon me French.'

'If you can give Harris a place to stay for a month, that'd be really good.' I bite my lip to stop my grin from breaking open any wider.

Mark lifts an eyebrow. 'What about Dennis?'

'What about Dennis?' Dad echoes quietly. He shakes his head over the bowels of Westie's Hilux. 'You think he might try and have a word with you?'

The smile flees from my face. Being so caught up in what Harris might say about all this, it never occurred to me to take Dennis Derwent into account.

Westie shrugs. 'He's not gonna get his jocks tied about a four-week stay, is he? And it's for the hospital. He can't complain about the hospital.'

Oh yes he can. Not like Dennis hasn't complained before. But maybe that's the angle I can take with Harris, that Harris can use with his dad: it's the hospital that's set it up, and it's only for a month. A month sounds short.

'He can blame it on us,' I say jokingly, my mouth a little dry. 'Barb can have a chat before Harris is discharged, tell Mr Derwent it's a requirement of release or something.'

'Yeah, I'd prefer if Dennis wasn't growling at me,' Mark says, nodding. He makes a gap-toothed grin. 'Barb's got his number, though. He doesn't yell at her.'

'Barb's pretty tough,' I agree.

'Bloody Dennis.' Dad picks through a greasy tin of bolts before looking up at me. 'Will he cause a ruckus? Should I have a word to –'

'No, no,' I say hastily. 'Best not to get too official about it. Let Barb have a word to Mr Derwent, I'll tell Harris he's got this as an option, and we'll take it from there.'

Mark and Dad both nod their approval. There's only one other thing I need to sort out, so I better get it over with.

'Mark, it's great of you to say yes, but have a think about it. I'll have to ask Harris first. And I don't know about the money –'

'The money?' Westie squints at me.

'Well, you'll have Harris for a month. He'll have to pay room and board, but I don't think he's cashed up. He hasn't worked for weeks and it'll be a fair while before he can get back to the quarry. I was gonna offer you fifty bucks a week for groceries and expenses. It's not a lot, but it's –'

'I'll chuck in,' Dad says.

'What?' I stare at him.

'I'll throw in a bit,' Dad says evenly. 'Why not? Keep Harris Derwent off the street and outta my hair for a month. Be worth it.'

But he's got his eyes on me and I know there's stuff he's not saying.

Westie snorts. 'Well, shit, I was gonna do it for free. But if you wanna throw in a bit, I wouldn't knock ya back.' He scratches his chest through his T-shirt and I hear the woolly rasp under the fabric. 'Right, then. Everything's sorted except the car.'

'Gimme an hour,' Dad says.

I go back into the house to put the kettle on again, make a plate of toasties. There's a light-winged feeling in my chest but it's competing with darker flutters of anxiety. This is more than bandaids and lollipops. I'm sticking my neck out for a guy who's pure chaos.

But I was the one who told Harris to keep fighting. I said I'd help work it out. Well, now I've set it up: I've given Harris options. The only question is whether he'll take advantage of them.

After Mark West revs the Hilux down our driveway and off into the distance, Dad wanders back inside, wiping his hands on a dirty rag.

'All good?' I'm cleaning up at the table, putting the remains of the sandwich makings back into the fridge, wiping up the crumbs. 'That engine sounded nice by the end.'

'Yep.' Dad leans on the kitchen bench near the sink. 'Satisfying, that is. Something's broken, you fix it, bloke drives off happy. It's a bloody far cry from police work, I can tell you.'

I smile at him. If Dad wasn't such a good copper he'd spend all day tinkering with cars. But he is a good copper. I actually think the tinkering has something to do with that.

'So,' he continues. 'You've set that all up nicely then, with Harris Derwent.'

'Yeah.' I focus on the tidying. 'Well. I just thought it'd be good, y'know? Give Harris a chance to get better properly.'

'Right.' Dad picks grease out of his fingernails. 'How well does he know Snowie Geraldson, y'reckon?'

'Dad!'

'Well, I wonder, don't I?' Dad abandons any attempt to look like he's worried about the grease. 'Westie said it was Snowie's mate he got in a stoush with at the pub. And I've had Harris down at the station plenty of times in the last few years – drunk and disorderly, driving unregistered, brawling –'

'Well, he came off second best this time.' I dump the dish cloth full of the dirty crumbs into the sink.

'I'm not saying he's a villain, love.' Dad straightens. 'But if he's hanging around Snowie...' He rubs through his hair. 'Maybe I could just ask him. Drop in at the hospital and ask Harris straight out.'

I put my hands on my hips. 'I know you're trying to get a line on Snowie, Dad. But do you really think Harris will tell you?' I'm sure my expression says he should already know the answer. 'You know how the local kids are. They won't dob in a mate. They'll cover for each other. That's how it works –'

'Yeah, but this is different. It was probably Snowie supplying

Craig Davies, and we know he was dealing ice to Gavin Donovan. If Snowie's dealing hard stuff, stuff that's hurting people, local families, then he's dirtying his own patch. I don't think anybody'd be sticking up for him then.'

'Maybe.' I rub my eyes.

'Maybe people don't know,' he suggests. 'They think Snowie's still just dealing pot. Sounds harmless, right? If they knew he was the one who sold ice to Gavin and Craig, he might not find himself with so many friends.'

'I dunno, Dad. You'd be putting Harris in an impossible situation, asking him to rat out a mate.'

'It doesn't have to be complicated. I could just go in and have a chat with Harris, ask him about the fight. He might drop something useful.'

I don't like the sound of that. 'Can't you just pick up Snowie for some small violation and talk to him in person?'

'If it were that easy...' Dad turns around to fill the kettle, lodges it back in its cradle and hit the switch. 'I'm trying to avoid tipping Snowie off. This isn't just about him, love. Snowie's only the dealer. He's small fry. CIU in Mildura, they're trying to find out how far it all goes.'

'So it's all coming out of Mildura?'

'Largely.' He leans against the bench. 'Little towns around here like Walpe and Five Mile and Ouyen, they're just the feeder towns.'

'How's that?'

He sighs, spreads his hands to explain. 'Okay, think of it like a pyramid. At the top you've got bikies and truck drivers bringing in the gear from Melbourne or interstate, or getting it made locally, and then distributing it to a handful of trusted Mildura generals. The generals break it up and pass it down to lieutenants, who break it up further for sale – the lieutenants have got their own little army of dealers and small-time distributors. Snowie falls into the 'small-time distributor' basket. Then you've got the buyers – the addicts. They're the large desperate community supporting the whole thing at the bottom of the pyramid, and funding some of their habit through things like B&E and muggings.'

'And ripping off your parents' car and laptop.' I'm thinking of Gavin Donovan, his sad family.

'And ripping off your parents' car and laptop, yes.' Dad looks at me gravely.

'So you could pull Snowie in for questioning but that'll just tip off the big fish, and it won't stop the drugs from coming into the area.'

'That's pretty much it.' He turns as the kettle reaches the height of its bubbling cycle and switches itself off. 'But if I get enough info I could bust Snowie properly. If Snowie loses his lolly at the thought of doing serious jail time he might tell me the names of more significant parties – find out who's supplying him from Mildura, and I could pass that onto Mildura CIU. They could put away a few of the people who keep the operation running. If we can take down big names, the whole structure starts to collapse.'

'And if that happens...'

'Then Mildura looks like a less interesting place to distribute your drugs. Which means less product coming into Ouyen and Five Mile and other local towns.' He pours hot water into our mugs. 'People like Gavin Donovan have a fighting chance to get off the meth for good and recover. There's no piss-ant dealers like Snowie waving it under Gavin's nose on a Friday night.'

There's a lot of information to absorb but I'm thinking about what it means now. 'You could clean up all over the district. All the petty burglaries and assaults and ODs would stop, hospital admissions would go down...'

Dad nods. I can tell he's excited by the idea. 'If I could manage that before I hang up the uniform, I'd be a happy man.'

'So you're hoping to catch Snowie somehow. But what could you get out of Harris Derwent?'

Dad shakes his head, passes my mug over. 'I don't know, love. Like I said, maybe nothing. But Harris has been on my radar for a while for different reasons. The idea of him and Snowie getting matey...'

'You're worried about Harris,' I say, realising suddenly. 'You're worried he's gonna get mixed up in it.'

'Harris has been on a knife-edge most of his life,' Dad admits. 'He's coming from a bad place – his upbringing has weighed the scales against him. But he's not an idiot, even though he sometimes pretends to be. He's got potential. He had a good job at the quarry and he had Mark West in his corner. It was starting to look like he was digging his way out. Then he traipsed off to Melbourne and this shooting business happened –'

'And he went back to his dad's,' I finish.

If I'm going to say anything, now's the time. But I don't know if I want to share the news about Dennis Derwent's illness with my father. It's not like I've signed a patient-nurse confidentiality agreement or anything, but Harris told me about it in all privacy. I practically had to drag it out of him with forceps. Passing it on to Dad would be a breach of trust.

And if Dad went in to see Harris and let word slip... I honestly don't think Harris would ever let his walls down again, not for anybody.

I have to phrase my words carefully. 'Dad, there's stuff going on... Harris has told me there's problems with him and Dennis at the moment.'

'So Harris is talking to you?'

'Sometimes.' I contemplate my tea. 'That's why I've been trying to help him out. I mean, I know it's not really my business but when he came back to hospital the second time he was really struggling. He needs some space to recover, or he's going to end up returning again.'

Maybe to die. I flash on when I went into Harris's room on Saturday and found him lying there with his lips dry and his eyes unfocused... I don't want to remember how he looked at that moment, but the memory won't leave. I wonder if Harris remembers the look in my eyes when I told him my story about the coloured sand. I asked him for something true, something real, but I'm starting to realise that sharing truth with someone is like osmosis: a dual exchange.

'I think what you're doing is good, love,' Dad says quietly. 'And fixing up Harris with a place to go... I hope it helps. I really do.'

I nod, relieved to have my father's approval. This will be so much easier if I know Dad's on my side.

But he's not finished.

'Just be careful, okay? Harris is an each-way bet. I don't want to see you disappointed, but some folks...' His expression is very serious, and a little sad, and makes a dreadful hollow in my stomach like a tiny black hole. 'Sometimes things just don't work out for the best, no matter how hard you try.'

9

harris

I'm staying at Westie's place.

My brain was kind of spinning around inside my skull all week with the question of what I was gonna do once they discharged me. I even reached a point where I considered picking out my stitches to buy myself some time. *Just a couple more days*, my brain squawked, *a couple more days to sort this out...* Being desperate is like being drunk: even stupid ideas seem plausible when you've reached the bottom of the barrel.

The closer I got to discharge day the more claustrophobic I felt. That's how Amie found me crutching around near the picnic table beside the nurse's housing unit – the outside exercise was my physio's orders, but being outside was kind of necessary.

'Harris!' Her face was lit up like fireworks. 'Now, don't get mad, okay? But I've got a proposition for you...'

Where has this girl come from? Seriously, who does this shit? Who goes out of their way for a total stranger? Okay, not a stranger, but still – I'm no family to her, just some guy from ancient history. We barely crossed paths in high school.

But...I trust her. I trust her, and I don't know why.

Maybe it's because she trusted me first. She didn't have to tell me that memory about her mum, didn't have to visit me that night at all. Jesus, the last time I left the hospital I blanked her. In my experience, kicking someone in the teeth like that means you have to watch out for the kick back. But not this girl. For some reason, Amie doesn't seem to play by the usual rules of engagement.

Now it's Friday, and Amie's giving me a lift to Mark West's place. However this happened, I'm glad for the breathing room. There's still Dad to deal with, and his debts, and the information I'm owed about my mum and my sister. I've gotta get back on my feet, I've gotta find a job.

I don't tell Amie all the 'gottas' as I collect my crap from the side table. My jacket, my wallet, a white paper bag of antibiotics and wound dressings and sterile swabs – that's it. I'm the only guy in the whole hospital who doesn't have a bag to pack. That should make me feel depressed; right now, it just makes me feel light.

Amie's smiling as she passes my other crutch over. 'Glad to be leaving?'

'Like you wouldn't believe.' I don't mention I'm even gladder the place I'm going to isn't mine.

Barb Dunne gives me a clipboard of paperwork to sign. 'Yes, Mr Derwent, it was nice of you to drop in, but don't be offended if I say we'd prefer you visited less often, all right?'

'I'll do my best.' I grin, sign where directed, hand back the clipboard.

'Wonderful.' She gives me a pat on the shoulder. 'Take care of yourself, Harris.'

Out in the hallway, Amie gives me a prod. 'You've got all the wound care supplies from Barb, that's good. What about your appointment schedule? Your physio sheets?'

'Yes, ma'am. All sorted.'

'Remember, if you need anything you can give the hospital a call, or just drop by whenever you like. Mark's place is only a few blocks away.'

Which seems like as good a moment as any to point something out. 'You don't have to drive me, you know. I could walk over just as easy.'

'I don't mind,' Amie says. 'I'm off shift now, anyway.'

'I crutched eight kay along a dirt road for a beer. Pretty sure I can handle three blocks.'

'I want to,' she insists.

That gives me a little shine inside. The only sour moment comes when we get out into the foyer area. Nick Partridge is just clipping on his nametag as we pass by – Amie flags him with a wave. 'Another extra?'

'Another extra, yes.' He makes a tight smile, but maybe that's got nothing to do with me. He already looks tired.

Amie, by contrast, looks like she's glowing. 'I'm just helping Harris get to his new place.'

'So I see.' I dunno how he can see anything. He seems to be deliberately not looking in my direction.

Amie pushes a little. 'How's the car sale going?'

'It's going,' Nick says. Then he seems to chill a bit, makes a face. 'But, y'know, it's not a ute. I've had a few calls but not many folks want an automatic.'

'I want an automatic,' I say. It just pops out.

'What?' Nick says.

'Hey, that's right.' Amie looks at me. 'You can't get around in a manual, can you?'

I shake my head. 'Not unless I can use my crutches to operate the clutch.'

It's a crazy idea, but suddenly I want a car. I've had my license for years, but I've always been too broke to own. I'm used to walking around, riding a dirtbike, borrowing mates' cars, or in a pinch, hitch-hiking. But I remember how it felt to be out at the Five Mile house, stuck on the property with Dad because I couldn't simply drive away. Even that hard painful walk to the pub, the night I ended up back in hospital, was a result of my lack of transport.

So it's a crazy idea that's suddenly become hugely appealing. Could I pay off a car? A side-of-the-road deal, maybe. I've got enough mechanical know-how to fix something up. I could ask Mike Watts, or even Rachel, for a short-term loan... The idea makes me pause. But I'm kinda drunk on the thought of living away from Dad – anything could happen.

Amie nudges Nick's arm. 'Well, you're pricing pretty low, aren't you, Nick?'

'Ye-es,' he says.

'So that's perfect!' Amie says. 'You could sell your car to Harris.'

'Uh, yeah, Ames –' Nick says.

'S'okay.' I wave a hand, giving the guy an out. 'It's your car, man, it's your call.'

'Well, I am trying to get rid of it...' Nick's gaze slides over me, finally settles somewhere near my eyes. 'I mean, it's close by, and it's cheap.'

'Sounds pretty good.'

'It's a shitbox,' Nick admits.

'It probably just needs a tune,' Amie says.

'No,' Nick says, looking at me properly, 'it really is a shitbox. But it's a cheap close shitbox. So it's kind of up to you.'

'Even driving a bomb sounds better than walking right now,' I say, lifting one crutch a few inches off the floor. I have to balance on my good leg to do it.

'Fair enough.' Nick nods. 'I'm in town here, anyway. Amie's got my number if you want to come and have a look at it.'

'Excellent!' Amie pats my arm. 'Gimme a sec, I've just got to hand in my lanyard and make sure I've signed off.'

She walks further down the hall to the nurse's station. I don't realise how my eyes are glued to her until Nick clears his throat beside me. 'You guys know each other from the local FNL, yeah?'

'Uh, yeah.' I try to give Nick my full attention. 'Yeah, but it was a while ago. We never really had much to do with each other in school.'

'I know. Amie told me.' He's giving me a funny look, and I wonder what Amie's told him exactly. 'And then you arrived here.'

'Yep. Then I arrived here.' Which seems to pretty much sum up that whole mess. My gaze wanders back down the hall, where Amie is a small figure talking to another larger figure, the charge nurse.

'Right,' Nick says. The tone of his voice makes me look over, but he's just unslinging his backpack, getting ready for work. 'Good luck with your recovery. Hope it goes okay. Gimme a call if you really want the car.'

He walks off, not waiting for my thanks. Amie arrives by my side again as I'm wondering what the guy's problem is. I forget about it as Amie leads the way outside to the parking bay.

'Jump in,' she says.

I squeeze myself into the front passenger seat of her little two-door Holden, shifting the seat all the way back. Amie passes in my crutches one at a time until they're stuffed in between my knees, before running around to the driver's side.

It feels kinda weird being in a confined space with her, out of the hospital. I'm very aware of where my hands are, how much room I take up.

'You good?'

I nod. 'I'm good.'

'Okay, buckle up.'

Once she's sure I've done my seatbelt she starts the engine, pulls the car out. We pass the sign for the hospital at the exit and I can't help it: a smile breaks over my face. I must've gone past these old houses on Britt Street a million times, but it all seems like a new landscape now.

I wasn't joking when I said it was close. It takes less than five minutes to reach the white fibro place on Scott Street, near the old Masonic Temple hall. Amie pulls up on the verge.

'Well, this is me.' I unbuckle, open the car door. 'Thanks for the ride, hey.'

'No worries.' Amie passes out my crutches. 'You've got it all under control from here?'

'You bet.' Before I shut the car door, I bob my head. 'Um, thanks. Thanks heaps.' I should say more, show my gratitude. My tongue's thick in my mouth though. Saying *I think you might've saved my life* seems a bit overdramatic, but saying anything less feels lame.

She grins. 'Make sure you show up to your appointment on Wednesday. That's all the thanks I need.'

Then she's driving away, and I'm shoving my wound-care stuff into my jacket pocket as I crutch into Mark West's front yard. Westie's house is a flat-roofed fibro unit with some shrubby stuff under the eaves. Striped canvas blinds shade the north-facing windows. Wouldn't look out of place in a caravan park Permanent Residents' lot, but, hey, it's not my dad's house – it looks like paradise to me.

I climb the concrete step to the front door but no one responds to my knocks. Okay. I stand there blinking for a sec, then I remember – it's Friday arvo. Mark will be at the hall, teaching self-defence class.

Struggling off the step, I turn left to the corner and cross traffic-less Pickering Street. The hall across the street is tall red brick. I make my way around to the back of the building where the rear door stands open. Inside the cool air hits me, reminds me of the hospital air-con I've just left.

The light in here is muted, but the sounds of physical training fill the space: people grunting, boxing gloves hitting leather, heavy bags creaking on their chains. About a dozen people – kids, mostly, but a few older guys in training for local bouts – circle around the equipment stations. I smell sweat, and spot Westie: he's moving around the cavernous hall, checking folks on the punching bags, offering tips. *Put your feet here. Twist in the waist. Don't be afraid to hit hard.* My hands itch to grab a pair of gloves, to thump something. But the feeling doesn't rise out of my usual dark place. I'm just happy to be back here. It feels homey.

'Ha – the prodigal son returns!'

The voice makes me turn. Della Metcalfe is wearing a black crop top and a pair of hot-pink trackie pants, her exposed skin shiny with perspiration. She raises her gloves so we can fistbump. Then she laughs, shoulders inside my crutches and pulls close for a hug. Her bosom squishes up against my chest – she's got a lovely bosom, Dell – and it's bloody nice to see her.

'Dunno about prodigal,' I say. 'Isn't that when you apologise and say you're not gonna do the same stupid shit again?'

She pulls back to ruffle my hair with her gloved hands. 'If you tell me you've seen the light and changed your ways, I won't believe you. And I'll be pissed.' She nudges me with her hip, gives me a sly grin. 'Don't let anyone tell you to clean up your act, Harris. I like you better when you're dirty.'

I got a lot of time for Della. Used to have more time, in fact, until she called us quits about a year ago. Della's into on-again-off-again things, and I was cool with that – it made us a good match. It's great to see her. Apart from Snowie at the pub, it's been forever since I've spent time hanging out with mates. 'So you're helping Westie with training now?'

'Dick.' She play-boxes my ear. 'I help *teach* the class now. Someone had to take over when you left.'

It shows how long I've been away that I'm not up with this stuff. 'Well, I won't be good for shit for a while.' I shuffle my crutches. 'I guess you can spot for me in my absence.'

'So gracious.' She rolls her eyes, turns to bellow. 'Hey, Mark! He's here!'

Westie swivels and his weathered face lights as he walks over. 'Ah, great, you made it. You walked over from the hospital, did ya? On crutches?'

'Got a ride.' My face warms as I think of Amie.

'Well, great, good on ya. Dell, can you handle this lot while I nick home and get Harris settled in?'

Della nods, and Westie turns us both out of the hall. We make our way back to his house, where he lets me through to the living room.

'It's not fancy.' Mark blushes as he waves a hand around the little space. There's enough room for a couch, a big flat-screen on a side table, an ironing board set up at the back of the room, laundry piled on top of that. 'Not much of anything, really. Just a place to watch the footy on a Friday night – you watch the footy, right? But it's somewhere to crash, and you're welcome to it.'

I take the packet from the hospital out of my jacket pocket, settle myself on the couch. Westie's put a pillow and a pile of blankets on one end. It's true, it's not fancy. But it's not Dad's.

Which reminds me of the last loose end I have to tidy up before I can relax.

Once Westie returns to the training session in the hall, I use his landline to make a call. Even here, in a comparatively safe space, my hand twitches holding the receiver. I fucking wish I'd grow out of this, but with every *bbrrrpp*-ing ring my breath gets tighter. I close my eyes, open them again. It's easier, somehow, to stay cool when I can see the friendly mess around me.

The line connects. 'Yep.'

My throat swells shut for a second. I force the words out. 'It's me. Harris.'

There's a pause.

'Yeah?' Dad's tone is derisive. He sounds half-ripped already. 'Well, nice of ya to call. I run around like a bloody chook with its head cut off all week, tryin' to see ya, they fucking wouldn't let me in, would they? Next I hear that bloody fat bitch at the hospital has set you up someplace –'

'I'm staying at a mate's.' I keep my words measured, not caring that it sounds rehearsed. 'I'm sorry I can't come home. I know I said –'

'*You bloody said you'd be here!*'

'I know that's what I said, but I got crook,' I point out. Measured, calm. 'I can't look after you if I'm crook, Dad.'

'Where are you? Are you in Ouyen? I'll come in with the ute –'

I deflect that one. 'The hospital set me up with a place to stay, just for a month. The head nurse said she told you about it. I gotta be at the hospital every week or they'll send me up to Mildura for an amputation assessment.' I lean heavily on the next sentence. 'I don't wanna get my leg amputated, Dad.'

'Well, shit...' He can hardly argue with that.

I don't wait for him to wind up again. 'I'll be back in a month. And I'll be looking for work so I'll send you a bit of money when I can, okay?'

That seems to mollify him. 'Shit... Okay, then.'

'I'll call again soon, Dad. Don't stress.'

'Easy for you to say,' he whines. 'You're not the one –'

'I gotta go now, Dad,' I say. 'Dad, I gotta go. Bye.'

I disconnect. Then I sit on the couch for half an hour and wait for the shakes to pass.

'Take your jeans down.'

It's Wednesday, and a command like this is a bit early for a Wednesday. I kept my promise, made it to the hospital for my first appointment. When I arrived on time Amie smiled as if she'd known all along I could do it. But she quickly ushered me into a treatment room, put on her serious clinical face, and I was reminded this isn't a social visit.

I start to unbutton, hesitate. 'I've only got jocks underneath.'

She doesn't bat an eyelid. 'At least you *wore* jocks.'

'What, some blokes don't?' I find that a bit horrifying. 'So you're coming in to work every day, not knowing if some guy will be flashing his tackle at you?'

Amie raises her eyes to heaven. 'You don't wanna know. C'mon, then. If you need a hand –'

'No, no, I'm good. It's just...'

'Look, it's up to you. You can wear a gown if you prefer –'

'No gown.' Those things are the pits. It's like being dressed in a Chux.

'Here, then. Put this over you.'

She hands me a drape, which I wrap around my hips with one hand, while awkwardly dropping my jeans with the other. I manoeuvre back onto the examination table. Amie eases off the tape and the wound dressing, prods at the tender skin of my surgery site.

'It's a bit mucky,' she pronounces finally.

'Well, it's – *ow* – the stitches pull a bit, if I'm moving around –'

'You're not supposed to be moving around.' We're so close to each other we're practically eyeball to eyeball, and she's really dosing me with it now. 'You're supposed to be doing your physio exercises, but otherwise staying off it.'

'Seriously? I have to get up *sometimes*. I mean, I can't sit on Westie's couch all day, then sleep on it all night, I feel like –'

'Like someone recuperating from a gunshot wound and follow up surgery? Shocking.' She presses down on a spot along my thigh. 'Does that ache?'

'Ye-ow, yes, it does –'

'It still feels warm. Are you taking your meds?'

'Yes, I am, and –'

'Hold still.'

She starts on a round of obs, which I'm familiar with from before I was discharged: temperature, blood pressure, respiration rate, pulse. The BP cuff makes that familiar scream as it's Velcroed in place. Amie's hair is in a ponytail today and the shimmering fall of it spills down her back.

She keeps her focus on her work. 'Your pulse is a bit high.'

'Mm.' I concentrate on keeping still. I try not to notice that there seems to be a little force field surrounding each of us, and how, as she moves around me, my orbit seems to warm up in contact with hers.

She runs me through the range-of-movement positions the physio prescribed for me. 'It's okay. Your leg and the wound site don't seem to be tightening up too much. But you need to take better care of it.'

'I'm taking care of it –'

She puts a warm hand on my chest, gives me the take-no-prisoners stare. 'Harris, will you just trust that I know what I'm doing? How about we make that a permanent arrangement – you look after this to the best of your ability, and I'll look after it when you come in, and hopefully between the two of us we can get you better, okay? Then I don't have to call an RN to give you a full work-up if you come to your appointments with a nasty infected surgical wound.'

'Fine,' I say, abandoning resistance. 'I'll take better care of it.'

'Great. Now I just need to clean it and apply some more antiseptic, then re-dress it.'

'Okay.'

The cleaning and disinfecting are unpleasant, but it's harder to concentrate when she starts re-dressing my leg. While her fingers move on my thigh, I have to look away. I'm thinking about anything but the brush of her fingertips: cold showers, icebergs, the insides of fridges. God, it's been too long since I dipped my wick if I'm this sensitive.

'I've got another antibiotics script for you from Barb,' Amie says. 'Call the hospital if it starts to get painful again so they can book you in for an earlier appointment.'

'Huh? Uh, yeah, sure. I don't want to get another infection, that was bloody horrible.'

'You've got access to a phone? Maybe borrow Mark's, or –'

'Got one.' I fish my newest accessory – a phone with a hot pink case – out of the pocket of my jacket, waggle it in front of her.

'You got a phone?' She squints at the case. 'Nice. Bit glam for you, but –'

'Got it off Della Metcalfe. Bumped into her at Westie's self-defence class. She said I could have it. Her old one, she said.'

'Della gave you a phone,' Amie says, and her expression repeats it, with emphasis.

I shrug. 'Me and Dell, we've got a bit of history. She said she wanted to help me out. She's cool.'

Amie shakes her head at me, snorts. 'You're a bloody enigma, Harris, I swear to god. You've shagged half the girls in the district and still managed to stay friends with everyone.'

I make my best indignant face. 'Hey. For one, I have a charming personality. And for two, I haven't shagged half the girls in the district. That's an exaggeration.'

'Really.' Her fingers busy themselves fixing the final pieces of paper tape.

'Yes, really. You also might wanna remember there aren't actually that many girls *in* the district, so even if I *had* shagged half of them, it wouldn't end up being a very large number of girls –'

I stop when Amie starts laughing.

'Okay, you're good,' she says finally, still pressing her lips together to stop a grin escaping as she tidies up the wound dressing rubbish. 'I guess I'll see you again in a week?'

'Yep.' I get to visit Amie again next Wednesday. I'm oddly elated. Apart from the wound-cleaning business, these appointments could turn out to be more of a highlight than I'd thought.

'Oh, wait – you're going to Rathmine Street now, aren't you? To see Nick's car?' She looks a bit embarrassed to know that, but hey, he's her mate. I'm sure he's whinged in her ear about it. 'Could you say I'll meet him at the pub when I get off work? You're welcome to come too, if you'd like.'

'Cheers, yep, I'll tell him.' It's a nice offer, but somehow I just can't imagine having a friendly beer with Nick Partridge. The guy seems to think I'm a lower form of life than microbes.

I pull up my jeans and Amie hands me my crutches. 'It's good to see you back on your feet, Harris.' Her cheeks look a bit pink. 'I'm glad you're doing okay at Mark's.'

'It's good.' I still can't shape the right words, the ones I want to say. 'It's great.'

We stand there for a second, just looking at each other. I want it back, the easy rapport we had before I was discharged. No – I want that feeling I got when she sat with me that night, when we spilled our secrets out into the air and into each other. But that moment is gone.

We say our goodbyes and I crutch out of the hospital, make my shambling way along Britt Street. Turn at the corner of Rathmine, thinking the whole way. I'd like to get to know Amie better, but she's a police sergeant's daughter, and I'm a… Fuck, I dunno what I am. Things have whirled and changed so much I don't know where I stand anymore.

Okay, I'm homeless, jobless. Not without prospects: I've got Snowie's phone number on the coaster in my wallet. But is that the kind of job I want? Really? If I take that step, if I become a dealer, I'll never be able to look Amie in the eye again.

I try to screw my head on straight – I shouldn't limit my options. I can't eat good intentions. The question isn't do I want the job. The question is, how desperate am I?

And I dunno why I'm factoring Amie into this anyway. I only see her once a week now and maybe that's just how it's gonna be. Maybe that's for the best – especially for her.

By the time I get to Nick Partridge's place, I'm sweating. Sun scours the roof of the little brick veneer house behind him, glints off the metal of the car Nick's leaning against. This weather feels more like early summer than the end of the cold season.

Nick pushes off the car bonnet when I come closer. He looks quietly disbelieving. 'You made it.'

'I did.'

I've made a few phone calls since I saw him last, too. Mike seemed overjoyed at the idea of lending me money. I hated doing it, so I just stuck to the basics: everything's fine, but I need a car, could he front me a deposit. I didn't say anything about Dad or the debts.

Nick stands aside so I can walk – sorry, hobble – around the vehicle. When I'm done looking, and he's done being patient about me looking, I turn to him. 'It's a WRX.'

'Yes, it is,' Nick says.

'But not a cool eighties model.'

'Alas, no.'

The car is – I remember this word from when Amie used it – an enigma. Its advantages and disadvantages seem to cancel each other out. First of all, it's a shit-brown colour, which is nice and nondescript. Good for slipping under the radar. On the down side: it's a shit-brown colour. It has black racing stripes, which is cool, because racing stripes. Except on this daggy Subaru model, racing stripes just seem to make the car look embarrassed, like a shy girl in a red vinyl miniskirt.

'Does it run?' I ask.

'It…runs,' Nick says.

'You're filling me with confidence.'

'No, it goes okay. But Amie's right, it needs a tune. I mean, it pretty much constantly needs a tune. That's what I'm having trouble with.'

'Not mechanically minded?' I get him to pop the hood, have a look at the beast's innards. Can't see anything rusted out.

'I can manage the basics.' Nick shrugs. 'I got this car off my brother, but Grant's more of a revhead than me. I need something a bit less high-maintenance. So what do you reckon?'

'Start her up and we'll see.'

He slides into the driver's seat and we both listen as the engine chugs, catches, chugs again. Our eyes meet just as the car revs to life. Nick's expression is relieved. As I close the bonnet, he switches off the engine, gets out.

'How much you want for it?' I ask.

'How much can you offer?' He looks at me then, and I know he knows. I've been in and out of hospital, word gets around. People have figured out I'm not working, which means I'm broke.

I bite down hard on my pride. Think about what I've got. Mike offered me two grand – I caught my breath, kept my voice steady and said if he could put eight hundred in my account, that'd be plenty. Now I'm holding the money in the hand tucked in my pocket. But I'm gonna be living off it for a while. I want a car, badly, but I've still gotta eat.

Whatever I offer won't be enough, but Nick Partridge might be willing to negotiate. Amie says he's an okay guy, in spite of his bullshit attitude.

'How about nine? I can give you five hundred now,' I say. 'I got a bit more, but I kinda need it.'

'I was gonna ask for twelve.' He chews his lip, like he's considering his chances of getting a better offer. The car is kind of crap.

'I can give you five now,' I repeat, 'and another hundred every week as it comes in. I dunno when that'll be, but –'

'I can't go lower than nine,' he says.

I stick to my guns. 'That's your call. Don't do me any favours. This isn't mate's rates. We're not mates. Like I said, I'll pay you another hundred every week when I get work. And I've gotta get work.'

He hesitates, looking at me. I get the feeling he's trying to suss me out, can't quite place me in a category.

Then he holds out his hand. 'Five now, then a hundred a week when you're cashed up. Sounds all right.'

'Cool.' I shake his hand. We look at each other warily. I wonder if Amie's influence had anything to do with Nick agreeing to the low price.

I take stock of my new purchase. The car is like a pitbull terrier: kind of ugly, but functional. I'll do some investigating under the hood later. Right now I pass over the cash, try not to look pained when Nick takes the money out of my hand. Part of me wants to snatch it back. *I could pay off some of the debt with that. I could get Dad off my back.* I take a breath, control it.

'Shit,' Nick says, eyebrows lifting as he counts the notes. 'I've finally sold the car. Bloody hell.'

'At least Amie can stop ragging you about it now.' I receive the keys, run my hand over the racing stripes on the bonnet. In spite of my angst, a happy little bubble forms inside me and floats up into my rib cage: I've got a car. I'm free. And I remember Amie's message. 'Oh, yeah – she asked me to say you should meet her at the pub after she finishes work.'

'Uh, right. Thanks.' There's a pause. 'You like her, huh?'

'Yeah.' I re-focus and realise what he's just said, how I've just replied. 'I mean, yeah. Amie's good value.' I wince. We've just bartered over a car, and this is not a car we're talking about now. 'I mean, she's...she's great.'

Once again my brain and my mouth aren't working in unison. I know what I want to say but it seems too huge, too important to just throw around in casual conversation.

'I was at the hospital the day you were discharged, remember?' Nick's voice is so dry it makes me look back. 'You didn't have to check her out so obviously, y'know.'

I shove a hand through my hair. *Jesus*. Am I like a bloody neon sign?

'Amie's a nice girl,' Nick says. 'She's a nice person.'

'I *know*,' I say helplessly. I swallow, try again. 'I know. She's done a lot for me and I'm pretty bloody grateful.'

Nick holds my gaze. 'You just keep on being grateful, okay?'

My eyebrows hike north. 'You're giving me the talk? Seriously?'

'Look,' he says, 'I guess I can't say anything you don't already know. And Amie's her own person, she can make her own choices. Just...don't fuck up. She's not like all the other chicks you've screwed. Have a little respect.'

My face gets hot. 'I think there's a lot of bullshit going around about "all the other chicks I've screwed" –'

'I honestly don't give a rat's.' Nick stands there, staring me down. 'That's your business. But Amie's more than just my ex – she's my friend. She's had a crap run these past few years and I don't want to see her get hurt.'

I rein back hard on my instinct to front this guy. For one, he's taller, heavier, and in way better shape, and I'm stumbling around on crutches. And for two, he's talking about Amie like he gives a shit. Like he actually cares about her. Anybody who cares about Amie enough to go in to bat for her with a guy like me is already one up in my estimation.

I put some thought into what to say next. 'I'm not trying to screw Amie over, okay? Honestly, she's way out of my league. I'm just grateful for what she's done. I'm happy to be her friend. And I'm trying to keep it just friendly, whether you believe that or not.'

'Huh,' Nick says. He doesn't look convinced.

'Really.' I look away. I don't want to look at him when I say this next part. 'I don't think Amie needs the kind of shit I've got in my life right now. I wouldn't put it on her. I appreciate her enough as a friend to know that much.'

I lean back on my crutches and let him see my face. Chances are he still thinks I'm feeding him a line of bullshit, but maybe he'll realise I'm being sincere.

'Right.' Whatever Nick saw seems to have mollified him. He squints, folds the money I've given him into the back pocket of his jeans. 'Well, I guess there's nothing more to say.'

'Give Amie my best when you see her at the pub,' I say firmly.

He nods, almost formal. 'Good luck with the car. And I hope you find work soon. For both our sakes.'

'I will.' I consider the coaster with the phone number, find it harder to push the thought away now. 'I will.'

10

amie

Harris seems pleased with his new cane. Well, I don't know if 'pleased' is the right word; more like 'relieved to not be on crutches'. But that's something positive. God knows, with Dad chasing Gavin Donovan all over the district, Nani calling to ask me if I think Apu would like a new suit to wear to the wedding, Robbie harassing me about the residency and Nick's updates about his planned departure, the last week has had a serious lack of positive.

I finish re-dressing Harris's leg, then pull my lanyard over my head. Today's shift was draining: two patients on the ward have gastro. I just want to go home, shower and change my clothes before flopping on my bed. But I still have to call Nani tonight, and make dinner. Dad has said won't be back until late.

'Tired, eh?' Harris eases himself off the examination table, tugging the drawstring of his trackies tight again.

I shrug. 'Joys of nursing. And I smell like crap.'

'Nah, you don't,' Harris says.

'Yeah, I do.' I grimace. 'I mean, I literally do – bedpan duty. Don't worry, I've scrubbed all the way up to my elbows.'

'Joys of nursing.' Harris makes an amused face. 'You smell all right.' He colours, glances away. 'So you're heading home now?'

'Yeah. You're my last port of call.' I smile as he tries out the cane, takes a few tentative steps. Then I remember. 'Oh shit, I was gonna give you the keys.'

'The what?'

I tear off my glove, flapping a hand. 'Nick gave me the spare keys for the Subaru. He forgot to pass them on the day you bought it. I wrote it down, to bring them, but I've bloody left them behind.'

'It's okay. I'll just drop you home and I can get them. Or did you drive in?'

'Yeah, I've got my car.'

'I'll follow then.' He seems happy to be able to say that. 'I mean, if you're okay with me coming to your house...'

'Sure, it's fine,' I say, flapping again. 'Just let me sign off?'

On the drive back, I glance in the rear-view and see Harris following behind me. It's a bit weird seeing him at the wheel of Nick's car. But I don't feel bad about putting the hard word on Nick to sell low: Harris needed a ride and I know he's broke.

Harris has named the car the Pitbull, and it sounds as if he's spent the last week tuning the engine to a humming growl. The car seems to suit him. I don't know if it's had any other material effect, except to make Harris feel better, which I guess helps. But whenever I ask him about work, or his father, or where he's going from here, he deflects. Things are obviously still far from okay.

He's bloody gutsy, though, I'll give him that.

When we arrive at my place I show him into the house. 'I won't be a sec. The keys are in my room.' And I can go and get changed out of my horrible work clothes, into something more normal. 'You okay to loiter here?'

Harris leans his cane against a chair. 'I can loiter.'

'Great. One minute.'

One minute is all I need to dash down to my room, strip off my yucky nursing gear and pull on some cut-offs under a yellow sundress and a purple cardigan. No shower, but clean clothes will have to do. I'm balanced on the edge of my bed, slinging my boots on, when I hear Harris's voice in the hallway.

'Um, Amie?'

'Yeah?' I poke my head out, yanking the elastic band out of my plait.

'Your dad's not home, is he?'

'No, I don't think so.' I don't remember seeing Dad's stuff on the table. 'Sometimes he comes home at lunch to tinker on his cars, but it depends on what sort of day he's having.'

'Oh. Okay.' Harris looks nervous, listing in the hallway.

I grin to reassure him. 'He won't bite your head off or anything.'

'Sure.' His right hand shoves deeper into his trackie pocket. 'I just thought, y'know, he might not be cool with me being in the house –'

'Harris, it's fine. I invited you in.' I've got my hair mostly unravelled now. 'Oh – hang on. The keys.'

I dart back for them. While I'm still rummaging amidst the crap on my desk, Harris leans around into the doorway.

'Hey,' I smile over at him. 'They're here somewhere...'

'Mm.' His eyes travel round the small space. 'Your room, huh?'

'Yeah.' I see it through his eyes for a moment. 'Uh, I guess it's kind of bohemian in here.'

As in, it's messy: there are clothes on the floor and over the backs of chairs. A gold-beaded, toffee-apple-red dubatta curtains the big window beside my bed, keeping the room rose-tinted. Satin cushions plop on my bed and multi-coloured saris are draped over the walls, adding to the theme, which I've elaborated on over the years with candles in bottles, a hat-rack near the door, a fringed shade over the ceiling bulb.

I like my room: it's relaxing to be in, and has a sort of 'lady's boudoir' feeling which has discouraged Dad from invading. I've staked out my claim to one room in the house that isn't purely functional, that doesn't contain spare car parts or utilitarian appliances. Although, admittedly, my own utilitarian appliances – my camera, the charge cords that go with it, the lenses and chips and other paraphernalia – occupy a dedicated shelf in my cupboard.

I gesture at the mess. 'I think this room has been mine my whole life. We've always lived here. I was born in Ouyen hospital so I've never really strayed.'

'Huh.' I can't quite read Harris's expression: it's a mix of quiet surprise, curiosity and some other emotion. It's like he's looking at the landscape of another planet. When he speaks, his words are halting, almost shy. 'I was born in Adelaide. We moved here when I was a little tacker.'

'Still in the same house, then?'

'Yeah. But, y'know...it's Dad's house.'

I know straightaway what he means. His dad's house. Not his. Not him and his father peacefully co-habiting, like Dad and I do.

Harris licks his lips. 'Did a bit of couch-surfing before I went to Melbourne, when things got a bit...difficult.'

'Was that when you worked at the quarry with Mark?'

'Yeah. Dad wasn't always on board with me working with Westie.' He doesn't elaborate. 'Anyway, yeah, I squatted at Meary's or at the old Watts place when I needed a roof.'

...and now he's living on the couch at Mark's house. Suddenly I know what the expression on his face is saying. It's saying he's never had a home. Not a home he can feel comfortable in, the way I do in mine.

The understanding strikes me like a blow. Why does so much

shitty stuff happen to nice people?

I turn back so I can hide my face. My room really *must* seem like an alien planet to him. It must seem like Mars. 'Sorry — one sec.'

I fumble around for the keys, fish them out of the detritus. There's a moment's silence, then: 'Wow.'

Harris has listed over to the wall with my collage of pictures. I haven't pinned them up in any order. I like seeing them scattered on the wall, angled here or tacked up randomly there.

'What's that?' he asks, pointing.

I walk over to stand beside him. 'Um, that's Antelope Canyon. It's part of the Colorado Plateau in the U.S.' I scan the other pictures, nodding at the ones I look at all the time. 'And that's Machu Picchu in Peru. And that's the Himalayas.'

'In Nepal?'

'Yeah.' I smile at the picture. 'I like that one a lot.' I wave a hand at my pile of magazines under the tableau. 'I cut them out and stick them up. Mostly from old *National Geographics* – I gave you some of my stash when you were in the hospital.'

His eyes take in the stack at our feet. 'Are those travel brochures?'

'Huh?'

'You got some brochures tossed in there with the *National Geographics*...and is that a travel guide? Did you go overseas or something?'

'Oh, those.' I scuff the pile of old dreams with my boot. My inner voice wheedles: *If you were accepted for the residency...* I tell my inner voice to shut up. 'Nah, I was gonna go after school. But I put it off when I got the CNA job. Dad and the family kind of need me.'

'Right.' His eyes pause on my face, turn back to the wall. 'What about these pictures?'

He's pointing at some of my prints now. I feel my cheeks warm. 'Mm. The photos.'

'Did you take these?' Harris peers at them, leaning on his cane.

'Um, yeah. I kind of go off with the camera sometimes, just walking around and finding stuff. That's the gate near the Malcolm's place. And that's up near Pink Lakes.'

Harris leans in. 'Mistletoe – that's the stuff that infests the mallee trees, yeah?'

'Yeah, the framing in that one turned out really nice.'

He touches a finger to the edge of another print. 'Isn't that in Murrayville?'

'Some of them worked out good. Some of them are a bit boring.'

'No way. These are cool.' Harris seems fascinated.

I can't help but grin. 'You think?'

'Sure.' He nods at the ones higher up the wall. 'Those big landscapes are the best. They look really wild.'

'Oh –' I blink at the washes of light and colour in the high prints. 'They're really old ones. I haven't done open landscapes for ages.'

'So these are the latest?' He pushes up his hoodie sleeves and examines the pictures right in front of us. 'That's tight. You've got all the tiny details... That one's the old machinery at Kow Plains, isn't it?'

'Yep.'

'It seems different.' His eyes sweep around the whole display. 'Everything looks different.'

'Things look different in close-up.'

When I turn to say that I realise how close up we actually are. Harris's shoulder is right beside mine. I can feel his body heat. Me and Harris have been this close in the treatment room – I've seen him with his jeans off, for god's sake – but now I notice things about him as if I'm seeing them for the first time.

The tops of his cheeks are smooth, even though his jaw is golden with stubble. The golden is all over him: it's in his tan, his hair, the fine pelt on his forearms. He has a scent – that warm male scent I noticed the first time he was admitted, half perspiration and half something else... The scent of his skin, I guess. And his eyelashes are long, incredibly long. Wasted on a boy, Nani would say. They look soft.

My hands suddenly go sweaty. I rub them on my dress. Then I feel the metal under my palm and remember what I was doing.

'Right, um, keys.' I hold them up, dangle them in Harris's direction.

'Ah, cheers.' He reaches to take them and the moment is broken.

I gesture back up the hallway to the kitchen. 'So, you wanna, um, have a cuppa or something? Maybe a cold drink?'

'Yeah. Sure. A cold drink would be good.' His eyes dart around and I wonder if he's thought about my dad before replying.

The kitchen seems spartan after my room. Dad and I live a simple life. Four tumblers on the shelf, a few plates, half a dozen mugs, a smattering of cutlery – just the bare minimum. A workshop lamp hangs down above the kitchen table, which is hardly big enough for me and Dad to eat together. From the table you only need to walk about one step further in each direction to reach the benchtop, exit to the living room, or open the back door for the steps to the workshop.

I grab tumblers, and juice and ice from the fridge.

'It's kind of a small house.' I wave an unoccupied hand around at the space. Harris seems to take up a lot of it.

'Nah, it's nice. Cosy.' Harris is looking out through the back louvers. 'So your dad's a bit of a part-time mechanic, is he?'

He must've seen the workshop. 'Oh, yeah. He's pretty good at it, actually. Keeps our two-car fleet going. He tunes all the squad cars, too.' I settle the drinks on the kitchen table. 'Tinkering, he calls it.'

'Right.' He takes another look. 'That was my dad, too, originally. Diesel mechanic.'

I nod, sitting down. 'So it's just you and him? Over in Five Mile?'

'Yeah.' He clears his throat. 'Mum took off years ago. Went back to Adelaide, I think.'

'Right.' I push his drink towards his side of the table. 'Here you go.'

'Ta.' Still standing, he grabs the glass and drains off the top.

'No worries.' I watch him fidget for a second. 'You can sit down, you know.'

'Oh, right.' He fumbles his glass and his cane, puts down the glass, finally manages to seat himself.

'Harris, if Dad comes back, he's not gonna arrest you or anything.' I smile. 'We're just having a cold drink in the kitchen.'

'Sure.' He blushes, makes a snorting grin at himself. 'Yeah, sorry. I'm just more used to dealing with your dad when he's in uniform on the other side of the desk.'

'Don't worry about it.'

'Right. Anyway...' He searches for another topic of conversation. 'Your family's always lived here, you said?'

I nod. 'I grew up here. But it's just been Dad and me since Mum died.'

'Oh.' He looks directly at me, blinks. 'Shit, that was rude. I'm sorry –'

'It's okay. It was four years ago. Aneurysm.' I say it casually, like I don't think about Mum every day. 'She moved here from Mildura – I mean, her family is still up that way. I still see a lot of my grandma, and my aunt's family. Dad's family are sort of scattered, mostly in Queensland, so…'

'That's good,' he says. 'I mean, it's good you've got some rellies around.'

'My dotty nanna,' I say, grinning. 'Yeah, she keeps in touch a lot. They're her saris, hanging up in my room. Old ones, from when she was my age.'

'So your mum was from…'

'India, yeah. From the Punjab, originally – that's in the north. She and her sister came as students, and they brought my nanna over. How about you, you don't have any grandparents here?'

'Nah.' He rubs at a dribble of condensation on his glass. 'No idea about that. Could be in Adelaide, could be gone. Never really knew 'em.'

'Oh.'

He shrugs. 'It's okay. Don't miss what you never had, right?'

'Right. I guess.'

'Anyway,' he says again, eyes skittering towards my face, 'I've been meaning to say thanks. For helping me out with staying at Westie's. For the car –'

'Well, that was Nick,' I point out. 'He's been wanting to offload that car for a while.'

'Yeah, but… You looked out for me. In the hospital.' He takes another quick sip of juice. 'I just wanted to say thanks.'

I shrug and smile. 'That's okay, but come on. I mean, that's what I do. That's my job.'

'Not finding people places to live. That's not part of your job.'

'I did it cos I wanted to,' I confess. 'You wanted to get out of your dad's place, right?'

He lifts one shoulder. 'Yeah, I kinda had to.'

'Now you've got a good place. Barb's happy cos you're keeping your appointments, Westie's happy cos you're helping him out –'

'I dunno how I'm helping him out. I'm just taking up space on his couch, I'm not even paying rent...' Harris's eyes zero in on my face – goddamnit, I *have* to stop blushing, I'm giving everything away – which is when his expression changes. 'Shit. Amie, did you pay my rent money? What the hell?'

'It's not rent.' I fight against the blood in my cheeks, make my voice firm. 'It's just a few bucks for groceries, Harris. Would you have knocked Mark back if I told you?'

He scrubs his face with one hand. 'I fucking can't believe you did that.'

'Hey, forget it. It's no big deal, and I reckon Mark enjoys the company. Like I said before, everyone's happy.'

'It's all gravy.' He makes a humourless laugh, shakes his head at the tabletop. 'Yeah, that makes it sound easy, doesn't it? Some kind of easy simple thing.'

I'm not sure I like the sound of that laugh. It seems too lost, too helpless. 'Harris, what is it?'

He's still looking down. 'I been meaning to say this for weeks. But I could never put it together right.' He shoves his blond hair out of his eyes and finally meets my gaze. His face is very earnest. 'All this stuff... What you've done for me... I dunno if you understand what it means.'

His eyes are a deep verdant green, with little brown flecks in them. I suddenly get this powerful feeling, the same feeling I got that time in his hospital room: like the air between us, everywhere around us, is humming.

I put my forearms on the table to steady myself. 'What does it mean, Harris?'

He waits a long beat before replying. 'Amie, I –'

'Amie!' There's a shuffle from the hallway. 'Amie, d'you reckon you could get Nick to shift his car? I wanna –'

The sound of my dad's voice gets Harris moving before I've even registered it. By the time Dad steps into the kitchen and cuts himself off mid-sentence, Harris is out of his chair and standing beside it. His blank neutral face is firmly back on. Dad takes one look at Harris and changes expression in an instant.

'Ah. Right.' He glances between me and Harris, back to me. 'Sorry, I thought you were talking to Nick. I saw the car and I just forgot...'

'Hey, Sarge.' Harris stands, fidgeting with his cane.

'Hey, Harris,' Dad says.

'Dad, I'm sure Harris will be okay about moving the car.' I speak clear and slow, still adjusting to the rapid shift in emotional temperature, trying to lower Harris's tension. I gesture at the glasses on the table. 'Is it urgent, or is it okay for him to finish his drink?'

Dad takes in the table setting. 'Ah, sorry. No, sure, it can wait.' He seems to think for a second. 'Actually, I might get a drink m'self.'

'We're out of juice,' I warn.

'Milk, then. A glass of milk'll do.' Dad lumbers towards the benchtop. I have to move my chair around to the side so he can get to the fridge and bench cupboards. The kitchen suddenly feels a bit...cramped.

I sigh. 'Harris, can you sit down again? He's not gonna throw you out.'

'Ah...' Harris says.

'Yes, for god's sake, sit, sit,' Dad says, ushering with his hand.

Harris sits.

I swivel to look at Dad. 'What happened? I didn't think you were gonna be back home until later tonight?'

'Just had to drop off the other squaddie for a tune, I'm taking Jared's car back,' Dad says over his shoulder. 'I probably won't make it home for dinner, love.' He glances at Harris, perched on the other kitchen chair, and his tone shifts from casual familiarity to 'we have a visitor'. 'Right. So. Just a social call, is it?'

'It was.' I restrain myself from eye-rolling. 'Harris is picking up the spare keys for the Subie.'

'Um, yep,' Harris says.

'You're looking better than last time I saw you.' Dad pulls a tumbler from the cupboard. 'Although you looked pretty dire then, of course.'

Harris huffs a soft laugh. 'Yeah, well, I didn't feel that great, either.'

'Fair enough.' Dad swipes out his glass with a tea towel. 'Amie says you had another close shave recently – with your mate, Snowie Geraldson.'

'*Dad*.' I purse my lips. 'You're really gonna get into this *now*?'

'Snowie's not my bestie, but I know him,' Harris says. The tone of his voice makes me look over. He has a quiet set expression on his face. 'It was Marcus Anderson I had a run-in with. Snowie wasn't throwing no punches, he was just there at the pub.'

'But you don't want us to book Anderson?' Dad says.

'Nothing in it,' Harris says. 'Just a bit too much to drink. Nothing I'd be bothered making a big deal out of.'

Dad doesn't reply, but he glances at me. I feel like saying, *See, I told you*. But for a second I get a momentary flash of how frustrating it must be: nobody will tell him the truth, even though he's trying to help.

Dad nods sombrely, heads for the fridge.

Harris sits there for a long moment before suddenly speaking. 'Snowie offered me a job.'

My head whips in Harris's direction. *What?*

Dad has stopped dead in his tracks. Then he reaches slowly for the fridge door. Pulls it open. Takes out the milk carton. Closes the fridge.

I blink between Harris and Dad. It feels strangely like I'm

holding my breath.

Dad holds the carton in his hand, looking at Harris. 'Why'd you tell me that, son?'

'Just did.' Harris shrugs, as though it's unimportant. But his eyes are focused on my father. 'Snowie offered – I didn't accept. Said I'd think about it.'

Dad meets his stare. 'D'you know what there is to think about?'

Harris's pause is as small as his nod. 'Yeah. Yeah, I reckon I know.'

'And what do you know?' Dad asks.

Harris reaches for the glass in front of him. Doesn't raise it yet, just looks at it. Then he seems to come to some sort of decision.

He looks up at Dad again. 'Snowie's been moving gear around the stretch between Ouyen and Five Mile for a while. Nothing large – sticks of weed, pills. Friday night deals. But he's hooked up in Mildura now, he said. I get the impression he's moved business north. Started bigging up. And the product has changed. Ice, not weed.'

Air escapes my lungs, soft and shaky. Does Harris know what he's doing, what he's saying? Looking at his face, I'm pretty sure he does.

Dad makes a heavy sigh, as though Harris has just gone through a kind of test and Dad's relieved he passed. He puts the milk on the kitchen bench and pulls out the chair opposite Harris, sinks into it. 'Ice is screwing up a lot of people in this area, you know. A lot of families.'

'I know it,' Harris says.

He shares a glance with me and I have a feeling we're both thinking about the same thing: Craig Davies. But I'm still shocked. Dad is a police officer. Harris isn't stupid, he has to understand what sharing this information with my dad will mean.

Has Harris tried ice? Does he know about Gavin Donovan? My

head suddenly crowds with other questions, but this isn't the time to ask any of them. Some kind of bass chord has been struck between my father and Harris: a deep thread of communication I'm loathe to break.

'So Snowie's looking for a small-time dealer to fill his shoes down here,' Dad says.

'More like a few local mates to act as foot-soldiers in Mildura. That was the gist, I think.' Harris sips his drink, studies the tabletop gravely. 'Snowie's never been a real player. But he's trying to keep his dad propped up with the pub, and I reckon he might be getting in over his head this time.'

'His mate Anderson is going with him to Mildura?'

'Ando's not local, so he doesn't care where he goes. Ando's the muscle – and Snowie's where the money is. He'll follow Snowie, yeah.'

'All good to know,' Dad says. He waits a beat. 'Still begs the question of why you're telling me.'

Harris considers his glass. 'Well, Snowie's a mate. I don't want him to get sucked too deep into this shit. And you and Amie have always been straight with me, so I figured I'd return the favour.' His eyes dart towards me as he pauses. His teeth snag at his bottom lip again and again. 'But the main reason is because...I'm kind of fucked. I'm almost completely broke, but I can't live at home.'

He doesn't say why, and we certainly don't need him to explain.

'Someone fronted me the deposit for the car,' he goes on, 'which is a good escape plan, but I still owe money. And Dad... Dad owes money. Big money. I'm laid up with my leg, so no job prospects on the horizon for a couple of months. If I register for welfare I'll be waiting three months for my first cheque to arrive. But I can't live on Westie's couch forever. There's other stuff involved as well, personal stuff...'

Dad just looks at him. I look at him. I'd like to reach out and grab his hand, which is squeezing hard on his damp glass, but I don't think Harris wants me to do that. After a second, he continues.

'I don't have a lot of options.' Harris glances up, snorts. 'I mean, I never considered a career as a drug dealer, y'know? The whole idea seems kind of revolting. But I need the money. Like, really. And it would make sense for me to take this job.'

He stops then, like he can't keep going. His other hand comes up from his knee to rub across his mouth. His eyes look hollow. I have to press my lips together to stop myself from saying something, anything, to make him feel better. For a moment it's as if time is frozen, just the three of us grouped around this tiny table, like a cinematic still. Insects buzz in the afternoon light outside the kitchen door to the workshop.

Dad doesn't seem to know what to say either. He's frowning hard, his mouth a puckered line. Then he sighs through his nose.

'It would make sense. You're right.' He frowns even harder. 'More importantly, it would make sense to Snowie.'

'What?' Harris says it half a second earlier than me.

'It would make sense to Snowie for you to take up his offer.' Dad nods, almost to himself. 'And you should. You should say yes.'

Harris's eyebrows almost meet in the middle. 'Sarge, I'm telling you cos I don't wanna be a –'

'You should say yes, and then you should report to me,' Dad says.

That's when I do jump in. '*Dad.*'

'I'm authorised,' Dad says to me, 'and Harris isn't a minor.'

I hate the sound of this already. 'Dad, I know you want to make a difference before you retire –'

'This isn't about that.' Dad scowls

'—and I know you want to cut off the drug supply to the area. But he's a *civilian*.'

'A civilian is what I need.' Dad turns fully to meet my eyes. 'He's street smart, he's the right age, and most importantly, Snowie's already asked for him.'

Harris is glancing back and forth between us. 'Are you talking about me being...' His eyes settle on Dad. 'Are you recruiting me for information?'

Dad turns back, nods again. 'Yeah. Yeah, I think I am.' He sucks his teeth. 'I don't know what to offer you except a token payment when it's all done and dusted. It'd be like a police reward for voluntary information.'

'Okay – time out.' This whole out-of-the-blue concept is making my stomach roil. I may not get how the local drug system works, but I've heard enough war stories from Dad to know the risks. 'Can we just pause for a sanity check? Dad, you've told me plenty about the scene in Mildura. It's not *safe*.'

But Dad is focused on Harris. 'If there's a bust I can't guarantee you won't lose the cash Snowie'll pay you, because it's proceeds from an illegal business. But I'll see to it that you're recompensed somehow.'

'Are you for real?' Harris seems to be having a hard time getting his head around the idea.

I'm having a hard time myself. 'You can't let him *sell drugs* to get information!'

'Not selling,' Dad says, shaking his head. 'Foot-soldiering. Go-between stuff – delivering cash, setting up meetings, passing on info.' He looks at Harris again. 'Tell Snowie that's what you'd prefer to do. Tell him you need to get outta Five Mile, that you'd like to join him in Mildura.'

'Well the first part's true,' Harris mutters.

I jab the table in front of Dad with a finger. 'Did you hear me say "*it's not safe*"?'

Dad frowns at me. 'He'll just be a messenger boy, Amie. And if he gives me anything useful, I can pass it on to Ronnie Murphy up there.' He glances across the table at Harris. 'The Mildura CO is an old squad mate of mine. But I can't register you as an informant with the department because there's criteria, and you don't meet them.'

Harris squints as he works it out. 'So it'd just be old-school-copper style.'

'Yeah. You'd find out as much as you can about the operation, and who's bank-rolling the whole thing, and let me know.' Dad leans further. 'It's good you told me. But you should think about what I'm offering, too, before you make a decision. Because Amie's right, it might be dicey. Might not be the safest working environment.'

'Hey,' Harris says, 'I used to work at the quarry blowing stuff up, remember?'

'It's not the same,' Dad says. 'These are human explosives – a lot more unpredictable. The people Snowie's dealing with are bad people, I know that much about them. If it gets scary, you can back out.'

I groan, because now Dad and Harris seem to be occupying their own little bubble. Harris looks curious, surprised, and quietly excited. I'm *not* excited. Don't either of them recognise how dangerous this could be?

'You're serious about this, aren't you?' Harris says to Dad.

'Deadly,' Dad says. 'If you were younger, I'd say steer clear, I'll help you find a way out of the mess you're in. And I'm still happy to help you, either way. But you're grown now, and you've come here and spilled this to me like you want some advice on how to handle it. As a police officer, I'm telling you how *I* plan to handle it – by getting as much info on this bloody cancer as I can while I still have time, then pulling it out by the root. And if we help each other, then the job's done faster, and more effectively, and you get some benefit from it.'

'*Harris.*' I nearly grab his hand again. 'He said think about it. Will you please think about it?'

'I'm thinking.' He meets my eyes. 'I'm thinking you and your dad have done right by me plenty of times.'

'It's not about paying us back!'

'It is for me.' He looks at my father again. 'So...I accept Snowie's job offer and head up to Mildura.'

Dad nods. 'You go up, work it for a bit, see what you find out. When you've had enough – and how long that will be is up to you – then pull the pin, tell them your dog died or something, come back to Ouyen.'

'What happens if they make me?' Harris asks. 'What if I get arrested?'

'Let me know and I'll get you bailed. If you're worried you might be in danger, get outta there fast. I'll help get you out. You're not like a standard informant, I don't have anything over you. You've just told me off your own bat. That makes your safety my responsibility.'

'I can't believe you're doing this,' I say to Dad, but he's not looking at me.

Harris is caught up in the logistics of the idea. 'Who am I gonna pass word to? A cop in Mildura? Will you tell the station up there?'

'No, and that will make it more difficult, but you don't want any silly sideways glances from Ronnie and his crew giving the game away. The cops there won't know you. I'll do my best to keep you out of the shit here, but up in Mildura you'll be on your own.'

'Bit daunting.'

'Yes, it is. Like I said, you need to think about it.'

'So how's he going to pass on information?' I ask. I think my nostrils are flaring. 'Who will he talk to?'

Dad doesn't even hesitate. 'Me.'

'What, he's gonna have the local senior sergeant on speed dial?'

'I'll give him a different phone –'

'So he's gonna carry around a secret agent phone? That won't look suss *at all*.'

Dad frowns briefly. 'Okay, maybe it'd be better if he didn't call me. He could drive down to Hattah, or I could meet him at –'

'He can meet me,' I say.

I didn't mean to say that. I totally didn't mean to say that. But now the words are out there and I can't revoke them. I won't. Even though saying them has made me feel light-headed.

'What?' Harris stares. Dad looks like he's seen something that offends his sense of good taste.

It's a terrible idea. But I let Harris go back to his father before, and I won't leave him to do this unsupported now. And now I've said it I suddenly realise that – as a concept – it's actually got merit. Words keep falling out of my mouth like I've decided. I think I really am decided. And even though I'm making it up as I go along, I feel lighter and lighter with every word.

'He's gotta come back to the hospital for two more check-ups,' I say, gaining momentum. 'It will just be part of his normal post-op routine. He can write down the info or give me a verbal report. After a fortnight we can just say he needs more check-ups, and if Barb won't come on board with that, we can –'

'Not on your nelly,' Harris says, at the same time Dad says, 'Are you outta your *mind*?'

I finally lose my temper. 'If you two idiots are going ahead with this, it's the best way, and you both know it!'

Dad starts, 'I'm not exposing you –'

'Oh, so it's okay for *Harris* to risk his safety on your behalf, but it's not okay for me?'

'No, it's *not!*' Dad says. He looks at Harris, torn.

Harris raises his hands. 'Hey, I don't want her to do it either.'

'You're both being *stupid.*' I glare between them. '*I'm* not the one who'll be traipsing around with drug dealers in Mildura – I'm gonna be *here*, where it's safe. Dad, you *know* Harris can't call you or see you in person. People will figure it out, and word gets around so fast... You'd be endangering him just by contacting him.'

Dad knows I'm right. I can see it in his face. I push my advantage.

'When I'm at the hospital, I'm invisible. I'm not your daughter, I'm just another nurse. It's the simplest, least suspect, least dangerous way for Harris to get information back. I'm already in place, and I'm just as invested in keeping Harris safe as you are.' I don't stop to ponder what I've just said. 'Dad, you've gotta at least think about it.'

Dad has his eyes closed, head shaking. Harris is looking back and forth between Dad and me, but mostly at me.

'You don't have to do this,' he says. 'I'm the one who –'

'I offered.' I still can't believe I *offered*. But I'm not going to take it back now. Anyway, if Harris – who has nothing – can take a chance on this, then what's stopping me? I have to lay my palms flat on the table to stop them trembling, but I make a wobbly laugh as Dad's head comes up. 'I'm here and I offered.'

'This is crazy,' Dad says.

'This whole thing is crazy,' I snap back. I remember Nick's words: *You should do something crazy at least once a day.* Well, I guess this definitely qualifies. Then I soften. 'But, like I said, if you decide to go ahead with it, it makes sense to have me on board.'

'*If you decide to go ahead with it…*' Harris echoes. 'Jesus.'

Dad's face, as he turns away from me, has that peculiar time-stopped expression he only uses for really serious issues. It's a kind of official expression. 'Harris, say it and it's happening. Say no, and you walk outta here and go on your merry way. But I'd stay clear of Snowie, if I were you. I'm planning on catching up with him soon, regardless of what you've told me, whether you're involved or not.'

Harris closes his eyes. They stay closed for five long seconds before opening and staring right at me. My whole world is emerald with dark brown flecks for another drawn-out moment before he speaks. 'All right, I'm in.'

Which means *I'm* in. I'm in, and there's no turning back.

'God,' I whisper.

'Right.' Dad nods firmly. 'That's great. Thank you.' He frowns at me. 'Amita, you know I hate that you wanna be involved in this.'

'It's my call.' I swallow hard. 'And I'm doing it.'

'Amie…' Harris meets my eyes. When I shake my head to show he can't talk me out of it, he sighs. He looks at Dad and his eyebrows lift. 'So that's it, huh? We're working with the police. Jesus Christ.'

'Will you contact Snowie soon?'

Harris looks dazed. 'I-I've got his number in my wallet.'

'Okay. Good. Call him tonight. Tell him you're ready to go.'

This time I don't think about it. I reach across and squeeze Harris's fingers. 'What if Snowie wants you up in Mildura tomorrow?'

'Then he should go,' Dad says.

'What about Westie?' Harris asks.

'Tell him you got work in Mildura. Or don't tell him anything. The less you tell him, the better.'

'I can't explain any of this to him, can I?' Harris's voice is pained.

Dad shakes his head. 'I'm gonna try to keep this on a need-to-know basis.'

'Will you tell Jared, at least?' I'm trying to find the safety net for this operation, even a thin one.

'Yeah – we might need him at some point. And I want someone else to be aware of this, even if it's not official.' Dad faces me, his eyebrows smooshed together. 'How many people saw Harris come here tonight?'

I look at Harris, and he looks at me.

'I don't...' I start, can't finish it. 'I mean, I'm not sure. Just us. Maybe Barb. But she only saw us leave at the same time, she didn't know Harris was coming here.'

'This is it, isn't it?' Harris says softly. 'It's on already.'

'If you want it to be, son,' Dad says.

Harris nods slowly. 'Yeah. Yeah, okay.'

His eyes, with the dark flecks, travel over to mine. I'm still holding his hand – he's gripping my fingers – and right now, I don't think either of us wants to let go.

11

harris

On the hour-long long stretch from Ouyen to Mildura, the sun hammers down on the roof of the Pitbull. The spring breeze outside is fresh; the inside of the car heats up fast. Another minus for the Pitbull, but it's collecting so many minuses now I'm starting to lose track. It doesn't matter anyway – I've named the car. Once you name a car, you're pretty much stuck with it.

During the drive I think about what I'm getting ready to do.

The outskirts of the city will be the battle line. Once I arrive I'll be in it, and there'll be no retreat. In the rear-view, my forehead's creased and my expression's grim. Most people moving to a new place, with the prospect of a potentially lucrative job, look happy. I've gotta practise relaxing my face.

My crap is all packed into the duffel bag sitting on the passenger seat beside me. I left a note propped up on Mark West's kitchen table. Pretty soon everyone in the district will know I've thrown over a good situation to hook up with the seedy element. If they think I've gone bad it won't actually be too far removed from what they think of me already. In terms of my cover, it's probably better if Westie just thinks I'm an arsehole.

Even if he knew the whole story, Mark'd only try to talk me out of it. But it's too late for that. I've made a decision. It was based on a gut feeling, sure. But I reckon gut feelings are more accurate than people think. Your reptile brain gets all the same information your conscious brain gets. It rolls the information around and comes to its own conclusions. You end up with a feeling, an instinct. It might not be logical or reasoned, you might not even realise it's happened. It's not a conscious process. But that doesn't mean it's not accurate.

I have a gut feeling about this.

It doesn't make me less nervous.

The road from Ouyen is just yellowing miles of wheat with the occasional silo or power line. It's like driving through the desert. Then I look up and suddenly I've arrived at this oasis. The irrigation has kicked in and houses have sprouted up like brick-and-weatherboard mushrooms, grapevines growing behind them in long orderly rows.

Mildura is weird. Like a giant market garden with suburban housing and warehouse shopping malls sprinkled over the top of it. There's fucking palm trees and roses in people's front yards, for god's sake.

I clench my fingers on the steering wheel. Salted through my anxiety are flashes of Amie's face. The way her eyes widened when I volunteered to narc. The way she stood up for me and, before that, stood beside me, when we were shoulder-to-shoulder looking at the photos on the wall of her room.

I had no idea she was a photographer. Her shots are incredible, heaps better than those pictures she's clipped out of *National Geographic*. Each of her photos forces you to have a closer look at something you've taken for granted, like she's peeled back the layers of ordinary so you can see the beauty underneath.

My face relaxes thinking about Amie. Her scent, away from the antiseptic smell of the hospital. Her black hair falling loose over her shoulders, the kinks from her plait like the ripples on a sand dune. Her eyes are rich brown, shot through with a lighter gold near her irises. Long eyelashes. Cheeks that flush pink when she's angry or embarrassed. Lips the same dusky pink...

Okay, hold it. No thinking about Amie's eyes, or Amie's lips, or Amie's anything. *Head in the game, Harris.* Right.

Snowie flashes his lights at me from where he's parked beside the Red Cliffs Hotel. I pull the car over, give him a chance to swing around so he can lead me through the outer suburbs. The main drag into town is dead straight: four lanes with sky-scraping streetlamps down a wide centre island. I can already see how this place must be heaven for the Friday night car jockeys.

I follow Snowie's silver Celica past the hotel-motel strip. We're driving away from Coles supermarket and through a series of turns. The houses around us start to get smaller, lower to the ground. Then, seedier. More neglected.

Snowie's car turns into a suburban court and down a bit before easing to the curb. The gardens here still have roses, but they're tangled and dry, paired with ugly weathered shrubs. I slide the Pitbull in behind the Celica, clamber out of the driver's seat with my cane, lock the car. Better to lock it around here, I reckon. All my shit's inside it and I'm not in Ouyen anymore. The sign behind us reads Amblin Court. I don't know if I could find my way back here without help.

'Harris! Mate!' Snowie walks over from his car to meet me, gives me a slap on the back. 'You made it. Good on ya.'

'Yep, I made it.' My jeans are sticking to the backs of my legs from the sweaty drive. 'Thanks for meeting me. Bloody maze, this town, yeah?'

'You'll figure it out.' Snowie grins. 'Right, here you go. Come on in.'

Snowie nods his chin to show we're crossing the road, waves a hand at the cracked concrete path in invitation. The house itself doesn't look all that inviting. A flat-walled brick box in the classic commission style, plonked in a dry patch of weedy lawn. There's an old caravan in the driveway. Shit-loads of garbage – broken furniture, bin-bags of rubbish, mouldy blankets – is mounded between the end of the caravan and the side of the house. The front screen door wheezes on its hinges.

'You said someplace cheap, right?' Snowie holds the door open as I enter.

'Cheap is good.'

'This is the place, then.' Snowie grins broadly as he ushers me into the living room. 'Gotta warn you, though, it doesn't quite have a woman's touch.'

No shit. The living room is large and butt-ugly: brick walls, pub carpet. A moth-eaten brown velour sofa is dumped in the centre of the floor. The rest of the living room furniture comprises a standing lamp with a bare bulb, two green plastic chairs and a milk crate. The whole house smells like bong water.

Yesterday morning I was in Mark West's homey cluttered unit. Then at Amie's, seeing the jewelled cave of her bedroom, the clean cosiness of the kitchen. Normal houses, with people living normal lives. The contrast here is jarring.

The living room is deeply shaded by a batik sheet hung over the window. You wouldn't know it was a nice spring day outside. The sofa is currently occupied by a skinny guy, pale as milk, in a blue tank and trackie pants. His hair is tied in a top-knot, tangled dread ends leaking out sideways, and he's smoking a joint while he watches cartoons on a giant flat-screen to my right. His socked feet are up on a wooden coffee table decorated with cigarette burns, an over-sized ashtray, and a crinkled chip packet.

'Hey, Snowie.' He raises the hand with the joint in salute, gives me the eyeball.

'Kev,' Snowie says. 'Brought you a new housemate. Harris, this is Kevin.'

I nod, Kev nods, 'heys' are exchanged all round. I see Kevin checking out my cane. The sound of the cartoons is all over-bright voices and zaniness.

'You fellas can get to know each other later, eh?' Snowie

nudges me, points with his chin to a white laminex room extending beyond on the left. 'Kitchen. Oven doesn't work.'

'Uh-huh.'

'Come on through, I'll show you which room's yours.'

We cut in front of Kev's view of the TV as we turn into a dingy hallway where someone has tagged the whole of one wall in red spray paint. There's two bedroom doors on the left, and on the right, a white door with bubbled glass panels, half ajar. I see a white shower cubicle, a toilet, and a small hand basin, jaundiced with rust below the faucet line.

'Bathroom,' Snowie says unnecessarily. 'Ah, here we go.'

He moves one padlocked room further and pushes open a wood veneer door to show me the place I'll be living in for god-knows how long. A window, that's nice. No curtain to keep out the sun, though. It's like being inside a mirror ball in here – I have to squint. On the upside, everything's clearly visible. No bullshit. I can see what I'm getting myself in for.

A stained single mattress, flat on the floor in the corner. Another milk crate, with an old swollen copy of the *Sunraysia Daily* lining the bottom. Light fixture in the ceiling hasn't got a bulb. Someone's punched a hole in the plasterboard beside the mattress – I can tell it's a punch, because it's fist-sized. What fucking desperado lived here before me? I don't know. I don't wanna know.

'Right, here you go.' Snowie scuffs the corner of the mattress with the toe of his boot. 'You can see why the rent's cheap, yeah?'

'Um, yep.' I glance at him. 'You don't live here, then?'

'Me and Ando got a two-bedroom place closer to the main drag,' Snowie admits. 'Don't worry about the décor, mate. It's just a place to crash.'

'For sure.' I try to inject some enthusiasm into my voice. 'So there's a few other blokes around?'

'Well, it's a mixed bag. Kevin, you just met – he's a bit of a hippie. Barry's at work, you'll meet him later. Steph's probably asleep. She works nights.' He flashes me his teeth, so I have an idea what kind of nightwork Steph's doing. 'Coupla folks crash here sometimes – Jules, Reggie...'

'Mildura Motel, is it?' I say it with the right amount of dry humour.

'For now.' Snowie nods. 'This is just temporary, mate. Coupla weeks, you'll get some pay in your pocket and then we'll find you someplace decent, mark my words.'

'Yeah, all right.' *Just temporary.* I look around the ratty bedroom, careful not to sigh.

'Come on back out, you can get your gear.'

My first thought is, I don't know if I wanna leave my stuff in this house. Might be safer in my car. But my second thought is, it doesn't matter. I've got nothing of value, nothing but my clothes and my phone, and that I'll be carrying around with me.

When I return from the Pitbull with my duffel, Kevin gives me a cursory wave. He's friendly. I dump my bag on the mattress in the bedroom. As far as belongings goes, this is the easiest move ever. I wander back out. Snowie's in the kitchen, rooting around in the fridge.

'Ah, here we go.' He pulls out two coldies, passes one to me. 'You must be parched after the drive from Ouyen.'

'Yeah, cheers.' I wonder if there's anything in the fridge but beer. Something to investigate later.

'Have any trouble getting away?'

'Nah.' I don't elaborate on my previous living arrangements. Better not to mention Mark West's name. 'Dad knows I've shifted. He's happy if I'm sending him a few bucks from wherever.'

'Here's to being free of the dads, then, eh?' Snowie says.

'I'll drink to that.' We chink bottles, and it's the first time I've given him a genuine grin since I arrived.

The beer goes down nicely, very smooth and cold. I've already sunk about half of mine when a kid walks into the kitchen. His jeans hang off his hips in the accepted style, and he's wearing runners that are almost as old and taped-together as mine, plus a green hoodie that looks like it's seen better days. Dark shaggy hair with a plaited rat's tail at the back, brown skin. He's rangy: it's hard to tell if that's just his build, but I think he's probably missed a few meals – I know the look. He goes directly to the fridge and rummages inside as if he owns the place.

'Reggie, m'lad,' Snowie says.

'Hey.' The kid pulls a half-full bottle of orange Gatorade out of the fridge, thumps the door shut: the bottle has a piece of yellow electrical tape around it, with *Reggie* written in black Sharpie.

When the kid turns around I see he's not as young as I thought, probably closer to thirteen. His rat's tail is tied with a red lacka band.

He lifts his chin at Snowie. 'What's up? You feeding the same line of shit to this bloke that you tried with the last newie?'

Snowie smiles with shark's teeth. 'This is Reggie. He lives on the other side of the highway, but we put up with him when he comes over.' He noogies the kid with a free hand.

'Fuck off, Snow,' Reggie says good-naturedly, pushing Snowie away. He glances at me. 'You from outta town?'

'Near Ouyen.'

'You got a smoke?'

I open out my hands in apology. 'Not a one.'

'Shit.'

'Harris is gonna be staying for a bit,' Snowie says. 'Here in this lovely residence.'

'Right,' Reggie says. 'The lovely residence.' He glances at me. 'You got the *loveliest* room, then, did ya?'

'Yeah, for sure.' My lips quirk up. 'Bit of gaffer tape oughta cover that hole in the wall, I reckon.'

Reggie grins at me.

'Okay,' Snowie says, glancing between us before fixing on me. 'Looks like you're sorted. I'll leave you to get settled in. Meet up at the club later, about nine? I'll introduce you to the guys.'

He passes me something: it's a business card from a place called The Flamingos. The address is written on it. Snowie sculls the rest of his beer and fishes his keys out of his pocket.

'Cheers, then. See you at the club.' He winks at Reggie. 'Catch ya later, Reg.'

'Yep, see ya, Snow.'

Once he's gone, me and Reggie exchange looks.

'So,' Reggie says. 'You're gonna get settled in.'

'I dumped my clothes on the mattress,' I say. 'Dunno if there's much more to settle.'

Reggie makes this expression, where half his mouth lifts up in a lopsided smile and the opposite eyebrow raises at the same time. 'Well, that's probably more than the last guy brought with him. This house is a pit. You need stuff? You got a pillow?'

I confess that no, I don't have a pillow. Or sheets, for that matter, or a whole lot of anything else.

'You need to go to the op shop on Langtree Avenue.' Reggie swigs from his Gatorade as I take a pull of my beer. 'You can get sheets and stuff there for a few bucks. Don't even smell like piss – they wash everything before they flog it. You play footy?'

'Ah. Not at present.' I lift my cane in the air, try not to grimace.

'What happened to your leg?'

'I got shot.'

'Ouch.' Reggie's eyebrows shrug briefly, settle again, as if he's heard worse. 'Kinda crap, yeah, if you can't play footy?'

'No kidding.'

'If you weren't disabled we coulda gone to the ground up the road, had a kick.'

'You got a footy?' My voice sounds wistful, I'm embarrassed to note.

'Yep. Gotta play, yeah? Nothing else to do here but walk around, watch telly, and wank.'

'Not all at the same time, though.'

Reggie laughs, gives me a slap on the shoulder. 'You're all right, mate. What's your name again?'

'Harris.' I hold out my hand. 'Harris Derwent.'

He shakes with faux solemnity. 'Reggie McCloud. Pleased to make your acquaintance.' Then he caps his Gatorade and pulls the fridge open to toss the bottle back in. 'Gotta bounce. Stuff to do. Might catch you later at the club.'

Now it's my turn to raise my eyebrows. 'They let you in?'

'Snowie'll vouch for me. Anyway, club or not, if you're living here I'll see you round.'

He gives me that lopsided smile again, lopes off to exchange small talk with Kevin in the lounge room. I hear the front door open and shut. The walls in here are Kleenex-thin: I won't be calling Amie from my bedroom to give updates. We'll have to text each other to arrange meet ups, or handle emergencies.

I take the last swallows of my beer, look around the kitchen. The benches are peeling white laminex. The cupboards look like they were installed in the seventies. The table I'm sitting at wobbles: someone's shoved a folded TallyHo packet under the foot of one leg to steady it, but the packet has worked its way free. I lean over and push it back. The wobble lingers.

So this is it.

The decision to come to Mildura, to do this, seemed really clear-cut – exciting, even – when I was sitting at another kitchen table in Amie and Derrin Blunt's house. I'd thought I was stuck, that all my options were bad ones, but then I'd been given a third path. Amie offering to be my contact cemented the deal. It felt as if I was making a good choice. It felt *right*.

But now I'm in it, and this is no joke. Snowie, Ando, Kev, the kid Reggie I just met... These are real people I'm dealing with. Like an actor sunk in a role, I've gotta be switched on twenty-four-seven – I'm *living* it. And I can't afford to fuck up.

It's weird that Sarge Blunt and Amie are the only ones who really know what I'm doing here. But knowing they know makes me feel less alone.

I get up, dump my empty in the sink and make my way out. Give Kevin a polite nod, move through to the bathroom. Close the door and survey the grotty tiles and brown grouting landscape before splashing some water on my face at the sink.

I check myself in the mirror. I'm okay. There's nothing in my face that betrays how I'm feeling, what I'm thinking. I can fit in here. This is what I came to do. Settle in, sink deep. Pretend to be something I'm not.

I rake back my hair, put my game face on. Leave the flimsy privacy of the bathroom and go out to meet what's coming.

*

'Harris!' Snowie waves me over, a shit-eating grin on his face. 'Mate, good to see ya. Find the place okay?'

'Yeah, the big neon sign and the punters lining the pavement out front kinda gave it away.'

Flamingos is a pretty happening joint. Black and silver panels on the street facade, lots of patrons queuing. Mentioning Snowie's name got me the nod from the neckless Italian stallion on the door.

Inside, the club sinks down into the ground in three terraced rows, like an amphitheatre, with the dance floor laid out at the bottom. I've been in places like this before. Obligatory disco lights, dry-ice smoke, black vinyl couches, cheap tables. My own reflection bounces back at me a dozen times from mirror walls. People stand in clumps, move up and down the levels, laughing and knocking back beers, making enough noise to compete with the DJ. Through the speakers, Lana del Ray sounds like she's gargling acid in time to the beat.

I'm wearing my jeans and a clean T-shirt, with a black hoodie I got from the op shop where I bought my pillow and blankets this afternoon. I slide into the round-table booth. Ando slouches beside Snowie. His expression is approving as he pushes a beer across the table for me. 'There you go. First of many. Nice to see you could make it.'

Signing on, making the move here to Mildura, has obviously lifted me in Ando's opinion. But I'm not interested in his approval.

'Cheers.' I meet his eyes, hold them as I raise my beer. Ando knows I can take a punch, but the day will come when he'll find out I can throw one, too.

'Harris, this is Barry.' Snowie nods towards the guy sitting between us. 'You'll be seeing him around Amblin Court. Barry's our man on the ground. Talks to all our little friends. Barry likes to talk.'

The guy beside him guffaws. He's a bit older, with a dark flat-top haircut, a paunchy face, and below his rolled-up shirtsleeves, the hairiest arms of any bloke I've ever met.

He slaps Snowie's shoulder, turns to shake my hand with the enthusiasm of a Labrador. 'Harris, is it? Nice to meet ya, good stuff. Be cool to have a runner around.'

I raise my beer and grin. 'I gotta be the only 'runner' in town with a walking cane, I reckon.'

Barry yuck-yucks again, hunches over the table. 'Not gonna get homesick, are ya? You'll be right in Mildy, for sure, mate. Few more days, you'll feel like a local.'

'You bet.' I make a show of looking around the room. 'Nice joint. You live here or something, Snow? Or is it 'Free Mates' every night?'

'This is Leon's club.' Snowie gestures at the mirror walls, the punters dancing and shifting in the space of the club. 'Not bad business, eh? You'll meet Leon soon. He's the man. Giving the people what they want. And we're helping him out.'

For a nice tidy profit – right. So this Leon bloke is the general, and Snowie's one of his lieutenants. Ando's the heavy, Barry's the street dealer liaison...and I'm the runner. I drink on that for a moment.

We sit and bullshit together for a while. I can keep up this stuff all night: sinking piss and talking about nothing much, checking out the chicks in the club. I can't help comparing the ladies' dress code here – smoothed hair, skin-tight jeans or short skirts, high heels, shitloads of makeup – with Amie's homespun style.

I'm at the bar, buying the next round on Snowie's tab, when I see a familiar face in the mirror. Reggie McCloud is behind me, dodging patrons to slide in closer.

'Harris. My new friend.' He smiles, and all his teeth glow in the blacklight above the spirits shelf. 'Gemme a beer?'

I squint at him. He's just a kid. But when in Rome...

'Sure,' I say. 'But I'm gonna tax you for it – carry these ones to the table for me. I can't hold five beers in one hand.'

He helps me gather the bottles. 'You're pretty matey with Snowie, yeah?'

I shrug. 'Another Five Mile boy. I've known him since we were kids. How about you?'

He shrugs back. 'Wouldn't call it besties. I deal more with Barry.'

So now I know where Reggie fits in: he's a street dealer. Snowie must have Barry currying up a little team to distribute to customers. This is a real operation. And I've just scratched the surface.

'Reggie!' Snowie looks pleased to see the kid, although admittedly he's half-tanked. 'My man!'

'Yeah, yeah, I'm your man,' Reggie says, dumping the bottles on the table. He nods at Ando. 'Hey, Ando, how's it going? Keepin' your pecker up?'

Ando makes a nasty grin. 'Why? You looking to make a few bucks?'

Reggie strikes his chest dramatically with one hand. 'Ando, I'm cut. You're so gorgeous, mate, you know you'd never need to pay me.' He snorts at Ando's expression, makes a royal wave. 'Anyway, guys, nice to see ya, but Leon's asking for Harris, here.'

Barry nods. 'Ah, if Leon's asking, then...'

'Harris, you're on,' Snowie gives me the thumbs-up.

My spine straightens. Meeting the big boss on the first night wasn't exactly part of my game plan. 'So...what do I do? Just introduce myself?'

'He likes to vet the people he's working with.' Snowie grins, like he's trying to be reassuring. 'Go on, mate, he won't bite. Catch you when you get back.'

I paste on my smile, keep it there.

Reggie tugs on my sleeve to get me to keep up as we weave down the levels to a matte black door near the DJ's booth. I press hard on my cane. 'Any words of advice before I meet His Highness?'

'Don't call him Highness,' Reggie shoots back. 'He's just Leon. That's it. Keep the trash talk down, he's a serious man. Apart from that... I got nothin'. I don't hardly see him. Ignore Mick the Leb. He's Leon's minder, and he's a meathead. Just keep your eyes on Leon and try not to look like an idiot, that'd be my best advice.'

We push through the door into a rabbit warren of grotty dark-painted halls decorated with peeling band posters. We pass the toilets, move further. All this black paint is off-putting. I feel like I'm entering some sort of basement dungeon from a torture-porn horror flick. This Leon bloke must run the joint from his manager's cave: sorting out booze supplies, setting up bands, hiring and firing employees...and, apparently, strategising for the distribution of crystal meth in his patch.

Reggie leads me until I'm standing in front of another black door. He knocks, gives me an encouraging slap on the back. 'Have fun.'

I roll my eyes, Reggie scarpers, then a voice sounds from behind the wood veneer – 'Come!' – and I'm pushing through the door to meet Leon.

He's in his early fifties, I guess, and he's swarthy. Thin crop of salt-and-pepper hair, small eyes, face like melted cheese. Leon sits in an office chair, his body swelling over the sides, white business shirt straining at the seams. A cigarette sends up jet-stream from his right hand as he talks on the phone in his left.

Behind the door, a stocky guy – black hair, black monobrow, black leather jacket – sits on a wooden chair reading a girlie mag, one ankle crossed over his other knee. I'm assuming this is the minder, Mick the Leb. Everything is gloomily lit by a tall standing lamp in the corner of the tiny room.

Leon's leaning on a metal desk. The desk is normal-sized; Leon makes it look like a kiddie toy. But it seems to go with him. It's completely covered in crap, as if someone nicked a wheelie bin from behind Officeworks and upended the contents onto the metal surface. I dunno how he finds anything in there. Maybe he has a system. The Fucking Mess System.

At the moment, he's putting out orders for his bookie. I stand in front of the desk while he makes the call so I get the whole thing in stereo.

'Yeah, number four in the tenth. Fair Warning, it's called. *Fair Warning*. Yes. Yeah. No, mate. Fuck, mate, I dunno, I just back 'em.' He glances up at me and snaps his fingers, changes the snap into a writing gesture.

I find him a pen under the clutter on his desk, hand it to him. He makes a short scribbled note on a scrap of paper, pockets it. At least it won't get lost in the blizzard on his desk.

He disconnects, barely glancing at me. 'Harris, is it?'

'Yep.'

'I'm Leon.' He stubs out his smoke, makes another call. 'Yeah, mate, he's here.' Leon finally looks at me, standing in front of him with one hand on my cane and one in the pocket of my hoodie. 'Seems all right. I dunno, mate. You're the one vouching for him. You tell me.'

I straighten a little, keep my hands tight. I'm being sized up in this moment. Plenty of times I've been sized up. I've been eyeballed by the cops, slouched before potential employers. Fronted barneys at the pub, staring down bigger guys who think they can take me. They probably could take me now. It'd be easy.

I'm supposed to be projecting. *I need this job. I need the money.* None of that is bullshit. I've got thirty bucks left in my wallet, which is barely enough to tank up the Pitbull for the drive back to Ouyen.

I ignore the prickle of tension from having my back to the minder guy, keep my eyes on the wall behind Leon's head. Try not to look desperate. Try to look casual instead. The wall is black, and there's an aluminium-framed window with the blinds down. Thin venetian blinds, the kind that give you a paper cut if you try to wipe them clean. These ones need a clean. Nicotine-brown

170

stains line their edges, from dust, and years of passively absorbing exhaled smoke.

This place is a shithole. I try not to make value judgements, as a rule, but seriously. What am I doing here?

'Yep. Yep. Good on ya. Right, mate, cheers.' Leon finishes his call, thumbs off and tosses the phone on top of a half-buried ledger.

He appraises me as I bring my eyes back to where they're supposed to be. I'm supposed to look attentive, eager. Not too eager.

'Right.' Leon pulls another smoke out of a pack of Longbeach, lights it fast. He has thick stubby fingers but he moves quick. 'Snowie says you're an okay bloke. Sound about right?'

I slip out of my skin and into someone else's. Someone more cold and confident than I am. 'Guess so. If Snowie says.'

'He does say.' Leon's eyes are bright, beady, amongst the lizard rolls of fat on his face. He might be smarter than initial impressions suggest. 'So I'm gonna give you a go, all right? Nothing major. Just a little errand to run. You reckon you can do a little errand without fucking it up?'

I don't bristle. I don't. 'Sure.'

'Good.'

Leon exhales smoke, takes the ciggie out of his mouth with his left hand, grabs down for the handle of his desk drawer with his right. Again I'm struck by how he resembles a reptile – still for long seconds, then *bam*, he's moving. Shifty.

Now he tosses a parcel onto the ledger. It's a gold A4 envelope, folded in half. 'Here you go, then. Delivery job. Nothing fancy, like I said. Just take it to the place, drop it off. Handle that, you reckon?'

'Yep.' I don't say *Easy* or *No worries*. Don't wanna look cocksure. He wants to know if I'll fuck it up. Better to come over as efficient. A simple yes will do.

'Right. You take it to the pizza place on Pitt Street. Go round the back to the kitchen, deliveries door. Ask for Melon.'

'Melon. Okay.'

'Give it to him. Straight to him, okay? Don't leave it with someone to pass on, none of that shit. Melon's not there, you bring it back, go again later. No probs?'

'No probs.'

'Off you go, then.'

I reach for the gold envelope. Leon snags me as I'm picking it up.

His eyes are like black marbles, unblinking. 'You do this, come straight back here, I'll give you a nice tip. We'll talk about more work. You take it, fuck off back to Ouyen with it, I've got blokes I can pay to get it back. You understand me?'

Sweat freezes in the small of my back. Do I understand him? Uh, yeah, I think I do. He's got blokes he can pay to get it back – the way he drops it so casually into the conversation, as if it's not a direct threat. As if one of those blokes isn't sitting right behind me. As if Mick the Leb wouldn't come to my house, put a gun to my head, gaffer-tape my feet down on the coffee table before he smashed my knees in with a piece of two-by-four –

Suddenly I feel very...breakable. Now I know what Reggie was talking about when he said Leon's a serious man.

I wet my lips. 'I understand. Delivery for Melon at the back of the Pitt Street pizza shop. I won't screw it up.'

'Good boy.'

I slip the envelope into the front of my hoodie, zip up. Wonder what I'm supposed to say next. Nothing, as it turns out.

'Right.' Leon butts out his smoke on a black plastic ashtray with burn marks on the rim. 'Fuck off, then.'

I turn and limp out, close the office door behind me. Stand

there for a second, clutching the handle of my cane. The carpet in the hallway is stiff with years of spilled drinks and ground-in cigarette ash. A pearl of sweat melts off the ice-block in the small of my back, dribbles down into the waistband of my jeans.

This is some crazy shit I'm doing. What did Derrin Blunt say? *If it gets scary, you can back out.* I scoffed at him when he said that because I thought being scared meant you were weak.

The envelope crinkles, warming against my body. Delivery for Melon at the Pitt Street pizza shop. Who the fuck calls himself Melon? I keep my mind focused on that as I go out through the jarring loud front-of-house, wave to Snowie in passing, step into the harsh fluoro light on the street.

12

amie

Harris has lost weight.

He was looking stronger by the time he left hospital, better still after some time at Mark West's. Now he's been in Mildura for six days, and his face is getting that leanness again. In another week, he'll look angular.

It bothers me.

'What else happened?' I ask.

'That's it.' He spreads a hand. The other one is helping him to stay propped on the outpatient bed. 'Leon calls me when he needs money or messages delivered. Or Snowie calls me if he wants to see Leon, or deliver something. Not product – I mean, if he wants to organise a meeting with Leon, or pass back cash, or put in an order.'

'Why doesn't Snowie just deal with this guy himself?'

'Snowie's driving all over town, seeing his distributors. He's got folks lined up all over the place, yeah? So he's busy. Plus, there's limited direct contact. That's the most important reason.'

'So you're the go-between.'

'I'm the go-between, yeah.' He nods at the floor. 'I'm used to slipping under the radar. Dodging the cops. Being just another scruffy bloke on the street.'

'This is a bit of a departure for you, isn't it?' I raise an eyebrow. 'Being the good guy.'

Harris scrubs a hand across his stubbled cheeks. 'I guess.'

'But you've worked with the police before,' I say. 'That quarry business –'

'That wasn't... I wasn't working with the cops. Rachel had a problem, which the police were involved in. I was helping out a mate.'

'Well, this is kind of the same. You're just...helping my dad out. And a few other people in town who don't quite know what's good for them.'

His eyebrows lift. 'I guess that's true.'

'So that's it? Four deliveries, gold envelopes, four different places. You get the addresses written down?'

'Here's the last one.' Harris scrawls more on the back of the pamphlet I gave him about post-op care, hands the pamphlet to me. 'Tell your dad I'm just working my way in. If he goes gangbusters now, he'll miss out. I haven't seen anything solid, only cash in envelopes. That's not what he's after, I'm guessing.'

He looks tired. His blond hair has gotten longer, greasier, what Nani describes as 'flypaper hair'. It's flopping in front of his face, obscuring his expression as he talks. I don't know what it's like, the stuff he's doing in Mildura, but it's wearing at him. I wish I could push his hair out of the way, ask him how he's really going.

I put the pamphlet in my pants pocket and wheel the tray over, plump the pillow on the right. 'You want to lie down for this?' The outpatient bed is shorter than he is, and quite hard, but he looks as if he could do with a lie down.

'I'm good.' He bites his bottom lip. 'Can I, like, rest my back? Lean, or something?'

'Recline.' I smile. 'You can recline, yeah. One sec.'

I adjust the bed so the head end is at a forty-five degree angle.

Harris swings his legs up onto the flat end of the bed and leans his shoulders back as I wrangle the pillow. Close up, he smells of raw perspiration, unwashed clothes, cigarette stench. There's dirt in his pores, and he's warm. I'm tempted to put my hand on his forehead, check if he's got a temp.

'I came prepared this time,' he says.

'What?'

He grins, his lips thin and pale. 'Found a pair of these at the op shop on Langtree. Didn't wanna inflict my jocks on you again. Check it out.'

He reaches forward to the knee of his khaki pants, unzips at the leg. The whole bottom section of his pants leg zips right off. I help him tug the separated section away, pull it down towards his boot.

'Nice.' Then I open the dressing, see his wound. 'That's not so nice. It's... We've kind of gone backwards here, Harris. What's going on? I thought we had an agreement. You're supposed to wipe it and re-dress it every morning, or I can't –'

'Amie, I live in a sharehouse shack with a bunch of drug dealers.' He stares at me. 'Roaches come outta the taps. Last time I was in the bathroom, there was a chick vomiting into the sink. Let's just say it's not a clean hospital environment, okay?'

That makes me blink. 'Are you taking your medication, at least?'

'I'm taking my meds, yeah.' His shoulders release and his eyes close. 'I'm doing what I can. But I can't keep off my feet much as I should. And you don't know these people. You show weakness, you're roadkill. The leg – I tried to get some of those antiseptic wipes, clean it out and stuff, but if they knew how bad it was...'

The leg. I put my hand on his shoulder to get his attention.

'Harris, look at me. It's not 'the leg'. It's *your* leg. D'you get that? *Your leg*. And if you don't take proper care of it, you'll lose it.' I take my hand away. My eyes should be enough. 'Do you want to come back for an amputation? Seriously?'

'No.'

He looks sulky. I need him to get past that. 'No? You sure? Because if you want a prosthetic, you're going the right way about it.'

That seems to sink in. 'I don't want a prosthetic.'

'Good choice. But if you want to keep your leg, then you need to clean it and dress it every day, like we agreed. You've gotta do it – no, look at me for a sec. You're miles away, without proper care if you don't visit the hospital in Mildura, and you're walking around on a post-op injury that could easily take a turn. Find a place. In your car, at a truck stop, in a public toilet – wherever you can, all right?'

He nods, glancing away.

I wonder if he's really getting this. If my voice is firm enough, serious enough. 'I'll give you antibiotics and extra supplies, okay? I'll give you everything you need. Sterile wipes, bandages, tape, distilled water, whatever you –'

'Pain stuff?' He presses his lips together. 'Can you give me more pills?'

'Are you in pain?'

He nods again.

'On a scale of one to ten? Gimme a number.'

'Five.'

And I know straightaway he's not lying. The wound is healing slowly; it still looks very tender. It's at that level where you can cope if you keep really busy or preoccupied, but let your guard down and the constant hum of it gnaws at you. I wonder if that's why he's tired, if it's keeping him up at night.

I start slow. 'Harris, you're supposed to get an assessment for pain meds. Barb's supposed to have a look at you.'

But if Barb has a look at him, she'll go the whole hog. She'll probably want to admit him. Part of me thinks he needs to be admitted. He's not keeping up with post-op care, he's in a high risk living situation, he's underweight and probably at risk of infection…

'I don't want an assessment,' he says firmly. 'I'm close, Amie. A couple more weeks, I'll have the info your dad needs. I can feel it. Fine, I'll start looking after my leg, I'll get on it.'

I'm still torn. 'I can't prescribe pain medication for you, Harris. All I can tell you is to get some extra codeine-based painkillers from the chemist. But if you look after your leg properly, it'll get better faster. The pain will ease.'

'Then that'll have to do me. I guess I'll have to pick up my game.' He looks at the exposed wound on his leg. 'I'll…I'll try to rest it every day. I dunno how I'll do that, exactly, but I'll try.'

'Okay.' His eyes are so honest when he looks back up that my stomach clenches. 'I still have to dress this. Um, hang on –'

I cut myself off, start cleaning out the wound. My fingers fumble with the sterile wipes. Harris makes a faint hiss.

'So I've given you all my info.' He grimaces, looks at the ceiling. 'What've you got for me?'

'You mean from dad?'

'Nah, not that. Just… anything.'

'Anything, huh?' He's after a distraction. I can see it in his face.

'How's the photography going?'

I try not to startle. He remembered. 'It's going good. I took a couple of nice ones near the saltworks, and I bought a foldaway light deflector for bouncing natural light.'

'You're pretty into it, huh?'

I'm so into it, I got an opportunity to do it overseas but I'm too scared to open the information folder about it. Crap. There's no way I'm saying that. How can dealing with a few papers be scarier than being a narc's contact? But it is, somehow.

I focus on what I'm doing. 'My first camera was an old one of Mum's. Some of her shots were really good. She had a decent old SLR and she handed it on to me.'

'They're expensive, huh? Good cameras?'

'Yeah, like, really. I had to save up for ages for the one I use now.'

'You must really love it, the photography thing.'

'It's...something I need to do. When I'm shooting, I forget about everything else.' I think about it as I work. It's true: regardless of opportunities or validation, making images is important to me. I don't worry about anything when I'm out with the camera. 'There's something about it I find really energising. But it's weirdly peaceful, too.'

He nods, and I wonder if he understands or if he's just humouring me to keep me talking. But maybe Harris gets it. Maybe *peaceful* is something he's only ever had in short supply.

I try to explain further. 'It's just me and the camera and what's in front of me. The next shot, and the next, looking for the right framing, the colours... And you don't really see until you check the frames on a big screen and print it up, it's all just trusting you've got it right. It's capturing the unexpected.' I smile as I tear open a sterile swab packet, grab the Betadine solution. 'Plus you come out of it with something you can look at, and remember.'

'It's a bubble of time.' He winces as I dab a tender spot. 'You can go back to it.'

'I guess.' I feel myself flush. *This* is unexpected. I hardly ever let myself get overenthusiastic about my pictures in conversation.

'But you changed,' Harris says. 'You used to do those big landscapes, big sheets of light and colour –'

'Your style changes as you grow up.' I didn't mean that to come out so bitey. I swallow, rephrase. 'I stopped doing landscapes.

They just felt a bit…naïve. Now I do close-ups.'

'Of broken stuff. And suffocating trees.'

'I thought you said you liked them?'

'Hey, don't get mad, they're good, those ones. But I like your old photos.' Harris isn't looking at me and his voice is gruff. 'The space in 'em. Like you could jump into the background and fly.' I'm still staring at him when he changes the subject. 'And, um, how's your nanna?'

But I'm thinking about it now. Those spaces, those big sheets of light and colour… They stopped about four years ago. Did Mum's death really change my style that much? I've never considered it like that before. What else about me has narrowed down?

Flustered, I swipe my hot cheek with the back of my hand, concentrate on sizing the wound dressing. 'You seriously want updates about my relatives?' I conjure a smile, shrug. 'Nani's fine, I guess.'

'You guess?'

'She's… Well, you know how I said she's my dotty nanna?'

He nods.

'She's been acting a bit more dotty than usual.' I clear my throat. 'My cousin is getting married next week. Everyone's running around, getting the wedding organised, and I don't know if they've noticed how Nani's going. She's started talking about my dead grandfather like he's still here.'

He tilts his head to see my eyes. 'You're worried about her.'

My smile tightens. 'I'm kind of close with her. I spent a lot of time with her and my cousins when I was a kid. My mum used to take me up to visit a lot. And after Mum died, Nani was really supportive…'

Harris waits until it's obvious I'm not going to go on. 'Hey. I'm sorry about your mum.'

'It's okay.' I blink my eyes a few times to remind them not to do anything stupid. Unpeel the plastic off a roll of bandage. 'What I mean to say is, me and Nani have a connection. I look out for her.'

'Don't your cousins help her with stuff?'

'Yeah, but she's getting older and more forgetful. She needs more help these days. Like Dad.'

'Your dad?' Harris cocks an eyebrow. 'He seems fine to me.'

'Dad has a heart condition.' I see Harris's face. 'It's not major. It's just something he's developed as he's gotten older. That's why he's retiring.'

'That's gotta be tough on him, having to hang up the badge.'

'Yeah, he's not thrilled about it.' I adjust his leg so I can wrap the bandage, assess his expression before I ask the next relevant question. 'So how're things going with *your* dad, now you've shifted?'

He sighs. Since we had the conversation around the table at my place and he agreed to narc, it seems like he just can't be bothered glossing it up.

'We've talked on the phone a few times.' He shrugs. 'I called him – figured it was better to get it over and done with. He cracks the shits every time I call, but it's easier than dealing with him in person. At least I'm not standing right in the line of fire, y'know?'

I can't nod or agree with him: I've never had to handle anything like that. I don't feel like my physical safety is ever in doubt when I'm at home, or with family.

'I'm sending him some money,' he continues. 'And helping pay off the bills. That's placating him a bit.' He looks at me. 'It's not just the cancer or the booze, yeah? That makes it worse, but he's been like this since I was a kid. He's just...mean.' He shakes himself suddenly, as if he's shaking off a bad dream. 'Anyway, I'm not living with him anymore which is a helluva relief.'

'You're living in a sharehouse shack with a bunch of drug

dealers instead.' It's staggering that he considers his current accommodation an improvement on the one he had before. I tug the bandage end, fix on an elastic fastener. 'I'm sorry about your dad.'

He snorts at how I've echoed his sentiments back. 'Hey, I'm not bereaved. But sometimes, I can't help thinking ...'

'...that it'd be easier if you were?' I suggest softly.

He looks at me, looks away fast. I've hit a nerve, and maybe he's just realised that implying you wish your parent was dead in front of someone whose parent died isn't the height of sensitivity.

But I don't know how his father's illness is progressing, and now I feel guilty. 'I'm sorry, that was bad manners –'

He makes a low laugh. 'Don't apologise. It should be me apologising. I didn't mean to say that. I don't know what comes outta my mouth sometimes.'

'Well, don't hold back for my sake.' I keep my tone light. 'Anyway, I get the impression the way I was with my mum and the way you are with your dad are very different things.'

'Yeah, that's possibly the understatement of the year,' he says evenly. He pauses. 'I'm just happy I had the guts to cut loose.'

'God, I think you've been incredibly gutsy so far.' That came out a bit more honest than I expected. I redirect. 'Look, make sure you're being careful in Mildura. I'd hate to think of all this first-rate nursing going to waste.'

He pats his now-bandaged leg. 'Don't worry. I got my own personal well-being in mind at all times. The last thing I want is Mick the Leb breaking my kneecaps.'

He hops off the outpatient table with more energy than he had climbing onto it, tests out the bandaging, taking a few steps around with his cane. I'm chilled by the thought of Harris having his legs broken because of what he's agreed to do. What he needs more of, though, are people around who give him support.

I make my voice firm. 'It looks better – more comfortable for you. Make sure you look after it like we discussed.'

'I will.' He zips his pants-leg back into place, looks at me. 'Thank you. It's just...good to talk, y'know? There's nobody else I can talk to about any of this.'

I bite my lip. 'I guess you have to go now.'

'Yeah, it's a long drive back.'

I say the next bit hurriedly. 'Harris, remember to stay in touch.' I smooth my hands down the sides of my work pants. 'You've got my phone number.'

'Okay. I will.' He pulls his hood up. 'Good luck with your nanna. Hope it works out okay.'

We have this weird moment, when it seems like our simple acknowledgements aren't quite enough; I feel like hugging him, or giving something more than just a formal goodbye, and Harris seems to feel the same way. He hesitates, reaches out with the hand not on his cane. My fingers slip into his and we both squeeze, just for a second, before releasing. That's about as demonstrative as we can be in public anyway. Our eyes make up the shortfall.

Then I open the door of the Examination room and watch him limp off towards the hospital foyer and the outside doors. I get busy again when I see Barb coming towards me from the opposite direction. She enters the Examination room while I'm gathering together all the wound-care scraps.

'That patient of yours has been up to mischief, I hear,' Barb says.

'What?'

She helps herself to supplies from the cupboards. 'I heard Harris shot through from Mark West's place. That he'd gone to Mildura.'

I keep my expression appropriately mystified. 'Who'd you hear that from?'

'Came in to do my shopping yesterday, ran into Delphine, Mark's mum. She was telling me what she'd heard from Mark. According to her, Mark said Harris is in Mildura. He said it was a shame Harris took off, that he seemed to be getting better.'

I try to look dismayed, as if this is all news to me. 'Then...he came all the way down for his appointment. That has to count for something.'

Barb raises her eyebrows, shrugs. I know what the gestures mean. I'm starting to understand what Harris meant when he said people are happy to assume the worst about him.

Barb's already commiserating with me. 'You've got to let it go, hon. He'll come to his appointments or he won't. I know you've tried hard for that boy, but sometimes people don't want your help as much as you want to give it.'

'Maybe if he skips here he'll go to the hospital in Mildura,' I suggest.

'Maybe he will,' Barb concedes. She shrugs again. 'Maybe he won't. Like I said, best to just let it go.'

As Barb walks off I realise something. Me and Dad are the only ones who know exactly what's going on. I'm going to hear people slagging Harris off a lot more often over the next few weeks. He already has a reputation in this community and posing as a drug connection in Mildura will blacken it further. Peoples' opinions of him are only going to get worse.

And he *chose* this.

The fact that Harris is making a sacrifice to do this makes me think it must mean something to him, something important. What is it?

Maybe he wants to prove he's not like his dad, not a heartless bastard. Or it could mean Harris doesn't care what people think about him – he's been living with other folks' bad opinions his whole life. Maybe he doesn't give a toss what people say anymore.

184

I know he doesn't let people in often. He must feel very much alone.

But there's another scenario, and this is the one that worries me most. It's the scenario where Harris has stopped caring about what he does and what the consequences will be. Whether he lives or dies. I thought that darkness had melted out of him after his last admission to hospital; maybe it just sank deeper, burned down into the core of him. He said he's being careful, but he's throwing himself into dangerous situations up in Mildura, double-crossing drug lords who don't mind a spot of knee-capping, or worse...

Maybe Harris has a death wish.

It's easy for me to fake disappointment for Barb at the idea Harris might have gone off the rails. But it'll be even easier to act worried about what might happen to him as a result, because I'm one of the only people who knows what's really going on in Mildura.

And I know enough to understand that Harris's death wish could become a reality, with very little effort at all.

*

'Wow, you've got a lot of gear.'

'You should've seen all the shit I left behind,' Nick says.

It's Friday. We're on the verge in front of my house, and Nick's got almost every possession he owns stuffed inside his new second-hand car. He's crammed three boxes of gear into the backseat and there's two suitcases plus more in the boot.

'Last chance, now.' Nick eyebrows lift expectantly. 'You sure you don't want to climb aboard this train? You know I'd be cool with you crashing with me for a while, if you wanted to come down to Melbourne.'

His tone is joking but he looks hopeful, and I flash on my conversation with Robbie: *he's still into you*. There's so many reasons why I would never take advantage of Nick that way, but I don't want him to feel bad about it.

I squeeze his arm. 'If I ever decide to make the move, you'll be the first person I call.'

His expression becomes resigned but he disguises it by shoving his hands in his pockets. 'Be nice to Barb. She's helped me a lot, and it was pretty cool of her to give me references and pay out my leave on such short notice. I feel like a bit of an arsehole for that. But Grant said these guys in Preston are okay for me to let the room in their house, and now I've got wheels...'

'You should strike while the iron's hot.'

'This is all happening a bit faster than I'd expected,' he admits.

'Yeah,' I say gently, 'but you've been thinking about it for as long as I've known you. Now you get to do it – go out into the world and be awesome.'

I grin at him even though my eyes feel prickly and my head is full of nostalgia. Nick is standing there in his daggiest sun-bleached jeans and a white T-shirt. His black fringe falls in his eyes – all the Partridge boys have the same dark hair. It was one of the things I noticed about him when we first became friends, years before we started dating. I didn't realise then I was letting into my heart another person who was destined to leave.

But people are impermanent. I should've figured that out by now.

'Promise me something?' His eyes hold mine. 'If I take my awesome to Melbourne, you have to make up the difference here.'

'Or there'll be an awesome imbalance?' I joke.

'I'm serious, Amie.' He looks serious, too. 'Go get that residency. You're shortlisted, that means you have a good chance. Have you signed up for an interview yet?'

'Um, I'm still just checking out the paperwork.' I lean back on the car – a white Ford hatchback – and let the heat from the metal bonnet warm me. I'm doing some disguising of my own.

'Amie.' Nick extricates a hand and tilts my chin. 'You've only got one life. And it's yours, not your dad's or your nanna's.'

'I know that.' I bite my lip.

'Then stop worrying about everyone else and go live it.' Nick presses a kiss to my forehead, releases me. 'And sign up for an interview before the deadline.'

I ease off the car. 'There's a deadline?'

He snorts, shakes his head. 'Just make sure you keep following my recommendation. One crazy thing per day, remember?'

'I'll…I'll do my best.' It would be interesting to tell him about the Harris situation, if only to see the look on his face. But that's not gonna happen.

Nick's expression shifts into a smile as he tucks his thumbs in his belt loops. 'You'll come see me in Melbourne, right? I want to take you out on the town in the Big Smoke, show you what real living's like.'

'Hey.' I poke his arm. 'Real living is right here, every day. But sure, you can take me out. On a tram, or something.'

'On a tram…' Nick guffaws, but I think he's just doing it so he won't get maudlin. He reaches for me, reels me into a hug. I squeeze him, because I think this might be the last hug for a while. Soon it'll be time to let go.

'Don't cry,' he whispers. 'Don't you dare.'

'I won't cry,' I say, sniffing.

'If you cry, you'll just start me off.'

'I won't cry,' I repeat, my voice muddy. 'I'm happy for you.'

'Now say "Bye, Nick, see you round," just like we always do.'

'Bye, Nick,' I say. 'See you round.' I swallow hard and taste salt. Everything is blurry – the street around us, the houses, the sun.

'See you round, Amie.' Nick releases me, and his eyes are red. 'I'll see you soon.'

He moves over to the driver's side, slides into the seat. Guns the engine and pulls the Ford off the verge. I step back as the car drives out. Stand there, waving, until I see the car turn the corner and disappear.

The kitchen seems very small when I go back into the house. Everything seems gloomy inside, after the glaring afternoon sun in the street. Dad is at the sink, doing the washing up. I'm supposed to be drying.

'So Nick's off and away,' Dad says, over his shoulder.

'Yeah.' I wander over to the tea towel rack, touch each cloth to find the dry one. 'Off and away to rescue some poor patients in Melbourne hospitals.' I pull the cloth off the rack listlessly. 'I shouldn't be sad. He's gonna be great in the city. And he'll be a good nurse.'

'You can still be sad,' Dad says. He lets me lean against him, tilt my head onto his shoulder, as his voice rumbles on. 'People end up all over. And you can tell me, y'know. If you're ever thinking about it.'

'Thinking about what?'

'Shifting to the city.'

I un-tilt my head, step back to look at him. 'Dad, I'm not thinking about shifting to the city.'

'Maybe you should.'

'What? My god, it's like everyone I know wants me to leave home...'

'Amita.' Dad pulls the sink plug, takes the tea towel out of my hands. 'Sweetheart, I've watched you these past few years. A lot of your mates are leaving. You've become more isolated.'

'You don't have to worry about me, Dad.' I shrug. 'I'm fine. I've got a job here.'

He hangs the tea towel on the back of the nearest chair. 'But you're not happy here.'

'I am!'

'Love, I don't mean you're not happy.' Dad pulls out the chair and encourages me into it, settles his own bulk onto the chair opposite. 'You're a happy, easy-going person. You get along with everybody. You –'

'I've got a position at the hospital,' I point out. 'I've got friends.'

'I know that, love. I know you do. What I'm saying is that you might want to see a bit of the world. Go to the city. Travel, like you planned before your mother...' Dad trails off. He frowns at the kitchen. 'Y'know, this is my place. This is where your mum and me settled. But that doesn't mean it's the place *you* want to settle.'

He's right: I'm not in the same position as a lot of rural kids around here, compelled to stay with the family farm. I'm not tied to the land here. But the idea of leaving Walpeup, leaving Dad alone in this little house...

I feel my face screw up. 'But I want to be where you are!'

'And I like having you around, don't get me wrong.' Dad pats my forearm on the table. 'But that doesn't mean I think you should live with me forever.'

But who will look after you if I leave? I can't sacrifice dad's health for some photography pipe dream. I won't. More importantly, if I go, he will have lost another person. I don't think I could do that to him. And what about my family in Mildura? What about Nani?

'I-I don't know, Dad.' My hands are clasped in my lap. 'My mental picture for the last four years has always just been of you and me, here.'

'It's pretty normal, I think, for kids to move out of their parents' house at some stage.' Dad's look is dry. Then he leans back, starts picking at the table edge with a fingernail. 'I've been anticipating it. You, leaving. It's not like I haven't thought about it.'

I can't do anything except reach over and clasp his hand. Because since Robbie and Nick told me about the residency, I've thought about it, too. It's been tormenting me.

But if I let go of this picture I've always had, of me and Dad and this house, and Nani in Mildura, what will flood in to fill the gap? All those photos in *National Geographic* – they're just scenery. Not places where you arrive, step out, breathe in the air or feel the sun. It's been a long time since I imagined myself in any of them. They're two-dimensional and they don't feel quite real.

This – this feels real. Sitting in the cool dingy kitchen with the mozzie zapper buzzing outside. The smell of tonight's dinner still hanging around, settling into the curtains over the sink.

Dad's hand, grimy with engine grease, curled around mine.

*

I don't know what time it is. I fell asleep on my bed, in the middle of reading through the papers in the purple folder Robbie gave me. Then my phone chimes again and I realise what's woken me.

I push my hair out of my face and grab my phone off the dresser. The first text from Patient #451 – which is how I've saved Harris's number in my phone – says *Need to schedule new apptmt. Pls get in touch*. It's from ten minutes ago. The newest message is the one that just woke me; it reads *Call if available*. It's our pre-arranged signal: it means Harris is out of his sharehouse and free to talk. But this is the first time he's used it.

I hit Call, anxious there might be some emergency. 'Hey, what's up?'

'Ah, hey. Sorry to wake you.' Harris's voice is gravelly. He sounds like he's been drinking.

'It's fine.' I rub my eyes. 'How'd you know I'm not out raging?'

I can hear his smile down the line. 'It's one in the morning. I know you're not on shift, cos it's Friday. And...you sound different. Sleepy.'

I huff out a laugh, settle myself back on the pillows. 'Yeah, I'm a bit sleepy. It's okay, though. What's happening?'

'Friday night, hey? Parties all over – it's a busy time. Look, I thought your dad might wanna know Leon offered me a gun.'

I sit up again. 'He wants you to carry a gun? Why?'

'I'm the runner, yeah?' Harris sighs. 'I'm cruisin' around town with bundles of cash stuffed down the front of my shirt. And Leon's not the only game in town. The big bosses, they fight over turf all the time. According to Snowie I'm nuts if I *don't* carry.'

'But if you get busted by the Mildura cops with a gun –'

'That's what I'm talking about. I said thanks but no thanks. Bad enough if I get hauled in by the cops with a cash delivery, let alone if I'm sprung with a pistol down the back of my pants.' He makes a snort. 'I told Leon I was worried I'd accidentally shoot myself in the arse.'

'And what'd he say to that?'

His tone changes. 'He said it was my funeral.'

'I think you did the right thing.' I marshal my thoughts, try to keep my voice light and even. 'I'll let Dad know, but I reckon you're much less likely to cop a charge if they bust you and you're unarmed. And yes, less likely to shoot your arse off.' I think about it more seriously. 'But Harris, do you need to be carrying some kind of weapon? If there's a situation, and you feel threatened –'

'Hey, if there's a situation and I feel threatened, I'm gonna drop the cash and run. I'm not gonna throw myself in front of a bullet to protect Leon's profit margin. If that ever happens, you'll know I've switched sides.' He pauses. 'The money these guys throw around, Ames... It's crazy. Ando's bought himself a new car. Some bloody ridiculous Land Cruiser thing, he's driving it through town, parking it in Amblin Court. Like, Jesus, why don't you put up a big sign saying *Drug Dealer In Da House*?'

I know I shouldn't, but I can't stop myself from laughing. Harris laughs too, as if I've surprised him. It's one in the morning, we're both tired, and we're laughing over this insane thing... The laughter brings me back into myself, reminds me of why I think Harris has volunteered to do this. It isn't for the money. It's never been just about that.

'What are you doing right now?' I ask softly.

I get a shiver when he sighs again, long and low. 'I'm up near the milk bar. I've only got a minute, hey. But I really needed to get out for a bit. It's good to hear your voice.'

That makes the shiver spread inside me, all the way down to my toes. 'Are you okay?'

'I'm okay,' he says. 'But I'm living right in the middle of it.' His voice drops into a huskier register. 'That house, Amie, it gets to me. This girl comes over from down the street, she's got her baby on one hip, and she's coming for a hit off Kev's pipe. Last night I woke up and I could hear the baby crying in the living room...'

His breath hitches, and there's quiet on the line for a minute. I let him have the quiet before I speak because sometimes you just need to say it, just need to send it out there. But I don't let the pause go on too long.

'Harris, you only have one job, remember? You can't do everything. You can't save everyone.' Which I realise is something Barb has said to me, on so many occasions. I push the thought away. 'Just do the best you can with what you've got. And keep yourself safe.' *Because that's the most important thing* – I stop the words from falling out of my mouth just in time. To cover the blank space I say what's been on my mind. 'Nick left town today.'

He doesn't make a joke, although I know it must be tempting. 'He's your friend, yeah? I'm willing to bet you'll see him again.'

'Yes, he's my friend.' I can't stop a sigh escaping.

'Amie, you've got more than one friend in your corner,' Harris says quietly. 'Gimme a call, if you need me.'

'But you're –'

'I'm here. That's all I'm saying. Text me and I'll find a place to call.' He exhales. 'That's self-interest talking, by the way. Sometimes, I think touching base with you is the only thing keeping me from going crazy up here.'

'Harris –'

'Hey, I've gotta go,' he says quickly. 'I'll see you Wednesday, okay? Stay real.'

'Stay alive,' I blurt, just before the line drops out.

I hope he heard me. I hope he's taking my advice.

13

harris

I think I've finally figured out the deal with the house.

Basically, it's a bus terminal for small-time distributors, the grunts in this little army. Ando and Snowie call in from time to time, usually only long enough to drop off a package. Kevin hangs at the house, goes out when he gets something to deliver to his cadre or when he needs a break. Barry's name is on the lease, but he's never home. His room is just a front. That room, and the caravan, are just way stations for the small privates like Reggie and Dil and Jules, whose own homes are so bad or whose lives are so erratic that they sometimes need a place to crash. As the go-to guy, I qualify as a sergeant in the ranks. Kevin uses his status to boss the kids around. I mainly use it to give myself some privacy.

A few nights ago I met Steph, the other member of our motley household. Walking back from the kitchen with a bowl of cereal – I seem to be living on Weet-Bix a fair bit these days – I noticed the door after the bathroom, the one closest to mine, was ajar. It's been closed tight with a padlock on every other day. My curiosity got the better of me, and I poked my head in for a gander.

The walls were dark with the curtains drawn, crap everywhere. A full set of motorbike leathers lay draped over the back of a chair, a bike helmet perched on the seat. Someone was sitting on a mattress on the floor, lit by a desk lamp. At first I thought it was another bloke, but then the person looked up from the thick hardback book in their lap and I realised it was a girl.

'Yes?' Definitely Indigenous, with a sinewy look, her black hair was chopped rough around her face like she'd done it herself with blunt scissors.

I found myself caught on the back foot. 'Ah, hey. Sorry. Didn't know anyone was –'

'I got that.' Her expression was parched dry. 'Who're you?'

'Harris.' I detached a hand from my bowl to wave. 'Hi.'

'Steph,' she said.

'Right. Nice to meet ya.'

'Sure.' She put the book aside – the mattress was covered in paperwork – and got up to walk over. For a second, I thought she was gonna shake my hand. 'Harris, you said?'

'Uh, yeah.'

'Okay. Stay the hell outta my room, Harris.'

She closed the door in my face.

When I tell Reggie about it later, he laughs his head off.

'Ah, fucking Steph, she's a classic.' He guffaws as we walk. 'Snowie probably told you she's a hooker or something, did he?'

I shrug. Snowie had certainly implied that much.

Reggie laughs harder. 'Steph's not a hooker, mate. She's a driver. Drives down to Melbourne in the little van, grabs a package, drives back up. Or she goes on the motorbike. And get this – she's *studying*. Goes to night classes and stuff.'

So I'm not the only person in the house who's trying to do something meaningful while surrounded by shit. I file that info for later examination, keep following Reggie. Over the last week and a half I must've heard him whinge twenty million times about how nobody would have a kick with him. Today I finally relented, said I'd walk up to the Mildura South footy ground and keep him company.

He badgers me the whole way, practically skipping with excitement. 'Who d'ya go for?'

'Brought up a Magpie. Me dad's a Magpie.' I shrug. 'But mixed loyalties, hey. Me mum's from Adelaide. I should probably support the Crows.'

'Shit. You can't support the Crows, mate.' Reggie makes a face as we come in sight of the ground. 'You should do what I do. Screw everybody and barrack for Essendon.'

I snort. 'You're a Bombers man?'

'Underdog team, that's me.' Reggie grins. 'They're in the doghouse now, eh? Not to worry, they'll be back.'

Underdog team. Yeah, right. I squint at his dark complexion. 'How are you a Reggie? You don't look like a Reggie.'

He points a thumb at himself. 'Recep. Reggie. Same diff, yeah?'

'Shouldn't you be playing soccer, *Recep*?'

'Fuck off. Soccer's for wogs.' He bounds ahead, rattling the fence as he gets to it. 'You can't climb, can ya? No worries. There's a low place we can skip over.'

It's actually a relief to get out of the house. The fuggy smells and sounds of Amblin Court seep under the door to my room, get under my skin. But I'm outside now and the day is cold and fresh. A brittle sun makes the details of the Mildura South footy ground snap into focus. Reggie shows where we can slip over the fence, then we're tooling around out on the ground.

Reggie isn't one of those cute kids you see on Tourism Australia ads. His face is narrow. He's got thin lips, and he's all skinny arms and legs. He's got good eyes – big, and so dark they're almost black – but they're his standout feature. The rest of him is just average.

But shit, can he play footy. I handball it to him, he receives on the fly, kicks it a mile, runs to fetch it back. Most kids his age can't kick over a jam jar, but Reggie has real power in those little sticks of his. He's fast, does a good feint, and talks strategy like a pro. If he was playing in the local league I'd back him for sure.

He seems more like a kid when he's doing this. When he slouches in at the house – watching TV with Kevin, picking up whatever he's come to pick up, shooting the breeze with Steph in the kitchen – he seems older. He's got a good line in bullshit patter. He flops on the couch, smoking cigarettes he's cadged and making snarky commentary, for all the world like a street-smart kingpin. But now, watching him drop the ball onto his boot, kick it like he's in the Grand Final, gallop around with a grin on his face accepting the imaginary applause of the MCG crowd, I can see how young he really is.

I dump my cane to do a bit of receiving, nod my chin at him. 'Why d'you throw down with Ando all the time? I mean, you don't seem like a complete idiot. But around him you act like you're looking to get your head smacked in.'

'Ando's a dickhead.' Reggie shrugs, kicks unerringly.

The ball lands right in my hands. 'Jesus. Stop the press.'

Reggie laughs. 'I dunno. He's too easy. I mean, what, he's gonna get upset about something *I* said? And he's so up himself. Just cos Leon gives him private jobs he thinks he's King Shit.'

I handball back, my Spidey senses tingling. 'What kinda private jobs?'

'You read the papers?' Reggie glances at me, rolls the ball laces-up to drop another shot. 'Gotta read the papers around here, mate.'

'What?' I almost fumble the catch.

Reggie lopes over, pulls a folded newssheet out of the back of his jeans, shoves it in my direction. It's a page from a recent copy of the *Sunraysia Daily*. 'Check it out.'

I read the headline on the page Reggie's folded over. *'Man hospitalised after home invasion.* What's this?'

Reggie waggles his eyebrows. 'Not a break-in, that's for sure. Your fella, Ando. That's his work.'

'Ando's not my fella,' I say, distracted. I scan the first paragraph of the article. 'This guy got a punctured lung? Christ.'

Reggie whisks the newspaper away, tucks it down the back of his jeans again and covers it with his T-shirt. 'Just so's you know, yeah? It's not all beers at the club. You're playing with the big boys now.'

'I knew that.' I nod, but my forehead's creased, I can feel it. 'I mean, yeah. I knew that. We're not in Kansas anymore.'

'What?' Reggie screws up his nose.

'Forget it.'

'Just...' Reggie scans around before looking at me. 'Watch it, okay? Ando's risen up the ranks real fast around here. Now he does the tidying up for Leon. Someone gets shirty, Ando straightens them out. Someone can't pay, Ando makes sure they pay. I heard he knocked a bloke in Buronga. When Leon wants something done, Ando gets it done.'

'He knocked a bloke?'

Reggie makes a little gun-finger, shoots it at the turf. 'Fffttt. You're gone. They send you back to Five Mile in a box.' He slaps my shoulder with his gun hand, grins. 'Hey, don't get the wind up. Just passing on useful info. Go back to Flamingos tonight and give Snowie a smile, eh?'

'Yeah, sure.' But these new facts have my mind running fast. I thought Mick the Leb was Leon's muscle, but maybe that's not the real story. Mick must be just Leon's security. Ando is the real standover man. And, on special occasions, the hit man. The sarge will wanna hear about it – but do I need proof or something first? I can't just go on hearsay, can I?

And if Ando's that heavy, what's Reggie doing stirring him up?

I catch Reggie's eye. 'You should watch out, too. Unless you wanna end up with something punctured yourself. Hospital, mate – s'not all it's cracked up to be, I can tell you.'

Reggie laughs. 'I look after meself. I can play the good boy – and I can run a lot fucking faster than Ando can. What about you, though?'

'Hey, I'm Teflon.' I tap my chest. 'All the shit slides off.'

Reggie's eyes get serious. 'What about bullets? They slide off, too?'

All of a sudden the day looks less bright.

Things pick up, though. I do two late deliveries, and the last package of the evening is to a guy at a house in Red Cliffs who sends back a handwritten note that seems to make the bossman happy. He leans back in his chair at the metal desk with his hands behind his head, massive elbows out, looking frighteningly like Jabba the Hutt in a party mood.

'Finally,' Leon says. 'Some fucking good news.'

The sweat stains under his armpits are like dark maws. I try not to stare. Bass from the club is deadening the carpet beneath my feet and light from the streetlamp outside filters in strips through the filthy blinds.

'Here ya go.' Leon releases his hands, reaches down to his desk drawer and comes out with a thick multi-coloured bundle. 'Bonus points. And if you're as smart as I think you are, you'll listen to this pearl of wisdom – don't go blowing it all at once.'

He tosses me the bundle. Small bills, but a lot of them. There's about a grand there. That's my car paid off, and another payment on Dad's debt. I can almost taste the flavour of release.

'I won't.' I look from the bundle to Leon. 'I mean, I won't blow it. I got a use for it.'

'So I hear.' Leon looks at me speculatively.

I stopped feeling like I want to piss my pants in Leon's presence a while ago, but this comment makes me swallow. What does he hear? From who? I'm writing a mental list of what Snowie, or Ando – or even Reggie – might have said about me.

I try not to feel the prickle in my shoulder blades when I shrug. 'Got bills to pay, hey.'

'Not your bills, though.' Leon's eyes are beady. 'You don't gamble.'

I'm gambling right now, aren't I? 'Yeah, well, the bookie doesn't care where the money comes from, so long as he gets what he's owed. Thanks for this.'

Leon doesn't say *You're welcome.* He just inclines his head. I make a quick escape, find Snowie talking on his phone outside the club.

'Ando's at the tatt place getting a touch-up.' Snowie snaps his phone back into his pocket, sees my expression. 'Not that kind of touch-up, ya dirty bastard. Come on, it's a few blocks down.'

We catch up with Barry at the Mildura Hotel, where he's sinking a few beers to line his stomach in preparation for more alcohol later, then wander past the palm-treed traffic island to the corner of Eighth Street. The little shop Snowie's heading for is flanked by another op shop and a place that sells bikes. It's black on the outside: all the dark glass reflects the red and green and white flaring from headlights, stop signs. Barry spits into the the street and lopes behind Snowie, tugs my sleeve to follow.

In spite of my man-of-the-world attitude, I have never actually been inside a tattoo parlour before. The place is small, a long corridor with checkered lino on the floor, a counter on the left and vinyl waiting seats on the right. On the wall above the seats, laminated pictures of tatts are displayed in all their razor-sharp colourful glory: cars, tribals, Japanese waves, titty girls, fauna and flora.

The long counter separates the walk-in area from the business side of things. It looks like a barber's shop, that part. I see mirrors, a bench of white melamine holding neatly shining equipment, racks of ink bottles, desk lamps, white hand towels. A bloke with shaggy ginger hair, wearing latex gloves, is hunched over Ando's stuck-out leg. Ando's in a black tank and trackie pants, sitting in what looks a helluva lot like a dentist's chair, getting work done. The buzz of the needle is loud, like a really big pissed off mosquito, and the tattooist moves smoothly: *buzz*, wipe, *buzz*, wipe.

'How's it going, mate?' Snowie leans over the counter to check out the action.

'S'going good.' Ando, voluble as ever. He's got a stubby in one hand. He and Snowie exchange some chat while I check out the flash.

Barry pokes me, pokes a finger at a picture of a busty blonde riding a pistol barrel. 'Whaddya reckon? I'm thinkin' of getting that done next.'

'Uh, yeah, looks good.' What else am I supposed to say? 'This mate of my old boss, he got "Angel" written on his bicep. Only the tattoo artist was tanked, so now he's got "Angle" spread all over his arm for the whole world to see.'

Barry makes a face.

I scan the shop, but my eyes keep returning to the pictures. The designs look flat and weird divorced from their flesh backgrounds. Some of the tatts have a distinctive realistic style: I figure it must be the same artist. There's photos of newly completed tatts – I squint at them, find them more familiarly real than the flash, if a bit sore-looking. Maybe it's the time I've spent in the hospital, but looking at these photos makes me hear Amie's voice in my head explaining which kind of wound dressing would work best, which paper tape to use.

'You haven't got any ink, have ya, Harris?' Snowie calls to me.

'Huh?' I'm pulled away from contemplating a photo of a koi fish, in lurid golds and reds, gliding over some girl's back. 'Ah, nuh. Nothing like that yet.'

'*Yet*, he says.' Snowie makes a big grin and lifts his chin at me. 'Thought you woulda signed up in Melbourne?'

'Nah.' I make something that could look like a disappointed face. 'Never did. Always too broke, hey.'

'You got cash now,' Snowie challenges.

'Yeah, well.' I shrug.

I got money in my pocket now, sure. But I had some plans for it – like food, maybe, petrol. Some of it will go to Nick's forwarding address, some of it will go to Dad, and the bookie, and sorting out the Five Mile bills. I got no plans to decorate myself with it. I'd be better off buying a new shirt.

'Tell you what,' Snowie says. 'I'll cover you for it.'

'What?'

'You, getting some ink.'

The fuck? I want to say. I don't say that.

'You ripper!' Barry whoops. 'Harris is gettin' his ink on!'

I'd tell him to shut the fuck up but that might come over a bit extreme. I look at Snowie. 'You're gonna pay for me to get a tattoo. Bullshit.'

'No shit, mate. You should go for it. Get Leela to do it.' Snowie is practically crowing. He leans over the counter, gets the attention of ginger bloke. 'Leel on tonight? She up for a greenhorn, you reckon?'

'Yeah, she's out the back,' Ginger replies, stripping off his gloves after fastening a bandage to Ando's leg.

'Hang on –' I start, but don't get to finish.

'Leel!' Ginger calls to someplace over his shoulder. 'Leel! Come out, you got a customer!'

'Snowie –' I try again, but Barry is already slapping me on the back.

'Aah, awesome! Leela's great, she did me arm, wanna have a look?' He rolls his sleeve and waves a garish cowgirl at me. His arms are so woolly, it looks like the cowgirl has a hairy chest.

'Sounds good.' Ando's all done now, easing the leg of his pants down over the bandage as he leans against the counter. 'Whatcha gonna get?'

'Buggered if I know,' I mutter.

'Have a look at the flash behind you,' Ginger offers. 'See something you like, or maybe you got something in mind, Leela can draw it. She's good freehand.'

I hear the clump of boots on lino and the chick in question, who is apparently 'good freehand', dips out suddenly from behind a black velvet curtain at the far right behind the counter. She's smoking a cigarette and her dyed red hair is slashed just below her chin.

She's tiny, even in chunky black boots, and she's good-looking. Older than me, pierced eyebrows arching over kohl-darkened eyes, other piercings at ears and lip. All her silver looks immaculate, like she polished her studs and ball-bearings just this morning. Fingerless fishnet gloves, a kind of rockabilly-goth thing going on with her wardrobe, juicy curves. She's standing there, looking me over like she caught something interesting on her line.

'You the newbie?' She blows out at the ceiling, looks at Snowie. 'This your idea, was it?'

'Sure,' Snowie says, grinning, 'but Harris is keen. You're keen, aren't you, mate?'

I look at Snowie, at the tattooist chick. Feel the eager stares of Barry and Ando.

'Sure,' I say slowly. 'Snowie said he'll cover it.'

'Right.' Leela ashes her smoke on the floor. 'You got anything in mind?'

'Ah…' I make a wave of my hand.

'Take your shirt off,' Leela says.

'What?'

'Take your shirt off,' Leela repeats. 'Turn around and let me look at you.'

This has got to be some rite-of-passage thing: I feel it when I stand my cane against a chair to comply. All the other blokes nudge and snort and stare, make jokey comments. I pull off my hoodie and my T-shirt and turn in a slow circle, my hands held out a little from my sides. I don't feel embarrassed – I know I'm outta shape after the last five weeks, but I've still got a bit of lean muscle on, and enough scars to prove I'm not completely soft. But I've never paraded in front of a girl before with this feeling of being deliberately sized up.

'You don't want any tribal crap, I'm guessing,' Leela says. The bangles on her wrist chime together as she draws and ashes again.

'Dunno,' I say.

'What *do* you know?' Leela stares at me hard.

I shrug, make a face. 'Engines. Quarry work. Lizards, rocks. Dusty shit.'

'Lizards,' Leela says contemplatively. 'Frill-necks?'

'Get a few out our way,' I admit.

'Hm.' She squints a little. 'But you don't look quite like a…' She trails off, begging the question.

'…like a lizard man?' I suggest. 'Nah, never was a big Doors fan.'

Her face is surprised into a grin. 'That's right – the Lizard King! How'd you know about that?'

'My dad. He's into the Doors.' It comes out gruff.

'But not you?'

'Not really.'

She steps closer, absently hands her smoke to Snowie, who takes a long drag. Leela puts her hands on her hips, looks up at me. 'You got nice eyes.'

'Um, thanks.'

'Yeah, but you're not gonna be inkin' his *eyeballs*, are you?' Snowie says, rolling his own eyeballs.

'Shut up, Snow.' Leela makes a little pirouetting motion at me with one finger. 'Lemme see your back again?'

I turn obediently.

'You're never gonna go to fat,' Leela says quietly. She could be talking to herself. 'Not the body type for it. Maybe get a little thick in the gut, when you're older. But your back'll always be nice. Something here, I reckon.'

When she traces one short red-painted fingernail from my shoulder blade to my kidneys, I feel it.

'Something sinuous... Not a lizard.' Her hand turns me by the arm. 'Ever thought of a dragon?'

I shrug, but my face must show my distaste. Dragons are for wankers.

Leela's eyes narrow. 'What about a snake?'

My eyes drag back to the flash on the wall. There's snakes there, all types. Some of them punch out of flesh, fangs bared. If I'm gonna go through with this, I don't want anything grotesque.

'Not like that,' I say.

'Nah, but look at this.' She points at a picture high on the wall. 'King cobra. No colours, just monochrome. Or this.'

She taps another picture. I see a stark angular head, muscular brown coils.

'You put that on many people?' I ask.

She smiles, showing teeth. 'Only you, baby.'

Sounds like bullshit to me, but she's walking back behind the counter now, grabbing latex gloves. She pats the dentist's chair invitingly. 'C'mon up here. Straddle backwards.'

'Nice choice,' Ando says, nodding his approval.

I baulk. 'You're just gonna ink it straight on?'

'Draw it first.' Leela snaps into the gloves. 'Check the fit, then we start.' She looks over at Snowie. 'Two sessions. He'll need touch-ups and shading next week. Three hundred.'

'Jesus.' Snowie looks reluctant for the first time. 'C'mon, Leel. Don't I bring business in?'

Leela shrugs. 'Two-fifty.'

Snowie gives me a look of appeal. 'You don't wanna go for something smaller?'

Leela makes a disgusted noise. 'You want him to get a tramp stamp? Fucking hell, Snow.'

I raise my hands, like I'm helpless. Actually, I'm kind of enjoying watching Snowie squirm.

The dentist's chair has been wiped clean with Windex, or something that smells like it. The vinyl is cold on my stomach. I straddle the seat awkwardly, shoving my left leg into place, balancing my cane. Leela appears in front of me, swivelled forward on a wheeled office stool, pulling her hair back with a band.

'Little accident, was it?' She nods her chin at my denim-covered leg, at the cane.

'Something like that.'

'He got shot,' Barry pipes up. Jesus – if his mouth opened much wider, all his teeth'd fall out.

Leela lifts her eyebrows, making the ball bearings dance.

'It fucking hurt, is all I know,' I grit.

Leela swivels back to someplace behind me. 'Right. Well, this is gonna hurt, too.'

'I figured,' I say drily, and she laughs.

The tracing on takes about twenty-five minutes. Snowie gets bored in that time, and he and Ando go up the road for another beer. By the time they mosey back I'm standing side-on to the mirror, trying to see over my left shoulder. Barry's holding a hand mirror helpfully to one side.

'Looks awesome,' he enthuses. His mouth might always be flapping, but Barry's party spirit is kind of endearing. At least he's keen.

Even Snowie seems to catch a bit of it. He leans on the counter, lighting a smoke. 'Yeah, value for money, I reckon.'

Leela tilts her head critically. She angles me this way and that like I'm a hanging cut of meat, pushing my arm up so she can see the shape move. 'Yeah, I think it'll be all right. This bit over your hip looks good. I'll add most of the detail with the outline now. It'll look even better when the shading's done.'

'C'mon, get on with it then,' Ando says, grinning. 'We wanna hear him squawk.'

So I sit back in the chair with my legs dangling in front and my chest against the vinyl. I cross my arms on the headrest, lean my chin against them.

'Have much to drink?' There's a snap as Leela dons fresh gloves.

'Um, not really. Just a few beers. Should I have had more?'

She snorts. 'Booze makes you bleed.' She pats my arm with one latex-covered hand, picks up this thing that trails wires. It matches the chair: some kind of drill for sadistic dentists. Now she's got my full attention. 'Okay, this is it. You sure?'

I nod.

She gives me an intent look. 'Be sure. This is forever.'

Forever. Forever and a day. Until my blood and bones and skin all pass away. Something for this moment, and for every other moment to come. My decision, my mark, my choice – something *I* chose, not something my father chose for me.

I nod again, more firmly.

She scoots back around and I hear the buzzing of the needle ignite, like a hive of bees. And then the pain starts.

*

'You got all that?'

'I've got it,' Amie says, as she fixes the tape on my leg. 'The part about Marcus Anderson will be the part Dad's really interested in. Now are you gonna tell me why you've got a massive dressing on your back, or are you just gonna let me guess?'

Driving down to Ouyen for my final appointment, my shirt felt strange against my skin. The extra padding from the bandage made me squirm. Or maybe I was squirming at the idea of Amie realising what I'd done.

'I got a tattoo.' I'm torn between being pleased she noticed and preferring to show it off when it's finished. 'You done with my leg?'

'You got a – yes, I'm done, put your pants back on.' She waves that away. '*Harris.* Did you say you got a tatt?'

I slide off the corner of the table to zip, manoeuvre back on to do my socks. 'Yeah, it's nothin'.'

'It's not nothing, it's something.' Amie leans around to catch my eye, and I'm relieved to see she's grinning. 'Can I look?'

'It's not finished yet,' I protest.

'Please? Can I peek?' Her fingers brush my neck as she eases the collar of my T-shirt back. 'Oh, I can see the edge of it. It's, ah, a big tattoo, Harris. Can I take the dressing off? I'll tape it up again, I promise.'

'Yeah, I guess.' I'm self-conscious about it all of a sudden. 'I s'pose you could check if it's healing okay. I can't really see it properly to tell.'

She snorts. 'Well, yeah, it's on your back.'

She moves behind me and suddenly I feel this mind-blowing sensation, which is *Amie taking my shirt off*. The air is cool on my chest and back as she slides the fabric off me. She makes me lift my arms up, angles her head to give me a quick grin. We're doing this together, this undressing. For a second, I get dizzy, like bells are clanging hard in my head. I can't think. My breath comes in short.

'Here,' she says from behind me, 'let me unstick this. I don't wanna hurt you –'

'You're not...you're not hurting me.' My voice sounds weird. The bandage sticks in a few spots. The sharp tugs on my skin bring me back to myself.

'Oh my god,' she breathes.

'Is it okay?'

'Haven't you seen it?'

'Tell you the truth, I've been a bit scared to look,' I admit.

'It's *amazing*. Hang on, there's one more piece of tape... Holy crap.' I can hear the smile in her voice. 'My god, who did this? It's incredible.'

I shrug my unmarked shoulder. 'Just this tattooist on Eighth Street.'

'Well, it's frickin' *cool*. And it's *huge*.' She leans around again, her smile lighting up her face. 'Harris, you've got a massive naga on your back.'

'Naga?'

'A snake. A naga, a samp – that's what my Nani calls them. They have a lot of meanings in some Indian religions.'

'Like what?'

She stands at my shoulder as she explains, her hands moving

excitedly. 'Snakes are supposed to be powerful. Most of the old stories portray snakes as sacred beings, either for good or evil. Sometimes it depends on how they're depicted. Sometimes it depends on the number of heads they have.'

That makes me grin. 'This guy's only got one head.'

She raises an eyebrow, grins back. 'Well, that's an odd number, so it means infinity. Like my name. Because everything in the universe came from One.'

'Like your name?'

'Yeah. Amita. It means...' She searches for the best word. 'Boundless. Limitless.'

'*Limitless*. I like that.'

I do like it. It's a great word. Lots of promise. I like the way Amie blushes when she talks about it, too. She ducks around behind me again so I can't see.

'It's healing up fine.' I feel her prod at the tattoo edge. 'Is it irritating you?'

'Nah. Well, it's itchy sometimes. But it's okay.'

'Are you putting Bepanthen on it?'

'Yeah. Trying to, anyway.' I twist my head sideways to squint at her. 'How do you know about it?'

She colours. 'Oh, well – Nick. He's kind of obsessed with tatts. He's had some work done on his back and legs, from some guy in Melbourne.' She tugs gently on a lower piece of tape. 'There's more bandage here.'

'Yeah, it goes over my hip.'

'That's why your jeans are slung so low.' She nods as if she's contemplating that. 'How far down does it go?'

Her hand darts for the waistband of my jeans. I grab her wrist just in time. 'Far enough.'

Holding her wrist lightly only reminds me of the places she's not touching. I don't think I could keep up a conversation if she touched me there. In fact, it's probably better if I don't even think about it.

'Oh, right. So it's okay for the tattooist to see it, but not me?' She shakes me off, her eyebrows raised. 'Harris, I saw you when you came out of surgery.'

I startle. 'Not all of me.'

'You had a drape.' She shrugs.

I relax enough to snort. 'Yeah, well that's not all of me. This goes underneath my jocks, so I think we'll just leave it at that, hey?'

'Fine, then. Prude.'

'Prude?' My own eyebrows go up. 'Really? I been called a lotta things, but that's definitely a new one.'

She pouts, her lips making that pillowy shape...aaand I think it's time I put my shirt back on.

'Hang on, let me fix the bandage...' Amie fusses with the tape as she re-fastens the white padding. 'You're kind of getting into the role, then, getting a tatt.'

'Snowie paid for it,' I admit. 'But it wasn't just for the job. It was for me.' I ease my T-shirt carefully over my head, my back. 'I haven't really had that for a while.'

Amie's expression changes as she comes around to face me. 'You're a good person, Harris. You know that, right?' I snort, and she becomes insistent. 'No, it's true. Don't blow it off.'

'I'm no more good than anybody else,' I say firmly. 'I mean, look at you. You're committed, too.'

'I'm not living in it – you are. You're doing a really full-on thing. You need to be so careful.' She's concentrating on her hands as she packs away the medical supplies. 'I used to believe if you're a good person, good things happen to you. But I was kind of proved wrong when Mum died. She was good, and then she died. Just remember, *good* doesn't equal *safe*. I've heard plenty of

211

stories from Dad about shitty things happening to nice people.'

It makes me feel warm, that Amie thinks I'm a nice person. But I don't want her to be disillusioned when she realises the truth. 'Well, I get that. My mum was a good person, too, but Dad made her life really miserable. She left before it got too serious.'

'Too dangerous, you mean?'

I examine my hands. 'Yeah, I guess. And my sister was so little...'

Amie stops where she stands. 'You have a sister?'

I didn't mean to mention that. I move on quickly. 'Anyway, I can understand why my mum left. How stressed she must've been.'

'But...she left you behind.' Amie looks genuinely shocked.

A sudden smarting pain smacks me in the chest, deep inside. 'Yeah, but my dad didn't really give her any say in the matter. He set terms.'

'And...you were part of the terms,' Amie says.

This isn't as much of a revelation for me as it is for her, but it still makes the pain in my chest thrum. I clear my throat but my voice comes out husky. 'Being a nice person has never been something I've learnt to see as an advantage.'

Amie's eyes hold a challenge. 'So why do you keep trying to be one?'

'Who says I'm trying?' I half-grin, squint at her. 'What about you? Who are you being good for?'

She shrugs, like it's not as important as we both know it is. 'For Mum, I guess. And for my dad. But I don't believe anymore that being good automatically immunises you from harm, or brings you luck.'

'Well, you can't play it safe all the time.'

'I guess. I just...' Amie seems to be avoiding looking at me. 'I worry about you.'

'That's...' Probably the nicest thing anyone's ever said to me? Can I say that? But I reckon I need to spell something out to her. 'Amie, that means a lot. But you don't have to carry all my shit.'

'But –'

'Seriously. Don't go getting all responsible. You've got enough on your plate. Feel free to look *out* for me – it's nice, and I appreciate it. But don't look *after* me. I can look after myself.'

I leave the hospital, and Amie, a few minutes later, flop into the car for the drive back to Mildy. The wheat fields on every side of me are darkening into a cold yellow sea. Sunset seeps up, hits the arses of the clouds and tans their hides pink.

Amie worries about me. Now there's a concept. She worries about a lot of people, though: her dad, her nanna... I'm just one of many. I don't want to be another load she has to shoulder, another person her thoughts spin pointlessly around.

I try to keep my mind on the reality. She's got her problems and I've got mine. I need to stay loose. I got Dad, I don't need anything else tying me down. When this job is done I'm cutting outta here – to Melbourne, to wherever, as far away from Dad as I can manage. Find Mum and Kelly, if I can. Stoking the fire in my belly over an unattainable girl isn't gonna get me anywhere.

By the time I get to Hattah, I'm so tired that the red-and-white road markers are making neon tracers in my vision. Like those glowsticks me and Mike used to buy from Metcalfe's grocery when we were kids – we'd put strings on them and spin them around our heads to make a firefly lasso...

That's all I can think about as I'm driving home: fireflies spinning, circling endlessly through centrifugal force around the person at the centre. And the question keeps returning again and again: who am I circling around?

14

amie

'...there will be decorations to hang, and food to prepare, and your auntie is working all day on Sunday –'

'Nani, I'm coming, okay?' I tap my pen on the keyboard in front of me. 'I said I was coming, it's just I've got Sunday night shift until six-thirty the next morning. But I promised Auntie I'd drive up straight after.'

'You will be tired,' Nani says. 'Driving after working all night.'

She's right: I'll be stuffed by the time I make it to Mildura on Monday morning. Although if I get in early I might be able to wrangle a nap before Hansa needs me in the kitchen. I can worry about that later. This bloody wedding – it's still five days away, but Nani must be stressed about it if she's calling me on my mobile.

'I'll be fine,' I reassure her. 'I'll drink a lot of coffee and I'll definitely be there.' A car pulls into the emergency ambulance bay, which is strictly not allowed. They'd better have a good excuse. 'Nani, I have to go, I'm staffing the front desk at work. I'll call you again tomorrow, all right?'

I swap hurried goodbyes, and I'm just slipping my phone into the pocket of my uniform pants when a gnarled hand slaps the blue counter top.

'I'm sorry, but you can't –' I start on the standard spiel, jerk to a halt.

A pair of red-rimmed brown eyes stare into mine. *'Tell me where he is.'*

Dennis Derwent has cheeks like sandstone caves, and antipathy seems to seep out of his pores. Plus booze – booze is a sour constant with Mr Derwent, as if he's wearing vodka cologne. His clothes are dusty and there's dirt under his nails.

I think quickly: Barb is not on shift. Penny is in Exam Room Three, dealing with an Urgent Care case. Unless another staff member walks past, I'm on my own. I consider whether to press the security buzzer.

'I know you all *know*.' He lays the snark on thick. 'Now I'm not gonna stand here and listen to some bullshit about –'

'Mr Derwent,' I say evenly, 'you can't park in the ambulance bay. I'm happy to talk to you but first you need to –'

'Tell me where my son is!' His hand thumps on the counter again, fisted this time. 'He can't stay hid forever. He's *my* son. *Mine*. You got no right –'

'Mr Derwent, I'm sorry, but I don't know where Harris is.' The lie falls out of me easily. I back it up with truth. 'Even if I did, we're not legally permitted to pass on patients' personal information without –'

'Don't you gimme that crap about legal permission!' Dennis flicks my words away. 'That fat cow said a month, and it's been a bloody month. I know he's around someplace – is he in Ouyen? Or has he gone back to Melbourne?'

The thick counter stands between us and I should feel protected, but I don't. I've dealt with irate patients and their families before. Dennis Derwent is in a different class.

But the way he speaks to me, the way he speaks about Barb, and his own son, lends me some steel. 'I can't give you Harris's address, Mr Derwent.' I steeple my fingers against the desk top, push down hard. 'Please go and move your ute out of the ambulance bay.'

Dennis bears forward, venom sparking out of him with every word. 'Fuck the ute. I'm not bein' ordered around by a bloody teenager.' He shakes his head. 'When I catch that boy, I swear...'

That boy. I stood next to that boy only a few days ago, heard some of his history. I think I'm starting to get a fuller picture of how Harris became the person he is now. The armour he's constructed around himself, piece by bleeding piece, and why he needed it so badly.

My voice goes flat. 'I'm sure Harris will tell you where he's living when he's ready. He can make his own decisions.'

'Harris? Make his own decisions?' Dennis thrusts himself so far over the countertop, I see his wrinkles and whiskers in close-up. '*I'm* his fucking father. *I* make the decisions. It's not your job to interfere, it's got nothing to do with you. Now gimme that ledger –'

He grabs for the daybook sitting open on the desk in front of me, which is ridiculous because it doesn't even hold personal records. I'm not gonna let him snatch it, though.

'Hey, give that back!' I grab for the ledger. The pages scrunch and tear as I wrestle Dennis for it, and I feel it when my fingernails scrape his hand.

'Shit!' He holds up his red-marked hand, his expression thunderous. 'You rotten little bitch!'

For a sick old alcoholic, Dennis moves like lightning. He grabs my shirt front in his fist, yanks me against the counter. His lips are wet with spittle. He looks demented. I'm half-stunned that it's escalated so fast. Then my hip whacks against the edge of the desk and I react without thinking: I rear back and smack him hard across the face.

His eyes bulge and his cheek goes white. Before it has a chance to redden, he lifts his arm, fist balled –

Another hand grabs his wrist.

'*Right* – no you don't.' Mel Stubbins twists Dennis's arm up and back until he yowls and releases me.

I stumble, right myself; I've never been so glad to see the flash of Mel's white uniform shirt.

She has a hand sunk into the scrawny meat of Dennis's nape. 'Back off *right now*, Dennis, or I'll break your bloody arm.'

Dennis struggles. '*You fucking –*'

'Right now, I said! I put you outta here last time, and I'm happy to do it again.' Holding Dennis's arm at what looks like a very painful angle and ignoring his cursing protests, Mel nods at Allan Waugh, the other security manager, as he comes running up the hall.

'You right, Mel?'

'All sorted, Allan. Might be good if you stick around, though.' Mel frog-marches Dennis over to the waiting seats, spins him around and pushes him down. 'Sit down. *No* – don't you bloody move. What a dickhead you are, Dennis, I swear to god… Amie, are you okay, love?'

I'm actually a bit winded. The hospital can be a challenging place, but this has never happened to me before. I watch Dennis sneer and writhe under Mel's arm. My god, how did Harris live with this man for twenty years?

'I'm fine. I'm okay.' I straighten, smoothing myself down. One of the buttons on my work shirt is only hanging by a thread. 'He was trying to take the daybook –'

'She fucking slapped me!' Dennis's eyes are still wild.

Mel rounds on Dennis. 'You shut your mouth. *I'll* slap you in a minute if you're not careful.' She presses on his shoulder with one strong hand before looking back at me. 'D'you wanna call your dad? Cos if Dennis spent the night in the lock-up it wouldn't be the first time, and you'd be well within your rights –'

'I just want him gone.' I glance out at the ute in the ambulance bay. 'Put him in his car, but if he comes back here, go for it.'

'We'll see him out, no worries,' Allan says.

I walk around the admissions desk until I'm right in front of Harris's father. My voice is shaking, but I enunciate very clearly. 'What you've done is illegal, Mr Derwent. If you come back here we'll call the police. And if you come anywhere near me again, I'll have you charged. Do you understand me?'

He mutters under his breath, looking baleful, with Mel leaning on him.

'Do you understand me?' I repeat. His lips purse over a curse. I feel my own lips curl down as I look at Mel. 'I think he understands. Get him out. There's people here trying to get well.'

Mel and Allan escort Mr Derwent to the ute and bundle him in. He mutters and swears the whole time, then finally gives up – slams his own door, guns the engine and takes off for the exit with a squeal of rubber.

'What a pathetic man...' Mel says when she returns. 'Press the buzzer next time, darl, if you need me.'

'There wasn't time.'

She puts a hand on my back. 'Sure you're okay? You look like a ghost, and no wonder.'

'I'm okay,' I say, but I can hear in my voice how all my limbs are suddenly tired.

'Allan, could you get Amie a nice hot cuppa?' Mel asks. 'That'd be great.'

Allan disappears, and Mel walks me back to the desk. I sink into the wheeled office chair, push it away from the counter; I don't want to sit near any space Dennis Derwent has just occupied.

Mel hovers to the side. 'You'll need to give me a statement, love. He's already been in strife here, we need it for the record. Just in case.'

My shift finishes an hour later. I spend the entire drive home mulling over whether to tell Dad what happened with Dennis Derwent before deciding it's unavoidable. He'll only hear about it on the grapevine anyway, and he'll be hurt I didn't let him know.

'He grabbed you? Like, really grabbed you?' Dad asks.

'And then I hit him, yes.' I glance at Dad's expression as he puts his mug of tea down on the table. 'Please don't go all Dirty Harry on me, Dad. I've had enough of that aggro rubbish for one day.'

But Dad is still glowering. 'Don't tell me how to do my job. If anyone deserves a personal call, it's that bastard –'

'It won't change anything. Dennis will still be a bastard after you leave.' Harris's comment about his father – *he's just mean* – seems pretty bang-on. 'If he comes back to the hospital he'll be evicted on sight. And he doesn't come in from Five Mile often enough for me to run into him on the street.'

'But –'

'You'd only be making it worse. Dad, it's over. I handled it. Let it go. There's too many bastards in the world to bother about them all on a case-by-case basis.'

'You've pretty much just nailed my job description,' Dad says, but then he stops, sighs out his nose. 'Okay, fine. I'll leave it. But you're heading for Mildura on Monday morning, aren't you? For the wedding? I want you to skip your next shift and go tomorrow.'

'Dad –'

'No. That's it. You're going. Give yourself some space and give Dennis a chance to cool down. I can't guarantee I'll be friendly next time I see him.'

It's a concession, but one I'm prepared to live with. I ring work to give them the bad news, then Nani, who thinks it's fantastic. I also contact Robbie to let her know we should get together while I'm in town.

'Whoo, baby!' she exclaims. 'This will be ace. I wanna go to this club in town…'

'Sounds good.' It's the last thing I feel like right now, but whatever.

'So have you signed up for an interview yet? Girl, if you get that residency I'm gonna tell everyone how your career as a famous photographer was all because of me.'

Famous photographer – yeah, right. 'I'm, uh, still working out a day.'

She crows down the line. 'They'll take you, Amie. I can feel it in my waters!' Her voice turns speculative. 'Hey, have you seen Harris Derwent lately? Is he out of hospital now? I thought I saw him on Langtree Avenue a few days ago, but it might've just been someone with a resemblance – he's probably back in Ouyen, doing the dirty with Della Metcalfe, am I right?'

My limp smile changes. 'Uh, he's out of hospital, yeah. You might have seen him, I think he has mates in Mildura. But I don't know what he's getting up to with Della – none of my business.'

I finish the call, my stomach churning. I should be worried about Robbie spotting Harris in Mildura, but I'm not. It's the other part of what she said that got me. I remember Harris's pink phone, the words that went with it – *me and Dell have some history*. I joked about it then. Why don't I feel like joking now?

Later that night I text Harris: *Hospital appointment changed – call for further details.*

He gets back to me within an hour. 'You're coming to Mildura? When?'

'Earlier than expected. I'll be arriving tomorrow to help my cousins get ready for the wedding.' I consider whether to tell him about the scene at work with Dennis, discount the idea just as quickly. If Dad got that angry about it I'd hate to think how Harris might react. 'We'll need to figure out a place to meet.'

He's silent for a second, then his voice goes warm. 'The river. There's plenty of quiet places along the banks, near the old pipe factory. I'll meet you there, and we can drive further in. Lemme suss out a day and time and I'll text.'

I finish the call quickly. I can't deny the soft pulse of excitement inside me, like a heartbeat. Harris and I will get to meet in private, away from prying eyes at the hospital. Just the two of us, sitting on the Murray River's bank.

But I need to flatten that feeling, squash it back down. Harris and I have become friends. We've shared some personal details with each other. It doesn't mean I should let myself think our relationship is personal in a different sense. I will not be *that girl* – that dewy-eyed girl.

Harris has his own life, his own agenda...and a long torrid history. He doesn't need me mooning and sighing. He knows plenty of girls who'd be happy to do that for him.

*

My aunt's house is a single-storey double-brick with a fortress-like fence. An elaborate yellow-painted gate, much taller than me, lets you through to the front yard. In the gardens on either side of the concrete path are loquat trees, jasmine trailing everywhere, plenty of greens and pinks, flowers in bloom with the season. My aunt lost her husband, Deepan, to a drunk driver more than fifteen years ago. She plants a new rose in his honour every spring.

When mum died I spent a lot of time here at Hansa's. After Mum's funeral, Dad did his best to keep it together at our place.

Things began to get on top of him though. I remember coming home from school one afternoon and finding Dad still slumped in the same chair at the kitchen table he'd been in when I'd left that morning. The love of his life was gone, and his whole world had fallen apart. Just like mine.

That's when it was decided I'd go up to Mildura to live for a while.

It wasn't until I arrived at this house that I realised how quiet my own had been. Here was conversation, colour, routine, and – for bonus points – two female cousins who let me sit in their room and look at their magazines and gossip with them. Jasminder would plonk me on her bed and brush my hair. It wasn't a replacement for my mum, but it went a long way towards salving the wound.

So this house means a lot to me. Beyond the rosebushes on the left is the rising driveway and the carport, which provides a covered walkway to a brick studio. The studio is supposed to be a guest room bedsit, but it's only ever been used as a place to store junk. My aunt tried to do it up once, with a nice day-bed and couch for Nani, but there was no way Nani was ever going to live anywhere but right in the thick of things, so she has her own room in the house.

Auntie Hansa waves a hand at the studio as she ushers me through the front yard. 'Beena has cleaned up there for you if you want to stay outside. But I thought you might like to stay inside, in Jasminder's room.'

'Beena cleaned up the outhouse?' That was always what we used to call it, amongst ourselves.

'I wouldn't really call it *cleaning*. More, *pushing things over to the walls*.' Hansa helps me get my suitcase through the doorway. 'But come in, have tea first, and then you can decide.'

I've barely dumped my suitcase when my aunt pushes me

through the living room with the enormous portrait of Guru-ji above the mantelpiece, and into the kitchen. The kitchen is basically the soul of the house. Hansa positions me on a high stool at the kitchen island and bustles to get me a drink from the fridge. It's mango cup, one of Nani's specialities, with a liberal quantity of ice. It tastes like home.

'Now, tell me how your father is,' Hansa asks as she moves from sink to electric kettle to crockery cupboard, collecting the tea things. 'And Nani says you have a friend leaving town.'

I give my aunt the potted versions of all the news, including a debrief on the CNA job. My aunt is Head of Nursing at Mallee Health here in Mildura, so she knows the ins and outs of the job. It was something she and my mum always had in common: they both knew the nursing life.

When it's her turn, my aunt shares all the excitement about the preparations for Jas's wedding. I find it all a bit staggering. 'My god, Mami-ji, there's so much organisation involved!'

'Not to mention the cooking, and the shopping, and the cost. Oh my god, the cost!' Hansa shakes her head. 'Ah, well, these are my daughters. I do my best for them, yes?' She smiles, brushes back my hair. 'And one day, with your father's blessing, I will do wonderful things for you, also.'

The idea I might be expected to go through something like this myself at some point is more than I can imagine right now. I take a breath, set down my glass. 'Mami-ji, is Nani going okay? When I've been on the phone with her lately she's sounded a little...disoriented.'

'Nani hasn't been in the best of health,' Hansa confesses. 'She's all right, but she's getting older, Amie. We're keeping an eye on her.' She changes the subject quickly. 'Now, you should find a room and unpack.'

'Is it okay if I take the outhouse? Beena's already gone to the

223

trouble of cleaning it up. Jasminder has her hands full, and she'll probably need her sleep. She doesn't need to be tripping over me in her bedroom as well.'

By lunchtime I'm installed in the little bedsit studio, and already busy helping Hansa prepare dinner. Then Beena arrives back home and there's a lot of hugging and squealing.

'Oh my god,' Beena says breathlessly, 'you have to show me what you're wearing for Mehndi Night. And then you have to tell me what I'm wearing doesn't look too over-the-top.'

'Bee-bee, she's only just arrived!' Hansa rolls her eyes at me. 'She's been waiting for you to come.'

Beena drags me back down the hall to her room to do a fashion audit. She shows me the jewellery she's borrowed for the wedding. 'Mum is wearing Nani's, and I'm wearing Mum's, and Jas is wearing some from the boy's family and some from Nani, so everyone is being placated. Are you wearing a sari to the ceremony?'

I actually have two options, a sari and a salwar kameez, so it's good to have someone to consult about what to wear.

'I think the sari for the wedding,' Bee confirms, 'and the salwar kameez for Monday. And great, you're wearing your mother's jewellery. What about your shoes?'

I show her. 'Are you working this week?'

Beena is studying nursing – our family is chock-full of nurses, my god – and has been working at Mallee Health, in a different unit to her mother, for about a year.

But now she shakes her head. 'I took two weeks' leave, starting last Sunday, and thank god I did. Mum's been running around like a lunatic, and she doesn't finish work herself until tomorrow – they couldn't spare her. I've been doing most of the organising and shopping.' She grins. 'It's so good you arrived early. Now I have someone to whinge to. Jas won't hear it, and Mum doesn't have time to deal.'

'Where *is* Jas? And where's Nani?'

'They're together. Jasminder wanted to look at dinner sets, and Nani insisted on going, too.' Beena re-folds my Mehndi Night kameez, lowers her voice. 'Hey, are you going out this week? Like, to a club or something?'

'Well, I told Robbie I'd catch up with her at some point...' I almost don't want to explain because I think I know where this is going.

Sure enough, Beena makes a pleading face. 'Then will you take me along? Please? Amie, I'm dying, I need to get out. Mum keeps saying we should just concentrate on the wedding, but all I've done for a month is work, wedding-plan, go to college, and sit with Nani in front of the TV in the living room. If I have to watch *Devdas* one more time, I'm gonna spew.'

I hesitate, reluctant to be the meat in the sandwich. 'Bee, if your Mum doesn't want you going out –'

'But if I go with you, and we say we're meeting Robbie, I'm sure she'd be okay. I mean, Girls' Night Out. That sounds pretty sedate, right?'

I pause, then nod. 'Okay, I'll do my best. But it depends on your mum.'

She hugs me ecstatically. 'Amie, you're a lifesaver!'

Nani and Jasminder don't get home for another hour. When I hear Nani's quavering voice saying, 'Is she here yet? Has she arrived?' in Punjabi, I take my hands out of the bowl I'm mixing roti in, wipe off fast and go out to greet her.

'Amita!' Nani's arms are outstretched. 'Ah, bebe, come here to me!'

She's thinner than I remember: her pale yellow salwar kameez billows over her bony edges, and the sharp line of her nose seems more severe. Her hair, under her dubatta, seems more white than steel now, and the arm of her glasses is held on with tape. I take in all of this in an instant, like I've clicked the shutter on a memory.

I do namaste, and a quick '*Sat sri akal*', but we're both more excited to exchange hugs. 'Oh, Nani-ji, I've missed you!' My eyes well up, although I promised myself I wouldn't make a scene.

'Ah, my girl...' Nani's own eyes are shiny with emotion, and she squeezes me hard. 'My girl has come back home.'

Later, after family dinner is over, Hansa helps me shove around some extra junk in the outhouse to make it more habitable: my aunt has an enormous collection of plastic storage boxes. I'm just making up the bed with fresh sheets when there's a knock on the open door.

'Turn on the heating, Amita,' Nani's standing there with a giant pillow, a pillow case and towel balanced on top. 'You will get cold out here.'

I walk over and take the things out of her hands. 'It's warm enough, Nani-ji. It's the middle of September.'

We stand in the doorway for a moment looking across the carport to the house. The smell of cumin and star anise lingers on my hands. The eaves of the house are bright with fairy lights to mark the approaching wedding.

This house isn't only where I recovered from my mother's death. It's also the place where I realised how deeply my parents had loved each other.

For my mother to move out of her family and community and follow a white Aussie policeman to a dusty rural blip like Walpeup... And for my father – then only a senior constable staffing a tiny cop shop that served all the surrounding countryside – to woo and marry a young nurse from a culture and community so different to the one he was raised in... It really must have taken something powerful, something heroic, for both of them.

I squeeze the pillow in my arms as I study the fairy lights. 'My mum and dad had something special, didn't they?'

Nani reaches up to touch my hair. 'When you fall in love, you will know. You will feel it, like it is a part of you that has always been searching, and now it has found a home.'

I think of Harris's green eyes, push the thought away. 'My mother had to find her home in a new place, though. Away from everything she knew.'

'Your mother was very brave.' Nani traces my cheek gently. 'She knew what she wanted, and when she found it, there was no turning back.'

My mind tumbles with a dozen different things as I look at her: Barb and my job, Nick's expression before he left, Harris's husky voice over the phone, my father's weathered face, Nani's own health, the deadline for the residency paperwork I've brought with me in the purple folder all this way... The deadline is the end of next week and I still don't know which way to jump.

'I get scared sometimes, Nani,' I whisper. 'What if I have to be brave, take risks like Mum? I'm no good at taking risks. What if I don't have the courage to do it?'

'Amita, stop worrying,' Nani chides. 'Or worry now about catching cold out here in this draughty room.'

Nani takes the pillow back, walks over to the newly-made bed and starts struggling the pillow into its case. I hold the corners to make it easier for her. Watching her, my eyes get all leaky. 'Nani, I'm sorry it's been such a long time since I last visited –'

'Shh, no, let us not say sorries. Let us only be happy you've come.'

I blink at her use of the collective 'us', keep my gaze on the pillow-battle. 'Nanaa-ji is happy too?'

'Of course,' Nani says. 'Didn't you see him smiling all through dinner?'

*

The next few days blur into one another in a riot of silken dubatta, golden jewellery, the smells of dahl and fresh roti, as we prepare for the onslaught of the wedding.

Mehndi Night starts on Monday afternoon. Beena and I both get our mehndi done early; we need to have hands free to help with serving food. I need my hands for the camera, as well – I've brought it with me especially to do the photography for the wedding, on Hansa's request.

By six it seems like the entire female Punjabi population of Mildura is occupying the living room. Women sit on the furniture or on the floor cushions, drinking, eating, crooning suhaag and making teasing jokes. *Mehndi Laga Ke Rakhna* is jangling from the dock, mixed with the sound of dozens of voices talking at once. The mehndi artist works her way slowly around the room, used to the demands of pre-wedding crowds and jittery brides-to-be.

Jas is patient at first, but she gets cranky once she realises she'll have to sit still for the next four or more hours, while we dab lemon-sugar solution on her hands and feet.

'I can't even feed myself!' She slumps back in her comfortable spot on the sofa. 'I feel like a giant baby.'

I smile at her, teasing as I take another photo. 'Lap it up, Jas. You'll be looking after your own house and taking care of a husband after this, with no one to fuss over you.'

'Exactly!' Hansa sits on her low stool, feeding her daughter bite-sized chunks of samosa with a grin. 'Enjoy it while you can!'

There are no men here tonight so the conversation in the living room quickly turns naughty. Jasminder has to sit on the sofa, pretending to look demure, while listening to all the suggestions and advice dished out by the older women. I don't understand everything they're saying in Punjabi, but what I do understand makes my face go red.

'What about this girl?' one of the elderly aunties says, lifting her chin at me. 'Is she engaged yet?'

'Not yet,' Hansa says, giving me a smile. 'Amita is only the same age as Beena.'

'My son is a nice Sikh man looking for a wife!' another auntie cackles.

Bee nudges me with the tray of mithai sweets she's carrying. 'So are you seeing anyone, really?'

My cheeks are already like a furnace. 'Ah, um –'

I'm saved by the chime from my phone. I look down at the screen and am shocked to find a text from Harris: *New appointmt Tue 25 @3pm ok?*

Bee gives me a grin. 'Is that your boyfriend?'

'What?'

'You're blushing.'

I don't meet her eyes. 'Hard to avoid around here right now. This room is hot as a sauna.'

I scrabble a quick *Ok* in reply. Everyone will be busy and distracted tomorrow afternoon during the preparation for jaago. I shouldn't have too much trouble slipping out for an hour.

*

'What's that?' Harris is looking at my hands. 'You been drawing on yourself or something?'

'It's mehndi.' I put my camera down on the ground beside me and stick one hand out, palm up, for display. 'For the wedding. I had to help at a party for my cousin, the bride-to-be. Like a bridal shower.'

The old pipe factory was signposted. Harris insisted the place was too exposed for us to talk, drove us both in the Pitbull to a spot further along the winding dirt road that follows the river.

The place we're sitting now, under trees near the water, is secluded enough for privacy. The day is bright so it's hard to understand his caution, and the light here is so nice I want to use the camera as more than just an excuse to get out of the house.

'A bridal shower.' Harris leans back against a log. 'Where they draw on your hands.'

'It's like a temporary tattoo,' I explain. 'You mix henna powder up with hot water, or black tea, or lemon juice –'

'Lemon juice?'

'To make it darker. Then you trace it on, leave it for a while, rub it off with mustard oil, and you've got this.'

'Right.' He sits up, grabs my hand and leans forward to look more closely. 'It goes over the top, too.'

'Yep.' He's cradling my right hand in both of his. A light warm humming has started in the small of my back.

He circles my wrist with his fingers, tracing the dark lines. 'Show me the other one?' I line up both my palms together, and now he's starting to get it. 'They match.'

'Um, yeah.' The pads of his fingers tickle on my skin. I clear my throat. 'They're mirror images, see? And then you put jewellery on – bangles and stuff. You get more jewellery around your ankles, sometimes on your toes.'

'That's cool.' He releases me, sits back. 'You're going to a wedding.'

'I can't really get out of it,' I admit. 'My cousin, Jasminder, and her family... I lived with them for while after Mum died. They took care of me.'

'So you feel obliged.'

'Yes, but I want to go. A wedding is a big deal for the family. Dad's driving up early tomorrow to attend. And Nani's putting the thumbscrews on me to dress up properly, and put on all the make-up and jewellery...'

'You'd look good, all dressed up and stuff.' He catches my eye.

'I mean, not that you don't look good without it –' Now his face has gone all rosy. 'I mean –'

'It's okay, Harris. I get what you mean.' I grin, rest back on my elbows on the grass and leaf litter. 'The downside is the wedding will be exhausting. It's, like, all day, and into the evening. We had the mehndi last night, and tonight is jaago, kind of a pre-wedding party. Then tomorrow is the ceremony. It's just...really full-on.'

'I've never been to a wedding,' Harris says, contemplative.

'If this is the last one I go to, I won't complain.' I see his amused expression. 'I mean, it's lovely, but I don't know if getting married is high on my list just yet.'

'Fair enough.' He frowns. 'What *do* you wanna do? I mean, you just finished high school. You skipped the chance to go travelling... There must be something.'

'I don't know.' I study the sun on the river before making my confession. 'Nick and Robbie put my name forward for a photography residency.'

'What's that?'

'Like a scholarship. They pay for your travel and living expenses and stuff. The deadline to sign up for interviews is next Friday. It looks amazing, but...yeah, I can't do it.'

Harris baulks. 'Well, that's bullshit – why can't you?'

I frown at him. 'I've told you. My family needs me here. Dad and Nani aren't well, and my auntie –'

Harris makes a noise like he's personally offended. 'Come on, don't give me that. You're really good. You could study photography, go overseas like you planned. You wouldn't have to be stuck here –'

'I'm not stuck anywhere,' I say firmly. 'I have a job, and I have friends, and I have people who rely on me. Why would I throw all that away for some unknown quantity?'

'But this residency thing, it's a big deal, right? You musta

231

thought about it.'

'Sure, I've thought about it.' I look elsewhere. 'But there's no point thinking about something that can't happen. Photography is just a hobby. And I have responsibilities here...'

'But you're not gonna stay in the Mallee, living at your dad's forever.' His expression, as he glances away, is horrified. 'Christ, I couldn't imagine anything worse.'

I don't know if I agree with him. 'My cousin, Jasminder, is doing it. She was born here, and she's married here, and she'll grow old here. Some people are happy exactly where they are.'

'Not you, though.' He examines my face. 'You got that look in your eye...'

'What look?'

'Like you're searching for the horizon.'

'I don't know about that.' I sit up, cradling the camera in my lap. This conversation is making me restless so I pass back his question. 'What do *you* want to do?'

'Get out.' His response is immediate. 'Get as far away from here, from anywhere my dad is, as fast possible.'

My head feels scrambled by the intensity of his words. 'So you really want to go.'

'Fuck, yeah.' He looks away to the river.

'And I have to stay.' It comes out more plaintive than I intend.

He bites his lip, looking at me. The moment is awkward until his gaze returns to the water.

'Sorry. Didn't mean to fire up.' He reaches for a dried leaf on the ground, crumbles it into dust. 'Guess I should tell you the big news. Leon has started batching. I mean, obviously not Leon personally. He's got blokes to do it for him.'

I squint at him. 'What's batching?'

Harris picks at the gumnuts on the ground, his hands agitated. 'Homegrown meth. Get the right gear and you can cook it up yourself. Leon's planning to start up a local crop.'

'And you know for sure it's happening?'

He flicks gumnuts towards the water. 'Saturday, I had to deliver a package. I know it's an important package, cos Mick the Leb comes with me –'

'How do you know he's Lebanese?' I cut in.

Harris shrugs, flicks another gumnut. 'I dunno. His name's Mick, everyone calls him Mick the Leb. Anyway, I get a big fat envelope from Leon, and Mick does the driving –'

'You're being chauffeured now?'

'Special occasion. So we drive out to this shed north of bloody nowhere, and there's a guy with a van. Here's the plate number, I wrote it down.' He passes me a slip of paper, which I pocket, and continues. 'I wait in the car while Mick goes to have a look, then when he's checked it all out, he gives me a nod. I give the van-man his money. He says to tell Leon he's waiting on some equipment, but the first package will arrive soon after that.'

'What's Leon paying for?'

'Chemicals, my guess. S'pose there'll be a couple of boys cooking up the whole mess in that little nowhere shed, far enough away that no one's gonna smell any fumes.' He looks at me. 'If I was your dad, I'd wait until the first batch is ready, then when the delivery day comes... Nail 'em.'

Harris's face is hard when he says that. Sometimes the stuff he tells me, the things he's doing – this thing we're *both* doing – seem so divorced from real life I have trouble reconciling it all in my head. But this is real life too, just like the sari and jewellery issues I've been dealing with over the last few days... The juxtaposition makes my brain hurt.

He lifts his chin at me, at the camera. 'You gonna take some photos or what? Your auntie'll get suss if you come home without any, won't she?'

'Huh?' I blink. 'Oh. Yeah, I s'pose.'

He looks at me sideways. 'You could photograph me. I wouldn't mind.'

'Oh, I don't take photos of people,' I say quickly. 'I mean, I'm taking shots for the wedding, but I don't really –'

'Why not?'

Good question. 'Well, you saw – all my work is in close-up. And I like the small details with people, too. The buttons on their shirt, or the corner of their mouth –'

'Go on then. I don't care.' He grins, gently teasing. 'Put the pics in with your residency application.'

I consider. The tension of our first exchange has passed, and the light here really *is* pretty... 'You don't think it's weird? If I only photograph part of you?'

'Depends on which part.' His eyebrow kinks up.

I give him a look as I pull myself into a kneeling position. 'Can you sit still?'

'Sure. Long as you like.' He settles back against the log with his ankles crossed. 'Makes a change from draggin' my arse around all day.'

Harris stretches his shoulders. He's stripped off his hoodie and I can see how lean he's gotten – he still looks strong, but he's become streamlined, his muscles defined from lack of body fat. He's trimmed his beard close, and ditched the cane: he limps, but his gait will get more natural as his leg fully recovers.

I'd be lying if I said he wasn't photogenic, though, and now I'm intrigued by the possibilities. What the camera might show, with *this* light, *this* subject. I bring the camera up, sight through the viewfinder. This isn't like the micro set-ups I'm used to: I have to find a different angle. I shuffle around, trying to find something that speaks its own language.

Then I see it – just a glimpse, at first. From Harris's cheekbone, down the side of his whiskered jaw, further. There's a long stretch of tanned neck to his collarbone where the edge of his T-shirt sags away. Over his shoulder, the rough log, and away behind that, the river is on fire: all glassy sparkling ripples. Harris's hair shifts in the whisper of breeze off the water.

I broaden my field, open the aperture. Let my focus expand. Light is coming down through the gum leaves above us, spangling every surface. I take an experimental shot.

'Is that okay?' When Harris speaks I see his throat move.

'Tilt your head to the left.' I sight again, focus. 'That's it – stop.'

For about five minutes there's only the sound of my shutter. I stare at this combination I've discovered in the viewfinder: fiery stars on the water, the grey texture of the log, the smooth length of Harris's skin.

'This is nothing like mugshots,' Harris jokes.

I snort. There's another pause, with clicking.

'I heard you went in to bat for me with my dad again,' Harris says. 'I heard he objected quite strenuously.'

I wait a beat, clicking the shutter button on my held breath, before releasing. 'How did you find out?'

'Dad told me about it last time we spoke on the phone.' His eyes glance at me, although the rest of him stays still. 'I've been putting him off, finally had to let him know I was in Mildy with a sketchy job – told him best he wait for me to visit. He'd been whinging about it. He said he went to the hospital to *give those bloody interfering nurse bitches a piece of his mind,* and why wouldn't they bloody pass on my new contact address?'

I sigh a little as I reframe. 'I told him we weren't allowed to give out that information by law.'

'He said he tore strips off the young black-haired chick at the desk.'

I like how Dennis has only given him part of the story. 'Did he tell you he grabbed me by the front of my uniform? Did he tell you I slapped him?'

'*What?*' The sight in my viewfinder changes, everything going wonky as Harris sits up. 'Christ, what happened? Are you okay?'

I lower the camera. His expression has gone flat and pale, and his hands grip the earth either side of him. This reaction, more than anything else, gives me a true insight into what his relationship with his father is really like. I try not to show how much that shakes me.

'It's okay, Harris.' I put my camera down in my lap. 'I'm okay. He scared me, but I stood up to him.'

He schools his features immediately, but I think he knows it's too late. 'Well…good.' He releases his hands, scrubs them together as he looks away. 'Okay. Good on you.'

'He's been like that with you your whole life, hasn't he? God, Harris, why do you put up with it?'

There's a long pause. I've given up any pretence of using the camera, and now I watch his eyes move as he struggles to explain.

'My mum and my sister.' He slowly sits back against the log again. 'I've wanted to get back in touch with them since…always.'

'And your dad knows how to contact them?'

He nods. 'That's how he got me back home. But I think it was just bullshit. If he told me how to find Mum and Kelly, he wouldn't have anything to hold over me, y'know?'

The flare off the river ignites in my head. 'Harris, my dad might be able to find your family.'

For a split second, Harris's expression is completely armour-free: hopeful and wanting. But the hope is extinguished just as quickly. 'I've tried, hey. It's not that easy.'

'At least let me ask Dad when I see him tomorrow?'

'I dunno.' He looks away as his tongue untangles. 'I dunno if my family'll still want to see me. If they still…' He breaks off – the words *care about me* must be somehow too hard – and shrugs.

'Maybe I shouldn't contact them. Maybe I'm too fucked up to be with them again.'

I shake my head. 'How can you say that?'

Harris gazes out over the river, his voice soft. 'I just wonder, y'know? Did my dad get so mean cos of what *his* dad was like? I'm a rough-head and I'm a drinker, and I can get mean. What if I get back together with Mum and Kelly and I can't put that part of me to bed?'

'You're nothing like your dad, Harris. You know that, right?'

That doesn't seem to console him. 'But what if it's like Wash, Rinse, Repeat? I mean, what if I make a family one day, and have a kid, and then I just...'

His words dry up and I can't look away from his expression. I shuffle closer on my knees and put my hennaed hand on his. I'm trying to think of what to say, something more significant than just platitudes, when the phone in my back pocket chimes.

'Oh shit.' I check the time. 'It's four o'clock.'

Harris clears his throat, releases my hand and starts to rise. 'Gotta get back to your nanna's, huh?'

'Um, yes. Dammit.' I hook the camera around my neck with the strap, push myself up with the log. The tough bark scrapes my palm, and I remember. 'Harris, I'm going home on Thursday afternoon.'

He looks crestfallen for the briefest moment before shifting into neutral again. 'Oh, right. Sure. You just came up for the wedding, yeah?'

'Yeah. So, I won't get to see you –' I stop, rephrase. 'We won't get to touch base again before I go.'

He shoves his hands in his jeans pockets. 'Right. Well, good luck with your residency stuff. And have fun at the wedding.'

'Thanks.' I give him a little smile.

'Don't get married yourself, by accident.' He colours, walks to the Pitbull.

After he drops me at my car, I drive back home to Nani's house, the sun beating down from above. I think about Harris and the conversation we had. Lately it's as if everyone I know wants to talk about what I'm doing with my life. And I don't have any answers. I only know I can't leave. I won't turn into another missing person in my family's photo albums. It would be like a mini-death.

Harris has a plan – a getaway plan. The idea of him shooting through makes my chest feel tight. But he's determined to escape his father's clutches, and who could blame him?

I haven't really been around anyone like Harris before, who's so full of despair. There's got to be something in me he's seeing, some spark of hope. I survived despair. My dad survived it. We didn't become closed-off and broken. Maybe Harris sees the possibility of an ending to sadness.

But I worry that he's seeing a false positive in me: I don't know if he can judge his own recovery by me or Dad. Our sad time was sudden and finite, while Harris's started from childhood and went on and on as he grew into a person.

I don't know if I've ever gone through what he's feeling. And I don't know if anything I said to him will resonate. I'll talk to Dad about finding Harris's family: maybe some good will come out of that. But will it be enough? Barb's words roll over in my head: *You can't save people – you can only give them the encouragement they need to save themselves.* God knows I want Harris to save himself. It surprises me to realise how deeply invested I am in that wanting.

I'm hot and sweaty by the time I get back. I need a nap. What scares me a little though is that I want to lie on my bed *pretending* to nap while I think about Harris Derwent's bottom lip. The fullness of it, curving into this tender luscious shape.

How it matches his top lip perfectly, with the little indentation there, right in the middle. How it catches on his teeth when he bites it.

I shake my head to clear it as I pull into the driveway of the house. Jaago preparations will be a distraction, Robbie wants to meet tonight in town, and there's plenty to do.

The drowsiness is all through me, though. I shouldn't be thinking about Harris's lips, or wondering if he'd let me photograph them. I don't want to check my camera for the shots of his neck – I know it'll only make the feeling worse – but I don't think I'll be able to help myself. Because I want that vision through my lens. I want to hear its liquid foreign tongue. I want to see that sight again...

Harris's sleek warm skin.

The rugged tree bark.

Flame on the water.

15

harris

Big Ball of Cranky

That's what Reggie called me, in disgust, after I lost three hands of poker at the kitchen table and did my block at him. That was at nine, and I was killing time before going to the club. Reggie departed for the CBD corners, and Steph – making a rare evening appearance in the kitchen – told me to take my tanty outside because some people in the house were trying to work. Then I told her to shut up, and then we insulted each other some more until it was more than I could stand, so I hauled myself up and left.

Now it's nearly eleven and I don't know if being in Flamingos is making it better. Beer has taken the edge off, but I still feel restless. Barry's gone to do some job so it's just me and Ando and Snowie making small talk, confirming what I've always thought: that there's a limit to how much you can hang shit on each other, and talk footy and fucking before it starts to sound like fingernails on a blackboard. I'm hoping Leon will call me for a delivery – something, anything – before I lose my mind.

I'm trying not to dwell on the conversation with Amie at the river this arvo. I'm damned if I know what made me so maudlin, and I wish I could take it back, every bloody word. Nobody needs to know it, nobody needs to hear it, especially not her. She's got enough going on. And I can't fucking *believe* Dad fronted her at the hospital. I've been battling the urge to jump in the Pitbull, drive back to Five Mile, and slug him on her behalf. *Here's one for the black-haired chick on the desk.* That'd be disastrous, but it's what I feel like doing.

So I guess I'm riled. And the thought of Amie leaving Mildura is bringing me down. Which it shouldn't, cos I don't *want* her this close to the action. But...I like seeing her in person. I like knowing she's around. It's selfish but I can't seem to help it.

'Hey, check it out,' Ando says. 'Curried wogs.'

A very bad feeling makes me look up, follow the line of his eyes, and suddenly...

My first thought is *Oh shit*. Following hard on its heels is my second thought, that this is really not my night. And then I think *Oh shit* again.

Because I can see Amie.

She's standing at the bar with two other girls: an Italian-looking chick and another girl who's most likely Indian. Amie's got her hair twisted up and eyeliner on, and chunky-heeled boots, and some kind of sparkly purple top which she may be wearing as a dress. She looks so fucking amazing I want to get up and go over to her immediately.

But I want to do that anyway because of the *absolute goddamn panic* that churns inside me as soon as I spot her. She smiles at her mates, does a quick scan of the place. I can tell by the way her gaze lingers on me, for the briefest second, that she's realised I'm here.

Snowie guffaws at Ando's joke, then smiles at the girls huddled by the bar. His eyes narrow with a predatory glint.

'I know that chick.' He leans towards me. 'Harris, d'you know that chick? The Paki chick in the purple dress – what's her name? Copper's daughter.'

I can't let my face give anything away. I slow my breathing, keep my eyes down. A burning sensation starts somewhere in the back of my throat, like the beer is repeating on me.

I force myself to sound off-hand. 'Yeah. The sarge's kid. I've seen her around.'

'You know her?'

'I've seen her. She works at the hospital.' I take a long swallow of my drink, set it down. 'Don't know her personally.'

'She's cute, for a Paki.' Snowie nods contemplatively. 'I could just about take a bite of that.'

'Great tits,' Ando agrees.

The desire to lunge across and slam both their faces into the tabletop comes upon me so suddenly, so violently, I'm almost blinded by it.

Snowie lifts his chin at the girls. 'I should have a crack, whaddya reckon? Blow some smoke up the sarge's arse, eh, if I got a taste of his baby girl!'

I have to breathe a couple of times before I trust myself to unclench my fists.

'Nah, mate. Not worth it.' My voice sounds like I've been dragged across barbed wire by the throat. 'But if you really want the sarge breathing down your neck every time you leave Mildura, hey, go for your life.'

Snowie makes a face. 'Yeah, I guess.'

I gulp beer like I'm dying, finish my bottle.

'Fuckin' thirst, mate!' Ando stands for the next round. 'Anybody else want one?'

'Yeah, me.' But Snowie's still looking at the girls. 'Y'know what I reckon? I reckon I'm gonna ask her to dance.'

And I'm gonna do something I'll regret, any minute now.

I stand up abruptly. 'Fuck off, Snow. You always take the hot chicks and leave us the dregs.' I produce a large fake smile. 'Let's ask her. You and me – see which one she picks, eh? Ladies' choice.'

He tries to chuff his way out of it, but when Ando starts hassling him he gives in. So it's the two of us who walk up to Amie and the girls, Snowie slithering to a halt in front of them. I squeeze in beside him just as Amie turns around with her beer.

'Ladies.' Snowie leers. 'Nice night for it.'

'If you reckon,' the Italian girl says, passing another bottle off to her friend.

'Hey, we were just having a conversation, me and my mate,' Snowie says, skewering Amie with his next glance. 'We were saying we thought you were an Ouyen girl. Is that right, you from over that way?'

'Um, yeah, over that way,' Amie says stiltedly before glancing at me. 'Uh, hi... Yeah, I'm not really from Ouyen. But I know a few people along that strip.'

'You'd know my dad, then,' Snowie goes on. 'Col Geraldson, at the Five Flags.'

'Oh, yeah, right.' Amie makes a forced smile. I don't think she's putting this on. 'Yeah, I guess. Oh, yeah, so you're Snowie. Right, great.'

'Thought you might be up for a bit of a dance, then,' Snowie says, waggling his eyebrows. 'Take a turn on the floor, yeah?'

Which makes it sound as if he's gonna waltz with her, and I know that's not what he's got in mind. Not unless waltzing involves copping a feel at the same time.

'Or you might like to dance with *me*,' I suggest, giving Snowie an obvious nudge. 'You're hogging the mic, mate, give it a rest. D'you wanna have a dance with me?'

I turn a desperately neutral face towards Amie, and she takes the hint straightaway.

'Oh. Um, yeah. Sure. I'll have a dance, um...'

'Harris,' I supply.

'Harris! Right!' Amie says, and this girl deserves a fucking Academy award. 'Sure. Shall we...'

She offloads her beer with her friend, the other Indian girl, and leads forward to the dance floor. I give Snowie a smirk as I follow her, just to maintain the illusion, then me and Amie are jostled together by the press of bodies, and we can talk.

I start with, '*Do you know where the hell you are?*' and she starts with, '*Shit, I didn't know you were gonna be here!*' and both of us are sort of whispering and glaring while trying not to look too suss.

In this situation, though, my panic wins out. 'Amie, you've got to get the fuck out of here.'

'Don't you think I bloody know that!' she hisses. 'Shit, Bee wanted to come out with me after jaago –'

'D'you know how close I just came to clobbering Snowie when he spotted you?' I cup her elbow. 'I nearly had a fucking heart attack.'

Amie turns us both, keeping up the pretence of dancing. 'I'm sorry. Shit. This is bad. Robbie dragged us all here and now we've bought drinks –'

'You need to go.' I push myself towards her. 'Like, right now. Take your mates. Snowie knows you're the sarge's daughter, it's not safe –'

'How the hell am I gonna do that?'

'Easy.' I press in close as I can, close enough so it's obviously not just a consequence of being thrust forward by the crowd. God, she smells incredible.

Amie's voice goes breathy. 'Harris –'

'This is how you're gonna do it,' I say. 'First, I'm gonna do this.'

I snake a hand around her waist, settle it just above her tailbone, and rub it slowly back and forth. The purple fabric of her dress makes smooth bunches under my palm, and the friction makes my eyes shut of their own accord. Then – god help me – I slide my hand down lower.

Lower.

Amie stiffens against me. I lean my face down so my mouth is nestled under her ear. 'Now you're gonna look shocked.'

Amie pulls up short. 'You want me to look shocked?'

'Yep.' I glance at her expression. 'That's pretty close. Now you're going to push me back, and slap my face.'

'*What*?'

'That's the perfect look. Do it now. Slap me hard as you can.'

Amie looks aghast. 'Then what?'

'Then you stomp over to your mates, grab them by the arm, and drag them self-righteously the hell outta here. You got it? So do it.'

Amie rears back, her eyes horrified, but she does it. She winds up and open-hands me, right across the cheek. It bloody hurts. My head whips, Amie gasps, then I feel her barging away.

I give it a few seconds, stagger off the dance floor, do a quick surreptitious check around. Amie and her mates are bolting out. My cheek stings like buggery but the rest of my body relaxes. I make a 'what can you do?' gesture at Snowie and Ando, who are pissing themselves laughing at the table, before lurching to the men's.

Splashing some water on my face helps, but the adrenalin of the last few minutes has me shaking. Plus the memory of cupping Amie's arse... I've run my hand under the tap twice, but it's like my fingers have been napalmed. I stand at the grotty men's wash basin for another two breaths, getting my shit together, before I've got enough in me to go back to the table and make raucous jokes about it with Snowie and Ando.

It's another hour before I can finally make my excuses and piss off. I don't go home straightaway though: I pull over a couple of blocks before Amblin Court and yank my phone out of my pocket, send a quick text and hope Amie isn't asleep already. I chew my thumbnail as I stare out the windshield at the night, then jump when the phone brays in my hand.

Amie sounds breathless, like she did in the club. 'Harris –'

'I'm sorry,' I cut in quickly, 'God, I'm sorry, I'm probably waking you up, I just wanted to check –'

'You're not...' There's a little pause. 'You're not waking me up at all. I'm glad you texted.'

'Shit, Amie, about the club –'

'It's okay,' she says.

'It's *not* okay. I just freaked the fuck out when I saw you. I didn't mean to stuff up your night out –'

'*D'you really think I care about my night out?*' Her voice is shaky. 'For god's sake, Harris...' I hear her exhale deeply into the line before her voice levels out. 'Seriously, I was worried I'd blown your cover. I didn't even know we were *going* to Flamingos until the last minute, and I came this close to dumping you right in it.'

It sounds like she's trying to forgive herself for that. I only hope she forgives *me* – for feeling her up on the dance floor. 'Amie, listen. I didn't want to offend you, or see you get hurt. I'm sorry I did what I did. And you only slapped me cos I asked you to, so don't stress about that. It was just... It was a bad situation.'

'It was supposed to be this civilised night out with my cousin...' She sighs, but there's a bit of genuine humour coming back into her tone now.

My imagination is only too happy to supply a vision of her sitting in bed in her pajamas, raking back her hair. Except she's not in her room in Walpeup now, she's in her nanna's house in Mildura –

'So, um, did you make it home okay?'

'Yeah.' I close my eyes, but my brain won't let up. 'I mean, yeah, I left the club about twenty minutes ago. But I'm not home yet. I just stopped to make sure you're all right.'

'I'm fine.' She pauses. 'Is your face sore?'

That gets a laugh out of me. 'It is a bit tender, now you mention it.'

'Oh god –'

'It's no big deal, I've had worse.'

There's a bit of silence down the line. I can't help but think that, putting aside the first trumpeting blat of panic at seeing her in the club, what I remember most is when we were pressed up against each other in the crowd. The way we moved together. The soft roundness of her, cupped in my hand...

'Stay safe, Harris.' Her voice is quiet. 'I'd better go. It's late, and the wedding's tomorrow. My auntie will be wondering why I'm still up.'

I force myself to snap back. 'Good luck for the wedding.'

'Thanks.' Now I can hear her smiling.

'Watch out for roos on the drive back to Walpe.'

'Will do. And I'll tell Dad what you told me.'

'Okay, good. And text me...' I swallow, hope I don't sound too eager. Ah, fuck it. 'Text me when you figure out a way to meet up again.'

'I will. Go home, get some rest.'

We say our goodbyes and I tuck my phone back in my pocket, turn the key for the drive onward to Amblin Court. The idea of meeting up with Amie, of seeing her again, sends an orange fireball ricocheting through me. But that moment may be a while off.

Until then, I'll just have to burn.

Seven-forty-five next morning, the house gets raided.

I jerk awake to hear a lot of banging around and shouting from down the hall. At first I think it's the start of a fight, but part of me registers that the shouting's too structured.

I hear, '*Down on the floor – get down on the floor!*' and then my door seems to explode open. Two guys in black – uniforms, flak jackets, helmets – almost fall into my room. I think they were expecting the wood veneer to offer more resistance. Their service weapons are out and one of them yells, '*Hands on your head! Lemme see your hands!*' so I do exactly as I'm told.

The sheets and blankets fall down to my hips and I'm half-kneeling on the bed. Apart from fighting general fogginess and confusion, and the strange heart-attack feeling of being woken with a bang, I'm thinking a couple of things. One is, I'm super-glad I told Leon I wouldn't carry a weapon. Because if I'd agreed to it, the gun might've been in the room with me right now, and that would be problematic. The other thing I'm thinking is, I'm bloody relieved I don't sleep commando.

'*Hands!*'

'I'm doing it, mate, I'm doing it –'

'*Don't you move. Don't you fucking move a muscle.*'

'I got my hands up, see? I got 'em up.' My hands fumble at the top of my head.

'*Stay there.*'

'I'm stayin' here, okay? I'm staying here. I need to sit down, but.'

One of the officers – the older one – nods at the other officer, who comes over and quickly tugs my sheets and pillow onto the floor. His eyes light on the bandage on my leg. He covers me with his weapon the whole time. I've never had a police pistol stuck right in my face before. It makes me sweat.

'Sit down right where you are,' the guy says. 'Do *not* fucking move.'

It's one of those funny police moments where they tell you to do two completely opposing things at the same time.

'I swear to god, I won't move.' I sink my butt back on the bed with relief. My sore leg stretches out over the edge. 'Thank you. Shit, that's better.'

The older cop points a finger at me. 'Stay exactly where you are. Just stay there.' He glances at the younger cop, holds his gun with one hand as he lifts a hand-mic on the shoulder-side of his flak jacket and speaks into it. 'We've got one in the far bedroom. Yep, holding.'

Shouts come from down the hall. I hear Kevin say, '*Get the fuck off, you bastards!*' and Steph yell, '*I'm fuckin' doin' it!*'

'What's going on?' I ask quietly.

'Shut the fuck up,' the younger cop snaps.

The older guy frowns at him, looks at me. 'It's a bust, son. Suspected drug activity in the house.'

Well, applause all round. I wonder how long it took them to work that out. Blind Freddy could've told you there was drug activity in the house.

'Okay.' My arms are getting tired from keeping my hands on my head. 'But I don't think I'm the droid you're looking for, yeah? I just moved in here.'

'We'll see,' the older cop says. 'We'll just wait and see.'

The radio mic on his jacket squawks.

'Hold him here,' he says to his younger buddy. He exits abruptly.

'Seriously,' I say. 'I've only been here three weeks. Go through my stuff and have a look.'

Young Cop sneers. 'Thanks, we'll do that.'

I don't think he needed an invitation. Young Cop tosses the

249

room. I have to lie face down on the carpet in my jocks while my duffel gets upended. All my wound care stuff goes flying.

'Medical supplies, hey?' Young Cop says.

'That's for me leg.' My voice sounds muffled, because of the carpet.

Young Cop moves around behind me, steps over me. 'That's it? Nothing else?'

D'you think I'd tell you if there was? I don't say that.

Maybe my lack of solemnity is in my posture, splayed out here on the floor. Young Cop crunches through my sterile wipes and stuff until I catch his shadow looming near my head.

'C'mon. You've gotta have something.' He steps on my fingers. It hurts.

I tense my arms. 'Ow.'

He shifts position. The toe of his boot nudges my wounded thigh. 'You guys think you're so fucking smart, dontcha? So fucking smart.'

I've met cops like this before: young, dumb, and full of attitude. They like to let you know who's boss. Change the uniform into a Jim Beam T-shirt and jeans and this guy would be indistinguishable from Ando.

And he likes to play with his food.

'You're a stupid shit, aren't ya?' Young Cop hunkers down so he can hiss above my ear. He raps the back of my head with the butt of his gun. 'Aren't ya?'

If he really expects me to reply to that, he's dreaming. My teeth clacked together when he whacked my head, and that's how they're gonna stay. I keep my nose pressed to the carpet.

Boots clomp towards us from down the hall. Young Cop stands up fast, but before he moves he kicks the side of my prone leg. His toes are steel-capped, and it takes a lot of effort not to cry out as a localised white explosion shoots through my thigh. *Fuck*, that fucking *hurt*.

'Sorted,' Old Cop says as he returns. 'You find anything?'

'No, sir,' Young Cop says meekly.

My shoulders relax even though I knew there was nothing to find. Now the other cop's here, I think it's safe to speak. 'Can I get up now? This carpet is bloody rank.'

'What're you doing here, son?' Old Cop lets me up so I can sit on the milk crate.

'I live here.' I'd thought that was pretty obvious. I stretch my leg out, rubbing my thigh and throwing glares at Dickhead Junior. 'I come up from Ouyen, looking for work.'

'You picked a dodgy place to move into,' Old Cop says flatly.

'It's cheap, that's all I know. And I didn't know where else to go. Like I said, I've only been here three weeks.'

Old Cop raises an eyebrow.

'I used to work at Ridgeback Falls quarry,' I insist. 'Stuffed me leg, so now I'm looking for a new job. That envelope on the floor there, that's my references. Check it out yourself.'

Old Cop goes through my wallet. 'Driver's license says your name is Harrison Lucas Derwent, is that correct?'

My face warms as I nod. 'Yeah. But it's just Harris, hey.'

'Well, just-Harris, why don't you put a shirt on and we'll sort it out.'

His name badge reads *Murphy*. This is the guy Sarge Blunt told me about: the Mildura CIU guy. I check him for funny looks, but he doesn't so much as twitch at me. The sarge was true to his word then – the cops here don't know me. Inconvenient in the long term, but definitely a plus in a situation like this. Let me be arrested with the others. Let Snowie think I'm part of it all.

'Sorting it out', like the Murphy guy said, takes the better part of the morning. I slap on some clothes, get cuffed – *'Nah, go ahead and cuff me if it makes you feel better'* – and am handed off to the cop shop. They take my fingerprints and process all my gear before I'm put in a holding cell with Kevin and Steph, plus the girl who usually brings the baby. She's on her own this time, crying and obviously strung out.

'I didn't do nothin', I didn't do nothin'!' she wails.

'What the fuck're ya here for then?' Kevin snarls. Kevin's been done for possession. He's not such a happy-go-lucky guy when he's stressed.

Reggie's not in the cells – I'm relieved. I sit beside Steph on the cold concrete floor and knead my bruised leg. 'You all right?'

'Yeah.' She rubs her hands together. 'Bit desperate for a ciggie. And I wish I had me jacket, it's bloody freezing in here.'

I've got a flannie on so I offer her my hoodie. 'What's the story, you reckon?'

She gives me a wary look then accepts my hoodie, pulls it over her threadbare T-shirt. 'Dumb bust. Dunno what they expected to find. Nobody's batching, and nobody sells outta their bloody *house* – unless they wanna get robbed.'

'What about Baby Mama over there?' I cut my eyes at the crying girl.

Steph makes a 'pfft' sound. 'Neighbourhood troll, hunting for freebies. She knows Kev will do anything for a root. And she'll do anything for a pipe.'

'So why the bust?'

She shrugs. 'Best guess, they know something's up. They know the house. They're probably trying to rattle Snowie's cage.'

I think she might be right on the money. Steph doesn't use, Barry's not a resident, I'm clean as a whistle. Kevin was the only idiot with gear in his room, and that was for private consumption. No quantities. If the cops were hoping to find some million-dollar drug lab in the Mildura suburbs, they've screwed this up royally. On the other hand, if they were just trying to shake up Snowie's household, see what fell loose...

We've already been here two hours when suddenly Baby Mama starts screaming. It takes another twenty minutes to get sense out of her, and that's when we find out the baby is back at her place. Alone. She left a six-month-old alone in the house while she went to score – that was four hours ago. The cops are nice enough to send a car over. I cross my arms over my chest and tuck my chin into my neck as Baby Mama cries like her heart's gonna break. The whole thing makes me feel sick.

They let us all go, except for Kevin and the mother of the baby, a few trying hours later. Baby Mama gets her baby back, carries it with her into an interview room. We're asked if we want to make a statement, which we graciously decline. Kevin'll have to go through the grinding process of court appearance, but they've got nothing to hold me and Steph on.

But something is different. Something has definitely changed. Because I'm in the system, now: I've been name-checked, fingerprinted, processed. My current place of abode has been noted. When I went to sleep last night I was 'under-the-radar just-Harris'. But now...

Person of interest. Known associate. Material witness.

The cops have lots of polite names for it, but none of those count. The one they use amongst themselves, that's the important one.

I'm officially a scrote.

16

amie

The wedding is over.

Parties were had, prayers were said, and after the reception on Wednesday night, Jasminder left for her new husband's house. It's only five minutes away, in the next suburb, but we all bawled our eyes out during vidai.

Now it's Thursday morning and there's no sleeping in. Dad offered to drive back with me but I said I'd help with the post-wedding clean-up before heading home this afternoon. All hands are needed on deck. Hansa gives me a list of tasks, asks me to wake Nani.

I knock and enter the room with a steaming mug and a plateful of warm puri, the local newspaper folded under my arm. The room is shadowed by curtains, and smells of old lady and incense. Nani is snoring gently. A little shrine to Guru-ji is in the corner, a small pile of poetry books by the bed.

'Nani-ji?' I set down the mug and plate and paper on the nightstand as she stirs. 'Hey, I'm sorry to wake you.'

'Daya?' Nani blinks up at me. 'Daya, is that you?'

It's the unexpectedness of it that cuts: I'm not ready. The sound of my mother's name slices through me, and I jerk, turn to the window.

'Oh, I had a dream...' Nani says, her voice sleepy. 'Of you, Daya, with your baby girl...'

I ease the curtains back. I try to be sensible about it: seeing me just after waking, with my hair loose like this, it's understandable Nani is confused. Everyone says I look like Mum.

I'm still blinking the wet out of my eyes when I turn and smile at her. 'Nani-ji, it's Amita. It's me.'

'Hm?' Nani sits herself up. 'Oh goodness, where are my glasses?'

I give them to her off the nightstand and she fumbles them on.

'I've brought you breakfast in bed,' I say lightly, swallowing hard and keeping up my smile. 'I'm sorry to wake you but you said nine o'clock.'

'Indeed I did.' Nani settles herself on the pillows, arranging the blankets. 'Thank you for waking me. Will you share some puri with me?'

But her voice still sounds odd: tentative and polite, as if she's not sure who she's talking to. I sit on the side of the bed near her quilt-covered legs.

'Nani-ji, I'll be happy to share with you.' I tilt my head to catch her eye. 'Nani, it's Amita. Do you remember?'

She looks at me, her eyes focusing behind her glasses. Then her expression clears and her voice becomes more natural. 'Amita! Oh, Amita, you are a sweet girl. You've brought me breakfast! Yes, yes, this is good. But where is your mug?' She beams as I pass her the tea.

'Oh, I've already had mine.' The fear in my stomach is a cloudy-white lump. 'This is just for you.'

Watching her sip, I suddenly feel awful. I wanted to spend time with Nani while I was here in Mildura. It's the thing that was on my mind when I drove up, more than mehndi and saris and celebrating. But I got caught up in the wedding whirl, and been as neglectful of Nani as everybody else. And I'll be going in a few short housework-filled hours, without doing what I came here for.

'Here's your newspaper, Nani-ji,' I say, unfolding it with a guilty flourish. 'You can read it while you're –'

I stop because I've seen the headline. It's not the lead story, but it's still on the front page.

Police raid nabs drug offender.

I scan the paragraph at the top of the article, stand up. 'Nani, I'll be back in just a sec, okay?'

While Nani looks at me, bewildered but mollified by her tea, I slip out of the room, yanking out my phone. I tap a quick text – *Pls contact hospital immediately for test results* – and hit Send. I go to the bathroom, splash water on my face, squeeze my hands together. While I'm standing at the sink, I get a reply.

Available @4pm for meeting re: test results.

First comes the relief: I heave a giant sigh. Then I realise the timing's perfect – right about when I'm leaving Mildura. I can see Harris and get details about what the hell happened on the way home. I text back *Ok* and return to Nani, hoping her quiet presence will calm me before the day's craziness rolls on.

*

'...so that was basically it. I spent six hours in the lock-up yesterday, and by the time I got back to the house, I couldn't say I was feeling hugely sympathetic towards police process.' Harris grimaces. 'Anyway, Snowie passed word around last night that we should all chill until we get news from above.'

Icy breeze off the river whips my hair around. The sky is like smoky quartz, the river a dull sluggish reflection: it's as if Tuesday's spring brightness never existed. Harris and I lean against the Pitbull's bonnet, which at least keeps our butts warm.

'Okay, I'll let Dad know,' I say. 'You probably could've called him from Mildura station, but it doesn't sound as if he would've been much use to you anyway.'

'Maybe the opposite,' he admits. 'It was good — everybody knows I got busted, just like the rest of them, and they know I didn't say nothing. It makes me a solid part of the crew.'

'Sinking deeper,' I murmur, and he knows what I mean.

'Yeah.' He nods, as though he's accepting how entwined in this he's become. 'Snowie and Leon shouldn't have any suspicions now.'

'What about Ando?'

The cold transforms his shrug into a shudder. 'Ando's suspicious of everybody, all the time. He only trusts himself. Nothing I do'll make any difference.'

'Okay, then.' My voice sounds weary. I've been cleaning and packing up all day, and I still have to drive back to Walpeup.

Harris looks at me, seems to realise what he's forgotten in all the drama. 'Ah shit, how was the wedding?'

Having almost forgotten myself, I'm surprised into a laugh. 'Mad. Indian weddings are always organised chaos. My sari kept slipping, Hansa wanted photos of every single person at the reception, and Jas looked like she was going to throw up at one point. At least jail is quiet.' I grin at him. 'But thanks for remembering.'

'You've still got a bit of stuff around your eyes...' He reaches out as if he's about to touch my face.

'Kajal, yeah.' I rub under my right eye with a finger, but that's probably only smearing it worse. 'What about the other people at your house? Are they all okay?'

He tucks his hands into his hoodie pockets, like he's keeping them there for safety, but it's probably just to stop them from freezing. 'None of the kids were there, which was lucky. Kev's still in the clink. I don't think he gets bailed until tomorrow. And the girl with the baby looked really strung out. Actually, I felt more sorry for the baby.'

I clutch my windbreaker at the neck where the breeze dips in. 'I still don't get it. What is it about drugs?'

He raises his eyebrows in my direction. 'You've never been drunk? Smoked pot? Taken anything?'

I shake my head. It's not something I should be embarrassed about, but I feel embarrassed somehow. I think the embarrassment is more that I'm revealing my own naiveté.

Harris looks amused, shrugs. 'Well, drugs are nice, for lots of reasons. That's one of the things they don't tell you in those classes at school. Like, they say, 'Don't have sex before you're old enough', 'Don't do drugs cos they're bad for you'. But what they *don't* tell you is that drugs are bloody nice. I mean, that's the attraction, for some people. That it's forbidden, but it feels so good.'

'Well, I understand getting high is supposed to feel nice –'

He stops me. 'Drugs do three things when they're inside you. First of all, they change your energy. So if you're feeling uptight, they chill you out, or if you're feeling tired, they give you a burst.'

I'm hyper-aware of how near we're sitting, together on the car bonnet, when Harris leans closer. 'Then the second thing they do, they make you feel good. Here, under your skin.' He pulls his hand out of his pocket and runs a fingertip slowly from my thumb to my wrist. The way he looks at me, his light soft touch, brings my skin alive. He grins. 'Like that.'

I can feel myself blushing. 'What's the third thing?'

'The third thing is the most important.' He uses the same finger to tap my temple gently. 'They take away every doubt or fear or insecurity you ever had. Everybody's got something unhappy inside 'em. Drugs seem to clear all that away. They make you feel like you're the best person you ever imagined being. They make you feel like hot shit.'

He snorts softly, looks out at the river. I don't know whether I agree with his ideas about drugs – I've heard too much about the reality, from Dad – but I want to keep Harris talking. I focus on the shifting grey water, the cold air, and remind myself we're only huddled together for warmth.

'But you've never...' I have to work out how to say this. 'You've tried them. And you obviously liked them.'

'Yeah, sure.'

'But you never got addicted.'

His hands are back in his pockets. 'Well, I think you've gotta like them on all three levels to get hooked on them. That's just my own opinion, mind you. I like the energy, and the feeling, but I can get that in other ways.'

'What about the 'getting rid of self-doubt' part? That seems to me to be the most attractive thing about it.'

'Sure. But hey, I like being self-doubting.' He grins. 'If I thought I was hot shit all the time I'd be kind of unbearable, I reckon. Being a bit insecure, it's not such a bad thing.'

'Really?'

He looks at me and his expression changes. 'Being righteous is kind of a fucked up world-view. I only know one person with no self-doubt. Who thinks everything he does is completely justified.'

'Your dad.'

He nods. 'My dad liked to tell me he'd rather kill me than let my mother have me. Cos, y'know, he's the only one who can make the rules. Now that's righteous.'

He gives me a twisted half-smile. I can only shake my head at the horror of it.

He goes on. 'And the other thing with drugs is, whatever your drug of choice, if you really get into it hard, ultimately it's gonna kill you. My dad's already said he'd be happy to kill me. Why would I wanna get addicted to something? I'd just be doing his hard work for him.'

The drive home feels long, and the whole way there my mind churns over what Harris said. The way he said it, so matter-of-factly. When I drag my suitcase into the kitchen and find Dad home, it's a relief to have someone I can talk to about it.

'Nobody should ever feel like that,' Dad says. I can tell from the way he's wiping his spanner so meticulously with the oil rag that he's seething. 'Nobody should ever feel like they're not safe with the people who're supposed to take care of them. Your parents are supposed to support you, be there for you –'

'I think it's been a long time since Harris felt safe with anyone.' I sit on the wooden steps below the kitchen back door, squeezing my forehead. The fluoro light above the steps is softly buzzing. 'Should we really be asking him to do this, Dad? I know he volunteered, but he's already been through so much...'

'Should we be worried, d'you mean?' Dad places the spanner carefully back in its spot on the pegboard near the wall. 'About whether he can hold it together? Do you think he's pushing himself too far?'

'I'm worried he's tempted,' I admit. 'I'm worried he's exposed to stuff up there that will change his mind about what he needs to get by.'

I've explained Harris's theory of addiction to my dad already, and now he sighs.

'There's another reason why people get high, Amie. It's because for some people, their lives are so awful they don't want to think about it. Some of them don't want to exist anymore. So they're going into it because it's an escape.' He wipes grease off his hands with the rag. 'Do you think Harris is like that? D'you think he feels he's got nothing to live for?'

I hug my windbreaker around myself with both arms. 'He has something – his mum and his sister. He's excited that you've offered to help find them. But he's scared about meeting them again, too. I just hope his bad opinion of himself doesn't push him into doing something stupid.'

Dad frowns. 'I guess Harris is vulnerable, yeah. But he's toughed it out most of his life, and he's toughing it out okay so far in Mildura. Next time you speak to him, though, remind him he can pull the pin any time. That's what I said, right from the start.'

The reminder that Harris has an 'out' if he needs one makes me feel slightly better – but only slightly. 'God, Dad, how do you deal with this stuff all the time? It was easy when I was just handling Harris's medical treatment, but this is...'

Dad walks closer, squats down in front of me and puts a hand on my shoulder. 'You're listening to him. That's important. But it's difficult to just listen and not do something.'

'*Yes.*'

'And the external stuff is easier than the emotional stuff.'

I nod, feeling too emotional to answer.

'That's the way it is, love. And mostly, it's only the external part of the equation we can really do something about. I can try to find his family, sure. But what Harris is feeling, how he works it out for himself... That's kind of his show.'

'He's fighting,' I say. 'I believe he's fighting. I just wish I could do more to help.'

'You're supporting him, Ames.' Dad gives my shoulder a squeeze. 'You're doing everything you can. Just remember, it's not a battle you can fight for him.'

17

harris

The Lay Low period is officially over.

'You did good,' Leon says, and I know what he means by it. *Good* means keeping your mouth shut. *Good* means taking one for the team.

'Well, it was a dumb bust, yeah?' I shift on my feet, eyeing off the package he's got on the desk. Bullshit small-talk makes me impatient. I don't need a pat on the head. Get on with it already.

Leon notices, snorts. 'This here – another delivery for Red Cliffs. Go round the back this time.' The gold envelope he hands me feels weighty.

I leave the office, but something makes me hesitate in the hall. The impatience I felt a second ago, in the office, has been replaced with this treacle-y lethargy. It scares me, for some reason.

I walk down the hall, turn left into the men's toilet, go into a stall, close it. Sit on the lid of the toilet. Take the envelope out of the front of my hoodie, unfold it. The flap isn't stuck down, makes it nice and easy to check inside.

The money in the envelope is stiff, clean, fresh. Fifty dollar notes, the polymer shining. This is a decent chunk of money. It sits nicely in my hand, this chunk. I don't like to make value judgements, but if I had to take a guess, I'd say there's about five grand here. Another matching chunk, its twin, still sitting in the envelope.

Ten grand, here in my lap.

Just looking at this much money makes me dizzy.

I lift my head. The toilet stall is painted black. There's silver tagging and old playbills on the inside. The doorknob is falling out as the chipboard disintegrates; the door is actually kept shut by a slide bolt that goes into a drilled hole in the jamb. The slide bolt is new. It's still shiny.

Ten grand. My breath comes out shaky. *Ten thousand dollars.*

For the space of two breaths, I think crazy thoughts.

All my debts repaid. Dad's bills sorted. The monkey off my back. I could go to Melbourne – no. Further. I'd need to go further than that. Brisbane, maybe. Or overseas – hell, I could live overseas for a long time on ten thousand dollars –

I catch myself before I start to spin loose from my moorings.

Getting involved with this narc business is high risk. I've never had any illusions about that. But the reality of it is sinking in: ten grand in a gold envelope, toilet doors with the knobs falling out, the smell of urinal cake. These things feel very real right now. I bet if Leon told Ando to knock me, that would feel pretty real, too.

I put the money back in the envelope the way I found it, fold the flap down, tuck it back in my hoodie. Then further, into the waistband of my jeans. I feel nauseous. I need to talk about this. Just to get it off my chest. Because the alternative is a heart attack or something.

I consider pulling out my phone right now and calling Amie. Explaining that I'm sitting in a black-painted toilet stall in a skanky club in Mildura, with ten large pressed up against my skin.

But I can't call her now. That would be fucking suicide. I stand up, press the flush button and get out of the stall, wash my hands at the little pitted sink, dry them on my jeans. Look at my face in the rust-spotted mirror above the black and white checkerboard tiles.

I still look okay. My lips are a bit white, I'm a bit thinner in the face, but I'm still me. I lick my lips, press them together. *Don't overthink it, Harris.*

I get the hell out.

*

After my panic attack in the dunnies at Flamingos, the delivery turned out to be very simple.

Without that wad of money under my shirt, I feel calmer, less cloudy, even though the weather has turned to drizzling crap. I stop off home to change clothes – 'always change clothes after a delivery' was one of Snowie's tips – and walk into the house to find Reggie watching TV.

'Hey, Reggie.' I shake rain out of my hair. 'What's happening, mate?'

Reggie leans over the back of the couch, his plaited rat's tail flopping loose. 'Yeah, just watching the game, eh? Watching Carlton lose.'

I check the teams on the telly screen. 'Shame they're not losing to Essendon.'

Reggie shrugs. 'I don't mind, I'll take it. I just like seeing those snobby bastards eat it.' He drags his eyes away. 'Whatcha up to?'

'Got an appointment.' When he raises his eyebrows at me, I shrug. 'The girl at the tatt place said I've gotta come in for touch-ups, to finish off me back. Come for a ride if you're bored.'

He makes a face. 'Can't. Waiting for Kev, hey.'

I change my shirt and hoodie in my bedroom, head back out to the Pitbull. Eighth Street is only a five minute drive away, and the tattoo parlour is deserted on a Saturday afternoon.

Leela is sitting sideways on the dentist's chair, blowing smoke at the ceiling and swinging her legs. She's wearing navy three-quarter pants with a big black jumper. 'Didn't think you were gonna make it.'

It reminds me of what Nick said when I went to buy the car. Why do people always assume I'm gonna be a no-show? 'No point getting it done if it's not done right.'

Leela grins. 'I like your attitude, boy.'

She hops down, dabs her smoke into an ashtray on the counter, waves me over. The air in the tattoo parlour is freezing. When I pull off my top layers, I get goosebumps.

'Baby,' Leela says, pouting. She sits me backwards on the cold dentist's chair, prods the skin of my back with a gloved finger. 'This is looking all right. Been taking care of it, have you?'

'I'm kind of used to the medical stuff.' I nod towards my leg.

She lifts an eyebrow. 'Gonna tell me that story one day?'

'Yeah, one day,' I say, which is nice and vague. 'You gonna tell me how you ended up working in a tattoo parlour in the Mallee?'

'Oh, that's a long boring tale of woe.' Leela uncaps the little black and brown bottles, lays a white hand towel over her knee. 'So you're happy with the ink?'

'Yeah, I'm rapt. Thank you.' I grin at her in the big mirror we're both facing. 'I mean, I can't see it most of the time, but I reckon it's good.'

Leela gives me a wink. 'The beauty of back tatts – you can't see 'em, so you don't get sick of 'em.' She hooks up the needle to the wires. 'And how about Leon, you happy with him too? He's treating you all right?'

I go still. It's only when the buzz starts and the needle comes down that I flinch. 'Well, I dunno who you're –'

'Oh, save it.' Leela waves the hand she's not using on my back. 'You think I don't know what's going on? I've worked here for six years, inked more local scrotes and bully boys and skaters than you can count. Heard all the horror stories, the sob stories. And I don't truck with the cops.' She gives me a significant look in the mirror. 'That's why I do good business. It's not my milkshake that brings all the boys to the yard, y'know what I'm saying?'

'I guess.'

'So what's your arrangement?' she asks casually. 'You deal?'

I try to ignore the feeling like there's a white-hot poker inching its way down my back, think about what to say. Snowie and the boys wouldn't come here if they thought there was a danger.

I decide to just be honest. 'I run.'

Leela makes a dry laugh. 'Not fast enough, apparently, if you're still mixed up in this shit. D'you use?'

'Nah. I'm clean.'

'That's how they all start out,' she says quietly. In the mirror I see her shrug. 'Well, it's a good preliminary survival strategy, anyway. How'd you end up here in Mildura?'

'Ah. That's a long boring tale of woe.'

'Okey doke.' She doesn't seem bothered I'm withholding info, tilts her head in the mirror. 'You want some advice from an old hand? Someone who's acquainted with the industry but not involved in it?'

'Sure.' Considering I feel like I'm making it up as I go along most of the time, any advice is welcome.

'It's just you seem like a reasonably intelligent guy...'

'Tell me whatever you think'll be useful,' I say, leaving things open.

'All right. Here's some distilled wisdom for you.' She cleans the tip of the needle, loads more ink and starts a new area on my back. 'Three pieces of advice. Number one, don't mix your loyalties. You're part of Leon's crew, so don't forget it. There's two other crews in town, under Little Toni or Mazerati, but if you start turning tricks for the other bosses you'll have a very short shelf life. Got it?'

'Sounds legit.'

'Okay. Number two, don't get on the gear.'

I roll my eyes. 'That seems pretty obvious.'

'You'd think so, right?' She swipes down my back with a sterile wipe. It stings. 'Well, that's the advice I give everybody, but they never listen.'

I wince against the pain, control the urge to jerk when the needle dips in again. 'And what's the third piece of wisdom?'

'Don't get sucked in by the money. Get out before this business kills you.' Leela concentrates on her work. 'Nobody takes that advice either. They're always, like, "Oh, I need to do one more job", or "I've just gotta pay off the blah blah". Forget the blah blah. Get in, make whatever money you can, get out. If you can do those things, in that order, then you might be the last man standing when the shit goes down.'

Suddenly the dizziness I got this morning holding that money rises up inside me like bile. Is this chick psychic? How did she know? Then I realise: she doesn't know. She's just seen my story play out dozens of times before. Other boys, other lives, same tale of woe.

I take a big breath and let it out. 'How d'you know it's gonna go down?'

There's a moment's silence and all I hear is the buzz of the equipment. When I look up, Leela is staring at me in the mirror. Her perfectly-made-up mouth twists into a sad smile. 'Oh, honey. Haven't you figured it out yet? In your industry, there's nowhere to go *but* down.'

Half an hour later I leave the shop, my skin still smarting, a new bandage on my back. The work's all done now and it won't take as long to heal this time, Leela said.

But I'm thinking more about all the other things she said. I'm just another anonymous cog in this machine. It'd make me feel low if I didn't have an ace up my sleeve. This isn't all of me. Amie and the sarge know what's going on. I'm doing something here, something important, and when this job is done I'll walk away, light and clean as Teflon, just like I said to Reggie. That's what I keep telling myself, anyway.

I push through the door and walk into the lounge room, still thinking about it. Then I see something that stops me dead.

The lounge room is dim and muggy, like always. Kevin and Reggie are sitting on the sagging couch, lit by the jaundiced glow of the TV. They're watching the shopping channel. Kevin is in a trackie jacket, with a sarong wrapped around his skinny waist, smoking a cigarette and gesturing at the screen, saying, 'But why would you wanna cook without fat, eh? Fat makes it taste nice.'

And Reggie is having a pipe.

I dunno if he's seen me. He's sucking on the glass teat, using the lighter off the coffee table to keep a flame under the bowl. The bowl turns white as the smoke swirls inside it.

My brain turns white as well. Something inside my chest breaks, and I feel an ache. Leela's words punch me again: *Honey, in your industry there's nowhere to go but down.*

In your industry. *Your* industry.

Kevin looks up and sees me. 'Yo, Hazza! You're back, mate.'

'Um, yeah.' I have to ignore my chest, ignore the ache. Play it cool. Act normal. 'Tools-down time.'

Reggie makes a little cough. The white smoke trails around his face as he raises a hand. 'Hey, dude.'

'Hey.' I nod on automatic.

Kevin gives Reggie a pat on the back. 'Don't cough, mate, you'll waste it.'

'Shut up.' Reggie's grinning. He clicks the lighter again, raises the pipe.

I lick my lips. 'Right. Leave you to it then.' I walk off down the hall.

Once I'm in my room I let myself exhale. Let the ache out. Leela is right. Every other little shit-bird crank peddler in town is using their own product; I don't know why I imagined Reggie would be any different. But I did imagine it. And I was wrong.

My view of the world has suddenly been flipped on its arse.

Reggie is using.

I'm living in a house full of drug dealers. I'm surrounded by the business of shards, baggies, pipes and skaters. It shouldn't be a big deal. But seeing that kid – he's just a kid! – suck up a hit of ice was like listening to a song played in a minor chord.

Shit, when I was his age I was well on my way: stealing booze and smoking weed and getting hammered every chance I could get. It's not the same, though. Ice fucks you up. Turns your skin inside out. Gouges holes in your brain. Rots your teeth. Destroys sleep. Makes you feel like the king of the universe, while it eats you alive.

I dunno what to do, what to think. Reggie's using, and it's normal for him, and it's everywhere here, and I have to act cool about it, like I'm okay with it. And I'm not okay with it. And I'm part of the bloody system that's *delivering* it to him.

Fuck.

Fuck.

I have never hated this job, this whole fucking *industry*, as much as I do right now.

18

amie

'This,' Harris says, 'is product.'

He's holding up a little plastic bag he's scrounged out of his pocket. It's just a normal ziplock bag. But the contents are not normal. I see a few grams of brittle off-white crystals that would seem innocuous if they were stored in a jar on your spice rack.

I squint at the bag. 'It looks like rock salt.'

Harris cocks an eyebrow. 'Yeah, you probably don't wanna sprinkle this into the spag bol or anything.' He lays the baggie on our kitchen table.

It's Sunday, just after two in the afternoon, and I got home from my shift to find Harris in our house, having a cuppa with Dad, like it's the most normal thing in the world. I've only just had time to get over the shock of seeing him here, and change out of my work clothes; now I'm sitting in on this little business talk, and Harris has produced the bag of ice, like a party favour.

Something has happened, though, since I spoke to him last. He's still working the same grungy street look in his dirty jeans and boots, the black hoodie. His surfer hair is tangled, like he's raked it back with his fingers too many times. But it's not the outside of him that's different. It's the expression on his face, the way he carries himself. The vulnerability I saw in him last Tuesday by the river seems to have been whittled away. He seems more purposeful, more directed. The anxiety in his eyes has been replaced by a cool determination.

I can only wonder at the change, file it for later. Now the conversation is all about the 'product'.

Dad leans across to examine the baggie. 'This isn't local?'

'This is from Melbourne,' Harris says. 'About five hundred bucks worth – there's five points in there. More expensive, this stuff. The local product isn't ready yet, and it won't be as clean.'

'They're stepping on it pretty heavily?'

'Yeah, they're gonna chop it up with Epsom salts or something. Wouldn't want to stick it up my arm, personally.'

That makes me gape. 'You inject it?'

'Yeah.' Harris shakes his head. 'Sounds crazy, right?'

'Or they smoke it,' Dad says, to clarify. 'Either way, it's not gonna do you any good. Who gave you this?'

'Snowie,' Harris says. 'Leon's happy with me, I've been doing a good job as a cash courier, and when Snowie said he needed to make a delivery down here I offered to make it easy for him. Said I needed to come see Dad anyway, drop in at the hospital...'

'You're still sticking to the hospital story?' I ask.

'Yep, although I made it sound like a chore.' His gaze holds mine. 'This'll be the last time I get to use that as an excuse.'

'Tell me about local production,' Dad says.

'Well, apparently, there was a big bust about three months ago, cleaned out a few of the more reliable cooks.'

'Yeah, Mildura CIU broke up a party in Irymple a while back.'

'Right. So Leon's got his out-of-town suppliers, plus he's bankrolling this new lab. Two boys from Swan Hill have got things cranking. Not much I can tell you except it'll be big quantities, and delivery should be happening soon. Dunno dates, dunno details yet. Won't be too hard to find out though.'

'Just keep your questions low-key. You don't want to seem obviously nosy.'

'Or I'll get my nose cut off – yeah, I figured that out already.' The way Harris says it so casually, snorting at the joke, makes me shiver. He lifts his mug in Dad's direction. 'I'm being low-key, hey. It's not that hard to get info. One of the guys I'm working with has a mouth like a sewer trap. Vomits words. Snowie's not so good at subtlety himself. All I have to do is sit at the table, drink my beer and keep quiet, and the others all fill in the blanks.'

'Good,' Dad says. 'Better if you're a listener, not a talker.'

I touch the bag with the tip of my finger. 'What about this stuff? You're supposed to offload it, right?'

Harris nods. 'Some of it is for me to distribute as I see fit. And some of it's on order for Gavin Donovan.'

I look quickly at Dad, who returns my look before nodding at Harris. 'Right. You been given any names for who to pass the rest onto?'

'Said I knew a few parties who'd be interested. Nobody who'll report back, except for Gavin.'

'So you give Gavin his share –'

'Dad!'

Dad turns to me, one hand raised. 'He's gotta do it, Amie. If Snowie realises Gavin missed out he'll get suspicious of Harris.' He looks back to Harris. 'You give Gavin his share. Then after you leave, I'll bust him. Not for this – I've already got an excuse for picking him up. This'll just be the icing on the cake when I get him for violations on his car.'

Harris sucks on his bottom lip. 'No guarantee he won't whack it up his arm before you catch him.'

'I'll just have to risk it. There's a fair bit there – if I move fast he won't have a chance to use it all before I search him.'

'Is arresting Gavin really the only way?' I ask.

'Far as I can see, yes.' Dad sips his tea, sits back in his chair. 'Amie, if I bust Gavin for possession, he'll get referred to a rehab clinic. And it'll be expedited and mandated by a court order, so he won't have to wait and he won't be able to skip out. If the judge is sensible, they might even mitigate his jail sentence into custodial-plus-rehab. Trust me, that's a good outcome for Gavin.'

Harris leans over the table towards me. 'Could be a lot worse, Amie. Gavin's gonna sweat, but he'd be doing that anyway. Better he sweat it out in a rehab place.'

'The rest of it...' Dad flicks a finger at the ziplock bag full of drugs on our kitchen table. 'You return that to me, Jared can put it in impound. Meanwhile, I'll give you what you're owed. You go back to Mildy looking like a good boy.'

Harris nods. Dad's face gets that satisfied look, the one he always wears after he's solved a particularly tricky tinkering job. 'Harris, you're doing a good thing. Get more info on the local batch and I'll pass it on to CIU. If we can break up the operation before delivery, that'll be a great help. That'll make a dent.'

'Mildura will start to look unappealing as a drug-holiday destination,' Harris says.

'Exactly. And if this guy, Leon, goes down, then even better.' Dad's mouth makes a bitter twist. 'I hate guys like him. Local kingpins acting like the bloody mafia. They saw *Breaking Bad* on the telly once and decided they'd give it a go – get-rich-quick scheme. Top up the old superannuation. They're like a poison. They don't give a shit about the community they're living in, the community they're destroying. It's all about the money.'

'Leon's a poisonous bastard, I know that much.' Harris's lips curl in a similar way. His face has a zealous anger. 'I wouldn't mind seeing someone knock him off his perch.'

'Well, you could be the little rock that brings Goliath down, mate.'

'Sounds mighty appealing.' Harris stands, pushing back his chair with a creak. He swipes the plastic baggie off the table.

I'm glad it's gone, out of sight. That doesn't mean I'm not still thinking about it. 'What're you doing now?'

'Gotta make delivery,' he says, shrugging. 'And I've gotta get outta here, hey. I parked miles away, and snuck in quiet, but the less time I spend here, the better.'

'Good,' Dad says. 'When's your next check in with Amie?'

'Dunno.' Harris looks at me. 'How're we gonna work this? Like I said, this is my last trip to Ouyen for a while...'

I'm honestly not sure. I rub my forehead. 'We need to work out a new system and we need to talk about it. If you're dropping that off to Gavin, then meet me after. In about an hour, say?'

'I gotta stop and see my dad, too,' he says, very deliberately not frowning. 'Gimme an hour and a half. Not here, but.'

'At the rez, past the old Lutheran Church? We can walk in from different directions. I'll take the camera so it looks legit.'

'Cool. See you at the rez a bit before four.' He ducks out.

Dad turns to me, looking quietly triumphant. 'And you're still worried about him?'

I cross my arms over my chest. 'Yeah, actually, I am. He seems stronger today, sure, but it's not always like that.'

'But it's working for him, Ames. You can see that, right? And he's good at it. He's a bloody natural.'

Harris does seem more relaxed, I'll give Dad that. But I'm thinking about the bigger picture. 'So, I guess you'll be arresting Gavin Donovan soon.'

'Yeah, I'd better ring Jared and give him the heads-up.' Dad slugs back the rest of his tea, pushes out of his chair. Sees my expression. 'Don't stress about Gavin. This'll be good for him. He might not look at it that way, but it's true. And don't stress about Harris. Did you see his face? He looks like he's finally found his calling.'

Dad's face is lit, too, with that strange fire, just like Harris. They're both glowing with this energy, eyes on the prize. And they get off on it: it's the Secret Agent dream every six-year-old boy has. I'd almost be excited about it, too, but I saw Craig Davies. He and his sister will have those scars – mental and physical – forever.

Harris has enough scars. He doesn't need to add to the collection.

*

When I arrive at the rez, hiking socks rolled down and my camera in my hand, I discover Harris is already here, sitting half-hidden under a big tree. He's taken off his hoodie, and his threadbare T-shirt has spots of red on it. There's a butterfly closure on a cut high on his forehead, near the hairline. The skin around the cut looks red, puffy.

'What the hell happened?' I plonk down beside him, dump my camera and reach over to examine the cut. It's not bad, but it's fresh.

Harris shies away. 'S'nothing.' He sighs. 'Dad got pissy when I showed up. He was in the middle of having a shit-fit, then he got all gaspy and bent over and stuff. I had to take him in to the hospital. They've admitted him for observation, but I think he's gonna be there for a few days.'

'The cancer?'

'Yeah. It's in his liver. He looked really yellow. At least someone else is looking after him now.'

'And the cut?'

Harris colours, looks at the water of the reservoir. 'He threw a bottle at me.'

'Bloody hell –'

'It's my own fault. Shoulda ducked faster.' He picks at the flat stones on the ground between us, setting them on top of each other in a little cairn. 'Told the docs to call me if there's a problem. But I'm kinda glad he's in the hospital. Now I don't need to worry about what he's getting up to without me.'

'I still don't understand why you bother,' I blurt.

Harris meets my eyes. 'He's my father. And believe me, I've been uncivil in the past. But if I treat him like he's always treated me, then I'm as bad as he is.' His sober expression changes into a sad smile. 'I'm not tryin' to be holy. I just want him to know that real people, normal people, they don't act the way he does. I want him to know I'm different.'

'You *are* different.' I squint at him. 'In fact, today you're really different. Did something happen up in Mildura?'

He shrugs. 'Ah, shit... Yeah. I got some bad news, I guess you'd say. This kid in the house, he's one of the street dealers, I got to know him a bit. Then I found out he's on the gear. Kinda spun my head around.'

Now the expression of anger I saw on his face earlier makes sense. 'Fired you up about this narc work, did it?'

'Yeah.' He straightens, tucks his right foot under his bad leg, leans back on his hands. 'Anyway, I'm hoping that once this batch delivery comes up, I'll be able to pull out. The whole crew'll get done, Leon will get busted, and my job will be over.'

I pick at the stones he's abandoned. 'I can't say I'll be sad to see the finale.'

The idea that this ordeal might be finished soon gives me a warm feeling inside. But then I remember: once the job is done, Harris will be gone. That puts a dampener on my fuzzy glow. I remind myself this isn't about me and Harris, and the final outcome is still far from decided.

Harris seems to be considering an end to his involvement

though. 'Apart from the general awfulness of it all, I'm bloody sick of sitting in Flamingos, listening to the boys piss and moan. I mean, it's not as if they really like each other or get on. They're just hanging out together because of the job. I guess they'd say they were mates. But they chip at each other all the time, and dish shit... Sometimes I feel like they just put up with each other, and with me, because they have to. Because they're stuck with it.'

'Yeah, that sounds kind of weird.' I lean back on my own hands. The afternoon is sultry. 'Most of the guys around here seem to get on with each other okay. They're blokey, but in a nice way. They're not aggro – they help each other out. They've got manners too, some of them.'

'Well, they've got manners when your dad's around, that's for sure.' He raises an eyebrow at me. 'I'm kinda amazed he let you hang out with any of the local guys, considering he knows the dirt on all of them.'

You included, I think, but I'm not gonna say that. I push my shoulder against his. 'Hey, if I wanna go out with someone, I'll go out with them. I don't need Dad vetting applicants. That would just be creepy, and unfair.'

He eases back onto his elbows. The sun from across the rez tints his face and chest gold. 'So he didn't vet Nick Partridge, when you went out with him?'

'No!' My shock-horror face has a blush to it, though, I'm sure. 'Well, not much.'

'I'll bet.' He grins. 'How long were you and Nick together?'

I arch one eyebrow. 'That's not really any of your business, is it?'

'I know.' He waves a persistent fly away. 'Sorry, I know it's not my business.'

But I don't want to close off this conversation. I take a breath, gather my courage. 'Well, in the spirit of sharing...'

'What, about six months?'

'Eight months,' I say quietly.

'Wow.'

I nudge him again. 'What are you "wow"-ing about? You got it on with almost every eligible girl between here and the border.'

'Yeah, well...' He purses his lips.

'But you never fell for anyone.'

'I fell for someone.' He looks away. 'She was involved with someone else.'

'When has that ever stopped you?'

That surprises a laugh out of him. 'Hey! Jesus, I'm not a complete hound.' He looks at me, away. 'I mean, I tried to tell her, but she just... She wasn't interested.'

'Are you talking about Rachel Watts?'

He shrugs. I get the impression the knock-back hurt, but he's not going to moan about it.

'Well, that's news,' I say.

'What, that I fell for someone?'

'Yeah. I always thought love 'em and leave 'em was your style.'

Both his eyebrows take a hike. 'My *style*? I have a *style*?'

'Around this district you do.' I grin.

'Jesus...' He laughs. 'But you, though. Eight months – phew. So you and Nick were serious?'

Which is a euphemism for sex, like sex is serious. I never got that. Sex has always been pretty fun, as far as I'm concerned, and I'm surprised Harris, of all people, would subscribe to a different philosophy.

'I guess,' I say. 'But me and Nick were never completely...' I sink back onto my elbows; I've tried to figure it out in my head before. 'I mean, a relationship isn't all breathy sighs and flowers, is it? It's more how you fit together. Whether you get on. Make each other laugh – and think. Whether you can talk about stuff with each other. Genuine stuff.'

He considers that. 'Whether you can both be your real selves with each other.'

'Yes.'

'But what if you're not a good fit in bed?'

I shrug. 'I think that's part of it. If you're a good fit in life, you'll be a good fit physically.'

'So you and Nick weren't a good fit? On either level?'

'No. I mean, Nick's a great guy. We fit okay with some things, which is why we were together so long. But mostly we were just...'

'Wrong pieces.'

'What?'

'Like in a jigsaw. Some pieces, they look like they should fit, but you get them together and they don't.'

'True.'

'But the sex was okay?'

I laugh because I can feel my cheeks heating up again. The setting sun is striking us square on, so maybe that's the warmth I'm feeling. 'I can't believe I'm talking about this with you... Yes. No. It was okay.'

'Just okay?' He makes the air quotes with his fingers.

I roll my eyes at him. 'Well, I don't have the vast range of experience you've had, so...'

He snorts and grins. 'Trust me, if it's good, you know.'

I squint at him. 'How do you know?'

There's a pause. He swallows, looks away. 'You know.'

'That's specific.'

'Fuck, I can't tell you how you...' He laughs, and the sound is slightly helpless. 'It's just... Your whole body feels alive.'

'But you've never had sex with anyone you really loved,' I point out.

'So?'

'So maybe it's different then.'

'I guess.' He shrugs again. 'Maybe it is. Maybe it will be.'

I want to look away when he says that, but I can't. Harris has my eyes locked up with his. The pause goes on and on, and my blood moves fast inside me. My pulse thunders in my ears. Harris licks his bottom lip, and I stare and stare, and –

Something else starts thundering. It's my phone.

The interruption jars me into full consciousness. When I fumble my phone out of my jeans pocket and see the name above the number, I get another cold splash of alertness. It's my cousin.

'Oh shit –'

'You better get that,' Harris says.

'Yeah, hang on –' I thumb the phone to accept the call. 'Beena?'

'Oh, thank god,' my cousin says. 'I was worried I'd only get your voicemail, and it's getting late in the day.'

'What, what is it?' The tone of her voice brings me sitting up. 'Are you okay? Is everybody all right?' I wince: I sound like my dad, and his 'all right's.

'It's Nani,' she says. 'No, no, please don't be anxious, okay? She's fine. I mean, she's fine now. But we had a problem today because Jas is on her honeymoon, and Mum was working, and I went out to the back garden just for a moment –'

My voice sounds odd and far away. 'What happened?'

'Nani wandered off. We still have no idea how she managed to walk so far, she was only in chappals, for god's sake –'

My eyes close on a heartbeat. 'Is she okay?'

'She tried to cross the road at Deakin Street, you know how busy it is there...'

For a second my stomach seems to fly up into my throat until I register that Bee's explaining further.

'...anyway, she must have got a fright, or heard a car horn or something, because she fell back onto the pavement. That's what

280

the paramedic said at the scene.'

'You called the ambulance?' When I glance over, I see Harris is gazing at me intently.

'Yes, Mum called them as soon as she found her. But look, Nani's fine, she wasn't hurt, just a bit shaken. And we're all a bit shaken. This is why I'm calling you, because Mum and I have work tomorrow, and then I have classes after lunchtime –'

'You want me to come and look after Nani,' I say, realising where this is going.

'Yes. I'm so sorry to call you about this, but Mum suggested you might be able to come up for a few more days until we can sort out a solution.' Bee exhales deeply after getting all this out. 'I know you've just arrived back home and I know you have work of your own. But we thought you might have a bit more flexibility.'

I don't hesitate. 'It's totally fine. Not a problem. I can be up by tonight, if you like.'

Beena sighs again, and this time it sounds more relaxed. 'Oh, Amita, thank you so much. Mum will be so relieved. I don't know what's going on with Nani, she's never wandered off like this before...'

'Don't worry, Bee, it'll be okay. We'll work something out.'

'Oh, thank you, thank you! Phew. I was so stressed, and we're all still a bit muddled after the wedding, and Nani, she'll be so happy to see you again. She talks about you all the time lately.'

'I know.' I'm surprised to find my voice has thickened. I get a hold of myself. 'Look, tell Auntie I'll be there eight at the latest. I'll get away as soon as I can.'

I round out the conversation with Beena and disconnect. My arm feels warm; Harris has moved closer to me. He's pressing his arm gently against mine, propping me up. 'Is your nanna okay?'

'She wandered away from the house this afternoon, and it sounds as if she nearly got hit by a car....' I see his expression and hurry on. 'No, she's all right. But Jasminder is still on her honeymoon, and Beena and my aunt both have responsibilities tomorrow, so they've asked me to come and help out.'

Harris frowns at the news. 'Is she really losing it, your nanna?'

'I don't know. She's become very absent-minded lately. She thought I was my mum last time I was there. But this wandering thing is new.'

'Will you be okay to drive? You've just come off shift.'

'I'll be all right. Anyway, there's no way around it. The family needs me.' I let my shoulders settle back, give Harris a rueful smile. 'So. It looks as if we're both going back to Mildura.'

He exhales softly and looks away, but not before I see the flash of his eyes.

19

harris

Driving back feels like flying, with the window down and warm air blowing in my face. The sky is still a deep aqua colour, so every black bush and tree looks like a shadow play.

Amie's coming back to Mildura. She's only a few hours behind me. The knowledge makes my brain hum. I don't want her there: it's too dangerous, too close. But I want her there *so bad*. Just knowing she's arriving later tonight fills my whole body with energy.

After she finished on the phone to her cousin, we sat on the dirt under the tree until our skin felt like liquid sunlight, and it was time for me to leave.

When I got up and dusted myself off, Amie stood up too.

'This doesn't have to be all your responsibility, Harris. You don't have to keep going with it. Dad's looking for your family. He said to remind you that you can pull out any time –'

I shook my head. 'It's nice he's trying to track Mum and Kelly. I dunno how far he'll get, but it's nice. As for the rest... People are getting hurt. More people will cop it if we don't shut it down.' I scuffed the dirt with my boot, looked out to the sunset on the other side of the rez. 'And I'm in it now. I'm gonna see it through to the end. I think I need to do that.'

Then something happened: Amie hugged me. Just grabbed me by the back of the neck and pressed herself in. I don't know what surprised me more – the fact she did it, or the feel of her against me. All soft, and skinny arms, and her face in my neck, and plump breasts against my chest. The shock of it made me freeze in place for a second before I unfroze and wound an arm around her. Both arms.

She squeezed me hard enough to make me gasp, then she pulled away. 'C'mon, I'll walk you to the car.'

We didn't really say much more before I left. She clasped my arm before I slid into the driver's side. She was still standing there by the trees near the rez when I looked in the rear-view. Then I pulled out onto the dirt road to the turn off, and she was gone.

I keep going over and over it in my head: the things Amie said, the easy way we talked, the whiteness of her teeth when she laughed. That moment she asked me how you know when sex is good, I almost said, *I could show you.* It was right there on my tongue's tip while I was looking into her eyes. But I wouldn't have managed the proper jokey tone. And the conversation was already so loaded I couldn't do it, I couldn't go there.

This isn't like the way I felt about Rachel. It's different. Rachel made me feel as if I was worth something. But Amie makes me face myself, the whole unvarnished truth of me. And she accepts me. The bad shit as well as the good.

Even the sensations I have around her are different: clearer, sharper, hotter. Definitely hotter. Hot enough that my skin feels too thin to contain everything. It's like I've been saving up the wanting inside myself, and it's so close to the surface now that if I let it go, I'll shatter.

I try to consider it in really concrete terms. I haven't had sex for a long time. Girls' bodies are nice: you can't help but think about them. This feeling, like I'm barely stopping myself from reaching for Amie every time I see her, it's just normal. I shouldn't wind myself up about it.

And I can't be a prick about this. If Amie and me... Well, let's just say I'm not interested in having Sergeant Blunt chasing me around for the rest of my life.

But if Amie and me...

I let the thought carry on. I can't touch, but I can fantasise, right? A guy can fantasise. Nothing wrong with that. Not a hanging offence, a bit of fantasy.

Christ.

*

Amblin Court is more of a disaster than usual when I rock back up. The kitchen is like a bloody bomb site and the couch is tipped over, lying on the living room floor like a giant brown cockroach on its back.

'Reggie and Dil,' Kevin says, shrugging. We right the couch together.

I clean up in the kitchen, then realise my own room is as much of a dump as the rest of the house. I shove all my dirty sheets and clothes – which is basically everything I own, except the stuff I'm wearing – into a bin bag, twist the top and take it out to the Pitbull. Food's a priority, and I'm planning to cruise by the club and see Snowie, let him know the delivery went okay. May as well make a stop at the laundromat if I'm heading into town.

Being inside the club before opening time is weird: everything looks a lot more squalid under harsh fluoros. Bartenders are setting up and some bloke is giving the dance floor a sweep. Music is playing, stop-start and down low, as the DJ preps her set.

Snowie is standing by the bar, sucking back a cold one. He's jittery. I've noticed he's been drinking a lot more lately, and I wonder if he's on the gear. It wouldn't surprise me.

'All good, mate, all good,' he says, when I tell him the news. His head bobs as he talks, and he lights another cigarette off his last one. 'Come back later and we'll see what else the bossman wants done. Hey, you haven't seen Ando about, have ya?'

'Nah, mate, I just got in. Feet have hardly hit the ground, y'know?' I wouldn't be keen to lay eyes on Ando anyway, but I don't need to mention that.

'Awright, no worries.' Snowie looks worried, though. 'Guess I'll catch up with him later.'

I get out of the club, pick up some takeaway and collect my laundry. Everyone is getting tight as delivery day for the big batch approaches. Tempers are starting to fray. It's like when I'm driving from Mildura to Ouyen and back again: I'm always on the lookout, I'm always scanning from one side of the road to the other, checking for roos. Because you can't predict when they're gonna jump. They just come at you with no warning.

That's how I feel now I'm back in the thick of things: like I'm always on the alert. I'm always scanning. It's kind of exhausting, being so alert all the time.

Later that night, after I've got orders to report back to the club tomorrow, I lie on my bed with the window open. I check the texts on my phone, return again and again to the message I got from Amie just before eight p.m.

Test results have arrived all clear. Contact reception for apptmts as rqd.

I'd like to call her, ask her how she's getting on, ask how her nanna's going, just listen to her voice... But the atmosphere around here at the moment is fragile. The closer I stay to the house, the better.

My clean sheets are soft from the laundry, and the breeze through the window is fresh. The scent of Ouyen, of wheat fields and dust, is gone: the aroma of car exhaust and suburbia has swallowed it up. But somewhere to the north of town Amie is breathing the same air. For now, that thought has to be enough to calm me.

*

I'm eating leftover noodles in the kitchen next morning when Steph clumps in, still in her leathers. Her black cropped hair sticks up from her head, and she dumps her motorbike helmet on the floor before making a cup of instant shit.

'Business or pleasure?' I ask, nodding at the helmet.

She glares at me over her shoulder. 'Harris, it's been a long fucking night, so if you're only talking to piss me off –'

'Jesus.' I check out the set of her shoulders as she turns around with her mug. 'Just making conversation, hey. My bad.'

She sighs, unkinks her neck. 'Sorry. I'm tired.'

'Sit.' I lift my chin at the other plastic chair. 'Drink your coffee.'

She flops in the chair, jacket unzipped in front, sipping slowly. Her face is sweaty from the helmet, cheeks flushed.

I eat my noodles, try not to look like I'm examining her. 'You got a good bike?'

'Yeah.' She seems surprised by the change of subject. 'I mean, it's okay. Running a bit rough lately, I gotta spend some time on it.'

'I could have a look, if you like.'

She turns the mug in her hands. 'I usually do my own work.'

'That's cool. Whatever.'

Noise from next door – a woman yelling, a little kid crying – seeps through the kitchen walls. I scrape up cold noodles with my fork. 'You're studying, right? What sorta study are you doing?'

'What do you care?' She sees my expression. Makes a bit of effort. 'Business management.'

'Business management?' I amend my tone quickly at the look on her face. 'Okay, business management. Sounds all right.'

'It's just a diploma.' She shrugs. 'Something to do, hey.'

'You like it?'

'I got a brain. I like to use it.'

I think for a minute. 'What sorta study would you do if you wanted to be a photographer?'

'What?'

'What would you study if you wanted –'

'You wanna be a photographer?' Steph stares at me.

'No. I mean, I don't wanna be a photographer. I just know somebody who's... I was just interested, that's all.'

'Harris, has anyone ever told you you're weird?'

Any reply I might've made gets shelved when Reggie gallops into the kitchen. He runs to the fridge and rummages for his Gatorade, spins around and slams the fridge shut with his arse. 'Yo, what's up? Whatcha talkin' about?'

His green hood slides off and I see his head. He's shaved off his hair. All that's left is the skinny rat's tail at his nape. It's a crap shave job: there's tufty-dark patches, bald patches, as well as red nicks here and there where the razor slipped. He looks hard-man tough and impossibly young all at the same time.

'Just saying how Harris is weird,' Steph says.

'No shit.' Reggie grins, gulps like he's parched, gulps until the bottle's empty.

I blink at him. 'What'd ya do to your hair, ya crazy fucker?'

'It was itching me,' Reggie says. He pitches the bottle at the sink, takes off with a snorting laugh.

There's a little silence in the kitchen. Me and Steph look at each other across the table, both our jaws clenched.

*

'Nice work,' Leon says, 'taking that packet to Ouyen.'

I shrug. I'm wondering how nice he'll think it is if he learns one of the receivers got busted. Or maybe he doesn't care – what's gone is gone. Not like anyone can trace it back to him.

'All right. Now go to this address.'

He waves a scrap of paper which I pluck from his fingers to read. 'What am I doing in...Tulane Road?'

'Let's call it collecting the rent.' Leon smiles, which looks unpleasant. Someone should tell him not to bother. 'Should be a packet for me. Bit of cash, and some product samples.'

'The new stuff?' My head lifts.

Leon is cagey. 'Just samples, like I said. Nothing substantial yet.'

If we're getting samples that means it's not far off. Could be a matter of days. I'll have to let Amie know.

'Talk to Skunk,' Leon goes on. 'Scruffy-looking guy, wears thongs. Be nice and he'll offer you a beer.'

'Great.' If his name's anything to go by, Skunk might offer me more than a beer. I tear the scrap of paper into pieces.

'Don't bring the whole package back here,' Leon warns. 'Give the samples to Snowie, then let me know when you're coming in with the rest.' He dismisses me with one hand. 'That's it. Happy travels.'

It's not until I'm in the Pitbull that it occurs to me: Leon and I sounded so casual. I've started to relax around him. It's unnerving because I thought I'd kept my guard up. I don't *want* to be comfortable around Leon. He's not the kind of guy you want to take for granted. And one slip by me when my guard's down...

I wonder what's caused the shift in me, then realise straightaway what it is.

Leon is a businessman. He does a lot of really bad shit, but it follows a logical pattern. He might have Ando break someone's legs, for instance, but it's not because he dislikes them. It's because he's trying to get what he's owed, or because someone's done the wrong thing for the business, or because they're a competitor. Sure, he might get pissed at them – maybe he takes it a bit personally. But for Leon, it's generally not personal. It's all business.

So his actions are explicable, reasoned. There's no drunken whims or paranoid delusions or volcanic eruptions of anger. He's a lot more predictable and considered than my dad, for instance.

And that's what's made me relax. Knowing Leon has a system, has logic, is easier to handle than my father by a wide margin. Dad's actions are erratic, explosive. Dealing with Leon is a cakewalk by comparison.

The thought is freaking me out as I get closer to Tulane Road. Clouds play tricks with the sunlight on the street as I park the Pitbull near the corner and walk in. Nicer part of town, this. Lawns are tidy, plenty of bottlebrush in flower on the pedestrian verge, roomy on the road. Not quite the Paris end of town, but getting there.

The house I'm heading towards is a pleasant-looking cream weatherboard on a rear-sloping block. Blue trim edges the window frames. The garden's overgrown but nothing looks out of place – except for a muddy chewed-up section of grass on the verge out front. Some idiot's parked his big-wheeled car here and then burned off. Bad manners, some people.

I open the gate, follow a concrete footpath around to the left – a closed-up look to the front entrance suggests it's rarely used. Past a Hills Hoist, wooden stairs lead up to a kitchen door at the backside of the house. Rosellas startle out of a jacaranda nearby, fly off in a shrieking whirl. It all seems very country-suburban.

I keep my hands in my hoodie pockets as I take the stairs to a white-painted door. I'm about to knock when I see the deadbolt on the door is snibbed: the door isn't locked. Friendly of them. I'm not used to friendly. And what the hell are any of Leon's people doing, being friendly? Something makes me stay my hand and call through the door instead.

'Ah, g'day? Mate of Skunk's here, come to say hi?' No answer but the rosellas' screeching call. 'Folks? Anyone home?'

That's when I lift my hand to try a knock. The door creaks back under my knuckles. I get a strange whiff of sourness, a sudden premonition, but it's too late. I can't unsee what I'm seeing now, as the white door swings wide.

It's the kitchen of the house, of course. Sink on the right, under the glass louver windows. At the end of the narrow room, the fridge. This would be a nice place to live: lots of natural light, airy, the blue-trim theme carried on inside the house in little details like the skirting boards and window frames.

On the left, an aluminium camp table with a dead girl resting her head on it.

She's looking right at me. Her skin is grey. She's wearing a long hippie skirt, and her dirty-blonde hair hangs down in the classic flower-child style. A hole in the middle of her forehead is coated in black blood. Flies are hovering around it, and around her chapped purple lips.

I notice these details, and I notice the smell – stronger now – and I notice that I don't seem to be able to do anything but stand here. My fist is still raised.

I lower my hand slowly, take deep breaths through my mouth. Take the step over the lintel of the house. I seem to do that without thinking. I stare at the girl and breathe. My skin is tingling.

A buzzing sound – my head swings sideways without volition. Another body lies on the floor to my right. A guy this time, in trackie pants and a tie-dyed T-shirt. The movement I've made, the change in the air currents, makes all the flies on his body lift and swirl around so I can see a mottled face, a beard.

I stand stock still. Listen. The whole house is quiet.

I should be looking for sample bags, loose cash, gold A4 envelopes. I need to do those things. If I don't...

Leon's black-marble eyes swim in my vision.

I make myself move. Walk through the kitchen, into a front living room. Again, natural light from the windows makes everything seem brighter. A mustard-yellow retro couch faces the windows, a bong standing on the coffee table in front of it. Flies circle a guy in jeans sitting on the couch, his hands splayed out to the sides and his brains soaking into the cushions behind his head. He's wearing thongs.

I hear Leon's voice inside my skull: *Talk to Skunk – scruffy-looking guy, wears thongs*. Right. Looks like I've found him.

Hands clenched, I move further to the left, into the hallway of the house. There are three doors along the hall. I open each door with my hoodie sleeve over my fingers. Behind the door to the first room: nothing. A messy bedroom with the maroon curtains drawn. In the second room: more flies. A guy is half-fallen off the bed, his body slowly sinking into the brown-stained carpet. The smell is powerful here, probably from a gut shot. I check the third door, find another empty bedroom. The bathroom is empty, too.

I go back the way I came, try not to jump when I pass the second room and the couch in the living room. The bloated buzzing of the flies seems to be merging with a hot electric prickle on my skin.

I get back into the kitchen. There's an ashtray, a set of electronic scales, a stubby, and two coffee mugs on the table near the girl's head. The chocolate-y liquid in the mugs is skinned over, drying. A pair of latex gloves sits in the congealed black puddle under the girl's ear. I don't look at the matted black crater in the back of her head.

I move around to her front. My brain feels dry. All my goosebumps are stabbing me with tiny needles. An empty ziplock bag is clutched in the hand resting in the girl's lap. No samples. No cash.

The buzzing in the kitchen swirls together with the buzzing in my head. I walk out the kitchen door, down the wooden stairs, turn left onto the concrete path. The smell of the house is still in my nostrils. I take the path through the creaky gate, walking as fast as I can with my limp. More than anything in the world right now I want to be in the Pitbull, clutching the wheel, driving.

I'm only two metres out the gate when a car passes me slowly on Tulane Road. It's a police car.

Shit.

I keep my head low, walk faster. The Pitbull is close. No, wait – getting into my car now is a dumb idea. They'll remember the car.

I limp briskly up to the car, pass it, keep walking. Turn the right-hand corner. Walk to the end of the block. An old man is sitting on a plastic lawn chair in his garden, watering his plants. I turn the corner, right again. I'm sweating. My hoodie is sticking to me.

What the fuck am I doing? I'm moving without direction. The police have seen me walk away from Tulane Road. Did they see me leave the house? I don't know.

I limp halfway down this block, then swing around, double back. The cop car is just coming out of Tulane Road. It noses onto the main drag, goes straight ahead. I wait until it's further down that street, then limp as fast as I can around the corner, until I'm at the Pitbull. I slide into the car, keep the engine quiet, peel off the verge. Drive in the opposite direction to the police.

Where am I driving to? Can't drive to Leon. If I lead the cops to him, he won't be best pleased. Amblin Court is out, too. Gotta get off the street, just for a few hours. But if I drive through town, every man and his dog will see where I'm headed.

My mental directory is coming up blank. Then I remember: Amie's Mildura house is a little north of here. Maybe only a few blocks away. I pull my phone out and call her, driving one-handed.

'Harris?' She sounds sleepy, like she's just woken up from a nap.

'Amie, I'm in trouble.' I can't keep the shake out of my voice. 'I need to get off the street, and I'm on the north side.'

She replies without hesitation. 'Number seventeen, Jubilee Court. No one's home but me and Nani.'

'Is that off Walnut Avenue?' I'm close. I'm so close I can almost touch her.

'Yes, but come in the other way, off Ontario. That's quicker.'

'Five minutes,' I say, and disconnect, because it'll be more like two.

I turn left onto Fifteenth Street, try to keep my brain disconnected from my body. Try to just act and do and be, without thinking.

I can't manage it though. The girl's face comes back to me, with the black hole in the middle of her forehead like a third eye. The smell in the house sits in my throat. The buzzing echoes inside me. It's infecting me, burrowing its way into my guts like a maggot squirming into dead meat...

I turn right onto Ontario Avenue, pull the car over. Open the driver's side door, lean and sick up onto the street. Cough everything out, spit, wipe my mouth on my sleeve. Take a shaky breath and close the door. Drive on.

Jubilee Court is only one block further.

20

amie

After all the recent ducking and hiding, it surprises me when the doorbell rings and Harris is right there.

'What's going on?' I pull him inside the cool hallway. 'You look horrible.'

He's sweating, pale-faced, with his hoodie up. His eyes look haunted. 'I've just been at...'

He stops when Nani comes into the hall, hot on my heels. 'Who is this? Amita, who is this strange boy in our house?'

'He's not a strange boy,' I say firmly in English. Best to normalise it, speak with confidence. 'Nani-ji, this is Harris. I know him from Ouyen. Harris, this is my grandmother, Amarjot Kaur.'

I demonstrate a namaste, and Harris copies me awkwardly, bobs his head. 'Uh, hi.'

I turn to Nani. 'Harris is living in Mildura now, and he was visiting a friend nearby but he started feeling sick on his way home. I told him to stop here until he felt better.'

'Ohh, yes, the heat,' Nani says, nodding. 'The heat can make you see spots.'

'Yeah.' Harris wipes his hoodie sleeve across his eyes. God, he looks like he's seeing ghosts as well as spots. 'Yeah, it's probably the heat.'

Nani nods some more then pulls on my arm. She yanks me down until my ear is close to her face. 'He looks like a sadhu!' she hisses, as if Harris isn't standing two feet away and can't hear every word she's saying.

'Nani!' I make a shushing calming motion. 'He's *not* a sadhu, okay? He's just...he hasn't had a bath for a while. But that's not his fault.'

'Can we discuss my personal hygiene standards later?' Harris grimaces. 'The car's still parked right out front.'

'Okay, okay...' I feel like I'm being split in two. 'Gimme your keys, I'll sort out the car. Nani, why don't you give Harris a drink or something, before he falls over. Just give me a sec.'

Snatching the keys Harris offers and extricating myself from Nani's grip, I head outside. Harris's car is parked sideways on the kerb, the driver's seat still warm from him. I twist the key, the car coughs to life, lurches gingerly up off the bitumen and into the driveway. I ease it all the way up, into the carport.

The rear of the car is still obvious because of the racing stripes. I angst about what to do for a second until I see a folded pile of old bed sheets Hansa has stacked on a plastic storage box near the outhouse. One of the sheets covers the backside of the car nicely. It doesn't look too weird, just someone who's protected their car's paintwork from the sun.

I run back inside, worrying about how Harris and Nani are getting on. Talk about worlds colliding.

They're in the kitchen, of course. Nani is perched on one of the stools at the kitchen island and Harris is sitting beside her. Nani looks tiny next to him, like a nut-brown doll. Harris is sipping from a glass of mango cup stuffed with ice cubes, a sprig of mint floating on top.

Nani's eyes are narrowed but she lifts her head to look at me. 'He likes the mango cup.' As if this is some sort of vindication of Harris's character.

'Everyone likes your mango cup, Nani.' I smile at her. If I seem relaxed she'll relax too. 'I've sorted out the car.'

'Thanks.' Harris is getting some colour back, but his hand on the glass still trembles. 'I'm sorry to call you, to come here –'

'You must come,' Nani says. 'You cannot drive when you are sick. That is how accidents happen.'

Harris looks at her, presses his lips. 'Yeah, you're right. Thank you for the drink.'

Nani beams. 'Mint settles the stomach.'

'Harris, would you like to use the bathroom to wash your face?' I suggest. 'I can show you the way.'

'Yeah, thanks.' He nods and rises, follows me down the hallway. I hear Nani bustling to refill his glass in his absence.

I push him in the door of the bathroom. 'What the hell happened?'

He rubs the heel of his hand across his eyes. 'I was in Tulane Road, picking up some cash for Leon. And samples – there were supposed to be samples of the new gear. And I got up the steps, and they were...' He stops, steadies himself at the bathroom sink. When he speaks again, his voice is a harsh whisper. 'They were all *dead*, Amie. Four people in the house, and they were all...'

My whole body chills. Harris leans over the sink like he's going to be sick. But he's just catching his breath before running the cold tap, full bore.

'Some kind of execution.' He plunges his hands under the water. 'Gunshot wounds. Hardly any struggle, I think. Must've been someone they knew, or maybe they got them late at night.'

'Jesus.'

'Yeah.' He stares at the two of us in the mirror, then shakes his head. 'Anyway, when I got back onto the street, a patrol car came past, and I just...I kinda panicked, I'm sorry. I shouldna come here –'

'Stop that.' I hand him a towel. 'Did the police see you?'

He presses his face into the towel, lifts it. 'Maybe. They saw me in the street, they saw the car. I reckon they'd put two and two together.'

'Then...you've got to stay here a while. Maybe overnight.'

'I can't do that.' He glances towards the door of the bathroom. 'Seriously, Amie, I can't stay more than a few hours, max. It's not safe for me to be here. You gotta think of your family.' He makes a weak grin. 'Not to mention I think your nanna might get a bit suss.'

'Okay, then...' I think, quick and hard. 'Then we should change your appearance. That'll work, won't it?'

His eyes narrow. 'What do you wanna do?'

'Cut your hair, for starters. Your hair is sort of distinctive. Change your clothes, if we can find some others that'll fit.'

'What about the car?'

'Maybe they'll recognise it, sure. But if they see a different guy driving it...'

He nods.

'I'll get scissors and a change of clothes.' I pat his arm, step out and pull the door of the bathroom shut behind me. Walk back up the hallway to the kitchen. 'Nani, I'm afraid Harris was sick in the bathroom. He's really not feeling well. I need to get him a change of clothes.'

Nani looks delighted to be consulted about this problem. 'Your Mami has a box of Uncle Deepan's old clothes... Now where is it?' She hops nimbly off her stool and begins the hunt.

With Nani safely on-task, I search for a pair of scissors in the kitchen drawer and try not to think about houses full of dead people. Mass murder in Mildura. I should call Dad, right now. My hands get a little wobble in them – I breathe deep, control it. That can wait. There's a different sort of emergency happening right now. I head back to the bathroom.

Harris is in the same position I left him, standing over the bathroom sink, only now he's shirtless. His hoodie and T-shirt are balled in the corner. His jeans are slung low on his hips.

'Hair-cutting, right?' he says. 'How we gonna do this?'

But I've been rendered momentarily speechless. I look at his bare chest for one more long second, then give myself a kick. 'We do this with you sitting on the edge of the bath.' I'm relieved at how steady my voice comes out. 'I'll stand in the bath behind you. Then we can collect the mess easy, and you can take a shower straight after.'

'Okay.' He still seems nervy. 'Okay, sounds good.'

'Take a seat.' I make sure the bathroom door isn't fully closed, so Nani doesn't get concerned, before stepping over the edge of the bath. Now I'm immediately behind him. His shoulders are incredibly broad and I see his tattoo: the great brown snake, coiled and sinuous, sleeping there on his back. It's an amazing piece of inkwork. I have to forcibly restrain myself from stroking it with my fingers.

I lay a towel across his shoulders. 'Gotta warn you, I'm not a professional hairdresser, okay?'

'Just chop it all off,' Harris says thickly.

I start snipping. I'm working in a hurry before Nani's voice "hoo-hoo!"'s out from the hallway. I'm really not very experienced at this: I've cut Dad's hair before, but that's usually with the clippers. I lift Harris's locks up and slice about two and a half inches off. Now I have to maintain this length all over. It's going to be a bit of a shaggy mop when I'm done, but his profile will be different which is what he needs.

His shoulders are still twitching. I don't think he's really focused on the haircut.

'I dunno why they were shot,' he says, avoiding his own gaze in the mirror. 'I mean, it was a drug house. Leon's money and the new batch samples – I was s'posed to be picking it all up.'

'So the delivery is close?' I ask.

'Yeah, it's close. I was gonna call you tonight. But the house...' He swallows. 'It looked like they were caught by surprise. There were some signs of resistance, but not...'

I stop mid-cut as I think of something relevant. 'Are you sure they were all dead? If someone was left with injuries –'

'They were dead.' He looks at me in the mirror. 'I checked all the rooms.'

The darkness of it clouds his eyes for a second, until he closes them, shivers. I put my free hand on his shoulder.

'Harris. It's gonna be okay. Just take a few deep breaths.' My training for dealing with patients in shock kicks in of its own accord. But my own energy jitters in response to his nerves. I smooth my hand over the towel around him, calming us both. 'Just take it easy.'

'I'm not feeling very easy.'

'Slow breaths.'

When he opens his eyes he stares at the floor in front of the bathroom sink. 'Those people... They were just some blood and bone that got in the way while someone was looking for the drugs and the cash. It was so clinical. They were expendable.'

He's saying something about himself, somehow. And I can tell we're both reacting differently to the whole scenario. The fear of it, of these killings, makes me want to hide here in the house. For Harris, it makes him want to run. To get out, get in the car and drive away as fast as he can. I feel the energy in him, the way he's containing the urge inside his body, the way it threatens to spill out.

I remember something my dad told me once about emergency situations: it's really hard to wait and take a breath, think about what to do, consider the consequences. It's hard to do nothing if you're a person used to action.

'We'll figure it out. Relax for a second.' I touch Harris's neck gently. 'Let me do this, then we can talk about it.'

He closes his eyes and exhales with a shuddering effort, as if more than breath is escaping him. I concentrate on what I'm doing. My fingers ease up from Harris's nape. His hair has a dark sheen at the roots, but the gold is splintered all the way through, like a lion's pelt. I'm not cutting the blonde out, just the whitened ends scorched by sun.

The bathroom is quiet, the low timbre of our breathing only punctuated by the crisp sound of the scissors. Hair falls in thick strands onto the floor, into the bath, into Harris's lap. I turn his head or shift sideways for a better angle, working quickly, running my fingers through to check the length. It's a choppy job but it's all we've got time for.

When I'm done, Harris doesn't look at himself in the mirror, just turns to me. 'How's that?'

'It looks…different.' *Better*, I want to say. His face is more open now. You can see his eyes. I wonder briefly if the curtain of hair he had before was useful, if he's going to miss the shielding that a fringe can provide. I hope he doesn't feel too exposed. 'I would've cut it shorter, but I didn't know if you'd want that.'

'As long as the cops don't make me, sitting in the Pitbull.'

'Amita!' There's Nani's voice, coming down the hallway.

I step out of the bath quickly, leave the scissors in the sink. Harris stands, nudges the hair trimmings closer to the bathmat with his foot, as I push the bathroom door fully open and step out. 'Nani, it's mostly cleaned up in here but I think Harris would like a shower. Were you able to find any clothes?'

Nani is cradling what looks like half the contents of a laundry hamper. 'Some shirts and things are here. Hansa had clothes in a plastic box.'

I take the armful Nani is thrusting in my direction. 'Oh, that's great. That's really good, thank you.' I pass the pile back to Harris, step right into the hall and close the door behind me. 'Let's give him some space while he's getting himself together.'

I walk back to the kitchen with Nani and wash my hands at the sink. The shower is running, water rushing in the pipes. I'm trying very hard not to think about Harris in the shower – this is not the time to be thinking about that at all – but when Nani speaks, I jump guiltily.

'He will be all right, this Ouyen boy? He looked white in the face.'

I consider the best way to reply. 'He should go home to rest. He'll feel better when he's washed and changed. Harris is new to Mildura, and he has no family to look after him.'

'Then he should come to eat here!' Nani looks aghast at the idea of someone struggling alone. 'You should invite him!'

I backtrack quickly. 'Well, that's a good idea, Nani. But...he's proud. He likes to think he can take care of himself.' I see her look. 'But I'll invite him. You're right, it couldn't hurt.'

When the pipes stop gurgling, I give it five more minutes then walk down the hallway to knock softly on the bathroom door. 'Are you right in there?'

'One sec.' There's a pause, then: 'Okay, I'm coming out.'

The door opens, and I have a brief dizzying moment when I'm hit by the smell of Harris's skin carried on the hot steam. Then he steps out into the hall and I don't know whether to laugh, or frown, or...

'This shirt's a bit much,' he says, still buttoning it up from the waist. 'What d'you reckon?'

I stare – I can't help it. The shirt is a wide-lapelled number, pale pink with a silvery pinstripe. Harris has used the scissors to cut his beard back to stubble, and towel-dried his hair. He looks fresh and clean. His trackie pants have been replaced by a pair of my uncle's old brown trousers: they're not bell-bottomed, but it would be ungenerous to call them boot-cut. They're tight at Harris's hips though. In fact, they're tight in so many interesting places I have to look elsewhere. His new haircut, with his smoother jawline and the pink of the shirt, makes his eyes stand out like green lamps.

I press my lips together against a smile, which doesn't work very well. 'I reckon if you grew out the moustache you'd look like an escapee from a seventies porno.'

'Thanks,' he says drily. 'Trousers are a bit, ah, snug.'

'Really? I hadn't noticed.'

'Uh-huh.' He eyes me, then his eyes track to someplace behind me just as I hear Nani arrive from the kitchen. She bustles forward, takes Harris's face in her hands.

'He is looking better.' She turns his head from side to side as his eyebrows lift. 'Mm. He is quite handsome. The green eyes. And tall, like my Anupam.' She holds Harris's head so he's looking at her level, lowers her voice confidingly. 'My husband. Such a man! He has a full beard, you know.'

'That's, um, good,' Harris says as she releases him. 'Ma'am, I'm sorry to impose on your hospitality. You've been really kind.'

Nani *tsks*. 'Kindness and generosity repay themselves.'

'Thank you for the clothes. I'll make sure to bring everything back.'

'Old clothes of Deepan's.' Nani waves a hand. 'This is no trouble. Nothing is too much trouble for my granddaughter's fiancé!'

I yelp. '*Nani!*'

303

Harris's mouth drops open.

Nani turns to me, smiling as if all her birthdays have come at once. 'For so long I have wanted to see you matched! And now you bring home this handsome boy...'

My face warms up like a space heater. 'Nani, Harris *isn't* my –'

'He wears his trousers like Shah Rukh Khan, hm?' She gives me a twinkling grin.

'Ah,' Harris says. 'Well, um, me and Amie, we're just –'

'Nani, we're not –' I start.

'Oh, you have made me a very happy Nani!' She grabs me and Harris and pulls us by the hands. Harris and I make matching goggle-eyed expressions at each other over the top of her head as we're towed towards the kitchen.

'Now,' Nani says to Harris, 'you have not told me your family name. And what is it that you do? Are you a student? Or perhaps you are working at the hospital, yes? Did you meet Amita there?' She pushes us both onto kitchen stools, slides glasses of mango cup in our direction.

'Uh...' Harris's eyes are round as goose eggs.

'Yes,' I choke out. Sweat is running down the small of my back. 'Harris met me at the hospital.' I give him a panicked glare.

'Um, yeah,' Harris says, nodding. 'But I don't work there. I came in...uh...'

I pick up where he falters. 'Harris is training to be a police officer.' I glance at him quickly. 'He had an accident during training and came in as a patient.'

'A police officer!' Nani exclaims. 'Such dangerous work! You must be a brave young man.'

'Harris is very brave,' I agree. I catch Harris's look. He's putting a brave face on this situation, that's for sure.

Nani swivels back to Harris, owl-eyed behind her glasses. 'Amita's father is a police officer, you know.'

Harris nods his head gravely. 'Yes, ma'am, I'm aware of that.'

'You are? Very good,' Nani says, and she leans forward to rub his cheek, smiling. 'Ah, then you are a good match for my bebe. How lucky I am, to see two granddaughters find husbands!'

I stand up. 'Nani, it's been lovely to have Harris visit but he really has to go now.'

'But you have not eaten!' Nani says. She turns as if she's about to head for the stove.

'*Nani.*'

Harris rises too, taking my cue. 'Yeah, I really do have to go.' He sees Nani's crestfallen expression. 'I'll come for a meal another time though. I promise. Sorry to be rude, but I gotta –'

'Harris has a – a – training class to attend,' I say. 'Yes.'

'Absolutely,' Harris says. 'Yeah, I better not miss that.'

Nani sighs, then nods. 'Ah, you must not miss your class, I understand. Amita will invite you to our house again, won't you, Amita? For a proper Punjabi dinner?'

'I – Yes,' I say. 'Harris will come another night for dinner. I'll make sure of it. Now I'm going to walk Harris out to his car, Nani, all right? I'll be right back.'

Harris makes his goodbyes, with Nani gushing over him, then I finally manage to get him out.

The door has barely shut behind us and I've already started apologising. 'Oh god, she's not usually this bad. Thank you. Jesus, I'm really sorry you had to handle that –'

'It's fine,' he says, grinning. 'It's okay, don't worry about it.'

'I should've expected something like this. She's used to the custom of bringing a fiancé home...' I squeeze my forehead with one hand. 'She probably won't even remember your *name* tomorrow.'

'Relax.' He looks at me. 'She's sweet, your nanna. You told me how she is.'

'It's the last thing you want to be dealing with after –'

'Amie, it's okay.' He turns to me so we both stop. We're nearly at the bedsheet-covered car, standing in the humid green shade of the plexiglass carport roof. 'Y'know, it kinda shocked me outta my own head for a minute, and that's all right. My head was a pretty stress-filled place when I arrived.' He puts his hands on my arms. 'Thank you. For everything. I'm sorry I screwed up and came here. I hope I haven't put you in a mess with your nanna.'

'What will you do now?' I ask softly.

'I dunno.' He looks away, back. 'Go tell Leon, I guess. That's what he'll expect me to do. It's not like I can report it to the cops.'

'You just did,' I remind him.

He blinks, shakes his head. 'Yeah, I forget, sometimes.'

'That I'm your contact?'

'That we're not just hanging out, down by the river and stuff.'

He holds my gaze for a moment. Then his hands move from my arms, one going up to scrub through his changed hair, the other digging in his pants pocket. It takes him a second to realise he's not wearing the same pants.

'Ah, shit, have you got the –'

' – keys to the Pitbull, yes,' I say, fishing them out of my own pocket and offering them up.

'Cheers.' He makes a pale grin. 'Are you still gonna invite me for a proper Punjabi dinner?'

That surprises a laugh out of me. 'I guess I'll have to, won't I? Oh god...'

'Don't worry about it.' He's still smiling as he opens the car door, slips into the driver's seat. 'Call me if your dad has a message, after you tell him the news.'

'For sure. And Harris, please be careful.'

He nods, utterly serious now. 'Always.'

I squeeze his hand on the window edge, pull the bedsheet off the back of the car as he starts the engine. I watch him back out. Then I return to the house. I have to contact Dad immediately, and I have to do Nani damage-control.

Standing with my hand on the door, I wonder if she'll lose this memory before Hansa and Beena get home. She's been losing time a lot more lately. The idea makes me sad.

But it also makes me stressed, the thought of what might happen if Nani *does* remember. Especially if she tells the rest of the family about my handsome trainee-policeman fiancé...

Goddamnit. I'm stuck.

21

harris

It's nearly four in the afternoon – the streets have an end-of-day feeling about them. I bolt from the Pitbull to the house, almost make it safely to the door of my room when I just about trip over Steph in the hallway.

'Whoah.' She looks me up and down. 'Nice threads.'

I shove open the door to my room. 'Not another word.'

Steph steps back, keeping her bowl of Weet-Bix out of the way. 'Hey, I think it looks good on you. And the haircut.'

'Shuddup.'

She stirs her cereal. 'I didn't even know you had a face.'

'I got seen by the jacks walking away from a thing,' I say over my shoulder as I hunt for a pair of jeans, a T-shirt. 'I had to change. And now I gotta fucking change again, so I don't walk into the bossman's office looking like –'

'Like you just walked out of a Bollywood movie?' Steph says.

I freeze, a T-shirt stuck to my hand. I turn to hold her gaze, and when my voice comes out, it's dropped a register.

'A friend lent me the clothes, okay? A friend who I really don't want to get involved with all this shit.' I squeeze the T-shirt hard. 'I'd appreciate it if you didn't say anything about it around the house.'

Steph locks eyes with me for a few seconds, then raises the hand not holding her bowl and does a zipping motion over her lips.

'Thanks.' I release the breath I didn't know I was holding. 'Now I gotta get changed.'

'Yeah, you gotta,' Steph says with a quick raise of her eyebrows. I put a hand on the door to close it, but she speaks again. 'What was the thing?'

'The what?'

'The thing. You said you walked away from a thing –'

My face goes wooden. 'You don't wanna know.' Then I realise I've gotta say something. 'Look, you'll hear about it. It was messed up.'

Her expression dissolves a little. 'What happened?'

'I don't know, okay? I don't know, I wasn't involved in it, I just found it. Now I gotta go work it out.'

She nods at me, very sober, like she's weighing up what I've said. She waves her bowl in my direction, giving me a Weet-Bix blessing, and turns away. 'Good luck.'

'Thanks.'

I change with fucking superhuman speed, then I'm back behind the wheel of the Pitbull. Better not to think about Amie's hand on my neck while she cut my hair, or the way she looked at me in the hallway. Better not to think too much before I do this. I put the car in Drive and do a uey in the street. Call the club on the way towards Langtree, tell them I'm coming in and I need to see Leon straightaway.

By the time I get inside the belly of the club, I'm lousy with sweat and my leg is stiffening up from fast walking. Leon summons me in, and the sweat gets cold on my skin real quick.

I tell him what happened in Tulane Road. I describe the people in the house, the things I saw. I use short sentences and try to sound clinical – I'm not telling him a story, this is real. Leon's face gets redder as I talk. He lumbers up to standing and lights a cigarette, finally interrupts me near the end.

'This is not a conversation I want to be having,' Leon says. 'We're at T-minus less-than-a-fucking-week until delivery, and this is not a conversation I want to be having.'

The tone of his voice and the set of his eyes nearly undo me. I firm my feet. 'I know. I know you don't wanna be having it. But it won't go away. Tulane Road's gonna be a fucking disaster area. There'll be cops, and ambos, and neighbours, and fucking journos, all lit up like a bloody Echuca paddlesteamer. It'll be all eyes on.'

'Did they see you? Coming outta there?'

I speak carefully. 'I spotted the squad car as I was walking to mine. I dunno if they saw me walk out of the house's front yard. I walked on, doubled back and took off when they got round the corner. Then I went and changed my clothes and hair and stuff before coming here.'

Which is all technically correct. I've just neglected to say where I did all this. I don't want to get caught up in a lie if he questions me again later. I'm hoping the thin lacquer of truth is enough to keep my expression guileless.

Still, he's not gonna be happy about the situation, or my involvement in it. I make myself talk straight. 'I didn't think you'd want to discuss this over the phone, and I don't trust any of the others not to blab, so I couldn't pass on a message. But I also thought you'd wanna know right away. If there'd been any other way to get word to you quick, that I could be sure was secure, I wouldn't have come.'

Leon's eyes are so soulless it's actually hard to tell when he's experiencing real emotion. But I think he's fully panicked and pissed off right now. I keep my sweaty hands inside my hoodie pockets, and pray he's not gonna shoot the messenger. There's a long silence as Leon turns to face the blinds, as if he's looking out the window.

'Right,' he says, turning back, and I have to work every fucking muscle in my body not to jump sky-high. He grabs his phone. 'I'm gonna make some calls. Go out front while I phone around, get yourself a drink from the bar. Then leave through the rear exit, and don't come back here again until you hear the word.'

And just like that, I know I'm okay. For the time being. Relief skitters down my spine on spider's legs. I remind myself the reprieve might only be temporary. The Leon I dealt with this morning is gone. He's still all business, but his system has been tested, found wanting. He'll be hyper-alert until this is sorted out, and I'm gonna have to watch myself. I've gotta stay on my guard.

I can't afford to slip.

*

Next morning is warm. The sun is already hot enough to make the dew steam and the air has a clamminess that tells you today will be a scorcher.

I got Amie's text twenty minutes ago: she wanted a fast meeting here, and there wasn't time to say no. The footy ground's deserted but it doesn't make me feel any more secure. I do a blockie before I feel confident enough to park.

I'm barely out of the car when I start talking. 'What's goin' on? Seriously, Ames, this is a shit place to meet. It's too close to the house, everyone's on the warpath, it's not safe –'

'Dad says you should pack it in,' Amie interrupts, her eyes fever-bright. She's wearing jeans and a white men's shirt over a purple tank. Her hair has curled with the humidity and I want to push my fingers through it.

'What?' I scan the length of the street, tug her over so we're half-hidden in the corner of the brick ticket booth. 'What are you talking about?'

'Dad says give them an excuse and come back to Ouyen.' She jigs on her feet, smiling and biting her lip. 'That's why I contacted you, that's why I thought we could risk a quick meeting close by, cos I wanted to tell you in person –'

'The fuck?' I step back, then forward.

'I figured you'd want to know as soon as possible.' Amie's expression falters as she looks at me. 'Come on, Harris, it's what you've wanted to hear, isn't it? You're free. You don't have to keep going with it, you can pull out –'

'I can't pull out now.' I frown, seeing her face. 'Amie, I *can't*. Delivery is less than a week away –'

'Harris, the police are covering Tulane Road like a rash.' She stares at me. 'It was all over the news, for god's sake! Dad said they're calling in homicide investigators from Melbourne. The whole town is getting hot, it's too dangerous –'

I step back again, shaking my head. 'But your dad wants the delivery dates for the new batch, I know he does. I can give them to him, if he'll just give me a little more time –'

'Goddammit, Harris, why are you doing this?' She circles around to face me. 'I thought you *wanted* to cut loose, I *know* you wanted it!'

'Yeah, but not like this!'

She sags, her shoulders sinking, face falling flat. How can she not understand this?

'C'mon, Amie. You really think I'd pack it in *now*? Make those peoples' deaths, all this work, for nothing?' I come in close, fix her in place with my hands, try to get through. 'Listen, I know I said I want this job to be over, and I do. But I can't just let it go, not now. I wanna *nail* these bastards. And it's so close – don't make me give up the prize just as it's sliding into my hands.'

It takes a moment before she musters a reply. 'I thought you'd be excited.'

'I am excited. I am. I want to finish this, just like you. But I want it to mean something.'

'Okay.' She scrapes back her hair as I release her. 'Okay. Shit. I get it. I don't understand, but I get it.'

I make a face, trying to break the tension. 'Are you that keen to see the back of me?'

'No!' she says fiercely. Her eyes drop to the concrete. 'I mean... Well, you know what I mean.'

'I know.' I tilt up her chin. 'Look, tell your dad thanks, but I'm staying until I hear word from Leon about the delivery. As soon as it's solid, I'll be outta Amblin Court before he can say, "You're nicked".' She doesn't look appeased. 'Amie, it'll be over soon. Real soon. I know you want it as bad as me.'

She nods and sighs. 'I guess I should go.'

'Yeah.' I hate seeing her look so disappointed. Then I realise something. 'Aren't you supposed to be with your nanna?'

Now she looks really low. 'Hansa's taken Nani to the hospital for a check up.'

'Is she okay?'

She glances down again. 'After you left yesterday, she had a dizzy turn. We're hoping it's just her blood pressure.'

I do what she did for me, what I've wanted to do since the second I saw her: I pull her into a hug. Amie's breath puffs out against my chest, through my thin T-shirt. Her arms slide around my waist, and she squeezes me tight.

'It'll be okay.' I don't know if it will be, but I want to say something. 'It'll work out.'

'I hope so.' She pushes back and smiles weakly. 'Thanks. You should go. And me, too.'

'Yeah. Go say hi to your nanna.' Then something occurs to me. 'Actually, no – do me a favour and wait here for a bit before you go. Just like at the river. Better if no one sees us peel out together.'

'Okay. Ten minutes. Then I have to get back.'

'You all right?'

'I'm fine. Go, go.'

The drive back to the house is quick: the footy ground is walking distance from Amblin Court, for Christ's sake. It's too close. My two worlds are starting to rub up against each other. It's not a comfortable feeling.

Inside, the house is muggy as the sun hits the roof. I wanna tear the batik curtain off the living room window, let some air in, but I don't do that. I go and slick my face with water in the bathroom, which makes me feel slightly better. As I come back out into the hall, Reggie appears, lolling at the edge of the doorway to the spare bedroom.

'Hey, Harris.' He props himself higher against the door jamb with one shoulder.

'Hey, mate. What's happening? Didn't see you at the club the other night.'

'I been busy.' Reggie glances around absently. 'Yeah, I been real busy.'

He looks like shit warmed over: dirty grey-brown skin, his awful shave job making his face look skeletal. I wish I could've had more time to keep an eye on him lately, but with everything that's been happening, I've been distracted.

I'm regretting it enough now to try to make up for it. 'Too busy to come for a kick later?' I wipe drips off my face with the hem of my T-shirt. 'Whaddaya reckon? Go out with the ball and –'

'Sounds good.' Reggie rubs at his flushed neck and face, pulls at his hoodie. 'Shit, I'm hot.'

314

'It's a warm one, for sure. Take your jacket off, ya goose.' But I look at him more closely. I don't think he's talking about the weather. 'You right, mate?'

'Good, all good, yeah...' He tugs at the hoodie collar, struggles with the zipper. 'Fuck. This –'

'Reggie?'

It's like he goes a little crazy for a second: he wants the hoodie off, it's gotta come off. He flails around, arms flying, elbows hitting the wall. His face is screwed up. Finally, he squirms out of the hoodie, shakes it away violently. Bangs against the wall again.

'Reggie.' I take a step nearer. 'Mate, don't get –'

His head bounces forward on his neck once, twice, and then he goes down.

Oh fuck. I bolt to catch him, miss, manage to get a handful of his T-shirt. It stops his forehead from connecting with the hard carpetted floor, but the rest of him is like jelly. I sling an arm around his front, flip him over.

'Shit, oh shit.' I half-kneel, cradling him in my arms. 'Fucking – *Reggie!* Reggie, wake up, man. Reggie, come on –'

God, he's thin. His arms and legs are floppy. They fall out of my grasp like he's falling apart. And he's hot as a furnace.

'Fuck –' I cast around for someone, anyone. '*Steph! Steph, fucking get out here!*'

I fumble to stand, try to keep Reggie in my arms. It's like trying to keep an octopus in a string bag.

Steph's voice sounds out suddenly behind me. 'Harris, what are you bloody –' She cuts herself off, and one second later she's next to me. 'What, did he drop?'

'What the fuck does it look like?' I snarl. 'Help me get him to the couch. Jesus Christ, he's fucking on fire –'

'Dump him,' she says quickly. 'Take him out to the street, put him on the pavement, I'll call triple-oh –'

'*Are you outta your fucking mind?*' I round on her, clutching my armful of OD-ing kid. 'I'm not fucking *dumping* him, all right?'

She grabs my bicep. Her short nails bite in. 'Harris, if the ambos come to the house and see an OD, they'll call the cops –'

'Jesus.' I close my eyes, try to breathe. Reggie shivers in my arms. 'Lemme think. Christ. Lemme –'

In a few fast strides I cross the living room, lay Reggie down on the couch. His shivers turn into jerks and twitches, like he's about to launch into a full-blown seizure. I'm not gonna dump this kid on the pavement. I'm not gonna have that on my conscience, no fucking way. Shit. *Shit.*

I dunno what else to do. I yank my phone out of my jeans pocket and punch Call.

'Harris?' Amie's voice sounds hollow down the line.

'Come to the house. We need a medic, there's been a... Jesus Christ, just *come to the house.*'

'I'm coming,' she says, and disconnects. God, does this girl ever hesitate?

'What did you do?' Steph pulls me around. '*Harris.* Who did you just call?'

'A friend.' I can't stand here, watching Reggie twitch on the couch. I pace in front of him. 'A nurse. Shit –'

'You called a *nurse*?'

'Get outta my face for a second, will ya?' I pace some more, pull at my hair. I don't know what I'm supposed to do. This is a bad idea. This is a good idea. I can't fucking decide. I think Reggie is deciding for me. He starts to convulse on the couch.

'Jesus –' Steph starts, then she tugs at him, pulls him off the couch. 'Move the table. The *table*, you dickhead!'

I clear the coffee table outta the way with one sharp shove as Reggie tumbles to the floor. His head hits the carpet with a thunk.

316

'Turn him,' Steph pants. 'Christ, will you hold him?'

'I'm holdin' him!' I get a sudden nauseating flash on some of the stuff the doctors and nurses said when I was first admitted to Ouyen hospital with my leg. My stomach rises, but I can't spew now. Things are too urgent for that.

There's a knock on the door.

'It's open!' Steph calls, which is weirdly neighbourly and hilarious, and I'm gonna throw up in a minute if I don't think of something else. Reggie's heels drum the carpet. My heartbeat drums with them.

'I'm here,' Amie says, breathless, and I need to glance at her, just to centre myself. She takes in the scene. 'Oh god –'

'Is this –' Steph takes one look at Amie as she sinks down beside us, immediately looks at me. 'The clothes.'

'Bloody –' I'm almost ready to scream by this point. '*No one gives a shit about the clothes!*' Turn to Amie. 'What do you need?'

She ignores me for a second, starts talking, almost like she's talking to herself. 'Okay. Okay – recovery position. Don't hold him Harris, let him go. Watch his tongue. Rapid shallow breathing. Pulse is...' She lifts her eyes to me. 'Timer?'

I grab for my phone, set it. She puts her fingers on Reggie's neck, watches the clock as she talks. 'I need cold – wet towels, ice, blankets. His temp's gotta come down.' She jerks back, we all do, as Reggie convulses and a spill of watery gunk comes out his mouth. Then she shuffles closer. 'A towel, something –'

I strip off my T-shirt, still damp from the bathroom, and thrust it at her. She wipes Reggie's vomit, slips her fingers inside his mouth, feels around. 'Okay, airway's clear –' Suddenly her eyes are on me and Steph, and her voice is commanding. 'Didn't I tell you I need cold?'

'I'll get towels.' I stagger off my knees, run for my room. Call out to Steph as she goes for the kitchen. 'Have we got any ice?'

'When do we ever have fucking *ice*?' Steph yells, but she goes to look anyway.

Towels, sheets, the blanket off my bed: I sprint it all through to the bathroom, dump it on the floor of the shower and spin the cold faucet to full. Takes ten seconds for the stuff to soak. By that time, Steph's come in with a red plastic bucket.

'In here.' She's still not looking at me. She waits for me to shove the sopping load into the bucket, then carries the whole mess back out to the living room.

As soon as it reaches her, Amie starts yanking the cold wet cloth out of the bucket and on top of Reggie. 'Help me. Here, on his neck, under his arms and knees –'

I drag out handfuls of wet sheets and stuff them around Reggie's limp body, swaddling him up. Reggie's stopped convulsing; now he just looks sick and awful. I can't think about what he did to himself, what it means. I can only concentrate on what's happening this second – the sound of my own harsh breathing, Amie's scared-looking face, the water soaking into the knees of my jeans.

But the cold is good for me as well as Reggie: I don't feel so airy now, my head is starting to come back online. 'Is he gonna be all right?'

'How long has he been unconscious?'

'Five minutes. Less than ten.'

'Did he have chest pain?'

'No. I don't know. What else do you need?'

'I'm not sure. He's breathing's still shallow, if he vomits again it might obstruct his airway. But his temperature's cooling and his pulse is starting to even out.' She shakes her head, like she's shaking a bad thought away. 'Look, I don't know. I'm just doing basic first aid. What did he take?'

I catch her eye. 'What do you think?'

'Okay, look, if he's not properly treated it could be fatal. He could have a stroke and get brain damage, or kidney failure. He needs a doctor, a hospital... Is the ambulance on its way?' She looks from me to Steph, back to me. Her face is all kinds of terrible. 'You *haven't called an ambulance*? Are you bloody *insane*? What are you –'

She grabs her phone.

'Hey!' Steph reaches out, closes her hand over Amie's, holding the phone. 'Listen. I dunno who you are, and I don't wanna know. But if we call the ambos they'll report an OD, and then the cops will show up –'

Amie snatches her phone-hand away. '*Do you want this kid to die?*'

'I *don't want* this whole house to get busted again,' Steph says savagely, 'not that it's any of your business.'

I'm torn between wanting to break them up, and wanting Amie to realise the stakes here are bigger than she thought. If the cops pull up here that'll be the end of everything. Me and Steph will get hauled down the station again, Leon will put off delivery, and if anybody remembers I was in Tulane Road... Amie looks at me and I think she knows it, although she doesn't want to.

Reggie starts coughing, which breaks the moment. Amie turns back to keep him rolled on his side, to rub his thin shoulder blades and speak softly into his ear. I touch his hands – they're cool now – as Amie starts easing the wet blankets back. I help as much as I can.

'I think...I think he's settling,' she says. 'We should get some dry wraps for him.'

'I'll get something,' Steph says gruffly. She leaves the room.

Reggie's face is damp, but I can't do anything about it. Amie stops fiddling with the wet blankets, and suddenly she doesn't seem to know what to do with her hands.

She sits back on her haunches, eyes glazed. 'He's okay. He needs a doctor, but he's okay, he seems stable.'

'Thank god.' I feel like I've just had a stroke. When Amie pushes off her heels and stands up, walks towards the hallway, I don't follow her for a second. Then I realise she's not coming back in. 'What – Ames?'

My eyes flick from Reggie to the hallway, which Amie's just walked down, but I don't think Reggie needs me at the moment and maybe Amie does. I get up and pass Steph as she's returning with a blanket off her bed.

'Put that around him, and wipe his face,' I instruct, and I keep walking all the way to my room. The door is open. Amie is in there, pacing, turning in circles, talking to herself. I don't think she knows whose room this is. I don't think she cares.

'I can't believe...' she whispers. 'Oh god, I can't believe I just did that...'

'What?' I try to fix on her, but she's moving around too much. 'Amie, you saved his life.'

She spins to face me. 'He should be in a hospital!'

'Amie, it worked out.'

'I'm not a doctor! I'm not even a qualified *nurse*! I didn't know what I was doing –'

'But it *worked*.'

'That was *pure luck*!' She's shouting. 'And you should've called an ambulance – you called *me*!'

Now we're both shouting. 'You were the only person I knew who could help!'

'What if he'd *died*, Harris? What would've happened then?'

'But he *didn't* die –'

'He *could* have! It was *stupid*, and *reckless*, oh my god...' She puts her hands to her face, throws them out again. 'You're the most reckless person I know –'

'I'm *reckless*? Is that the worst you can say?'

'You don't *think*, you don't think of anyone but *yourself*, you're a selfish –'

'Don't call me selfish.' My voice comes out stony.

'It's bloody *true!*' She steps closer and shoves me – puts her hands on my bare chest and shoves hard.

I stumble back. My whole body is heating up, like Reggie's did. 'At least I *acted*. I *did* something. You know, you talk so big, but you don't actually *do* anything.'

'That's a *lie!*'

'Is it? You sit at home, hiding behind your fucking photos, worrying yourself sick over everyone else, but you never –'

'You take that back!' Amie screams.

My breath comes in short and my throat is tight. 'You're so busy playing the fucking *martyr*, giving up your residency, giving up everything for your family. All the time you're freaking out about how everyone will cope without you, and it's just a fucking excuse to do *nothing*. You never risk anything, you hold yourself back, you never engage –'

'*I engage!*' Amie shrieks, and she's engaging now all right. She lurches forward and takes a swing at me.

I catch her fist and pull her in tight. 'There, you did it! You feel that? That's *emotion*. That's real fucking life in your veins –'

'*What do you know about it –*'

'I know it cos I *feel* it! What you're feeling right now.' When she whips her other arm back, I grab her wrist, drag her closer. 'You wanna hit me to make your point? Join the fucking queue.'

She's trembling with fury. '*Don't you touch me.*'

'You're shaking.'

'No, I'm not.'

'You're fluttering like a bird...'

We stand there, pressed together, both of us panting hard. My brain is white. The combination of all that stuff I said – that I'd never planned to say, not ever – and the feeling of Amie against me, it's swirling inside me so much right now it's like I went to sleep and woke up at the bottom of the river. Blood is rushing in my ears. Amie's so angry she's gasping, her lips pinched and pale. If I let her go I think she'd slap me into next week.

But I have to chance it when Steph sticks her head in the door of the bedroom. 'Reggie's awake. If you've finished your little shit-fight, d'you wanna come help?'

I nod, release Amie's hands. She yanks herself away, rubs her wrists. I'm surprised she doesn't try to flatten me. Instead she marches back to the living room, so I grab a T-shirt off the floor, pull it on and follow her out.

Reggie is awake, just like Steph said. He's still on the floor, legs splayed out, but now he's propped up against the cushions of the couch with a crocheted blanket wrapped around him. His eyes seem set inside black whirlpools. His skin is still grey. He doesn't look that much better but it's a hell of an improvement on convulsions and unconsciousness.

I go sit beside him. 'Hey, mate, how're you going? You had us all kinda worried there...'

'Hey, Harris.' He leans against my shoulder, like his head is too heavy on his stalk of a neck. His voice is like ash.

I put an arm around him. 'Reggie, I'm gonna take you to the doc, okay? You had a turn.' I remember Amie saying, *She had a dizzy turn*. She's had all the stress about her nanna boiling inside, and now I've just spilled all that mean shit onto her. I swallow. 'Reggie, I'm gonna carry you out to the car, okay?'

Amie sinks down quietly on the carpet on the other side of Reggie. 'Let me check him out first.' She takes his pulse, pulls back his eyelids. Doesn't even look at me.

Reggie focuses on her with difficulty. 'Who're you?'

'I'm Amie.' She checks his fingernails, listens to him breathe. 'I'm...a friend.' Then she nods the all-clear, never meeting my eyes.

This is me – this is me, feeling like a hundred kinds of shit, lifting up a weightless boy in my arms. This is me, waiting for Steph to tuck the blankets around him, so I can walk out into the over-warm day, out to the car I own, to put the boy in the front passenger seat so I can drive him to the hospital. This is me, watching the way Amie doesn't watch me, doesn't look at me, doesn't show any kind of emotion: blank-faced, blank-eyed, like a sign that's been painted out. This is me, driving, the boy lolling beside me.

I've felt like a criminal the whole time I've worked here in Mildura. But remembering the look on Amie's face, it's the first time I've felt guilty about it.

22

amie

'It was her blood pressure medication,' Hansa says, wiping her forehead with a handkerchief, 'which is what I've said before, that her medication needed adjustment. At least the doctor is listening now.'

I keep my voice low, outside the door to Nani's room. 'But it's not just the medication, is it?'

Hansa glances at the door, looks back at me. 'Let's talk in the kitchen.'

When we get to the kitchen I sit on one of the stools near the bench, like I've done a thousand times before. This doesn't feel like those times though. I clasp my fingers together as Hansa makes tea.

'You've been worried about Nani, haven't you?' She collects two mugs. 'I've been wanting to discuss this with you. I'm sorry we haven't had the chance to talk before.'

I had this all planned out, the words I would use, the right calm tone. All that fails me now. It's like my intestines have climbed up my throat to strangle my windpipe.

'Is it Alzheimer's? Is it...is it an aneurysm?' My eyes get teary before I can stop myself. 'You don't have to hide it from me, I know it's genetically linked –'

Hansa settles the mugs on the benchtop and clasps my hands. 'It's not an aneurysm, Amita. It's nothing like that.' She sits on the stool nearest mine. 'Nani has always been a little dreamy, yes? Now she is dreaming of the people and things she's always loved. She dreams them so hard and so well, they are starting to return to her. And she to them.'

Hansa must see the confusion on my face.

'We give it medical names,' she goes on. 'Senility, dementia, regression – because we're afraid of it. But it's not an illness. It's just old age.' She studies her mug. 'I hope I dream of the people I love when I get old. I hope I can dream them back to life with such certainty.'

My voice is halting. 'But Nani's going to need more care now.'

'Yes,' Hansa agrees. 'And that's what I wanted to talk to you about. I've wondered for some time what we would do when Nani needed support. In this country, old people go into nursing homes, but you know that is not our way.'

She shifts on her stool, steadies her mug, as if she's squaring up to do something more significant than just talk.

Her eyes are very serious. 'I've been trying to think of a solution. It's difficult, because I am the sole provider, so I need to work. Beena is still studying. And now Jasminder is married, her place is with her husband.' She finally looks at me. 'But you... Amita, you have more freedom. So I thought...I was wondering if you would like to become Nani's companion.'

My mouth goes slack for a second. 'Like a respite carer?'

My aunt shakes her head. 'No, Amita. I was hoping you'd agree to live here, with Beena and me, and look after Nani day-to-day.'

'I...' I have to sit very still for a moment. The dizzy confusion of a minute ago has retreated, but now I'm feeling something else. 'That's a big thing, Mami. I'd have to leave Dad to live with you, and he's not well, either.'

'Yes,' Hansa admits. 'But you'd be here, in Mildura, so you would still be close to him.'

'What about my job?'

'You would have to give up your job in Ouyen, it's true. But I could offer you a small wage for Nani's care, and if you pursue your nursing training, you could complete it here, at Mallee Health. Would you consider it?'

Would I consider it? In the hallway I'd have said and done almost anything to keep Nani safe. Now I'm vacillating without really knowing why. My head feels like it's been spun in a blender. 'I-I'll have to think about it, Mami. And I'll have to talk to Dad.' I look at the benchtop. 'There's other things, personal things...'

'Nani told me you've met someone.' Hansa angles her head to meet my eyes. 'Is that true?'

I manage to keep my expression from falling apart. 'It's not... Nani might have given you the idea it's more serious than it really is.'

Hansa colours. 'Oh, well, if you have an attachment, I'm sure you'll tell us about it eventually.'

When I go back down the hallway, I'm not intending to disturb Nani at all. Just a little peek to check she's still here, still breathing. But naturally she's onto me like a shot.

'Come in, child, don't lurk in the doorway.' Her silver hair is loose, fluffed around her face. How did she get so *old* all of a sudden? She waves away my apology with one bird-fine hand, makes me sit on the side of her bed, gets me to find her glasses. 'You look worried, dearest. Are you all right?'

'Am *I* all right?' I laugh, but the laugh sounds a bit hysterical, so I swallow it back down. Am I all right? I don't know. I'm still hurt. I can't think about Harris at all, and my insides feel bruised.

'I've been worried about you,' I say, which is both the truth and the only thing I can say.

'Well, that is a foolish thing to worry about,' Nani says, fussing with the glasses chain.

'I still do it.'

Now the chain is arranged to her satisfaction, she tilts her head. 'I suppose that is fair. I worry about you, after all.'

I huff out another laugh, a less fraught-sounding one. 'Why?'

She looks at my hand as she squeezes it. 'Because you are young, Amita, and your mother is gone.' Her voice is small but solemn, which is not like her usual tone at all. 'I see you trying to hold onto the threads of her all around you.'

A gasping noise comes out of me, like a kettle letting off steam. The steam clouds my eyes, and I have to blink it away. The scene with Reggie this morning, the fight with Harris, it all threatens to overwhelm me. And now Nani is talking about Mum, and I can't look at her for a moment. But I can feel her hand, holding mine.

'You should not be clinging onto what is gone, bebe,' she says softly. 'It is not yet time for that. You should be looking outward to the world, and forward to the life ahead.'

I shake the tears away, clear my throat. 'Life ahead...' My grandmother has gone to the heart of the matter again, as usual. 'I don't know, Nani. It's scary. I can't see that far.'

'Nobody can. That is the fact of it, Amita.' She pats my hand, her expression fond yet firm. 'But you cannot let yourself be afraid of it. You must only be energised by it. The potential of it. And it is yours – it is nobody else's. Nobody will ever live this life like you will.'

It's what Nick said, too. But the whole idea terrifies me. 'How will I know if I'm doing it right?'

'You will know *here*.' She lifts her hand and smooshes her palm against my breastbone, over my heart. 'And you will remember what we have said to you, your mother and father and I.' Which sounds really sensible, and should settle me down. Except what she says next, as she tidies her blankets, freaks me out completely. 'I have tried to live a good life. I have lived in different places and done many things. I have loved with all my heart. Those have been the important things.'

I feel like shoving my fist in my mouth, but I don't. I settle for hyperventilating a little. 'Nani, please don't talk like this.'

She regards me primly. 'I think I am old enough to have earned that right, Amita. Now you will stop your worrying, and let me rest. Surely you have something better to do than fuss over me.'

Reluctantly, I drag myself up and to the doorway. I'm almost outside in the hall when Nani quavers out again. 'Amita? Where is your Ouyen boy?'

Turning around to meet her eyes is almost more than I can handle. 'He's... I don't know. I don't know what's going on with him right now.'

'What is it? Did you have a disagreement?' She raises her eyebrows. 'Did you speak the truth to one another? Speaking truth can be painful sometimes.'

'Yes.' My own voice quavers. 'No. I don't know.'

'Well, when you have figured it out I'm sure things will be better.'

I go out. Everything seems faintly skewed – the hallway, the doors to each room – like a photo taken through a fish-eye lens. I wander back through the carport to the outhouse where all my gear still sits inside my suitcase. The purple folder with the residency paperwork lies on top. The Friday deadline for interviews is only a few days away.

The room is stuffy with the windows closed. I lie back on the bed. Trying not to cry is really exhausting, so I give in to the urge for a while. Then I wriggle up and blow my nose, force my brain to work.

I look at my hands: they resuscitated a boy at the house in Amblin Court just this morning. That seems to have happened a lifetime ago. The conversation with Nani is rolling around in my head, plus the talk with Hansa in the kitchen. I get up and push open a window, see if that makes me feel less stifled.

There's Harris to think about as well. It would be easier if I didn't have about a million voicemail messages from him. I check my phone but they're all still there. In every one of them he sounds pleading. *Amie, I'm sorry...Amie, I never meant to say all that stuff...Reggie's okay, he's gonna be okay...Please call me.* They get more desperate as they go along. *Amie, please...I know I screwed up...You don't have to forgive me, just let me know you're all right...Please, Amie...I can't do this on my own.*

There's no getting around it, I have to get in touch with him again. I made a commitment to be his contact and I can't just drop him in it; the outcome could be devastating. I don't think about who it would be more devastating for when I tap out a text.

Hospital meeting @5pm for outpatient evaluation if available

I hit Send, lie back on my bed, consider the next problem. Imposing mental order is somehow important. Okay. My aunt wants me to become Nani's full-time carer. I turn the idea over in my head. Oh my god, it's suffocating in this room. I jump up again and stand by the open window, close my eyes to breathe deep.

I could do it. In fact, I should *want* to do it. Don't I want to help look after Nani? Of course, of course I do. In lots of ways, I've been training for it for the last few years. And it would be kind of the perfect job for me. I'd be near enough to Dad, I could work towards completing my nursing training, I'd be right here to help Nani, support the family...

I look over and see the purple folder, the papers curling in the heat. The dizziness I felt outside my grandmother's room rises up in me again. A sticky nausea comes along for the ride. I clutch the aluminium sash of the window, hold on tight, wait for the nausea to subside – but it doesn't. Is this what I want? To live in Mildura, caring for Nani every day, never going anywhere else? Like Jas: growing up here, growing old here, dying here…

I've never questioned it before, and suddenly everything Harris said this morning comes crashing down on me.

You're so busy playing the fucking martyr, giving up your residency, giving up everything for your family…freaking out about how everyone will cope without you, and it's just a fucking excuse to do nothing.

Have I been hiding all these years? Even from myself?

I don't know. And the worst thing is, if it's true, I've cut off any means of escape. I've been so good, so *responsible*, for so long, I've backed myself into a corner: everyone expects me to do the right thing and stay with Nani. I feel guilty even considering another option. My aunt will be so disappointed with me if I choose differently, and Nani will still need care…

Has everything Harris said turned out to be right?

*

He's arrived at the river before me.

I see him pacing near the old pipe factory. When he notices my car, he stops. For a second I just take him in: his tall broad-shouldered stance, hands stuffed in his jeans pockets, his new haircut and shave showing off the angles of his jaw. I remember how we yelled at each other. He obviously remembers it too because, when I stand up out of the car, things get awkward.

'Thank you. For coming.' His words are stilted and low. 'I didn't know if you'd want to see me again.'

I keep my expression neutral. 'I didn't know either.'

'That's fair.' He flaps a hand at the Pitbull. 'Jump in.'

It's not comfortable at all, the silence in his car as we drive further in. The sun is nearly at the horizon, and all the trees are looming. I get sick of the tension and decide to be proactive. 'Tell me about Reggie.'

Harris seems to appreciate the conversation starter. 'He's okay. Not good enough to come home – the doc wanted to keep him overnight. He was dehydrated, apart from everything else. And yeah, obviously sending him home was a risk.'

'What about his parents?'

'Don't even know who they are. They've never been in the picture before and he didn't seem excited about getting in touch with them.' He cants the steering wheel gently, glances at me. 'You know you saved his life, right?'

All I can do is shrug.

Harris side-eyes me. 'You've got a bit of a habit of doing that, y'know.'

'What makes you say that?'

'You saved mine,' he points out, which kind of kills the discussion until he asks the next question. 'What's going on with your nanna?'

I fiddle with the strap of my seatbelt. 'She's...okay. For now. Can we not talk about it?'

'Sure. We don't have to talk about it if you don't want to.'

Harris finally noses the Pitbull into a spot near the water's edge. With evening coming on I'd like to stay in the car's warm interior. But the atmosphere is way too close in here so I get out. I hug my arms around myself as Harris emerges, his black hoodie stretched in front where he's pushing the pockets down with his hands. The giant gums surrounding us cast darkening shadows as the river water licks the bank.

Harris starts slow, keeping his distance over the other side of the car's hood. 'I know it's been a really full-on day. And I know you probably don't wanna talk to me. But I wanted to say I was sorry for all the stuff I said, for what I did. And I wanted to explain stuff –'

'You don't need to explain.'

'I think I do.' His frown is a collection of solid lines, like a closed shutter. 'I didn't know what to do, okay? I called you cos I was desperate. Steph was telling me not to call the ambulance –'

'Do you always do what Steph says?' It comes out more waspish than I intended.

'No,' Harris says, giving me a look, 'and don't get your gander up about Steph. There's nothing like that going on, and I get the impression guys aren't really her scene anyway. So it's not about Steph. It's about me.' He holds my gaze determinedly. 'It's just my history, okay? I've never been in a situation that was *improved* by calling the cops. That's just...not how it's ever worked with me.'

I throw my hands out. 'But you're *working* with the police *right now* –'

'I know that. I know it. But all I'm saying is it's never made things better before, to contact them. Those instincts just kicked in. And I'm not saying it was a good call – it wasn't, it was a shitty call – but in that particular situation, contacting the authorities would probably not have been a great idea.' He stretches his neck and exhales. 'I know it was fucked up. I'm happy to admit that. But at least phoning you was better than doing what Steph wanted to do, which was to dump Reggie outside in the street.'

I'm shocked by that. It must show on my face because the next time Harris looks at me his eyebrows are raised.

'That's the world I live in, Amie. It's what I'm part of, where I've come from. Did you think because I agreed to do this narc business that I was some kinda white hat?' His expression is bleak, unguarded. 'I've never been the good guy, Amie. Look at what I did. The way I acted with Reggie, all those crappy things I said to you –'

'You said what you thought was right,' I concede.

He shakes his head at the leaf litter on the ground around us. 'I dunno if it was right. Only you know what's right for you. I shouldna said it, that's the thing.'

I sigh. 'Well, don't get too mortified. Maybe some of what you said was true.' I don't meet his eyes when I qualify. 'I'm still working it all out.'

His lips press together until they go white. 'I seem to spend a lot of time apologising for all the stupid stuff I say to you. You've always been good to me, and I'm being an arsehole to you –'

'Harris, the fact you apologised means you're *not* an arsehole. You're not. And apart from a few hours ago when I was thinking a lot of horrible things about you...' I shrug at the admission. 'I've never thought of you like that.'

Harris's hands jerk his hoodie tighter. 'Then you should be more cautious. I've never been the knight in shining armour, Amie. If you think that you've got me all wrong.'

'I don't,' I insist. 'I don't have it wrong. You're a good person –'

'I'm not.'

'Excuse me, but I like to think I'm a reasonable judge of character.' I throw it back at him because, for some stupid reason, being called a decent human being is the only thing that seems to make a chink in his façade. 'And you're a good person who hides behind an arsehole mask. If you weren't a good person you would never have agreed to do this, you would never have stuck it out so long. You'd have taken the money and run –'

'If you knew how close I've come –'

'And you wouldn't give a shit about kids doing drugs, or whether the police arrest Leon. If you weren't a good person, you wouldn't get so cut about your dad –'

'Don't...' Harris frowns harder as his eyes drop to the ground. 'This isn't about my dad.'

'Harris, it's *everything*. Don't you see?' I keep my gaze fixed on him, willing him to listen. 'Everything you do, every minute of the day, is about making yourself different from your dad. *He's* the arsehole, not you. All I see when I look at you is this courageous, kind –'

'You can't say that shit about me,' he says flatly.

' – generous person, who has no idea of his own worth.'

'You can't...' Harris's eyes are screwed up tight. 'You can't just say that stuff, it's not –'

'Harris, the thing that drives me *crazy* is the way you look at yourself means you think it's okay to just dive into any situation, no matter how risky. I meant what I said, about you being reckless. You put yourself in danger all the time, it's like you don't care about your own life –'

'*Stop*, okay? Just stop.' His hand is out as if he's begging. 'It's all *bullshit*, yeah? You got this idea in your mind that I'm some kinda hero, but I'm *not*. I'm fucking *not*.'

'Tell that to Reggie.'

'Jesus, would you *stop*?'

In the cool dusk stillness, my whisper carries. 'Why is it so hard to for you to believe me –'

'*Because nobody's ever said it before!*'

Harris's expression is savage. His voice echoes on the river water. I watch him clutch at his head and spin on the spot. He looks miserable. If I was aiming to hurt him, I've hit the mark. But that was never my intention, and the sight of him tugs at me.

'Then *to hell with them*.' I stand firm. 'To hell with them. But you'd better start believing it.'

His next words are choked out. 'Amie, sometimes, I swear, I

don't wanna be anywhere near you.'

'What does *that* mean?'

'It means…' Harris slaps his hands across his forehead, like he's keeping his mental state from exploding out. But then he flings his hands wide, and the words explode out of him anyway. 'I don't know what it is, but you have something inside of you, like a key, that unlocks something in *here*.' He slams one hand against his chest. 'It's like…you unmake me. Every thought I ever had gets turned upside down. And I can't do anything about it. And you don't even know you're doing it. And it *fucking scares the shit out of me*.'

He paces as he raves, hands moving, his voice rising and falling and his whole body juddering. His face is anguished.

'You look at me and I just start talking, and all the stuff that comes outta my mouth… It's stuff I've never shared with anyone, *ever*. Do you know what that does to me? Do you know what it means? It's fucking *terrifying*. So there's a part of me that wants to bolt when I'm around you, okay? But it's like I can't help myself, I keep coming back and coming back…'

His words finally tail off, his hands covering his face, but I don't think the emotion is gone from him completely.

My voice comes out as shaky as I feel. 'Would it be easier if I wasn't your contact? Is that what you're saying? Do you want someone who'll tell you it's okay to throw your life away, just –'

'Why does it even matter if I'm reckless?' His body sags. 'What difference does it make?'

'*It makes a difference to me!*' I point my finger at the ground and let rip, as if raising the volume will make it stick. 'You've got one person out here who *cares about what happens to you*, Harris! I didn't mean to get caught up in all this, but I'm part of it now. And you can't be reckless with your life anymore, okay?' My face contorts. 'Because it's not all right with me. Because the last time I cared like this –'

I can't keep going because I've started crying, which is stupid, but oh god, now it's started it won't stop. The ache of it hollows me out, bends me towards the hood of the Pitbull.

Then strong hands are on my arms, turning me. Harris holds me, absorbing my whole soggy face with his gaze, finishing my sentence with soft words. 'Because the last time you cared, somebody you loved died.'

I let myself lean on him as he pulls me in. And then I'm bawling, in a way I haven't done for ages. I don't think I even cried this much at my mother's funeral, although I don't remember much about that time at all.

Harris hugs me through it, smoothing my hair with his hand. 'Ah, babe...' His words are muddy as the riverbank, 'Ah, Amie...'

When I'm all sobbed out, he leads me down to the river so I can wash my face under a canopy of dark branches. He splashes some water on his face, too. Then he helps me back into the car and we drive back to the place we started, with the headlights on. Frogs leap ahead of the light on the dirt road, and I tell him about my aunt's request and the disaster I've gotten myself into there.

'What will you do?' he asks in the dark car.

'I don't know. I honestly don't.'

'Amie, you keep telling me my life's important. But what about *your* life? What about your photography? I know you're worried about your family, but they're burying you alive...'

I don't have any answers. 'God, we're a mess, aren't we?'

'We are,' he agrees. His teeth shine in the light of the dashboard display. 'But at least we know it.'

'Tell me you'll be careful,' I say fervently, clutching his hand.

'I'll be careful.' His face is shadowed and solemn. 'I'll be careful as I can be, Amie.'

He brushes my forehead gently with his lips, like a parting gift, and when he's sure I'm okay to drive, he lets me go.

23

harris

'Leon wants a meeting?' Snowie repeats my words as a question.

'That's what he said.' I tip my stubby up to drain the dregs of my beer. 'And considering he's the boss, I'm assuming he knows what he's on about.'

I'm honestly trying to keep my mind on this conversation, on Snowie's presence here in the kitchen this morning. But I swear it's like my brain's got hives. It itches around, scratching for more distracting lines of thought.

All the things Amie said to me last night. The things I said back. How she let me hold her. All the feelings of it –

I can't think about feelings right now.

'Where's this meeting gonna be again?'

'Huh?' I look at Snowie properly. 'Um, just the club, hey. Dunno, it's like Leon lives there or something. Does he ever leave?'

Snowie shrugs, makes a face.

Reggie's head and shoulders appear around the corner of the kitchen doorway. He still looks washed out, with big circles around his eyes, but there's more colour in his face. Steph's crocheted blanket is draped around his shoulders like a cape.

'Hey, Harris, you up for another game of cards?'

'For sure. Just gimme a sec. Y'okay?'

'I'm bored shitless,' he confesses.

'Well, you shouldna knocked the telly over then, should ya?' I roll my eyes towards Snowie. 'That's what happens when you kick the footy on the couch.'

'He all good, then, is he?' Snowie says, as Reggie's back retreats.

'Yeah, he's fine.' I try to sound blasé about it. 'Checked himself out this morning, little bugger, when he got wind they were trying to sic Social Services onto him. By the time I went to pick him up he was already halfway down the street.'

Snowie snorts. 'Gutsy kid.'

It was Snowie's gear ripping through Reggie's system yesterday when he keeled over sideways. It's Snowie and Leon and the rest of the crew running this whole palaver. I have to focus on something else, on picking the label off my stubby, until the desire to plug Snowie in the chops dulls to a more manageable level.

'Okay, then.' Snowie stands up. 'Meeting about three this arvo. Guess I can work that in. Got any idea what's gonna come up?'

I shrug. 'Delivery dates, I s'pose.' I can't reveal how much that excites me. 'And the business outta Tulane Road. Word is, Leon's looking for whoever did the house and took his package.'

Snowie shudders. 'Tulane Road – that was some shameful shit. That's gotta be Mazerati's crew.'

I shake my head. 'Who knows, mate. No one's putting their hand in the air for it, that's for sure. But the jacks are out in force, so make your way in careful this arvo. Staggered arrival. Ando's gonna text the times.'

Snowie nods and sucks his lips, disguises his trembling hands by shoving them in his pockets.

338

When he's gone I text Amie to say I want to see her at noon so I can tell her about the meeting Leon's sprung on us. Actually, it doesn't matter I have a reason, I would still want to see her. It's dangerous, meeting each other again so soon like this, so often. But these sensations inside me are demanding. Seeing Amie, being around her, is essential now, like breathing.

I go play cards with Reggie, try to keep myself distracted.

*

'You're early,' Amie says, climbing out of her car. She's wearing cut-offs and a white buttoned shirt. 'I'm sorry I couldn't make it at noon, I had to –'

'Don't worry about it, it's cool. I've only got an hour, though. Leon's arranged a meeting of all the players at three.'

'You're cutting it fine.'

'I'm waiting on a text from Ando, so I've got an hour to kill.'

I grin at her as she slides into the passenger seat of the Pitbull. Some sort of barrier between us got broken down last night. Now, the day is hot, and nothing matters except I'm getting to spend some time with her before I go and face the shit.

I drive in to our usual spot, park for a quick getaway if necessary. The car is over-warm and I'm sweating: the last few days, it's like spring and summer have been fighting a turf war over who gets to blast Mildura first. We get out and plonk on the grass, close to the water.

'So what's the meeting?' Amie waves her hand like a fan, encouraging the cooler breeze off the river.

'Delivery dates, I'm hoping. I'd say that's one of the reasons. It's gotta be tomorrow or a few days after, yeah? Leon's got some of it ear-marked for Melbourne. But I think he's hoping to flood the local market, drive competition down.'

'What's the other reason? Tulane Road?'

I nod. 'Whoever did it's got Leon's money and his samples. He won't let that go lightly.'

She scoops the thick fall of her hair over one shoulder to give the nape of her neck some relief. 'He doesn't care about the people in the house though. What happened to them.'

'I don't think Leon understands what the word "care" means. The only thing bugging him about the murders is that now the cops are scurrying around town, which makes distribution harder.'

'Bastard,' Amie says with low venom, and she shakes her head.

'Hey, you don't have your camera,' I say, only just realising. She hasn't had it on her the last few times we've met, either.

'I forgot to bring it up,' she admits. 'It was all such a flurry when I rushed up here to help with Nani...'

'What excuse are you using to get out of the house, then?'

'I said I was going to the movies with my mate, Roberta.' She grins. 'Robbie'll back me up. Nani's gone to the shops with Beena. She said she was tired of lying in bed and she needed to move around. She should be all right if they stay someplace air-conditioned.'

'Yeah, air-conditioning. I wouldn't mind a bit of that.'

Amie laughs. I look at the river water. My shirt is sticking to me. The sun is burning. Everything about this place, this moment, is yelling at me to jump in with both feet. It's like the decision was already made inside my head and it's taken me until this second to catch up.

'That's it.' I stand up, grab for the hem of my T-shirt, strip it over my head. 'I'm going in.'

'What?'

'I'm going in.' Boots are next.

Amie gives me the owl-eyes. 'You're going swimming in your jeans?'

'Yep. In my jeans.' I pull off one sock, then the other. The grass between my toes feels fucking fantastic. 'You coming?'

'All right for some,' Amie says tartly.

'You've got cut-offs on,' I point out. 'Jeez, go in in your undies if you like. No one's around. Who's gonna care?'

Amie looks scandalised. I laugh, then I take a few quick steps and dive.

The instant my body enters the water, I feel transformed. All the worries of the last week – the shit-storm about Reggie, Snowie's anxiety, even my fear of Leon – they all sluice off me. I break the surface, grinning, flicking wet hair out of my face.

'This!' I shout to Amie. Water is running over my chest, sinking through the layer of denim over my legs. For the first time in days I don't feel sticky and sweaty.

She frowns with her lips pressed together, stands up at the water's edge.

I duck-dive again, emerge gasping. 'You're missing out!'

'Oh shit...' she says, then she shakes herself all over, blows out a big breath, toes off her Vans.

'Yes!' I crow.

She doesn't mince in: she bombs it, shrieking. Bobs up sleek, dripping laughter. I can see her bra strap through her wet shirt. It takes her about two seconds to start splashing water at me, and then I retaliate, and then we're whooping and I've got half the river on my face. Finally we stop horsing around, float in place.

'You think this was a good idea?' I say. 'I think this was a good idea.'

'I reckon you think all your ideas are good,' she says, squirting me with water out of her hands.

'This was an extra good one.'

She tilts her head back, dips her hair. 'Which is better, you think? Rivers or oceans?'

'Well, with rivers you don't get this.' I make little waves in her direction, so they break over her shoulders. 'Dunno about oceans, though. Never been to one.'

Amie rights herself, gasping. 'You've never been to the ocean?'

'Nup.'

'Not *ever*?'

I shrug.

'Harris,' she says, making a face, 'you've got to do something about that.'

'One day,' I promise. 'I like rivers pretty good, though.'

'At least you don't feel caked in salt afterwards,' she agrees. She sinks back down, letting the water embrace her. 'I think...I think I want to try all of them.' There's a new note of determination in her voice. 'The Amazon, the Nile, the Mississippi, the Ganges...'

'That's a lot of rivers.'

'I want to swim in them. Rivers from everywhere.'

'All the rivers.' I grin at her.

Her hands are moving back and forth in a spreading motion. I can't see her legs scissoring under the water but I can imagine them: firm and brown, kicking her weightless.

She frowns, looks skyward. 'When you see Leon today –'

'No no no. We're not gonna talk about that now.' I throw my head back and float. 'One hour of not talking about it, not thinking about it.'

She lifts her chin. 'Okay. One hour.'

We swim a bit longer, then we get out, wring off. Amie uses both hands to skim the water out of her hair. I throw myself down on the grass, lying on my stomach. Leftover water dribbles off me and I feel my back drying. This day is hot and bright and perfect.

Amie flomps down beside me, her clothes clinging and her wet hair like black ropes. She's still snorting off the giggles, lying back and basking in the rays. 'Should've brought my sunnies.'

'Put your arm over your face,' I suggest.

'Mm, that's better.'

The grass is warm. Frogs are pobbling somewhere on the bank, and the sun is soothing on my neck. I've got one arm curled above my head and one arm tucked under my chest so I can get up on my elbow and look around if I need to. But I don't need to. This place is quiet apart from us. The birds will let us know if anyone's approaching.

'My hair's gonna smell like river,' Amie says.

'Wash it later.' My voice has a lazy burr.

We lie so long, with the insects ticking in the grass and the sound of the air warming, that I almost forget where I am. I give in to this feeling, let myself doze. My jeans are softening as they dry. Maybe I could lie here forever.

It takes me a second to realise how close Amie is. My eyes are shut, so I sense it more than see it when she shifts. Then I feel a shadow fall on me as she reaches over. Her fingers touch my arm, the one nearest her.

'What's that from?' she asks softly.

It's the scar I got from the corrugated iron, the one I showed Rachel once, trying to impress.

'Accident.' My face is turned towards Amie but I've got it tucked into the crook of my elbow, so she can't see me flush.

Another touch. 'What about this?' She traces the old scar on my right shoulder I got years ago, falling off a dirt bike on Furlough Creek Road.

I remind myself to breathe. 'Accident.'

She touches another spot on my back carefully. 'Here?'

A different scar – she must feel me stiffen.

I pause. 'Dad.'

I don't know what made me admit that.

My heart thuds at irregular intervals. I wait for her to say something sympathetic or brusque, but she doesn't. She doesn't seem to react at all. Maybe this quiet beat is her reaction. I'm grateful for it.

Then she clears her throat quietly. 'A belt buckle, was it?'

'Yeah.'

Each of our pauses and hesitant words feel weighted, thick. My brain is firing slowly. Other parts of me catch alight faster. She touches me again, traces lines on my shoulder blade. My blood turns to golden syrup.

'Amie, what are you doing?' I try to say it casually.

Her voice sounds quiet and close. 'I'm looking at your tattoo.'

I don't know what else to say, and when her fingers slide gently down, over my ribs, I don't think I can say anything. All my skin feels stretched and sensitive, like the surface of a drum. My jeans are still damp. Grass tickles my face, my chest. The air around us seems to be heating up.

Her fingers reach the tender skin at my waist. Trickle, with infinite lightness, over the curves and whorls of the snake there. I can't pretend anymore. I press my mouth into the grass to muffle my gasp.

We are in a hot golden bubble. Amie leans closer and I smell her: below the smell of sun-warmed river, the scent of jasmine. Her fingertips have reached the waistband of my jeans, the lowest visible point of my tattoo.

'Show me where it goes,' she whispers.

I open my eyes. Amie is leaning over me. Her lips are parted, and there's a deep rosy flush on both her cheeks. She looks beautiful, with her serious heavy-lidded gaze, and glossy black hair falling forward. She's staring at me like she's hypnotised.

I am going to do this. Even before I move I feel it, like I felt before about swimming here. This sense of inevitability, of falling headlong into something already decided, already meant to be.

Amie watches as I move my hand from above my head, where I've been clutching at my hair, and drag it down to my stomach. Lower.

My body is angled now, facing her side-on. When I undo the button on my jeans I see her stop breathing, just for a moment, and the pleasure of it is like a zap of electricity. *I did that.* I hook my thumb into the waistband of my jeans and jocks, and ease them down.

Now my entire left side is exposed, almost to the curls at my groin, and she can see where my tattoo ends: where the snake curls fluidly over my lower back before twisting around my waist, to flick into a sharp supple tail that arrows down and lies flat in the inner valley of my hip.

Amie is motionless. Then she reaches out, and her finger traces the path. Her hand is shaking. My skin is on fire. When she arrives at the tip of the snake's tail, nestled in its soft private place, she turns her hand. Lays the back of it against me. I make a low noise, shuddering.

Her touch travels on from the hollow of my hip, up my stomach to my chest. She feathers the short soft hairs at my breastbone. Runs her whole palm further to my neck, curling around my nape.

I can't hold still anymore: I chase the length of her arm with my hand, plunge my fingers into her hair. Draw her closer. Look right into her eyes.

'Harris –' she breathes.

'Are you sure?' My voice is so husky and deep it doesn't sound like mine. 'Because if I kiss you, that's it. I don't think I can –'

'I'm sure,' she gasps.

I surge up and pull her to me, lip to lip.

Once, in science class, I saw magnesium burn. It went up so fast and white it was like watching a solar flare at close range.

I feel like that now. I've dreamt of kissing this girl, I thought I was ready for this –

I had no idea.

We fuse together. Our mouths are pliant, soft and wet. The taste of her makes my eyes roll back behind my lids, and it's like I know her taste, have known it forever. Something is happening inside me. Amie is keening into my mouth and I wanna tear my heart out of my chest and give it her.

Amie slides one leg over my hips and I clutch her tight. Everywhere we touch turns to flame, and suddenly we want to touch everywhere. Amie whispers my name, kisses my jaw, my eyelids. I smooth my hands down her back. She rocks against me, makes a noise so visceral I hear it echo in my own throat.

We kiss and kiss. I've pashed in car parks, smooched under covers, snogged in bars. This is nothing like that. Our lips move and meld – fast and frantic, then slow, slower. Languid. We're eating each other up. What started as an explosion becomes liquid wanting. We reach this incredible stage where our kisses are long soft-lipped conversations, and things I've only ever fantasised about actually happen...then suddenly some fuckwit starts braying at us and I realise it's my phone.

Amie breathes '*Don't*' into my mouth, and I breathe '*Shit*' and she moans, and I nearly don't stop, I come this fucking close, and then I do. I reach over for my shirt with one hand, flounder for it. Both me and Amie are shaking. I grab my phone, pull it over to see the screen, check the call I've missed.

'Oh fuck, it's Ando.' I drop my phone, let myself sink back on the grass. Try to steady my breathing with long slow inhales and exhales. 'I'm supposed to be at this meeting in twenty minutes.'

'God*damnit*.' Amie's shoulders are still heaving. She leans over me, propped on her arms, her mass of hair swept down one side of her neck to make a black pool on my chest.

Just being this close is too tempting: we kiss again, and I'm not imagining it, something ignites inside us when we do this. Our instincts take over. My hands are full of her hair, her skin, her *breasts*, oh god –

'Harris,' Amie pants. She groans when I suck down her neck.

Ando could be standing here in person right now, shouting at me, and I'd still struggle to give him my attention.

'Harris.'

'I know. I know. Shit.'

We have to push away together, or we'd never do it.

Amie gulps air. 'You've gotta go.'

'Right. Fuck.'

'Not yet,' Amie says. 'Later.'

She giggles, and I snort, and then we both laugh. Fall together. I run my fingertips across her cheek. We can't seem to stop looking at each other, touching each other. We've both been waiting for this for too long.

Jesus.

I didn't know it would be like this. I want to say *I think I've fallen in love with you*, but that would be crazy. Maybe it doesn't matter. Maybe we're both crazy. If this is crazy, I don't ever want to be sane again.

24

amie

I remember dragging my arm off my face and turning to Harris. My vision flashed white from the glare, and when I propped myself on one elbow to look around, everything was sepia-toned. Harris looked golden. It was like everything amazing about him was suddenly highlighted. I wanted him so much it was like a physical pain.

So I just...reached out.

He looked so beautiful, and the emotions were so strong inside me, and it was so easy. And the way we caught fire... I can't think about it without feeling it, deep inside. I can't stop smiling.

Harris puts his hand in my lap while he's driving so we can hold hands. I lean my head against his arm. We drove in with this companionable feeling, we were comfortable with each other. But now, driving out, it's as if something has melted in each of us and we want to run together. The early afternoon sun flares off the rear-view mirror, the visor, and we've got the windows down on both sides.

I put the radio on. It's the end of an old Nick Cave song, and Harris starts singing along. I'm somehow not surprised to discover his voice is a warm baritone. He smiles while he sings, hair blowing in his face, and he glances at me until I laugh and join in.

Is this the guy who was closed-off and broken? Seriously – is this the same guy? I can't say it's like he's let his personality out for the first time because that's not true: I've seen him, I've seen the real Harris, seen him laugh and think and feel, heard his nightmares and his dreams. But how much of each of us was caught up in holding ourselves back? It's as if we can finally relax around each other.

There are so many things I want. I want to lie on my bed with him, just touching. I want to start kissing him and never stop. I want this drive to last forever, but of course it doesn't. When we arrive at the pipe factory where my car's parked, we both sigh. As the Pitbull slows, Harris exhales so low his shoulders sink right down.

He pops the handbrake, squeezes my hand. 'How're you going? Are you okay?'

'I'm okay.' Once I'm smiling into his eyes, I can't look away. 'I'm great.'

'I really want you to be sure about this.' Harris leans his forehead against mine, watches his own fingers run lightly up from my knee. 'Lotta people would say you're insane to get involved with me. With all the shit I'm doing now, I'm inclined to agree with them.'

I lift his chin. 'Harris. You're a good guy. I'd be insane *not* to get involved with you.'

'I know I called you to the house with Reggie, but I don't want you anywhere near this stuff,' he says fervently. 'I wanna make sure you're safe. Your dad might be a cop but you're not, you didn't sign up for this.' His face looks slightly terrified.

'Harris, I'll be okay. I'm only on the periphery. We're being careful. I'm more scared for you, right in the middle of it –'

'Don't be scared, okay? Once delivery is sorted, I'm done. If things feel too hot after this meeting, I'll cut out, head back to Quyen. I can always disappear to Melbourne for a bit.'

'You could hide in my room for a few days,' I suggest, twining my arms up around his neck.

'Thanks.' He snorts, spans his hands either side of my waist. 'Your room, eh? What, under the bed?'

'*In* the bed.'

He colours. 'Shit, I'm sorry about the phone, we shouldna had to –'

I shut him up by kissing him, and he just...turns to liquid. His whole body melts under my hands. It's shocking and thrilling at the same time. His stubble scrapes my skin, and he makes soft needy noises as we kiss, and my belly and breasts start tingling. Now I'm the one who can't let go.

'Amie.'

'Mm.'

'Amie... Amie, I have to...' His voice is hoarse and his eyes are closed. I nuzzle his ear, and he whimpers. 'Ah, god...'

I glimpse the clock on the dashboard and realise his twenty minutes has turned into five. That breaks the spell.

I push him back. 'You have to go.'

'I...what?' He looks drunk. When I tap the clock display, he startles. 'Oh shit.'

I open my door, grab my shoes out of the footwell, slide one leg out. God, I don't want to go. And I don't want *him* to go, especially not back into that world that only knows the fake side of him, the armoured side.

I cup his cheek in my hand. 'Call me. About the delivery dates. But call me anyway. Let me know you're all right.'

'Okay.' His exhale comes out shaky. 'Okay. I will.'

'I want to hear your voice.'

He laughs suddenly, breathless. 'Will you get outta the car, please? Cos I haven't got it in me to make you leave.'

I don't kiss him one last time because I wouldn't be able to stop. I squeeze his hand and jump out, shut the door. He gives me a final look, swings the car around and drives away.

*

I'm a horrible person to be around for the rest of the day.

The clock ticks over from three o'clock, past four, towards five. I thought I would've at least had a text by now. I can't sit still. Nani finally stops me while I'm reading aloud to her from one of her poetry books. 'For goodness sake, Amita, what *is* it? You're like a dog with fleas.'

I throw down the book. 'I wish it *was* fleas. You can get rid of fleas.'

'What is bothering you, bebe?'

'What do you do when you're worried or afraid, Nani?' I try to clarify. 'Not for yourself. For someone else.'

She regards me. 'Don't you do enough of that?'

'This is different.'

'Well, then,' she says calmly, 'usually I pray. And when I've done all the praying I can do, I talk, or walk, or try to stay busy.'

I've done a little praying in my head already so I decide to take her other suggestion. I send off a text to Harris – *Pls contact hospital when available* – then go for a walk, tramping down the street in the dusk.

While I'm out of the house I call Dad. 'Harris says the dates should come through today.'

'Hallelujah,' Dad says. 'When does he find out?'

'He should've found out by now,' I say, fretting. 'I've been waiting for him to get in touch.'

'Maybe he's been held up,' Dad offers. 'He's been reliable up until this point, hasn't he? Just give him some more time. What else has been happening? Are you right up there?'

I haven't told him about the conversation with my aunt. Hansa keeps giving me sideways looks, waiting for me to give some sign I've come to a decision. Putting her off is getting more difficult.

'Auntie Hansa wants me to become Nani's carer,' I say bluntly. 'Nani is getting too frail to be left on her own, and after that wandering episode we're concerned about her. Hansa's asked me to quit my job and come live with them.'

'Really?' Dad sounds odd. 'Right.'

'I mean, I'm kind of well-qualified to look after Nani. She definitely needs someone.'

'And that someone has to be you?'

'I don't know,' I admit. 'But it would be better than dumping her in a nursing home. Hansa's offered to pay me a wage, and I could do nursing training up here...'

'Is that something you really wanna do?'

I hesitate. 'I feel sort of like I've been preparing for it. And, well, it's Nani.'

'I know you care about her, love, but...' There's a pause on the line. 'Look, I know about the residency.'

'What?' My stomach drops.

'I found some papers in your room...' Dad sounds pained. 'Sweetheart, why didn't you tell me?'

I can't reply, because of course I didn't tell him. I never wanted him to know I was weighing his health, our life together, against something as frivolous as photography.

'You should do it.' His voice has a gruff urgency. 'They want a reply by Friday, right? You should say yes, and you should –'

'Dad, I can't accept a residency.' I sound flat, weird. 'You know I can't accept it. With you and Nani sick –'

352

'*Amita.*' I can hear him glowering. 'Please don't say you're knocking this back. And don't use me and your grandmother as an excuse.'

'It's not an excuse!'

'Isn't it?' His words lose their sharp edge. 'Amie, I have a heart condition. It's not terminal and I'm not an invalid. I take my pills, I look after myself –'

I make a noise, which he hears.

'All right,' he admits. 'Maybe I don't look after myself as well as I should. But maybe if you weren't around to coddle me, I'd get better at it. I don't need a nursemaid. And I sure as hell don't want you refusing an opportunity so you can stay in the Mallee and look after me. Jesus, Amita. Your mother would tan my hide if I let you do that.'

My brain spins slowly on some invisible axis. 'Y-You don't want me to stay?'

'I only want you to be *happy*. That's all any parent ever wants for their kid. And I'm sure Nani would say the same thing. But you have to think about what *you* really want.' He sighs heavily. 'I know you're living up there, in the middle of it, and Hansa's probably putting the screws on you to make a decision –'

'Nothing's been decided,' I say weakly.

His voice stiffens. 'Just make sure you don't let anybody else do the deciding for you. It's your life, Amita. I've been trying to tell you that for years.'

The conversation ends with stilted goodbyes and by the time I click off I'm wishing I hadn't called. It's done nothing to make me feel better about Harris, and it's just added to my misery about the residency deadline and Hansa's request. Apparently, no matter which way I jump someone's going to get their feelings hurt.

The evening seems to drag endlessly. Where on earth is

Harris? My brain is full of anxiety and starts to cannibalise itself. I'm used to dealing with images, and now images are what I get: mental pictures of Harris shot through the head, his face beaten, legs broken. Sitting in front of the TV with Hansa and Beena and Nani becomes unbearable, so I make an excuse and go hole up in my room. Close to ten o'clock at night I finally tap out another text.

Pls contact hospital asap.

I check my phone at half-hourly intervals – well, okay, more often than that – until one in the morning, when I finally fall asleep. At five a.m. I snap awake, and there's still no news.

As soon as the hour gets respectable, I call Dad again.

'I know you're worried, love,' he says. 'But there's not a lot you can do. I can call Ronnie Murphy, get him to send a car around to Harris's sharehouse if you think there's a genuine issue –'

'No. That wouldn't be a good idea.'

'Then I'm not sure what else to say. I think you just have to wait for Harris to get in touch. He knew he was putting himself out on a limb after the Tulane Road homicides. Maybe he's being extra cautious.'

At nine, Hansa tells me she and Nani have another set of appointments up at the hospital after lunch. Beena is off to classes and then to a study group. So I'll have a whole three hours to myself, which is just what I need: three vacant hours spent waiting to find out if Harris is alive or dead. Then I realise something else: if I take the job here I'll be with Nani all day and surrounded by my family at night. Maybe vacant hours are something I should start to appreciate. I may not have many more of them.

At half past ten my phone rings. I excuse myself and take it into the bathroom.

'Amie, it's me,' Harris says. 'It's okay, I'm sorry I couldn't call, you won't believe the stuff that's been... Amie? Amie, are you crying?'

'No, I'm...I'm fine.' I straighten up from curling over the bathroom sink, grab a piece of toilet paper to wipe my eyes.

'Ah, babe...' His voice is soft. 'Amie, it's okay. Jesus, I'm sorry. I couldn't call earlier because there was a big meeting with Mazerati's crew and we all surrendered our phones.'

'It's fine. It's... I'm just glad you called.'

'I didn't mean to stress you out. I need to tell you what's been happening –'

'Can you meet me?' I've suddenly hit on an excellent idea. 'I mean, today? Around twelve-thirty? You can tell me about it then.'

'Sure, I can be at the river –'

'Not at the river. Here.'

'You wanna meet at *your* place?'

'Yes.' It's like I've been seized by a fever. 'Because everyone's going out after lunch and I've got the house to myself until half-past three.'

'Really?' I hear him swallow. 'Then...yeah. Okay.'

'Okay,' I echo, and I smile. 'Great. All right, I'll see you here in two hours. Do you remember the way?'

'Uh, yeah, sure.' He sounds dazed.

'Cool. I'll see you then.'

Hansa and Nani take ages to get organised. Nani has to find the right dubatta, then my aunt starts searching for her car keys. I watch the clock and dither around, making a mess of being helpful. Twice I hand things to Hansa she's already picked up and put down again.

'Are you feeling all right?' she says to me, casting a critical eye over my face. 'You look flushed. Are you sure you're not coming down with something?'

'I'm –' I start, then I see Nani, her eyebrows raised. 'Uh, well, actually, I do feel a little off. Maybe I'll just have a lie down while you're all out.'

'That's a good idea,' my aunt says. She pats my arm. 'You should look after yourself, Amita. You spend so much time looking after other people.'

There's no reply I can make to that, because I can hardly point out I'm about to make looking after somebody my full-time occupation. Also, if I reply it will mean more conversation, which will mean more *time*, and oh my god, they're taking forever to leave. It's nearly twenty past twelve. Shrieking at them and herding them to the door is starting to seem like a viable option.

Finally, Hansa and Nani exit for the car. I wait until I hear the engine turn over and the car back out, then I rush through to my room. I change into a fuschia-coloured tank and an orange buttoned shirt. My cut-offs are still okay. I've just dashed to the bathroom to unravel my hair from its plait when there's a knock at the door.

Calm, calm... I don't run to the door. I take a breath, reach for the door handle, and then Harris is there, and I –

Basically throw myself at him. Which is fine, because he hugs me back with equal enthusiasm. There's a lot of gasping, and I breathe into his neck, lean my cheek against his. I can't get over the fact I can touch him now. I squeeze the tops of his shoulders, needing to feel the solidity of him.

Harris clutches my nape and kisses me. His lips are firm, warm, and I get a sudden unravelling rush in all my muscles. My pulse beats in my fingertips. Before things go completely nuclear, we both ease back to inhale.

'Wow, okay, it's nice to see you, too,' Harris says, with a goofy grin.

'It's partly relief,' I say, 'but it's also just...'

'I know.' He runs his fingers down my arm until he's holding my hand, our foreheads pressed together. 'It's been hell on my concentration, I've gotta tell you.'

He's wearing jeans and a white T-shirt with his hoodie unzipped. He looks tired. His T-shirt is wrinkled but clean, I notice.

I push the door closed, pull him out of the entry way. 'Explain all the stuff that's happened. But do it quickly.'

He keeps hold of my hand. 'The batch is going out the day after tomorrow. Some of it goes to Melbourne, like I said. Ando and Snowie will shift the bulk of it – Barry's wording up a few new recruits.'

I nod for him to go on.

'After we met with Leon, we were told to wait at the club. Then, about eleven, we got the news there was gonna be a chat with one of the other crews. It all went down out in a shed east of the main drag. Our boys, their boys, everyone lining up on opposite sides. Weapons and phones surrendered into a bag until the chat was over.'

The thought makes me shiver. 'My god, that sounds freaky.'

'It was very very weird,' Harris says. 'I felt like I was in a movie. I dunno what I was doing there, to be honest, I don't think I look that threatening. Anyway, Leon and Maz talked in the middle of the room for a bit. A few of the words got heated and everyone started squaring up. Then the bosses stepped off and settled us all down, and that was it. Leon's not too happy, but some agreement was reached. Apparently there's nothing solid to say Maz's crew did the job in Tulane Road, and they've proved that to a certain level of satisfaction.'

'What was it that tipped Leon off in the first place?'

'I got no idea. Anyway, we all tramped back to the club and had a drink, cos we needed it, and by the time I got back to Amblin

Court it was nearly three in the morning. I didn't think I should call you at three in the morning –'

'Just *call me* next time, okay? I don't give a crap what time it is.'

'Noted. And that's the end of the story, apart from the fact that I slept until nine and I'm still a bit hungover from last night. Oh, and Reggie's looking better.'

'I'm glad to hear Reggie's looking better,' I say, but my eyes are focused on his lips. I trace his bottom lip with my thumb.

Harris swallows involuntarily when I touch him. 'God, it's nice to see you,' he repeats in a whisper.

The moment is broken when I hear the unmistakeable sound of a key in the front door lock. Before I can do any more than push Harris and myself a respectable distance apart, Nani comes tottering back into the house.

'Oh, Amita, I forgot my –' she starts, but her eyes widen when she sees Harris. 'Ah! You have a visitor!'

'Um, yes,' I say, waving a hand at Harris completely unnecessarily. 'Harris has dropped by. For a quick visit. To...return the clothes he borrowed.' My brain is working really hard right this second.

'Uh, hi, Mrs Kaur.' Harris does a slightly blushing version of a namaste in her direction.

'Well, this is very good.' Nani's cheeks are round with delight. 'I will find my handbag and then you will have time to chat.' She meanders towards the couch in the living room.

I exchange a fast frantic glance with Harris before rushing to help Nani. Harris trails behind. My grandmother's handbag is on the coffee table.

'Nani,' I say, as I pass it to her. 'So it's okay? Harris is just stopping by for an hour or so.'

Nani waggles her fingers in the air. 'Pfft, he may stay for a visit, that is all right with me. Your auntie and I might stop for tea after the hospital. We won't be home until at least four-thirty. But you are a good girl, I am sure you will be responsible like your father taught you.' Nani swivels back to Harris suddenly, skewers him with her saucer-eyed glare. 'Her father is a police officer, you know.'

Harris nods his head. 'Yes, ma'am. You told me.'

'I did? Very good,' Nani says, smiling. 'We have nice chilled mango cup in the refrigerator, Amita will show you. Now I must go. I don't like to make Hansa wait.'

Nani settles her handbag strap over her arm, adjusts her dubatta and toddles out of the house. We hear the door clunk behind her, the whack of the fly-screen door. There's the snick of Nani's shoes on the concrete outside, her quavering call to my auntie near the gate, then the sounds tail off. And then it's just me and Harris, standing together in the living room.

'Right.' Harris's eyes are dancing. 'Okay, then.'

'Hm.'

When we look at each other we can't look, because we keep cracking up.

'Your nanna,' he says.

'Yep.' I finally stop giggling. 'My nanna.'

Harris rocks on his heels. 'She's subtle.'

I completely lose it.

'You've got a subtle nanna,' he says, and I think he says it just so he can keep watching me laugh.

Then we both seem to subside on the echoes of our laughter and we turn to each other fully. Harris is looking at me like he wants to absorb my eyes, my whole face. I can't stop staring at him, either. He looks at my lips, open and waiting. Our hands reach out and when our fingers touch, these feelings inside us flare brilliantly to life.

We pull together, tumble together, and Harris starts kissing my lips straightaway. I can't seem to stop running my hands over him. There's so much panting and gasping I have to push back for a second, to catch my breath.

Harris looks at me with a stunned expression, his mouth open and his chest moving fast. 'We should take our time. She said until four-thirty, which means we've got hours, we should –'

I cut him off when I kiss him hard, unclasp our lips with a smacking sound. 'We should go slow.'

'Yeah. Yeah, we should.'

'We should go out into the back garden and have a glass of mango cup. Relax.' I start unbuttoning my shirt.

Harris watches my fingers. 'Absolutely.'

'Then cosy up on the couch for a while, until things get serious.' I'm working open the button on Harris's jeans. When he lets out a long shaky exhale, I feel his abdominals clench.

'Yeah.' He tugs his hoodie off, yanks his T-shirt up and over his head. 'Yeah, I don't think we're gonna do that.'

'No, I don't think so.'

'Nah, yep.' He pulls us both towards the hallway. 'Which way's your room?'

Once we make it to my room, Harris slides his hands into my hair, tilts my chin back. He nuzzles his way down from my throat, drops to his knees with a groan. Luckily, my legs are right up against the bed; I sink down with him, and we both squirm back until we're on the sheets, still kissing, half-dressed and desperate.

'Oh shit.' The words slip out of Harris's mouth. 'I left my shirt in your nanna's living room.'

I laugh even as I'm kissing him. 'Later. Go get it later.'

Harris's skin is tanned and smooth, with a lovely lustre of sweat. The sight of his golden cheek against my brown breast makes my heart feel like bursting.

Our sounds fill the room, expand outwards, and something inside me shouts that I get it now, I understand. Life, love, the way we all live, the way we intertwine, the way we move together.

Because this is how the world works. This is how all the terrible things people do is cancelled out: by the energy – the radiant sparks and flares – we emit during this exultant act.

25

harris

I cannot slow down. And I need to slow down for this girl.

But it's like there's lightning under my skin. I feel like my eyeballs are gonna pop out, all this blood inside my veins, this singing. Because I watch Amie as she lies beside me, and she's so beautiful it hurts. The sheen on her skin, her dark hair rippling around her face, the luscious curve of her hip. Like she was that day by the river with the sun on us. I didn't want to stop looking at her then, and I can't stop touching her now.

Our hands move, our lips sink together, and it's like I hear her voice again, saying *So maybe it's different then*. And I'm thinking she was right, because this feels different. It feels so *full*, so intense, so much like something I can't really control. It's like I have so much energy inside me, I have to push some of it out into the universe. When it's just our skin together, I start shaking.

I have been around town, I have done this dance with girls before, but I feel like a beginner again now. We're both just learning each other's bodies. Amie touches her hand to my stomach, presses herself against me, kisses my neck, and I can't even remember my own name.

I see stars. I've never seen stars before.

We end up having some of her nanna's mango cup, but we share it. And we have it in bed, not out in the back garden.

Amie sits on the pillows behind me in her tank and undies, her arms draped over my shoulders. She passes me the cool glass, slippery with condensation from the ice-cubes, before running her fingers up and down my back.

I grin at her sideways. 'You're a bit in love with my tattoo, aren't you?'

'Mm.' She slides her palm across the thick coils of the snake. 'And it's a good excuse to keep touching you.'

She leans forward and settles her cheek against the back of my neck, runs her fingers beneath my arms and onto my chest. Plays with the short hairs there. I'm having a lot of trouble concentrating on the glass. 'Ah, that tickles. Amie, I'll spill this...'

'We've only got a few hours,' she says sternly.

'Lots we can do in a few hours.'

She rubs her hands lower, across my stomach, and I arch, my eyes flipping shut. Might be wiser if I just put the drink on the nightstand.

I turn in her arms. Cup the back of her head, tease my fingers through her hair. Pull her in, kiss her. Keep on kissing her, until my lips go numb and our breathing gets muddled together.

'Jesus, I could do this all day' I say finally, pulling away, gasping.

'We don't have all day.' I think she learnt subtlety off her nanna.

I smile at her, then I go still. 'Amie, you can have me all day, any day. Any time you want me, or need me. For any reason. Just call for me –'

'Harris,' she says softly.

'I'm here.' I peck her quickly on the lips, wondering if this is too soon. 'I mean it. I'm yours. I never had this feeling before, like I'm...'

'Puzzle pieces,' she says, stroking my cheek. 'We fit.'

She gets it, and it makes me glow.

'Yeah.' Maybe she can hear the relief in my voice. I can't make myself disguise it. 'In here...' I trace a line across her forehead with my thumb. 'And here...' Run the tracing across her lips, down her throat. 'And...here.'

My hand travels south, until my palm is resting on her breastbone. Her heart beats hard against the gentle pressure and her legs are tangled with mine. The look she gives me takes my breath away.

She touches my hand on her chest, pushes my hand slowly down her body. 'I think you forgot a place.'

She smiles, and none of my fantasies have come close to this. I wanna give it back to her, some of this joy, cos that's what it is – pure unadulterated joy. Even as I'm surprised I recognise it, I realise I've gotta share it or I'll explode.

The beauty of it is, that's something I know how to do. I flip our hands so it's her own hand underneath, until she's cupping between her legs with my fingers covering hers. The heat of her radiates through me. I watch her eyes go wide as she figures it out, then I lower my lips to her ear.

'Show me,' I whisper. 'I want to know what you like.'

*

My T-shirt was behind the couch.

Amie opens the door of the house as I'm shoving my arms through my hoodie sleeves. Her face is ruddy but mournful. 'I miss you already and you haven't even left yet.'

364

'We can meet up –' She grabs me and kisses me, and my mouth is too preoccupied for talking. I give it a second try. 'We can meet up tomorrow –' Nope, still no good. I give it one last go. 'I'll call you as soon as I can, yeah?'

'Whatever the time,' she says firmly.

'Whatever the time. Midnight. Four in the morning.' It's after four now, I notice. My efforts with my clothes and boots get more urgent.

She grins. 'Call me when you want to kiss me.'

'I can't call you every time I wanna kiss you.' I stroke her hair, grin back. 'I'll be calling you a hundred times a day.'

'I'd like that,' she says softly.

'Me, too.' I hug her close. 'God. Only two more days until delivery.'

'Maybe you should chuck it in.' Her voice is muffled against my neck. 'Tell my dad you can't do it anymore because you'd like to start going out to the movies with me instead.'

I roll my eyes. 'Oh, he'd love that. "Sorry, sarge, I just found your daughter way more interesting than a bunch of drug dealers".' I pull back to watch her laugh. 'It'd be true. It'd also be suicide. But that's okay.'

She goggles at me. 'You think my dad would go you if he found out we were a couple? Come on, give him some credit.'

'I think your dad is a sensible bloke who understands the insanity of you getting mixed up with a guy like me.'

'A guy like you?' She smiles. 'And what kind of guy is that, Harris?'

I pull a lock of her hair away from her shoulder, lift it to my lips. My voice is husky. 'Your kinda guy.' I bury my face, so my mouth is right beside her ear. 'Your guy, Amie.'

Her earlobe is soft on my lips. When her body shakes, I feel it.

But I have to pull away. 'Lemme go now, babe. I don't wanna

get you in strife with your family. Tomorrow – I'll see you again tomorrow.'

'Tomorrow.' She nods, clasping my arm. Releasing.

I step out into the afternoon sun, dive back for a quick kiss in the doorway, wrench myself away. If I think about it I won't do it. I dig for my keys, look back over my shoulder. Amie's standing barefoot in the doorway, her brown legs stretching down from her cut-offs, black hair splayed over the orange of her shirt.

'Be careful!' she calls.

I nod firmly. Press the fingers of one hand to my mouth and cast my arm out, sending my kiss to her. Her scent is still on my skin. I carry it with me to the car. The inside of the Pitbull is hot, but the flush on my face has nothing to do with that.

Driving back to Amblin Court, it's like I'm so happy that everything pleases me. The bottlebrush in bloom – yep, that's nice. Pedestrians on the street – hi, how are ya. I drive slow, so I can enjoy it because I can't remember the last time I felt this mellow. In fact, I don't know if there ever was a last time. Like everything else that's happened today, this might be a first.

Nothing disturbs my level of happy, not even the sight of Ando's Land Cruiser parked on the verge outside the house. I can handle talking to Ando right now. I might even give him a smile. I can do anything today.

I park and walk to the door of the house, hoping Reggie's around so I can smile at someone who deserves it. When I get in the door, though, I see Snowie sitting on the couch. Reggie's sitting next to him. And he's not smiling.

He darts forward against Snowie's restraining hand. '*Harris, get out, he's gonna –*'

Ando steps out from behind the door and punches me in the face. After that I don't see nothing.

26

amie

I open my eyes onto Friday morning. Sun is patterning the room, and I feel fresh.

This day... This day is unlike any other day. And there's a long line of them in front of me: days when I get to roll out of bed feeling good, days full of potential. Days when I feel alive. Days with the promise of seeing Harris again. Whatever comes, I can handle it.

It's a good day for making decisions.

I've thought long and hard about it. After this week anything is possible. I can do anything, choose whatever I want, go anywhere in the universe. The idea of the residency, of freedom, doesn't seem as terrifying as it did last week, and today is the last day I can act on it. I'm still scared – my fingers shake as I fill out the forms, as I tap the laptop keys to upload additional photos, sign up for an interview – but it's nothing like the fear and nausea I experienced when I was contemplating Hansa's request.

As soon as it's done I feel a strange sense of peace. If I stay, I'll only be doing an impersonation of myself: good responsible Amie. With this decision, my best self and my real self are merging until I'm more whole than I've ever been before.

When I bring Nani her morning tea, she definitely notices.

'You're smiling, bebe.' She dunks her biscuits in her chai. 'That's better. You have been very low over the past few days.'

'I'm feeling better.' I settle myself on her bed. 'Maybe that rest yesterday was just what I needed.'

'Maybe having a visitor was just what you needed.'

I think I blush a little. 'I was glad to see Harris. He's...there's things about him...'

'You don't have to explain to me, child.' Nani waves her soggy biscuit. 'I have been in love.'

'You and Nanaa –'

'I know you think it is strange I talk to my Apu, but he is always with me. Even now.' She looks at me. 'I loved your Nanaa strongly, and I still do. He passed before you were even a spark in your mother's eye. But he was with me for the raising of two children until just before your mother and auntie came here to study, and he provided for their education overseas. He was a good husband and a good man. He is still always in my heart.'

'Harris is a good man.' Saying that was easy. Now for the hard part. I clasp her free hand, take a deep breath. 'And...I know you need me here for you, but I don't think I can stay in Mildura and look after you. I need to live my own life for a little while. I've been offered a chance at a photography scholarship. And Harris might have to leave town soon, so I think I'd like to –'

'Why would you stay and look after me?' She blinks at me.

'To be your carer.' Confusion is still written all over her face. 'To look after you here, full time? Like Auntie Hansa asked.'

'Your *Mami* asked you to stay and live with me?' Nani puts down her biscuit. 'To babysit me?'

'Not to babysit, Nani. To help.' Now I'm the confused one. 'Hansa hasn't told you about...'

'About the plan to have me taken care of?' Nani's eyes are

glinting dangerously. 'To be mollycoddled and fussed over and –'

'*Nani!* It's not like that!' Or is it? How much of this arrangement was Nani even informed of? I have a terrible feeling I've somehow dropped Auntie Hansa right in it, without even being aware of it. 'Look, everyone was concerned after you wandered down the street that day –'

'That is no reason for people to be making up plans to cosset me! Whose idea was this?'

'I don't –' I shake my head, not sure what to say now. 'I don't know, Nani. Auntie just asked me to stay.'

'Bah!' I have to rescue Nani's cup of chai when she flings her hands up. 'And you were going to agree to this foolishness? How long have I been saying to you, *"Go out and live"*? You think I meant staying *here*? Looking after an old woman, sitting amongst the doilies and making rice pudding –'

'That doesn't matter if *you're* the old woman I'm looking after!' I frown, shocked at my own directness. 'Nani, you spent yesterday at the hospital. How can you say you don't need more support when you have dizzy spells, and call me by my mother's name –'

'Your mother would never have allowed it!' Nani is glaring. 'I will not allow it either! Have you people never heard of domiciliary care? Senior citizens centres, home nurses –'

'Hansa can't afford to get a nurse in, you know that, Nani! She practically re-mortgaged the house to pay for Jas's wedding, and she's got another daughter to go. And would you really want a stranger looking after you? Don't you want someone who would care for you properly?'

Nani rolls her eyes dramatically. 'You think I haven't put something aside for myself? I can provide perfectly well for the services I need. Whether I choose a stranger to care for me is my own decision to make. I would rather that than have you stuck here in this house, pining for the life you won't get to lead!'

She leans forward and grasps both my hands in her own.

'Amita, I may be an old woman, and I may need attention sometimes, but that is not what I want for you. It is *never* what I have wanted for you.' She touches my cheek. 'Can't you see? You fuss and worry over the people you love, restrict yourself to make them happy. But you must stop holding yourself back. For the last four years I have been encouraging you to go out and make *yourself* happy.'

I'm trying to figure out why I feel so hurt. 'I thought you would want me to be here for you...'

'There may be a time when I call you to me, bebe, but that time is not now. Now is when you have the chance to be young, to have freedom to do the things that are important to you. I have had that time, and now I give it to you.'

Nani uncurls her hands from mine and I half-expect there to be something resting on my palm, like she's performed a magic trick. But there's no magic trick. It's just that she wants to kiss my hand, press it to her cheek.

The magic wasn't in her actions, but in her words.

'I wasn't...' My blinks are damp. 'I was going to stay, Nani. But I changed my mind.'

'Good,' she states. 'Then that handsome boy is having a positive effect on you.'

I laugh, dash at my eyes with the back of my hand. 'Yes, but it's more like... I guess he just showed me it could be done. Harris has had a hard life. So hard I can barely imagine it. He's had to fight for everything. But...he got free. He makes his own choices. If he can do it, after everything he's been through, so can I.'

'I told you he was a good match,' Nani says.

I laugh again. Then I think of something. 'What should I say to Mami? She might be upset if I turn her down.'

Nani shakes her head. 'It was not her decision to make. Maybe in five or ten years, when I am really "losing my marbles", as they say, she can decide then. But don't worry, bebe. Let me talk to Hansa. I will sort it out. Now, go. Don't you have someone you'd rather be talking with?'

She's right about that too. I kiss her on the cheek, make my way back out to my room and text Harris.

Contact hospital immediately for urgent care needs

It's not a particularly well-disguised message, but I'm hoping it will do.

*

Hansa is at work. Beena is at college, due home in an hour. I'm considering my options. It's nearly three in the afternoon, and I haven't heard from Harris.

I've texted him twice more, but I can't send a barrage of messages. It might seem weird if someone else looks at his phone. At that meeting he attended everyone gave up their phones: could he be stuck in some situation like that again? It's possible he's been held up with Leon, or Snowie, or any of the other characters involved in the house at Amblin Court. Maybe he had to take Reggie to the hospital again. Maybe there was an accident. Maybe he's been arrested.

Or maybe he's dead, sprawled in a ditch outside of town.

Apparently closing your eyes and squeezing them tight doesn't alleviate anxiety. Neither does snacking on Beena's homemade gulab jamun. Neither does walking: I've already taken a turn down the street and back with Nani.

I'm not ready to start praying again. That would make me feel desperate.

'Why don't you call him instead of sending those little messages?' Nani watches me pace, from her spot on the kitchen stool.

'I can't. He always lets me know when he's able to receive calls. Or he could get into trouble.'

'Ah, the police training,' Nani acknowledges, nodding.

I chew my lip, but I can't stand it anymore. It's like I'm ready to burst. 'It's not police training, Nani. Harris isn't training to be a police officer. That was something we said to make you feel better.'

Nani narrows her eyes. 'Then what is he doing?'

'He's –' I sit down on the stool next to her, close my eyes for the briefest moment. 'Harris is an informant. He's working with a local crystal methamphetamine cartel, and relaying the information he finds out back to the police.'

'*Drugs?*' She makes a terrible face. I think she's read plenty about crystal meth in the newspaper. 'He is involved with *drugs?*'

'Harris volunteered, Nani. I told you he's had a hard life. He was offered this job and he took it, on the condition he could work from the inside to bust the cartel.'

'My god, no wonder you are worried, this is... But he stays in touch with you?'

'I'm his contact. I send the information back.' Finally, I can say it out loud.

She looks horrified. 'Does your father know about this, Amita?'

'He was the one who set it up.'

She puts her hands over her face. I have a moment of panic. If she has a spell now, it won't be because of her blood pressure medication. It'll be all on me.

But then she drops her hands, clasps them together. 'So Harris was supposed to call you today.'

'Yes.' I check the time again. 'Only it's late, and I'm getting nervous.'

'And there is nothing you can do but wait?'

'No, there's nothing –'

I stop. There's not nothing. There's something. I know the house on Amblin Court, I know Reggie and Steph…Well, not exactly, but enough. I could go down there. Even just to see if Harris's car is outside. Even just to peer in the windows. I know where to go, and I can stay out of sight if I have to.

Sitting here and waiting again, like the other day…I don't think I could bear it. I have to act.

I stand up. 'Actually, you're right. There's something I can do. But Nani, I'd have to leave you here in the house. I can't take you with me. You'd be alone until Beena comes back.'

'That is my concern, not yours,' Nani says brusquely. 'I am perfectly capable of –'

'Nani, I mean it. I can't leave if I'm worried you're going to go off wandering the streets, or falling down in a faint again.'

'I am feeling all right.' She looks contrite. 'I will lie in bed and read, and wait for Beena. I promise.'

'Okay.' I'm not completely reassured but it's something. 'You tuck up in bed, and I'll get ready.'

As I change out of my cut-offs and into a pair of jeans, my brain snarls over all the things that could go wrong with this plan. What if Harris isn't home? Where do I search then? What if Reggie and Steph aren't at the house? Or worse: what if Snowie, or Marcus Anderson, are there? But I don't need to make myself visible, if it's not necessary. I can be sneaky…

I don't think about it. I just grab everything I might need – phone, keys, money – and stuff my pockets, then snatch up a jacket. I race back through the house, take the landline phone from the kitchen into Nani's room.

She's in bed, like she promised. 'Have you had any news?'

I shake my head. 'No news. Look, take the phone. If you're feeling ill, call Hansa at the hospital straightaway – straightaway, okay? Don't make me worry.'

'I will call if I need to.'

'Great. And...nobody knows about this except for Harris and me and Dad. Keeping it secret is really important, for Harris's safety. So if I'm not back, and people are asking, maybe you could make up a good excuse for me?'

'Certainly.' She beams. She seems happy to have something to do. 'I can be your accomplice.'

I almost smile. 'An accomplice is somebody who helps the bad guys, Nani. How about we say you're my deputy, okay?'

'Yes, a deputy. I will be a wonderful deputy.' She stops me with a hand on my arm. 'But Amita, if you are not home by tonight, I cannot make excuses. I will call your father.'

I don't want to say Harris and I might need a call like that. She might worry. 'That would be a good thing to do, Nani,' I say instead.

She pulls my head down and gives me a smacking kiss on the cheek. 'Go. May God help you find your Ouyen boy.'

'Thank you.' I kiss her in return, try to store the memory of her wrinkled cheek, her powdery honeysuckle smell. 'Hopefully, I'll see you soon.'

*

It's not until I'm swinging my car into Amblin Court that I realise I'm nearly out of fuel. I tap the gauge, swearing, and check the clock on the dashboard. It's three thirty-seven. Too late to turn around now.

The street is quiet. Sun escapes the swirl of cloud overhead and dashes itself on the windscreen. But I can see the Pitbull parked on the verge opposite the house. I cruise past once, turn around and pull up a little way further down.

Okay, Harris's car is here. What does that mean? If he's at the house, why hasn't he messaged? Maybe he's gone somewhere on foot: to the footy ground with Reggie. But he can't have been at the footy ground *all day*. Could he be sick? But if he's so sick he can't contact me, I want to know about it.

There aren't any other vehicles. The motorbike that was here the day I arrived to resuscitate Reggie – didn't Harris mention that Steph rode a bike? – isn't around now. Oh god, where could he *be*?

This is bullshit. I can't sit here in the car doing nothing, not now I'm so close. Harris is gone and there are answers in that house, if I've got the courage to find them.

I get out of the car and pull on my jacket, which makes me feel less vulnerable even though it's too hot. Locking the car, I check the street one final time, walk until I hit the path to the house. Somewhere in the neighbourhood a baby is crying. Maybe it's the same baby Harris has told me about.

Standing at the door I get another attack of nerves. What if no one's home? What if Snowie answers the door? But Harris said he drives a silver car, and Ando has a Land Cruiser. None of those vehicles are around... I dig my keys out of my jacket pocket and hold them tight in my fist. I'm a copper's daughter, I know how to defend myself. I knock, and pray I won't need to.

The door is yanked wide. It's Reggie, making a face like he thinks I'm selling encyclopedias.

'*What?*' His cheeks have more pink in them than last time I saw him. He looks at me properly, blinks. 'Shit. You.'

I make a little wave. 'Um, hi. Yep, it's me, Amie.'

He pushes into the doorway, towards me. His eyes have gone huge. 'Jesus, what are you *doing* here?'

I baulk. 'What do you mean, what am I doing here? I'm looking for Harris.'

'Get out, get out –' He steps forward out of the house, ushering with his hands. 'Are you fucking nuts? You can't *be* here.'

'Well, I'm here now.' I stand my ground. 'Where's Harris?'

'That's what I'm tryin' to tell you.' He pulls the door half-shut. His eyes are darting. 'Fuck, I can't believe you came here...'

I get a bad feeling in my stomach, which I try to beat down with a firm manner. 'Reggie, let's ignore the fact *I'm* here for a second. What I want to know is, is *Harris* here?'

'Shit, this is my fault... He's gone. That's what I been sayin' –'

'What do you mean he's gone?'

'They fucking *took* him, okay?'

'What?' Cold slices into me, through my jacket.

Reggie looks distraught. 'Ando and Snowie came and they gave me the fucking third degree about being in the hospital, and I told 'em about you, but it was a total *accident*, yeah?'

'Reggie, *what did you tell them*? What happened?'

He pulls at his stubbled head. 'Ah, shit. I told 'em there was a girl here when I come to, a desi chick –'

The cold is burrowing into my bones.

' – and then Snowie asked if you had a name, and I tried to buy some time, but I had to tell him, I had to –'

'You told Snowie my name?' My lungs are shorting out. I take quick high breaths.

' – and then Ando and Snowie, they – ah, Jesus – they waited for ages, and then Harris got home, and when he got in the door, they –'

'Where are they now?' My voice is hoarse. My hands are clenched hard around my keys but I don't even feel it. '*Where's Harris*, Reggie?'

'He was here, all last night,' he sobs out. 'They had him in Barry's room. They... I think they messed him up real bad. And then this morning they took him. I dunno where, I swear I dunno. But you can't be here. Ando said he's coming back, and I dunno when he's coming but if they find you...'

I can't think about Ando finding me right now. My head is clamouring, brimful of all those horrible bleeding images of Harris from the other day. Only now I know they're real, and it's making all my limbs weak.

But I can't feel like that. We don't have time. Harris's time might be even shorter.

I grab Reggie by the arms. 'Is Steph here?'

He screws up his eyes. 'Whaddya wanna –'

'*Just answer the question.* Is Steph here?'

'No. She hasn't been back since Wednesday. I dunno where she is, probably on some driving job.'

'And Kevin?'

'How do you know about –' He sees my face. 'No.'

'Reggie, listen to me. Do you have any idea where they might have taken Harris? To the club, or a house, or a –'

'No, okay?' He wriggles in my grip. 'I dunno. Not the club. Snowie's got a place in town, but –'

'If they're dragging him around, and he's been beaten up, that sounds too exposed.' I let him go, chew my thumbnail. 'Would they take him to Leon?'

He shakes his head. 'They were talkin' about it. They know they're in the shit. They were freaking out about having to tell Leon that Harris has been a dog this whole time –'

'So what were they going to do? Wait?' I swallow hard. 'Were they going to kill Harris and dump him somewhere?'

Reggie shivers. 'They said it was better to keep him alive. Then at least Leon's got somebody else he can take it out on.'

I stagger back a step, looking at the weeds sprouting up beside the concrete path and seeing nothing. *Don't pass out, Amie, you don't have time for that –*

Reggie grabs my arm. 'Hey. Hey, you're all pale and stuff.

C'mon...'

'I'm okay,' I whisper. 'I'm okay.'

'He's your guy, is he, Harris? He's your guy. It's not just dog and handler, right?'

'Yes.' My vision is going pale, overexposed. I fight it. 'Yes, he's my guy.'

'He's a good guy, Harris. He's a mate.' Reggie straightens, still holding my arm. 'He looks out for me. I wanna help, I do, but –'

'Is there *any place* you can think of?' I'm clutching at straws now, clutching Reggie's forearm. 'Any place, Reggie. A room, or–'

'There's a caravan in Red Cliffs where Kev holes up sometimes. And there's a shed near the river where they keep stuff, but –'

'A shed.' That could be it.

'Yeah, but I dunno the address, I only went there once, with Steph driving –'

'Could you find your way again?'

'Maybe.' He looks at me, uncertain. 'I guess. You're gonna try and find him?'

'Yes.' I feel better saying that. Stronger. I repeat it, more firmly. 'Yes, I'm gonna try and find him. But...I'm going to need directions, Reggie.'

'Shit.' Reggie glances up the street, back to me. 'Okay. Ah, fuck. I try to keep my head down, mostly, y'know?'

'But it's Harris,' I point out.

'Yeah.' He sighs. 'Yeah, it's Harris. Okay, gimme a sec.'

He dashes back into the house and, for a moment, I think he's scarpered. Then I really will be stuffed, because I can't search every vacant shed along the Murray. But before I've even finished the thought, Reggie's back, a flannie shirt tied around his waist and a half-full bottle of yellow Gatorade in one hand.

'Just getting me supplies, yeah?' He pulls the door closed behind him. 'Which one's your car?' When I point to my Honda he looks appalled. 'Really?'

'It's just a car, Reggie.' Then I remember. 'Oh shit. I'm low on fuel. How far is–'

'Far enough.' He shakes his head. Then something occurs to him. He slaps the Gatorade into my hand, pushes back into the house.

I don't have time for this. 'Reggie. *Reggie* –'

But a minute later he's back, waggling both eyebrows. With his head shaved like that he looks a bit demonic.

'Got a better idea.' He grabs the Gatorade and tosses me a set of keys, keys I'm familiar with. 'You're outta gas? There's your ticket.' He nods at the Pitbull, parked across the street.

I blink. But I have to admit, the Pitbull does have 'getaway car' written all over it. 'Where'd you get the keys?'

'Swiped 'em.' He looks pretty pleased with himself. 'Come on, then. Let's get movin'.'

With a last look at my Honda, I jog across the street, unlock the Pitbull and slide behind the wheel. Reggie trots around to the passenger side, takes a swig of Gatorade as he shuts the door. The big engine starts without a hitch. It growls smoothly as I handle the car off the curb and onto the road, doing a U-turn to get back onto the main drag. The steering is about a million times more sensitive than my Honda, and I have to pay attention.

'Okay, head for the river,' Reggie says, putting his window down. 'It's a bit south from here. When I see something I know, I'll give you a yell.'

I yank my phone out of my pocket and hand it to him. 'Check for any messages – look under "Patient #451".'

'Nah, there's nothing,' he replies, after a pause.

'Okay.' That's pretty much what I was expecting. 'Now send a text for me. Go to 'Dad' –'

'They said your dad's a cop.' He looks wary. 'Is that for real?'

'Yes, he's a senior sergeant. Now say –'

'Shit. Will I get busted if this all goes down?'

'*Reggie –*'

'Okay, okay. Fine.' Reggie holds the phone gingerly. 'Whaddya wanna say?'

I think quickly. 'Say *Harris made* – full stop – *S and A holding in river location* – full stop – *Checking places now* – full stop – *Call Murphy asap.* Have you got all that?'

'How d'you spell 'location'?'

I spell it for him, repeat the rest until he's managed to get it texted.

'Why don't you just call him yourself?' he asks, handing the phone back

I turn off my phone and slip it into my pocket, keep my eyes forward. 'Because he'll only try to talk me out of going to find Harris, and I don't have time for an argument right now.'

We clunk over the rail line, passing corner stores and fish and chip shops, wheelie bins on street corners, mechanics' garages. Houses here on the edge of town are fenced with corrugated iron or chicken wire. Long rows of grapevines stretch out into the paddocks behind people's backyards.

'Here!' Reggie's hand jerks out. 'Turn here.'

I turn left, towards the river. This is like the back way I drive to reach the usual rendezvous point. Clouds high above are overwhelming the sun as we head closer to the Murray. Below them, the only tall things are the power poles and the occasional stand of gums.

We pass a guy fence-posting beside his ute, on the left side of the road. Reggie sits up straighter. 'This bit. There's a house up here and some vine sheds –'

He's right: the house is a cream weatherboard, lonesome amongst the acres of vines. A large tin shed hulks behind, and

Reggie points out where the road doglegs into another straight stretch. A collection of sheds stands halfway down on the right. Far at the end of the road, I see a T-junction, the intersecting road running parallel with the river.

Tension is bubbling below the surface of my skin, ready to crest high and send me reeling. Better to focus on what I'm doing right now. When Reggie swears hard, I startle. 'What? What is it?'

'Oh fuck.' His face has gone chalky. 'That's –'

He's pointing at another vehicle approaching the junction from the right, on the intersecting road. It's a Land Cruiser. Even from here it looks enormous, as if it should be pulling a road train or something.

'That's *Ando's fucking car*,' Reggie rasps. 'Oh Jesus...'

And I realise what we've done wrong as soon as the words fall out of his mouth.

'This was a mistake,' I whisper. Reggie grabs the sleeve of my shirt, but I know it. I can feel it. 'The Pitbull... Oh god, he'll recognise the car.'

Our eyes are glued to the Land Cruiser as it passes the T-junction, hoping against hope...

'He's passing,' Reggie says, almost whimpering.

But I keep watching. When the Land Cruiser slows, eases to the road shoulder, leaving enough room to turn around, I voice what Reggie and I are both thinking. 'Shit. He's coming back around. He's seen us.'

I should be shaking in my boots but I've moved beyond that now. I'm so scared, my brain has switched into some sort of self-protective SuperCalm mode, and I think I've figured something out. In fact, I'm sure of it.

I clasp both hands on the wheel in a ten-to-two position, just like Dad taught me, and keep my foot steady on the accelerator. 'Reggie, get ready. You're getting out of the car.'

'*What?*'

'I'm going to swing around near those sheds, like I'm trying to get away. And when I slow down, while we're facing the other direction and you're shielded from sight, you're going to slip out of the car. Okay?'

Reggie looks at me like he thinks I've gone mad. 'Uh, okay?'

'Take this.' I loosen one hand, pass him my phone again.

Reggie's face is frozen. 'What, you want me to –'

'It's not locked. Once you're clear, call my dad. Tell him exactly what's happened –'

'He's not gonna listen to *me!*'

'He will if you've got my phone,' I explain firmly. 'Then get to someplace safe. If you don't have a place to go, find your way to Tenth Street and go to Moira's Corner Cuts beauty salon and speak to Roberta Geraldi. Tell her I sent you.'

I make him repeat Robbie's name, and the name of the salon.

'Okay, you've got it.' The Land Cruiser is at the junction, and the sheds on the right are coming up fast. 'Are you ready?'

'This is a bad idea,' Reggie says darkly.

'I know!' I surprise myself by laughing. It's a sobbing laugh. 'Oh god, I know... But it's the best way I can think of to find Harris fast.'

'By letting Ando catch you.' Reggie shakes his head. 'Jesus, Amie, you are one gutsy chick.'

'Get ready,' I say in reply, then we're passing the sheds and I'm swinging the car in a wide slow U-turn.

There's no other traffic on this road, so I have plenty of space to turn. At the arc's furthest point, Reggie pops the door handle and scuttles out of the car. He's done it perfectly, concealing himself in a patch of shade behind some tangled shrubs near the shed entrance. I lean across and tug the door closed as unobtrusively as I can without slowing the car's momentum.

Then I pull away fast.

The rear-view mirror shows no Reggie in sight, and far back behind me, the world's most enormous Land Cruiser. Right – I'm being tailed by Optimus Prime. A giggle escapes me: I rein it in. I don't know where all this inappropriate humour is coming from.

Wind tears through the open window of the car with a sound like snapping flags. I plant my foot on the Pitbull's accelerator, watch in the rear-view as the Land Cruiser rapidly gains speed. I hear an engine rev loud, then Ando's car is behind me. Level with me on the right. Passing me. It pulls ahead with a powerful chugging surge, makes distance –

Then it's angling, boxing me onto the road shoulder. I hit the brake hard as the Land Cruiser screeches to a halt, blocking the Pitbull in front like something out of 'World's Wildest Police Videos'. The driver's door on the far side of the Land Cruiser flings opens and I see Marcus Anderson's hulking form emerge. He stalks towards me amidst a cloud of dust.

My whole body is shaking. I clench my fingers around the steering wheel and wait.

27

harris

When you're in pain, you focus on details.

Details are a distraction. They give your mind something to latch onto, so it's not spinning in circles going '*oh jesus god fuck that really hurts*'. And when every part of you is sensitive, when every part is searing, you notice the little things.

Last night, I spent a really long time looking at Marcus Anderson's shirt.

Black buttons, a thick weave in the fabric, the tiny green alligator sewed on the breast pocket... I could draw that fucking shirt from memory now. It got to the point where I was hoping Ando would go home and change, just to give me some variety.

By that stage, though, we'd moved on from establishing that I knew Amie Blunt, that yes, her father was a cop, and yes, I had indeed first met her at Ouyen hospital (all true). We'd arrived at meatier subjects: how did she know the house, what had I told her, was I fucking her. At which point I headbutted Ando, snatched my phone out of his hand and smashed it on the bed frame, and if that wasn't a confession of guilt, I dunno what else they needed.

Not much, as it turned out.

That was around the time I became intimately acquainted with the carpet.

I honestly don't know how long I was in Barry's room. The carpet there is fucking awful, but. A hard-pile weave, full of lint and old dust. Terrible on your throat, inhaling all that dust. All I could think was, this revolting carpet is in my room too, and I just put up with it.

Reggie came in with a mugful of water at some hour – I gave him the eye to stay out of it, and Ando chucked him out anyway. Reggie looked remorseful, but there wasn't nothing he could do. And none of this was his fault. How was he to know? I think he did his penance, anyway, listening to me groan through the walls while he was in the living room.

After a while, we ended up here. I dunno where here is, exactly, but I've had time to notice the details. The dirt on the floor is firm-packed, a nice shade of brown, and it smells of oil. It's possible farming equipment was once stored here.

The walls are tin, and there's a steel centre pole which I've become matey with. A pallet of concrete mix bags sits in the rear right corner. An old wooden desk occupies the other corner, and there was a wooden chair with a cane seat, but it didn't prove up to the task of supporting the weight of one grown man pummelling another guy. Snowie broke the rest of it up for kindling.

The fire was a good distraction, but after a while I couldn't look at it.

Now I got the fades. Normally, I'd fight it; lapsing in and out of consciousness can't be great for your health. But it's been nearly twenty-four hours, and I'm dry. My head's still pounding – from that very first punch of Ando's, I think – and my ears are ringing.

I don't have the energy to deal with all the hurts, so I've turtled down inside myself. It's what I used to do when I was a kid: find a refuge. A place you can go when everything on the surface of your skin and beyond is outside your control.

It's an enduring place. It used to be a grey empty place as well, but I've discovered someone here with me now, someone I want to see. I've got all these memories of Amie's face, the touch of her skin, the soft secret parts of her, the way she laughs... So there's something to sustain me. The pain is just pain, it'll come and it'll go again. I can hold on. I can endure.

It still hurts. But I have the memory of Amie's voice.

So when the *reality* of Amie's voice appears somewhere outside, I have trouble distinguishing one from the other. Then I hear Ando speak, and realise I have to pay attention.

'Turns out,' Ando says, 'that *he's* the dog, but *she's* the bitch.'

A scuffling sound, a gasp. The sound of feet spinning on the dirt. A grunt.

'Touch me again,' Amie says ferociously, 'and I'll kick you in the balls so hard you'll be pissing blood for a week.'

I can imagine her saying it. Then I don't have to imagine, she's right here. Her face is right in front of me.

'Oh Jesus, Harris...' She kneels beside me, puts an arm behind my shoulders, straightens me up where I'm listing against the centre pole. 'Goddamnit. Just...fucking *goddamnit.*'

You're not real.

'Oh, I'm real.' She gives me a grim look. 'I'm really real, and I'm really hacked off.' She turns her head. 'Give me some water. Yes, you, Snowie Geraldson. You should be bloody ashamed of yourself, and don't give me that look, either. When your dad finds out –'

'Dad's not gonna –' Snowie starts.

'Snowie, shut your mouth,' Ando interrupts. 'And *you*, you little Paki shit –'

'D'you want us alive for your boss or what?' Amie sounds

386

furious and wheedling at the same time. 'Cos Harris is gonna peak from dehydration any minute now, then *you'll* be the one fronting Leon –'

'Ah, *fuck*,' Ando says, his voice sullen.

There's a bit of moving around. Something flomps down on the dirt beside me. Amie snatches it up. I hear plastic unscrewing.

'Here,' Amie whispers. 'Just a little sip...'

God, that's cold. I hiss in a breath, choke a bit on the water, swallow twice. I can feel the inside of my mouth for the first time in a while, but it isn't much fun.

'Hold on, Harris,' Amie says.

Ando and Snowie are in discussion over near the doorway, but the conversation only comes in snatches, cos of my head. There's a bit of, '...*fucking mental? She's the bloody sarge's...*', and there's a bit of, '...*two birds with one stone, mate, Leon'll be fucking rapt...*', and then Snowie's voice says, '...*give herself up like that? Her dad'll be on the fucking warpath...*', and then Ando rumbles, '...*easy. They both just disappear, all problems solved...*', and then I come back into my body, and realise this is not my imagination. Amie is here with me.

This can't be happening. I try to get both eyes open. She looks solid. Strands of her hair have slid free of her ponytail, and her hands shake as she rips a piece of fabric off the bottom of her shirt. She's sweating.

Oh fuck, this is bad. This is worse than this morning, and this morning was the pits. But even when I was screaming I knew she was safe.

'A-Amie...' My voice is a weird wheezing croak that stutters on her name. 'What're y'doing here?'

'Don't talk.' She's whispering, wiping my face with the water-moistened cloth. She's not looking at my eyes, and her own eyes blink hard. 'Don't talk, just for a second. I can't do this if you –'

She bites down on her bottom lip, blinks and blinks as she examines me. 'Okay, I don't think your nose is broken, but your cheekbone might be. The bruising on your neck is what's making it hard to talk. Look at me – Harris, *look* at me for a sec.'

She takes my face in both her hands so I'm staring into her eyes.

'You can't be here,' I wheeze. 'You can't be here, you gotta –'

'Shut up. Harris, just shut up. You have a concussion.' Her eyes well up as she releases my face to tear off more of her shirt, and starts checking down my front. 'I think most of the blood is from your nose. Most of these cuts are superficial, but these other –' Her jaw tightens as her voice hisses out. 'These are burns. These are *burns*, and I'm going to fucking *kill* Marcus Anderson –'

'Hey.' I lean until my forehead touches hers, until my arms hurt from pulling against the pole I'm tied to. 'Hey. Seriously, you shouldna come.'

She eases back to look at me, eyes wide. 'Well, I wasn't just going to let them *take* you.'

It's the closest I've come to crying in the last twenty-four hours. She's beautiful and she's here, and I want to hold her, but I can't.

'I love you, y'know that?' It just pops out.

She gives me a wobbly grin. 'I want you to say that again, when you don't have your hands tied.' She cups my cheek, slides closer, her voice low. 'Dad knows. Reggie's got my phone.'

That's all the news she can share, cos right then Ando stomps over and grabs her by the hair. Her hands lift, scratching and clawing, and I make a piss-poor scrabble to stand, sliding my hands up the pole behind me, although my ribs feel like they're eating me alive.

'This is your root then, is it?' Ando pulls Amie up, but he's glaring at me. He shakes her and she shrieks. 'She's a fucking firecracker, mate. You usually got shit taste in women, Harris, but this one, I like. Maybe if she's real nice to me, I might –'

We never find out what he might, cos Amie reefs around and kicks him right in the nuts. It's a good solid boot, and Ando drops her like a hot brick. She sprawls with a whoofing gasp, and Ando is doing some gasping of his own.

'*FUCK!*' He lets out a strangled moan.

Snowie steps forward tentatively. 'Shit, mate, are you –'

'*Get the fuck away!*' Ando yells. He staggers, bent over, towards Amie. He kicks her viciously in the side and she curls into herself, coughing.

My legs shake and my vision's red as blood. 'You're a dead man, Ando. You know that, right? A dead man walking –'

'I like my chances better than yours, dickhead,' Ando snarls. He flings around to Snowie. 'Do something *useful*, why dontcha, and tie that fucking bitch up.'

Snowie scuttles for another length of the handy ole baling twine. Amie coughs some more as Snowie lashes her hands together in front. His eyes dart back towards Ando, who's swearing and catching his breath at the shed entrance. Snowie's forehead is beaded with sweat. I stopped feeling sorry for him a long while ago.

My body's trembling. I inch back down the pole as Snowie drags Amie closer. Maybe he thinks she's out for the count after getting booted in the ribs, because he doesn't tie her to the pole. Amie gasps and shuffles until her shoulders are beside me and her head rests on my thigh. I lean over her, like I'm shielding her, which is pathetic – I can't even brush her hair back off her face. But now our faces are close, and her warm breath fans me, and this is the best I've felt since yesterday afternoon.

'I warned him.' She clears her throat, wipes her eyes against my jeans. 'I did warn him.'

I almost grin. 'You did. Remind me not to take you on.'

'Okay.' She rubs her tied hands against my waist. 'Rest now. You should rest. I don't think we have much more time here.'

I don't know about time. I don't know about anything anymore, except this thing I've just worked out. Because these last twenty-four hours, these last twenty years of my life, it's been all about enduring. I got through on a steady supply of anger and sheer stubbornness, and when that didn't work, I phased out, took refuge in my head.

But I've got something to fight for now.

Snowie and Ando are back in conversation by the shed door. They think they've got me nailed. They think they've exploited my weakness, by bringing Amie here.

They couldn't be more wrong.

*

The next move comes as the sun lowers herself into the crack in the world. Me and Amie get pulled apart, bundled up, shoved outside – I'd started to forget there *was* an outside, and I drink in the sight and smell of it. Dusk gives the air a blue tone and a biting cold. I wish I still had my hoodie. My hands are re-tied in front, which is good, cos my shoulders feel like they're about to detach from my body.

In the rear seat of the Land Cruiser, I hold Amie in the circle of my shaking arms for the first time and we get about ten whole seconds unobserved.

She leans into my chest. 'What do you think's happening?'

'Dunno. Stay by me, yeah? Whatever happens, stay close.'

Snowie gets into the front passenger seat before Ando. He looks like he's found some new source of confidence. There's definitely a swagger about him.

'So what's going on, *buddy*?' I ask quietly.

He gives me a snarly grin. 'Sortin' it out, aren't we? Delivering you two as a present. Leon's gonna be rapt.'

'Is he now?'

'Sure he is.' Snowie puffs out his chest. 'Cheers, then beers. Not that I'm gonna take all the credit. But it was me who figured something was up, and Ando's not a limelight kinda man.'

I dunno whether to laugh or cry. Snowie's an idiot, sure, but using meth seems to have reduced his I.Q. by half again.

Ando bigs Snowie up all the way to the new location, which – no surprises – turns out to be the Nowheresville shed outside town where me and Mick the Leb met the van-man. It's nearly full dark by the time we arrive, and the Land Cruiser isn't the only car around. A white van is parked at the rear of the shed with its nose sticking out from the corner, and there's another car, a dark grey Volvo.

Once we've pulled in near the Volvo, Ando twists around in the driver's seat. 'You two good there? Nice and comfy? Maybe you wanna have a last little snuggle before we take you inside, eh?'

'Yeah, don't mind us, we'll sit here and watch,' Snowie drawls.

'Or you could take us out and shoot us now,' I suggest. 'Spare us the shit banter.'

Amie snorts. Ando makes a disgusted noise, opens his door.

The crack I made earns me a bit of manhandling: Ando yanks me out, shoves me against the side of the Cruiser, whacks my face against the door panel. My cheekbone yowls in protest. Exploding light-bulbs go off behind my eyelids, so I open them before I get the spews. I'm staring down at the side of the car and it's like a really *giant* light-bulb goes off, right inside my brain.

'Y'know, this car's got big wheels.' I say it like I'm remarking on the weather. 'Seriously, Ando. These are, like, the biggest wheels I've ever seen.'

'It's a fucking Land Cruiser, you moron.' Ando spins me round, pushes me against the car.

'Good burn-outs, with tyres that big. They chew up the ground, though, don't they. When you park on the verge, I bet they chew up the grass real bad...'

I hold his gaze, see something creep into him. Maybe I'm full of shit. Maybe I dunno what I'm talking about. But maybe – just maybe – I have a strong sudden memory of a house with blue trim, rosellas in the trees, a muddied patch of grass on the verge near the front fence...

And it all starts to come together in my mind.

Some idiot's parked his big-wheeled car here and then burned off... Snowie at the bar with his cigarettes, the day before I went to Tulane Road – *'Hey, you haven't seen Ando about, have ya?'...* Reggie waggling his eyebrows – *'He thinks he's King Shit...Your fella, Ando. That's his work...'*

How did I not figure this out sooner?

Just like that, I know. And Ando's looking right at me, so now *he* knows. Before I can even open my mouth, he grabs me around the throat, muscles in and squeezes hard.

'One fucking word,' he hisses, 'and I'll kill you where you stand. Leon be damned. D'you hear what I'm saying?'

He doesn't wait for me to reply. When Snowie comes around, holding Amie by the shoulders, Ando jostles me off the side of the car. All together, we march and limp and stumble inside the shed.

Maybe in the city you'd have more luxurious premises to make your drugs in. But this is the boonies. The shed's set over a concrete slab. Two rows of old tables, a mess of batching equipment – primus cookers, plastic jugs, flat baking trays, and I-dunno-what-else – sit over on the right. A generator squats on the floor behind that, to keep the whole place plugged in. I can't see the cooks. Maybe they've already been paid off and gone home.

Workshop lights glow above the tables. On the left, a little picnic arrangement of plastic chairs. The whole place smells rank. I'd make a joke about Health & Safety regs but I don't think anyone would get it except Amie.

She quails beside me.

'Hey.' I nudge her gently. 'Chin up. We'll get through.'

'I thought we'd see the cavalry by now,' she whispers back, shivering.

Have to admit, I'd been kind of thinking the same thing. Whatever happens here, we'll be flying by the seat of our pants.

My heart hammers in my chest. I bend my head closer so I can brush Amie's hair with my lips. 'Stay behind me, and stay alert.'

Ando growls, pushes us forward. Whatever retort I was gonna make, I swallow it, because I've just seen Leon.

He looks weird, different, out of the confines of the Flamingos office. You can see the edges of him. In the office he seems to spill out to fill the whole space, it's like you're breathing him in. Here, he's more defined. Cigarette in hand, greasy white shirt, an ugly sports jacket, the strange reptilian folds of his face. His trousers are baggy. He's wearing black leather shoes.

His eyes look dead under the workshop lights.

Amie edges in behind me. Her fear is a live wire in my stomach. Mick the Leb looks up from his phone, stills in his chair. Leon scans from me to Amie, to Ando and Snowie.

'What's this?' He exhales smoke. His eyes light on the baling twine around my wrists. There's a pause. He drops his cigarette on the concrete, steps on it. Looks up. 'You've all got about twenty seconds to tell me what the fuck is going on.'

Behind me I hear jostling. Snowie steps forward. He doesn't seem so sure about standing in the limelight now.

'Uh, Leon, hey,' he says. 'Gotta tell you something, mate.'

This cannot end well.

Snowie explains it all very simply. It takes less than twenty seconds. In that time, Ando seems to fade into the shadows near the wall. After the explanation there's another pause, much longer this time.

Leon looks over at Mick the Leb, who shrugs. Then Leon turns back to look at me and Amie. Then he looks at Snowie.

'Lemme clarify a sec. You're telling me this bloke –' Leon points straight at me. 'This bloke is a police informant. And the girl beside him is his contact. Who also happens to be the daughter of a top-cop in Ouyen.' Leon fixes Snowie with his gaze. 'Is this what you're telling me?'

'Well, uh, yeah.' Snowie jigs a bit. 'That's right. And I brought 'em here because I figured this was something you'd wanna know about, and you prob'ly wanna make your own decision about it.'

I can't really fault his logic. Leon seems to disagree.

'You brought 'em here,' he says. He's still staring at Snowie.

'Uh, yeah,' Snowie says. 'I brought 'em here, cos like I said –'

'Here,' Leon says. 'To this place. This facility.'

'Yeah.' Snowie blanches. 'Oh. Yeah.'

Leon moves away from Snowie, takes two steps towards me and Amie. Takes a pistol out of the inside his jacket – he must be wearing a holster. Amie jerks and makes a little noise. I lean my shoulder in front of her. The expression on Leon's face makes me shake. Even my breath is trembling.

'And now,' Leon continues, 'I gotta figure out how to get rid of an informant and a cop's daughter. Which – as you can imagine, Snowie – is a pain in my fucking arse.'

'Oh,' Snowie says. 'Oh shit. Leon, I didn't mean to cause you hassles, mate. I just figured you'd wanna –'

'I do wanna,' Leon says. 'But, y'know, usually blokes tell me if there's a little problem in their patch. Then we talk to people who can deal with it.'

'Right,' Snowie says. 'Right.'

He flicks his eyes towards me, back to Leon. He looks petrified. I dunno why he's looking at me. If he wanted me to help him out, he shouldna tied my hands together.

'Most of my fellas, they've got the common sense to talk to me first,' Leon says.

'Oh. Yep. I just –'

'You don't have a lot of common sense, do you, Snow?'

'Oh,' Snowie says. 'I don't, um. Leon, mate, I'm sorry, I –'

'I gotta get rid of the bodies now,' Leon says.

'Leon –'

Leon turns around and shoots Snowie in the head.

The shot is incredibly loud inside the tin shed. Sound bounces off the concrete floor, off the metal walls, reverberates inside my skull. Even though I'd been bracing myself for it, it hits me like a migraine.

Amie has not been bracing herself. Maybe she's watched enough TV to imagine how scenarios of this type usually end, but I don't think she ever thought this sort of stuff could be *real*. The shot takes her completely by surprise. She makes a brief high scream, which cuts off abruptly as her breath leaves her. Her knees go out from under her – I have to turn and grab her arm with my tied hands.

Snowie is quite obviously dead. Apart from the way he tumbled boneless to the floor, we all saw the red spray come out the back of his head. I can only look at him lying there for one second before I have to close my eyes.

Leon engages the safety on the gun and pulls a crumpled handkerchief out of his trouser pocket. He starts wiping the gun off with the hanky. When he's confident it's fully clean, he passes the hanky-wrapped gun to Mick.

'Get rid of that,' he says. 'Then make some calls. Release all the packets early. Everything slated for tomorrow goes out right now. Plus I want a clean-up crew here for the equipment.'

'You could just torch the place, boss,' Mick suggests.

And I hold my breath. This is the deciding moment. If Leon chooses to cut his losses, we're fucked – Snowie is dead, and me and Amie will be next. Everything we are will be reduced to a headline: three bodies in a burnt-out shed in the back of beyond.

It seems particularly shit because I've got something to live for now. If I'd been in the firing line even a few months back, I might not have minded. But the last week or so has made anything seem possible, even life. I don't want to go now. Things have only just started getting nice.

Leon stands incredibly still for the space of three of my tortured breaths. Then he turns and walks closer to me. Rakes me up and down with his eyes.

'You had potential,' he says.

I don't know what to say. Saying anything could be bad. I just nod.

Amie is beside me, weeping silently, shuddering. I lift my hands and tuck her into the circle of my arms and chest. Leon looks at us, sighs out his nose.

'I don't want these two done on any property connected to the club,' he says to Mick, over his shoulder. 'And a fire will only draw attention. Just get the crew here. And get the tarp out of the van.'

I try not to let my exhale escape too loudly.

Mick disappears through a door in the back of the shed, his phone pressed to his ear. He returns with a folded blue tarp which he dumps beside Snowie's body.

Leon turns to the left-hand wall, and it's like I'd forgotten Ando even existed.

'Boss –' Ando starts.

'Spare me.' Leon pulls his smokes out of his jacket pocket. 'The load in the van goes to Melbourne. Put the body in the back.

Put the whole fucking lot of 'em in the back. You follow behind the van. When you get to the saltworks, take a left and you can do 'em there, then get back on the road. I'll give instructions to the driver about the pit-stop.'

That's our death sentence, right there, and he's ordered it like he'd order a pizza. But it's bought us some time.

Ando wets his lips, steps forward. 'I want the girl.'

'*No*.' My head whips to face him.

'You don't *get* to say no,' Ando grinds out.

'*I* get to say no,' Amie says. She slips out of my arms, slides around behind me.

I raise my tied fists. 'You touch her and I'll fucking –'

My hot speech is cut off by the feel of something cold. Leon has a gun pressed to my temple. Amie is clutching my arm. Ando is grinning with sharp white teeth.

'Turn around,' Leon says.

I turn. Now the muzzle is pressed to my forehead and I can see Leon's face. His expression is blank. Amie is whimpering.

'You deceived me, Harris,' Leon says. 'You screwed with me.'

My throat is too dry to do anything but whisper. '**Yes**.'

'Yes,' Leon echoes. His eyes are dark, and full of my terror. 'You like this girl?'

I don't want to reply. I can't. Any reply I make will be wrong.

But if I'm gonna die anyway, only one reply will be true.

'*Yes*,' I croak out.

Leon looks at me for a long moment. I was off the mark when I said he was soulless. He has the soul of the devil.

'Payback's a bitch,' he whispers. He looks at Ando. 'Take the girl.'

28

amie

When Marcus Anderson grabs me, I scream.

Screaming is okay, y'know. Screaming is a perfectly acceptable response to the last four hours of nightmare.

If you're being attacked, scream, Dad used to say. *There's nothing wrong with screaming. It disorients your attacker and lets people know something bad is happening.*

Something bad is happening. I scream as Harris cries out, as Ando yanks me towards him and pushes Harris back. I scream as the big boss, Leon, winces and gives the gun back to his minder. I keep screaming until Ando slaps me.

But don't waste your energy, either, Dad says in my head. *If screaming doesn't bring help, use your strength.*

I fling my head back around and bite Ando's hand. Blood bursts in my mouth.

'Fucking *bitch*!' he yells. He shakes me off and I go sprawling.

Harris has turned, all the bruises standing out from his golden paleness, every muscle in his body tense as he faces off with Leon. 'You're trusting the wrong person. Ando was in Tulane Road –'

He's cut off when Ando smashes a punch into his face. Harris staggers, drops.

'*Shut your fucking mouth!*' Ando bellows. He punches Harris again – I scramble onto all fours as I hear Harris groan. Ando turns to Leon. 'He's a fucking liar. And he's desperate. He'd say anything –'

'Jesus Christ,' Leon says tonelessly. 'All this fuss over a piece of skirt.' But he's looking at Ando in a different way as he lights a cigarette. He blows smoke at the roof of the shed. 'When you get to Melbourne, disappear for a while. I'll pay you now so there's no issues. Put them all in the van. No –' He holds up a hand as Ando opens his mouth. 'Whatever happens at the saltworks is up to you. But she rides in the van.'

It's the minder who takes us outside – me first, then Harris, still half-dazed. When I stumble out of the shed, the night is so black it's like I've had my eyes cut out. The van is a white delivery unit with double doors. There's a row of stainless steel shelving inside on the right, and the only place to sit is on the cold metal floor. Leon's minder dumps the rolled-up tarp with Snowie's body near the door of the van. Then the doors close and we're lost in darkness.

'Amie?'

I think I'm in shock. I can't say anything for a second. Something brushes my hand and I jump.

'Amie, it's me. It's okay, it's me.' Harris's voice sounds thick and rumbling. There's movement in the darkness. Warm hands cover mine, I'm being pulled against a warm chest, warm arms come down around me. 'I got you,' he croons. 'It's okay, I got you.'

A weird high-pitched noise comes out of my throat and is swallowed up by the sound of the van's engine chugging to life. The van vibrates around us. I'm vibrating in Harris's arms, shaking so much I think I'm going to be sick. I cough and cry and wipe my mouth against the fabric of his T-shirt, trying to get rid of the taste of Marcus Anderson's blood.

'Oh god. Oh Jesus.' I keep my eyes closed, because the blackness behind my eyelids is somehow better than the blackness inside the van. There's a series of jolts as the van starts to move. 'Ando's going to...he said he's —'

'That,' Harris states, 'is *never* gonna happen.'

A shudder runs through my whole body.

'Come on, babe,' Harris whispers. 'Come on. We'll fight together.'

'I don't know why I'm crying,' I gasp out. 'You're the one who got tortured. Oh god, Harris, you told me...you told me about your world, and I thought I knew, but I... Oh Jesus —'

'Shh,' Harris says. He hugs me close.

'How did you handle all this?' I whisper. 'Every single day —'

'You,' he says simply. 'I had you.'

I curl in his arms, press my face into his neck. I want to kiss him, but I know his mouth is sore from the way he's talking. Now I want a light in here so I can see what's been done to him, help if I can.

'I have to stop crying.' I dash my face against my tied hands. 'We don't have time for that. We have to get out of here. And I'm bloody sick of this baling twine.'

Harris snorts. 'Now you mention it...'

I duck under where I think his arms are, manage to bump my nose on his elbow. 'Shit. Ow. We need a light. Is there a light in here? Do you have matches?'

'Light's busted. I saw that when Mick put me in. And Ando turned out my pockets,' Harris admits. 'I got nothing.'

I sigh with frustration. 'Right. Well, this is the first time I've ever wished I was a smoker.'

Harris's voice changes. 'Snowie was a smoker.'

We both realise what that means at the same time.

'Oh yuck,' I say, as Harris says, 'Shit. Great.'

400

But there's nothing for it but to do it. We both fumble our way down towards the rolled-up tarp. I'm glad no one can see the expression on my face. When I feel the plastic weave with the squishy weight inside, I jerk back automatically.

'Okay. Right.' The words are more for my own benefit. 'I've handled this before, at the hospital.'

'Just not so messy,' Harris says.

'Not so messy, no.'

I hear a rustle as Harris moves. We need this. And if Harris can be brave, so can I. Wriggling my wrists in their bindings, I ease my hands over the crinkling plastic of the tarp, trying to orient myself. It's one of the most bizarre and macabre things I've ever done.

'Here's the edge,' Harris says.

'I've got an edge, too.' I feel wetness, and hair. I recoil with a gasp. 'Oh god, I think this is his head.'

'Yep, I've got his feet,' Harris says. 'I'll do it – it's easier from this end. Just hold him steady.'

Strange crackling sounds of burrowing come from where Harris's voice was before. The van goes over a series of bumps in the road. Harris swears, I hear scrabbling, and then:

'I've got it.' Harris flicks the lighter; it sparks once, twice, then catches, holds.

That meagre light makes everything seem better and worse. Harris's face is a mess. He's all blood, bruises and shadows. But he's smiling.

'Something to light,' I say, fast realising the lighter won't last. 'Damnit. Here.'

It's a piece of paper from my jeans pocket: a shopping list from the day before the wedding. The scribbled words go up with a flare. I scan quickly for something else to burn.

Two empty cardboard boxes are stacked into each other on the bottom shelf. I break off pieces of cardboard for fuel, feed the flames carefully. I'm keeping the small light going on the bottom shelf, but the van keeps moving, and the cardboard wants to scoot around. Finally, Harris thinks of a slightly gruesome solution: using Snowie's shoe.

He eyes the shoe. 'Goddamn Snowie. He was working to get money for his dad to keep the pub going.' His mouth twists. I think he's trying not to think about it.

We burn our baling twine off: it snaps at the weakest point once touched to the flame. Harris's wrists are bloody, but there's nothing we can do.

'Leon said the saltworks.' I dab at Harris's wrists with my shirt-tail. 'That's about an hour away. But I've got no idea of the time.'

'Me neither.' Harris sinks back against the inside wall of the van. 'No phones.'

'No phones,' I agree. 'What are we going to do?'

'Sit for a minute.' He rubs through his hair. 'My brain's not catching up yet. I feel like I'm running blindfolded.'

I slip another curl of cardboard into the shoe and shuffle in beside him. 'What do we know?'

'Ando did Tulane Road,' he says without preamble.

'What?'

'I'm sure of it.' He nods. 'All these little things I remembered... Then he as good as confessed, just before we went into the shed. That scummy bastard – he's probably got an iron in the fire with one of the other bosses, offered to get the samples. The cash would've been a bonus, or maybe his fee. He killed all those people... I'm amazed he didn't just kill *me* when he and Snowie first caught me.'

'He wanted to make himself look good,' I say, piecing it together. 'To show Leon he figured out what you were doing.

Making Snowie look bad was a useful side-effect.'

'He encouraged Snowie to wait before bringing me in. And then to take us both to Leon.' Harris shakes his head at the villainy of it. 'He knew Snowie would cop it.'

'And Ando just likes hurting people,' I remind him.

'Yeah. We've always kinda hated each other's guts. Getting to lay into me was an added plus.'

I touch his bruised jaw carefully. 'When we get out…'

'When we get out,' he repeats, with emphasis. 'First, we need to think.'

'Reggie has my phone. He should've called Dad. I already texted Dad about trying to find you, just before Ando grabbed me. Help should be coming.'

'But they don't know where we are. That we're travelling. We can't rely on them to be there when the doors open at the saltworks.' He casts around. 'We need to check in here, see if there's a way out.'

But there's nothing. There's no window, just a tiny vent high in the roof, and the doors are firmly locked. All the seams are tight. How would we prise anything open anyway? The shelving is screwed down, and the cardboard boxes are the only things around.

'Should we yell?' I suggest. 'Bang on the walls? Let people outside know we're here?'

'I dunno.' Harris grimaces. 'Do we wanna get shot in the face? The van-man looked pretty serious that time I met him.'

'Then…what? We just sit and wait?' The idea is eating me up. Every minute we spend in here brings us closer to the saltworks, and Marcus Anderson's cold eyes.

Harris looks grim. 'I'm gonna check Snowie's pockets again.'

We find a switchblade, a packet of Marlboro Lights (Harris shakes his head. 'Low tar. Lotta good that did him.') and some loose cash. Nothing else useful.

'The knife is something,' I say.

'Ando will have something worse.' Harris eases back against the wall again. He's started shivering.

I take off my jacket, put it around him, snuggle against his chest. I'm thirsty now, which means Harris must be feeling it more.

'How's your nanna?' he says softly. 'She still making plans for that dinner?'

I make a tired smile. 'She's great. I told her about you – I had to tell her. She's probably back at the house, coordinating with Mildura CIU and making up a seven-course menu.'

He laughs but it sounds hoarse.

I tuck another slip of cardboard into the shoe beside us. 'Apparently my auntie's plan to have me stay on as Nani's carer was organised without consulting her. She said she doesn't want me to stay. She wants me to live my own life instead.'

'Is that what you wanna do?'

'Yes.' I say it with conviction. 'If we somehow manage to get out of this, I want to live. Properly, I mean. I booked an interview for the residency. I want to make my own choices and figure out the things that make me happy.'

'That sounds good.' Harris's voice is muted. When I look up I see his eyes dipping closed.

'Harris.' I shake his arm. 'Harris, don't pass out me. No sleeping until we get you to hospital.'

'Okay,' he slurs.

'Harris... You make me happy.'

I lift my head and kiss him gently. Kiss the side of his smile, the edge of his bruised cheek, the soft lobe of his ear. Kiss the blood-stained curve of his chin, the blue thumbprints on his neck... All the marked and unmarked places of him. By the time I return to his mouth, his lips are searching for mine.

'I can't believe you came for me,' he whispers.

'Any time you want me or need me,' I say. 'For any reason. I'm here. I'm yours. Just call for me…'

We kiss for a long time then. That seems to wake him up.

Which I think might be a good thing. The van is travelling smoothly now, no stop-starting for traffic lights or corner turns. This is the road from Mildura to Ouyen – the road home.

The road to the saltworks.

'We have the knife,' Harris says. 'And we can build up the fire.'

'We have a dead body,' I realise suddenly. 'What if we shove that out when the doors first open?'

As the van growls around us, we formulate a plan. There's a turn, a collection of bumps, the sound of tyres on gravel. Harris kisses me swiftly, moves into position. I add cardboard to our fire until the shoe looks ready to catch alight.

The van slows, trundles forward, stops. Footsteps rush outside.

Now I let the sight of the fire, the memory of kissing Harris, fill me up. I become red as blood, black as a moonless night. The door unlocks, my whole body tenses to spring, my throat roils with a berserker scream –

'Amie! Amie, it's me! God almighty – lower your weapons!'

Flashlight beams nail into my eyes, then one of the black patches in my vision moves, coalesces: a stocky figure climbs onto the back step of the van.

'Amie, please god, love, tell me you're all right,' my dad says, and Harris realises just in time. Dad's flashlight swings to take him in. 'Harris, bloody hell –'

'Dad?' I whisper, then my throat works. 'Dada –'

My father steps into the van fully. I dump my fiery shoe, and Dad and I collide in a hug, like we're competing to see who can squeeze each other tightest. His chest heaves, and he's shaking.

'Ah god...ah Jesus...' He turns to see Harris. 'Shit, Harris, you look like hell. Come outta here, you two, come on now...'

He pulls me gently towards the doors of the van, grabs Harris by the arm to keep him directed. There are about half a dozen uniformed police and a couple of plain-clothes CIU guys milling about out here, and once we're out, the first thing they do is secure the van as a crime scene.

Dad is still shaking. I clutch his arm. 'Are you okay?'

'*I'm* okay. Are *you* okay? Are you sure?' He takes a big breath and lets it out. 'Fucking hell, Amita. That took about ten years off my life.'

The energy is slowly fading from my body. I'm weirdly aware of colours – the pink dirt underfoot in the yellow glow of police car headlights, the strobing reds and blues. The white-T-shirted figure of Steph standing to one side, a set of keys in her hand.

She catches Harris's eye. 'Talk about fucking lucky. I had no idea you were in the back of my van until Reggie called me on Amie's phone.'

A police officer steps beside her. 'We'll need to take those keys, miss.'

'You can have 'em,' Steph says as she hands them over. She looks at my dad. 'So are we square?'

'We're square,' Dad says. 'Give your statement, then you're free to go. Appreciate the help.' He turns to me. 'That's how we got your position. Steph told Reggie which way you were travelling, and he relayed it to me. We knew you were stopping here.'

'There's drugs somewhere in that van,' I say dazedly.

'I dunno nothing about that,' Steph says, raising her hands.

'I'm sure you don't,' Dad says in the conciliatory tone he takes with people he knows are lying. 'After you've spoken to Constable Tulley, you can get a ride anywhere you need to go.'

'You're a driver,' Harris says to Steph, like he's only just

406

remembered. 'I didn't see who was at the wheel when we were loaded into the van, I didn't even think...'

'That's understandable.' Steph shrugs. 'Although I reckon I might be looking for a new line of employment.'

'Wise choice,' Dad says.

My breathing is still fast and high. 'But – Ando. Where's Ando? He was going to be here, he was –'

Harris puts an arm around my waist. 'I think he might have wised up, too.'

He nods to where the Land Cruiser sits, gargantuan in its spot-lit position a dozen steps away. Police are holding a guy near the bonnet, but it's not the tall muscle-bound figure I'm expecting to see. This guy is shorter, with a flat-top haircut and strident voice.

'I keep tellin' ya, I don't know! He just told me to catch up at the corner of Fourteenth Street –'

'*Barry.*' Harris looks at Dad. 'How was he driving the Land Cruiser?

'Anderson called him, apparently, to do a car swap just before you left Mildura,' Dad says.

'Ando knew.' I turn to Harris. 'He must have realised Leon didn't trust him after what you said about Tulane Road.'

'So he cut loose.' Harris nods. 'Ando's evil, but he's not stupid.'

'Are you saying Marcus Anderson was involved in the Mildura shootings?' Dad's forehead lines meet in the middle. 'Then finding him's just become more urgent. Once we get the plate number we can track Barry's car to Melbourne –'

'Ando'll ditch that car fast,' Harris says. 'And he could just as easily have headed to Adelaide, or north to Sydney.'

'I've gotta go talk to Murphy,' Dad says, stepping free before swinging back to me. 'Are you all right for a minute, love? It's going to be very complicated here, but once I've done this I can take you home.'

'I'm good,' I say, tucking myself into Harris's chest. 'We'll wait for you.'

'Right.' Dad's glance takes in the way Harris and I are hugging. His eyebrows lift and he snorts. 'Okay, fair enough. Gimme a sec. Go over to the paramedics and get them to check you out – especially you, Harris.'

He walks off and I feel Harris's diaphragm rumble with a suppressed laugh. When I look up, he's grinning. 'Well, that was easier than I thought it'd be.'

I grin back, squeeze his waist gently. 'Told you.'

It takes more than a sec, but within half an hour – super-fast, for police time – Harris and I are loaded into the back of Dad's squaddie. The ambulance officer wasn't excited about the idea of us taking Harris home instead of to hospital. We reassured her it would only be for a short time, so we can give our statements. I know Dad has arranged this so Harris and I can have a period of calm before the medical examinations and the questioning and the evidence-gathering process begins, and I'm grateful.

Jared Capshaw rides shotgun with Dad driving; there needs to be at least one other officer present, considering Dad and I are related. Jared is a skinny freakishly-tall guy with a head of bright orange hair. He has to scrunch his legs up to fit in the front passenger seat. The squaddie is warm inside, and it feels comfortable – I've seen this car being tuned out the back of our house more times than I can count – but I can tell Harris isn't wild about riding in the back behind the mesh grille.

'Yeah, this is a little *too* familiar, if you know what I mean.' He holds a wrapped icepack to his cheek, wincing.

I take the icepack from him, re-wrap and re-position it. 'It's only for the trip to Walpeup. Murphy said he's going to try to find the Pitbull once they've found Leon.'

'They had a lead on the Volvo out of Dareton,' Dad says over his shoulder. 'But Leon's no dumber than Marcus Anderson. He's probably got himself a new set of wheels by now.'

'Murphy said they're keeping an eye on light aircraft, too,' Jared says. 'He's checking the airfield near Wentworth. Harris, are you okay, mate?'

'I'm real tired, hey, but I'm okay,' Harris says, leaning against my shoulder.

Jared looks between me and Harris like Dad did earlier. Much eyebrow-waggling ensues. I'm pretty sure the local gossip mill will get mileage out of this for years to come.

Then I look out the windscreen and – oh, my house! My sweet plain house... It seems to shine in the squad car headlights, but that could be because my eyes are watering. Dad eases the car onto the grass near the fence, pulls the handbrake and leaves the headlights on.

He angles himself to talk. 'We've only got a little while, but you can come in and rest. Murphy's said he's sending a car over for extra security.'

That's when I realise Jared isn't just here to supervise me and Harris giving statements. Leon's reach is long, and we're witnesses. Until CIU get a bead on Leon and Ando, Harris and I are basically under police protection.

'You'd better let us out then.' I nod at the doors. The rear passenger doors in the squaddie don't have handles.

'Oh, yeah, sorry,' Jared says. 'I'll do it.'

He jumps out his side, closest to the house, probably relieved for the extra leg room.

'We have to call Nani,' I say, remembering suddenly. 'Dad, she knows about Harris, and she'll be worrying about us.'

'I'll see to it,' Dad says. 'You'll probably need to –'

The explosive *crack* of a gunshot at close range makes me jump, cry out. Jared Capshaw's body slams into the passenger window on my side of the car – I gasp as he tumbles to the ground.

'Shit.' Harris has already half-climbed over me, putting his body nearer the house – nearer the gun-shot side – than mine. I scream as the front passenger window shatters, and another shot fractures the night.

Then Dad is yelling, 'Out! Get outta the car!' and Harris is yelling, 'We can't get out until you let us out!' and I turn my head to see...

In the glancing light of the headlamps, Marcus Anderson stands to the right of my house, partially concealed behind the Holden carcass near the fence. He's aiming a pistol over the roof of the old car, aiming through the windscreen of the squaddie –

Aiming for my father.

'Dad, get down!' I scream, then the gun goes off, and everything gets jumbled around.

Dad drops out of the car through the open driver's door with a garbled curse, onto the grass and dirt. My ears ring with the report of the shot. Harris has scrambled back over me to hammer on the rear passenger window, until Dad reaches over and something clicks. The door opens and Harris and I both roll out of the death-trap seat, into dark air and gunshot claps that rend the fabric of time and space.

'Amie –' Dad starts.

'Are you hit?' I yell, ducking as another shot thonks into the side of the squaddie. 'Dad –'

He shakes his head, drawing his sidearm. 'No, but Jared –'

'I'll get him, if you'll cover me,' Harris says. 'Have you got another weapon in the car?'

'Only the shotgun.'

Two more claps of gunfire – the squaddie rocks a little with the last one. Hunkered in the dust, we hear Ando's scream of rage.

'That'll do,' Harris says grimly.

'Can you shoot?' Dad asks, before dismissing his own question with a swift shake of his head. 'What am I saying, I saw you knocking holes in speed signs when you were twelve.'

'Gimme the shotgun,' Harris says.

'I didn't hear you say that.' Dad scrabbles down low and pulls the shottie out of the front passenger footwell, passes Harris a handful of cartridges. 'And you didn't hear me telling you to arm yourself.'

'Got it.' Harris nods, checks the action of the gun as he squats with his back pressed to the car. 'What about Amie?'

'Jared's pistol.' My voice shakes, but I ignore it. 'Get him back here first.'

Dad flips the safety off his sidearm. 'How many rounds does Anderson have?'

'It's a Bersa,' Harris says. 'Fourteen in the clip, one in the chamber. He'll have another magazine, though.'

'Right. Harris, are you ready? Stay low.'

'I'm low, I'm low,' Harris says fervently, squeezing my panic-clenched fist before ducking to the left of the side we're on.

Dad squiggles over the driver's seat and the transmission to aim out the shattered front passenger window. '*Drop your weapon, Marcus!*' he shouts. '*Don't make me shoot you!*'

Another shot zings across the hood of the squaddie.

Dad returns fire, and there's another scream from Ando. I want to plug my hands over my eyes and ears, but I can't do that because Harris is crawling back, tugging and dragging Jared Capshaw's long limp body with him. I stay down as I help pull Jared to relative safety, then I'm plunging into action, yanking Jared's shirt aside to see –

'Flak vest!' I could cheer. 'Oh, thank god.'

Dad backs out of the squaddie to see. 'Jared, good man. Now if we could get this bastard to stop –'

There's a crack, and Dad spins, falls into dirt and shadow.

'*DAD!*' I shriek, lunge for him as he groans.

Harris stands smoothly, bringing the shotgun to his shoulder over the car roof. 'Ando, if you fire again, I'm gonna drop you.'

'Just shoot him!' Dad hisses, his eyes screwing up as I apply pressure to the black-red at his shoulder.

'*FUCK. YOU.*' Ando bellows. He punctuates each word with a shot.

Harris doesn't even flinch.

'Marcus.' He says it softly, but his voice carries in the preternatural quiet between shotbursts. 'This isn't knock-knock at the pub, mate. This is real.'

'*Don't you think I know that?*' Ando yells, his words choked. Through the shattered window, I see him stagger away from the Holden. His face is tear-streaked, almost human-looking. 'You fucking snake, Harris. You fucking double-crossing bastard –'

'Don't make me do this,' Harris says. 'C'mon, Marcus. Snowie was your mate –'

'Fucking Snowie!' Ando's laugh is gasping, desperate. 'And his fucking jokes! D'you remember?' He raises his arm.

'Marcus, *don't.*' Harris braces the shotgun. He's fully exposed now, over the boot of the squaddie.

'What's a redneck's last words, Harris?' Ando looks and sounds like he's in the grip of some hysteria. 'What's a redneck's last words?'

The gun in his hand goes off. I flinch hard as the boom of Harris's shotgun explodes into the night, as Marcus Anderson is thrown back like he's been punched with a wrecking ball, as Harris slumps, exhausted, sliding down the rear panel of the car until his butt hits the dirt.

He tosses the shotgun aside, covers his face with his hands.

'"Hold my beer",' he whispers. '"Hold my beer, and watch this".'

29

harris

When I wake up, Amie's here.

She's stroking my hand, just these feather-light touches, but I feel it in my whole body. I want to tell her that, but my mouth's not cooperating.

'Shh,' she says, smiling. 'Don't try to talk until the anaesthetic has worn off. Here, see if you can sip this.'

She holds a straw to my lips. I take a tiny suck because anything more seems to make my head reverberate. It's only enough to wet my lips, clear the stale taste out of my mouth.

'The surgery went great,' Amie says. 'Your cheekbone is repaired, and apparently after the bruising goes away you won't even have a scar.' The wattage of her smile dulls down a notch when she sees my eyes. 'I know you'll always remember, Harris. I'm sorry.'

I shake my head a fraction. How I ended up back in surgery, how Ando died... I think about it, mostly at night. Sometimes in my dreams. But it's not something we should both have to carry.

'I'm hoping...' Amie hesitates. 'Well, I'm kind of hoping that we can smother over the bad old memories with newer nicer ones.'

She gives me another sip of cool water. This sip is easier. She puts the cup back on the nightstand, leans over me. Her hair is loose and it falls on either side of my face, so I feel like I've walked into a charcoal drawing – shades of dark brown, sable edges, but mostly black. Soft glossy jasmine-scented black. Our own privacy curtain.

'Poor guy. Can't eat, can't talk...' Amie's brown-gold eyes are mesmerising, quirked with laugh lines at the sides. 'I guess we'll just have to think of something else for you to do with your mouth.'

Her head dips and her lips are soft, warm, slow as honey. She breathes into my mouth, teases me with the tip of her tongue. It's like there's nothing else she'd rather do than kiss me gently all day. And I am totally okay with that.

It takes some of the sting out of the fact I'm recuperating only half a ward away from my dad.

A few days later, when I'm better, stronger, and Amie and her dad have come to take me home, I walk into my father's room. He's only half-awake, and our situations are weirdly reversed: now I'm the one with the speech, and the revelation, and he's the one lying in bed, cringing at the shock of it all.

Dad's never been a great cringer, though. 'You can't fuckin' leave now!'

'I've paid off all the bills, Dad.' I gaze out the window. Barb Dunne is out there, sitting on a milk crate with another nurse, both of them having a smoke break. 'The rent, the pub tab, the groceries, the bookie – everything's sorted. I've done my duty, and then some.'

His face is mottled, pink and yellow. 'But I've got me treatment in a coupla months, you can't just piss off and –'

'Remember how we used to go to the rez, Dad?' I shift on my feet near the window. 'Remember how you used to pound me for skimming stones?' I turn fully because I need to look him in the eye when I say this stuff. 'What about that time you burnt me with cigarettes? Or the day I got into strife for nicking that bloke's ute – the belt buckle day? You remember that day?'

Dad wriggles in his bed but there's nothing on earth can stop me now I've started.

I straighten my shoulders. 'I remember *all* the days, Dad. All of 'em. And you know what it was that really got me? It wasn't the pain, or the times I ended up in hospital, or even the fact I gave up living my own life to deal with your shit. What got me, Dad? Was that you didn't care. You still don't care. You never have.'

'That's a bloody lie!' Dad spits.

'Is it?' I make a hoarse laugh, which is crazy, cos my eyes are welling up. 'Maybe it feels like a lie to you. But it feels like the truth to me. Because if you cared about me at all, you've never shown it, and that's all that really matters in the end. It's not enough to just think it, Dad. You've gotta make it happen. And that's what I'm telling you now. I'm gonna make my own life happen. And the only way I can do that is to not be around you anymore.'

Dad's lips are wet with fury, his eyes are bulging. In another time, another life, I would've been scared. But that time is over. As I head for the door he makes one parting shot.

'You'll never find your mother without me!' he yells. 'All that bullshit about meeting up with her and Kelly again, it'll never happen!'

I pause, my hand on the doorknob. 'I know. But I made my peace with it. And now I've made my peace with you, Dad. That's...kinda all I've got to say.'

He's still screeching when I leave the room. Closing the door cuts off some of the noise. Thankfully, Amie is standing within arm's reach. She hugs me hard. 'You're shaking.'

'It's over.' My arms slide around her back. My heart's going like a trip-hammer, and I'm glad, so glad she's here. 'Jesus.'

'You right, son?' her dad asks. He plucks at the strap of the sling holding his right arm, and I can't remember when he stopped being The Sarge and just became Amie's dad, or Derrin.

'I'm good. I'm all good.' I pull back, scrub my thumb across my eyes. 'It's done.'

'He was yelling a lot of stuff about your mum...'

It's hard to talk for a second. I sniff and shake my head. 'It's okay, hey. I've come to terms with it. Mum doesn't want to be found. And she set it up that way for a reason.'

The reason is still bellowing curses from the room behind the door, so Derrin ushers me and Amie further along the hall. 'You shouldn't have to give up your family just to be free of your dad.'

'Yeah, but...' I stop, let out a breath. 'I gotta let this go. If I don't, it's gonna eat away at me from the inside forever.'

'Look, sorting out problems is kind of my business.' Derrin's really frowning now. 'Like the way I sorted out a place for Reggie with Moira Geraldi – that's the stuff that makes this job worth it. As far as finding your family goes, I haven't exhausted all the options. Your mum's maiden name was McKinley –'

'Yeah, but she's gone to ground. Maybe she changed her name, or maybe she remarried or something, I dunno. I've tried to find her, I swear to god, I've tried every way I can think of –'

Derrin cocks an eyebrow at me. 'Harris, you know I'm a copper, right?'

His expression suggests that he's wondering if I'm really smart enough to be dating his daughter.

But when I look over at Amie, she's smiling like she just found out the world is made of rainbows.

*

416

'Are we close now?'

'We're close.' Amie glances over at me. 'I was going to get you to cover your eyes, but I don't think that will work.'

'You're right, it won't work. It would never work.' I couldn't keep my eyes shut if I tried. I want to see everything, all at once. My blood is churning in my veins. 'It's good you're driving. I mean, I can't stand it, but it's good.'

She snorts. 'I can handle the Pitbull. But can you handle me driving it?'

'For special occasions, totally.' I clench my hands on my knees. They're trembling too much to deal with steering. One of Amie's hands slides off the wheel onto my thigh, and I take a breath. 'Hey, concentrate on the road.'

'I am!' Her hand squeezes, and she grins.

'Amie –'

'All right, fine.' Her grin bubbles into a laugh. 'But if I can't distract you then you have to talk.'

'Okay. Okay, all right, I'll talk.' I watch the houses thin out, the trees and shrubs changing into different types, more salt-tolerant types. 'Last contact from Ronnie Murphy, he said they picked up Leon's trail just north of Sydney. But they're having some jurisdictional problems with the New South Wales police, so that's slowing things down.'

'But they're definitely getting closer.'

'Yep. It's just a matter of time now, Murphy reckons. He also said they busted two lieutenants from Mazerati's crew, which could be enough to break up the whole show depending on the info they get outta them. That'd mean Little Toni will be the last man standing, providing no outliers pick up the supply chain.'

'What do you think?'

'Honestly, I think it's winning the battle but not the war. Keeping the town clear of ice is a tough prospect. There's a lot of other factors, not just on the supply side. I guess we'll see how it goes.'

Amie nods slowly, like she's philosophical about it. She's driving about ten kay under the speed limit – way slower than I would be, but I might be feeling it more because every atom in my body wants to move fast. I try to watch the scenery, keep my mind busy.

'What about the results of your interview?' I ask. 'Have they emailed you about it yet?' I'm pretty sure she'd tell me if they had, but I was a bit preoccupied this morning. She might not have wanted to spoil the mood.

'Yes,' she says. She doesn't say any more, but she doesn't need to. I can see it in her eyes.

'They said yes, right?'

She smiles then, can't seem to help it. 'Yes, they said yes.'

I turn myself sideways in the passenger seat. 'Well, hey, that's awesome! Shit, shouldn't you be jumping up and down or something?'

'I can't do that while I'm driving!' She laughs, then sobers, and her hand slips onto my leg again, but it's a different kind of squeeze this time. 'Well, yeah, I'm happy, but... You know it means we'll be apart.'

'For six weeks – yeah, I know that. I knew when you went for the interview, Ames. It doesn't mean I don't want you to go.'

She swallows as she watches the road. 'Nepal is a long way away, that's all.'

I put my hand over hers, curl our fingers together. 'I know. But you should still do it, if it's what you want. *Is* it what you want?'

'Yes,' she says. 'After I've finished my month residency in Chitwan, I can go south to Amritsar. Nani suggested I get in touch with family there, which means I'll have accommodation for the last two weeks of my stay.'

'Amie, that's... It's gonna be amazing. Think of the photos. The rivers. The mountains...'

'The mountains,' she says, nodding. 'The horizon.'

Her eyes catch fire as she looks forward, through the glass, and I want to keep encouraging her. It's what she's always done for me. 'Nick said I can have the room at his place, so I'll be waiting at Tullamarine airport for you when you get back.'

She bites her lip at me. 'You might have a crew cut by the time I get back.'

I snort. 'Babe, I don't think you need to worry. Police Force applications take a fair bit longer than six weeks to process.'

'Promise me you won't cut your hair before I arrive home!'

She makes me swear it, even while we're laughing, but I think it's all part of her distraction technique. Because a few minutes later there's a sign to Silver Sands. Then we're driving into the car park, and I'm so close now I can feel my breathing getting light.

Amie parks the Pitbull and we get out. The breeze pushes past us, flips the black velvet mass of Amie's hair around as she locks the car and comes around to give me the keys. 'Your fingers are cold.'

'I can't feel my fingers, I'm that fucking nervous,' I confess.

She hugs me quickly, looks at my feet. 'Take off your boots.'

'What?'

'It's the beach, Harris. You've gotta take off your shoes.' She grins at my expression. 'Just trust me on this one, all right?'

So I pull off my boots and socks, and Amie slips off her sandals. We hold them in our hands as we walk up this little rise, which is *sandy*, I don't know why I'm so surprised. At the very top, I stop dead.

For a second I can't take it all in – it's so *big*. Blues and greys call out for attention. The ocean, I'm seeing the *ocean*, with waves and salt and shit, spread out there like a full hand of cards.

Amie squeezes my arm and suddenly something in me tugs to look along the beach. Just down there is a woman with blonde hair like mine, and a girl the same shade of gold. They're collecting shells, the girl's dress whipping around her knees.

Suddenly my heart lifts so high it's like I'm flying on this breeze, jumping into this sky, soaring on clouds. I'm expanding, spreading out but still whole, filling this seam of heaven and sea, weightless, limitless...

The moment they look up and see me is the moment I become infinite.

ACKNOWLEDGEMENTS

This book is like The Little Engine That Could. And I had a lot of people helping my engine get up the hill.

Thank you, first of all, to the women of The Vault: my tireless compadres, writers, mums, amazing women all – you know who you are, and I couldn't have done this without you!

Thank you to those who assisted in beta reading, research, and representation and authenticity aspects, including Rose DeMaria-O'Sullivan, Fleur Ferris, B., Andrea Maxwell, Balli Kaur Jaswal, Merna Bell, Harsh Sharma, Alisdair Daws, and the Mildura community. Thank you to Amita Trikam, for lending her name. Thanks to all writing buds who offered encouragement and material assistance, especially Amie Kaufman, Jay Kristoff, Vikki Wakefield, CS Pacat, Will Kostakis, Shivaun Plozza, Simmone Howell, Nova Weetman and many more. Danielle Binks helped me find the perfect Harris for the cover – the sacrifices we make, darl! – and has championed this book every step of the way. Kylie Scott has been an inspiration. Adele Walsh always deserves hugs. Sincere thanks to Allen&Unwin for their cooperation.

AJ Collins, Nicole Hayes and Alison Croggon should all receive medals, giant medals, for going above and beyond the call. My gratitude to all online self-pubbers who've lent their advice and support. And there are not enough superlatives for Andy

Johnston – thanks so much, mate, love to the fam.

A huge thank you to the fans, especially those who love Harris as much as me! And to readers everywhere – you folks made this happen.

Final thanks, as always, go to Geoff and my boys – love you all so much.

AUTHOR BIO

Ellie Marney is a teacher and author of YA fiction. *Every Breath*, the first novel of her YA romantic crime trilogy, the *Every* series, was listed in 2015 as one of the most-borrowed YA books in Australian libraries, and her books have won or been shortlisted for a bunch of other amazing awards. Ellie advocates for the #LoveOzYA movement, runs #LoveOzYAbookclub online, and is an ambassador for the Stella Prize Schools Program.

She lives in a little wooden house on ten acres near Castlemaine, in north-central Victoria. Her partner and four sons still love her, even though she often forgets things and lets the housework go.